A WEEK AND A DAY

A Novel

Hal Adkins

ACKNOWLEDGMENT

Much thanks and appreciation to Terry Nelson, author of, among many other fine works, the four-volume *Far Riders Saga*, an epic Western adventure spanning over 25 years. His guidance and support greatly contributed to the outcome of this project.

Things you can't even believe,
Or ever foresee,
Would happen to you,
Do.

For those who never came home.

PROLOGUE

It has been said, for everyone, there is the perfect someone. Once found and joined, the bond becomes complete and shall ever be restored across lifetimes, to eternity. Beyond time, distance, and war, souls will reunite through inexplicable providence. This is one such story.

He awoke to the familiar odor. The combination of fuel oil burned in the boilers, and aviation gas, mixed with exhaust fumes, seemed to permeate every compartment of the ship, every hour of the day. It was a constant reality of life onboard an aircraft carrier.

Painted grey, the two-man cabin was small and cramped; his berth, narrow and uncomfortable, made it difficult to get much, if any, adequate rest. Combined with the continual threat of Kamikaze attacks, it tended to make a person perpetually exhausted and on edge.

The absence of noise and seemingly never-ending ship motion, especially if the seas were rough, was all but forgotten. He lay in the half-light of one overhead bulb, the disturbing vision still unsettlingly fresh in his mind. The more he tried not to dwell, the more he relived it. Sitting up and placing his feet on the deck, he saw Lieutenant Bob Jacobs was already up and gone. As always, he smiled at the black-and-white photo taped to his locker, touching it; he said, "soon."

Bob had been his cabin-mate for just two days, although they have flown together many times. Before then, he had bunked with Lieutenant Dan Owens, his wingman, who was killed in action. Dan had become a good friend; his loss and how he was lost affected him greatly. Five days ago, he'd watched him spiral out of the sky in flames.

Bob Jacobs was an affable type, a good flyer, and he liked him but could not, would not, allow himself to become close, as he and Dan Owens had become. With any war, friends can be gone in an instant. Seldom was there time for prolonged mourning or sad remembrance. You had to move on. But the losses, the personal losses, and their effect on one's mind combined to take a bitter toll.

I'd better get something to eat, even if I'm not that hungry, he thought, *then one more time, and done.*

Donning his flight suit, he glanced at a small calendar near the photo and noticed the date, June first. It was his twenty-second birthday. The image reflected from a mirror attached to a bulkhead did not resemble someone of that age. With dark eyes, disheveled, sandy-colored hair, and an increasingly wrinkled forehead, it presented someone appearing much older. He shrugged it off. A person ages quickly in his current line of work. Things perceived as important only a few years ago, such as personal appearance, meant nothing out here in the middle of the Pacific, where death from a tenacious foe was an everyday possibility and reality of wartime life. Grabbing the rest of his gear, he headed down the passageway to the mess deck.

"How are you today, Lieutenant, Sir? Can I get you some coffee?" George, one of the attendants, asked. "This morning, we have some fine frozen bacon that can't be more than four years old, along with the most outstanding powdered eggs this here man's Navy has to offer."

"Good enough. Tired today, George, just feeling so tired," he replied. "But it's my birthday, and one more go'n up and get'n down, and I'm headed home."

"Back to your wife and that sweet baby girl, Sir?"

"Yes, I haven't seen them since my daughter was not much more than a year old."

"I'm happy for you, Lieutenant, real happy. You be careful out there, now. How old are you today, Sir?"

"Twenty-two but feeling older."

"Well, I hope and pray you and your family have a long and happy life together, Sir."

"Want nothing more than that; you know what I mean? Promised I'd be back and meant it. Do you have any kids, George?"

"Why, yes, Sir, I do. Got me a fine wife and two young boys at home I just can't wait to see again. We'll miss you around here, but glad you'll be leaving this awful place."

"Tell you what I won't miss, among a lot of other things, George, the fuel oil and exhaust fumes. I'm sick of it."

The USS *Bennington*, CV-20 was commissioned on August 6, 1944. She is an *Essex* Class aircraft carrier, displacing 27,000 tons and 872 feet long. She is known fondly as *Big Benn,* and it was her second tour of duty in the Pacific, now stationed off the coast of the Japanese-held island of Okinawa, supporting the American invasion. It is the last island before Japan itself would inevitably come under attack by the allied forces. The year is 1945. Her regular contingent of aircraft includes; thirty-seven F6F Hellcats, fifteen SB2C Helldivers, fifteen TBF Avengers, and thirty-seven F4U-1D Corsairs.

Lieutenant David J. Hamilton is a Marine Corps fighter pilot assigned to the VMF–112 squadron, known as the Wolfpack, flying Corsairs. It is his second time serving aboard *Big Benn* and his final combat tour of the war. He is due to rotate out, having flown his prescribed number of missions, all but one.

Weather and visibility had been less than optimal for two days, with no flights off the carrier being made. But the forecast on this day promised to be more than adequate. A request had come from

Marine Command on Okinawa for assistance in attacking and securing an area along Horseshoe Ridge. He loves flying, especially the powerful and fast bent-wing bird, the Corsair, but is ready to hang it up and go home, safe and in one piece.

David Hamilton is a good pilot, having shot down two Japanese fighter planes, known as Tony's, and effecting significant ground damage, utilizing strafing and rocket runs on various Japanese-held islands, including this one. He is well aware that even good pilots get knocked out of the sky, and some get killed. More than one friend and fellow airman has failed to return to the ship.

David considers himself lucky, blessed to have flown on this many missions, with only a few minor injuries and one aircraft damaged beyond repair. After his flight today, to wreak havoc upon that miserable island and its determined defenders, a transfer stateside will position him in the new and valuable role of instructor, training future combat pilots to carry on waging this seemingly endless battle. He will be able to live with his wife and daughter, happy to be back on firm American soil, away from the constant sights, sounds, and smells of an ongoing war.

Spotting Bob Jacobs sitting at a long table, he joins him. There was small talk with Bob and others in the mess as he reluctantly picked at his food. Mostly, he sat in silence, anxious to get the day's work over and done with.

The familiar nervousness began to let itself be known, but this time brought with it a heightened uneasiness he had never before experienced. Putting it down to last mission jitters may have explained some of it away; even so, he could not finish his meal.

"You okay, buddy? You're looking a little haggard, actually very haggard. Maybe you should call in sick today; I don't need you up there bumping into me," Bob said with a faint smile.

"I don't think calling in sick is much of an option, Bobby boy.

Besides, who's gonna hold your hand and help you find your way back to the boat? You can get lost in a phone booth."

"Funny guy. Seriously, maybe you should go to sickbay, see what the doc says. It's your last flight and all, and, well, you know..."

"Yeah, and don't think it hasn't been rolling around in my head, Bob. Probably bad luck even talking about it, so let's just...."

"You two gentlemen want to take your coffee with you to the briefing?" George asked.

They hadn't noticed him walk up.

"That would be great; just top it off, if you would," said David.

"Me too," Bob chimed in as they both got up.

While he poured the steaming liquid into David's cup, George said, "I'll be praying for you today, Sir. Trust in the Lord, and re-member what He says in the Good Book, 'for I know the plans I have for you, they are plans for good, and not for evil, to give you a future and a hope.' Everything will work out, one way or the other, Lieutenant."

David looked at George to thank him, his usual good-natured smile was gone, replaced with an unfamiliar seriousness that made him uneasy. Turning away, he headed down the passageway to-wards the ready room.

It wasn't long after settling into one of the overstuffed chairs to receive the day's briefing; he felt a hand on his shoulder.

"How are you doing this morning, Lieutenant?" Major Hansen asked as he knelt beside David's chair.

"Fine, Sir, ready to get in the air and give 'em hell," he an-swered, with a slight, nervous smile as he began to stand up.

"At ease, Marine. Well, that's good," replied the Major. "I'm aware this is supposed to be your last flight before returning stateside."

"Supposed to?" David questioned, lowering himself back down into his seat. "Is anything wrong, Sir?"

"No, no, nothing wrong. But it is your last combat flight, and I know your last couple were pretty rugged. Your bunk-mate mentioned you haven't been sleeping well."

"Who does, in this business, Sir?"

"Roger that. It's just that, many pilots, at the end of their tour, get distracted, maybe even careless. Now, I am not saying…."

"I'm fine, Sir, really," David quickly returned.

Major Hansen put his hand on David's shoulder and said, "I'm sure you are David; I'm sure you are. What I'm trying to say, if you want to sit this one out, no one here would think any less of you. You've done a fine job and given us all you could."

David felt a certain lightness, and not a small amount of elation, upon hearing this. Nervousness and growing dread seemed to retreat. A feeling of relief washed over him as he began to imagine walking through the gate in front of the little yellow bungalow in Grand Rapids, Michigan, he and his wife, Macy, had rented nearly two years ago.

She would walk out of the red front door onto the small porch, holding their now year-and-a-half-old daughter, Jenny. After gazing at each other for a moment, he would drop his seabag and run towards her as she came down the steps to meet him, like the ending to one of the movies they used to see in the theater. They would meet, embrace with much kissing, and "*I love you's.*" A beginning, not an ending. Macy would be wearing her favorite perfume, the one he gave her; the last time they were together, he could smell the roses from her garden alongside the house and on the fence. It all felt so real, so very real.

The slight yet distinct odor of petroleum brought him back. He was a fighter pilot, trained to destroy the enemy, and was in for the duration of the war; his combat portion was yet to be fulfilled. Yes, he wanted to go home and be with Macy and Jenny, as soon as possible, to live happily ever after. But he did not want to let the squadron down and, just as importantly, himself. The uneasiness returned; he felt it in his gut.

"I'm fine, Sir; I'll be fine. I appreciate your concern, but this needs to be finished; gotta get the last one done. It's what I'm here for, what we're all here for, and I don't want to let anyone down," he told the Major.

David Hamilton had always been stubborn in this respect; something wasn't done until it was done.

"I understand," said the Major. "I'm proud of you, proud of all you guys."

"Yes, Sir," David replied.

Major Hansen stood up, as did the young pilot. They shook hands and saluted.

"You take care out there today, Marine. Do not, I repeat, do not take any unnecessary risks. Don't do anything stupid; hear me now, I mean that. Dump your ordinance on that shithole of an island, get your ass back here on this boat, and go home. Two passes, that's all. Two, no more, then firewall that son-of-a-bitch, and don't look back. That's an order, Marine. Do not look back."

"Yes, Sir," he replied and once more saluted the Major.

Well, there it was, David thought as he sat down; *I had my chance.*

"Okay, listen up," the Captain, giving the mission briefing, shouted out, "This is the shit you animals are supposed to go break and burn today."

There was no more time for thinking, only paying attention, taking notes, and preparing himself for battle.

David stepped out onto the wooden flight deck at 0900 hours; departure for the squadron had been set to begin at 0940. His Corsair's Bureau Number, 82628, twenty-eight for short, was one of three fighter aircraft he'd been assigned for combat duty and the one he had flown the longest. His first two mounts were F6F Hellcats, flown on multiple missions off another carrier before being assigned to *Big Benn* and Corsairs. *Macy's Magic III* was painted in white lettering on either side of twenty-eight's blue engine cowling. When David wrote home and told his wife what he had named the first fighter plane he took to war, two airplanes ago, she said it sounded lucky and would help keep him safe.

Jimmie Arcadian, twenty-eight's crew chief, was doing a preflight walk-around and gave David an update on maintenance items along with a few minor changes and repairs to the plane, but otherwise declared it good to go.

She was armed with a complement of six .50 caliber machineguns, three in each wing, sighted out to 200 hundred yards. Under those reverse gull-wings were eight, six-foot-long, high-velocity rockets, each packed with eight pounds of high explosives. They traveled to a target at over 900 miles an hour and could penetrate four feet of reinforced concrete.

The *Bennington* had been turned into a fifteen-knot wind coming from the west, to help facilitate take-offs and landings. Straight off the bow was the island of Okinawa.

With the preflight complete, David slowly walked to the railing on the carrier's deck and stared out over the lightly breaking waves. As was his custom, he took a few moments to calm himself while arranging his thoughts for the flight and grim work ahead. This time, he found it difficult putting those thoughts in order; typically, there was an anxiousness to get airborne. Today, it was almost a dread, and the feeling was foreign to him.

Topside, the air was fresher than below decks. This day, the sea breeze came directly from the war-torn island, carrying the stench of smoke and death; it was heavy in the air.

Mostly, his thoughts were of home. He was sick of war, sick of death all around him, and wanted his fight to be over. Jimmie Arcadian walked up, pointing at his wristwatch. It was time to mount up and finish this.

A large fighter plane, twenty-eight, was originally a darker blue, though now somewhat faded, with smoke-stain streaks from the gun barrels and exhaust pipes. Assorted patches were affixed to the airframe, primarily shrapnel holes from Japanese flack. There were few enemy fighters at this stage in the war to contend with. But the ugly, terrifying, black starbursts from the anti-aircraft shells were a constant threat and a reminder of just how dangerous it was flying against these Pacific island positions. Flak had knocked Dan Owens out of the sky five days ago. Flamed him, killed him, as David watched, and could do nothing.

Macy's Magic III sat with her wings in the upward, folded position, rocking slightly in the breeze and looking impatient to get airborne. She had a well-used, tarnished appearance about her. One of the three propeller blades was relatively new and shiny; the others faded and dull. She was no beauty queen but functional, dependable, and a great flyer, thanks to Jimmie and his crew. Above all, she was a warrior and deadly in David's hands.

Jimmie helped David into his parachute harness and put his flight suit in order. Before climbing onto the starboard wing, he put on his leather flying helmet, the goggles resting on his forehead. Using hand and footholds, he took three big steps up and into the cockpit. Jimmie also climbed up to assist David in getting the seatbelts buckled, and the radio wire hanging off his flying helmet plugged in.

A small, black-and-white photo of him, Macy, and Jenny, taped to the instrument panel, was the same image viewed the first thing every morning. He considered it his good luck charm. Received in the mail a few weeks ago, it was the only image of the three of them together he had. Jenny was barely a year old. *Wonder how big she will be when we get our next family picture taken,* David thought, as Jimmie finished pulling his seatbelts tight.

By now, several Corsairs on the flight deck were running; there was a growing roar and wind from the combined prop blasts. Jimmie looked at his watch and shouted to David,

"Should be ready to go now, Sir. You all set?"

David nodded.

Two crewmen, pulling the props through, were waved off, and David began going over his start-up procedure checklist. Cowl flaps open, *check*. Alternative air control, in, *check*. Prop control in low pitch, high rpm, blower in neutral, *check and check*. Mixture control, in the idle position, *check*.

Jimmie, leaning on the fuselage near the cockpit, looked on either side of the fighter, ensuring there would be ample room for the wingspread. He gave a thumbs-up to David, who put his hands together over his head, then pulled them apart to let crew members on the flight deck know the wings of twenty-eight were about to come down. The spread control lever was moved into the open position. Both men watched as the wings moved downward, slowly but smoothly. David pulled the handle, locking them in place; a light on the control panel signaled confirmation.

"Have a good flight, Sir. We'll see you when you get back," shouted Jimmy over the ever-increasing engine and wind noise. He saluted and, after shaking David's hand, hopped down onto the deck.

David returned to the checklist. Fuel selector switch on reserve, *check*. Set intercooler and oil cooler flaps, *check*. Set rudder and aileron tabs, *check*.

"Okay, old girl, let's see if you'll fire up for me, one more time."

He gave a thumbs-up to Jimmie, standing in front of the plane, who did a quick look around, then, with one hand in the air, gave a twirling motion. David flipped on the primer switch and pressed the starter button. With a barely discernible whine, the huge prop slowly began to rotate, with the usual mechanical clicking and clacking sounds coming from the 2000 thousand horsepower

Pratt & Whitney radial engine. It always seemed as if it was taking a long time to fire, and this was no exception.

Maybe it won't fire this time; maybe it won't start at all. Maybe it's busted. Would that be such a bad thing? Often, a few planes would not start or otherwise fail to launch. With scarcely any spare planes, the pilot would sit out that flight. He hated himself for thinking this. Perhaps, even wishing for it.

David heard loud pops and felt the plane shudder. Soon the prop blades were turning rapidly enough they could barely be seen, but for a dull, blue-grey blur. *Macy's Magic III* was soon puffing smoke and shuddering as the radial caught for good. After several seconds she smoothed out, and the smoking began to subside. All was well; Jimmie Arcadian had again given him a good airplane.

A number of Corsairs ahead of David had already taken off, and others were being moved quickly into the launch position. There would be only a few more minutes on this slightly pitching deck before he'd be in the air and heading directly towards Okinawa, his last step as a warfighter. Putting his foot onto the deck after his final carrier landing, would be his first step towards home.

He monitored the gauges, ensuring all the temperatures and pressures were moving into their normal operating range. The number of planes ahead was swiftly becoming fewer. David was drawn again to the photo on the instrument panel. There would be little time to do so upon reaching the island. Once over the target area, guns needed to be fired, and rockets launched. Things to destroy and people to kill. All in a day's work. And so it goes.

A quick thought came to mind; he wondered how many enemy deaths he might be responsible for. There was no way to know for sure and what difference would it make now; they deserved it. David Hamilton had no pity or compassion for the Japanese people and their waring ways.

Standing off to one side of the plane, Jimmie gave him three fingers, signaling how many planes yet to be launched were ahead. David confirmed the tailhook was up and locked. With the long nose of the plane and sitting in the tail down position, it was difficult to see directly ahead. What could be seen beyond the smoothly rotating propeller was a broken cloud cover, with increasingly large patches of blue sky.

Flying in marginal weather was never something any pilot welcomed. Still, the Mud Marines on the island were counting on the fighters for air support to get the job done, no matter what, and the conditions, thankfully, were becoming more than suitable.

Jimmie waved and held up two fingers. David acknowledged with a nod. Reaching out a gloved hand, he touched the photograph on the instrument panel.

He was standing behind his wife and daughter, sitting in a tree swing at their home in Michigan. It was calming and made him smile as he thought, *I'm coming home and will see you both soon.*

Jimmie raised one finger. David felt the prop blast of the plane ahead and heard its throaty bellow over the sound of his own idling engine. Jimmie twirled his finger and pointed left. David throttled up the engine and put in hard left rudder as the plane began to move. He maneuvered towards the catapult launch position as the cable was reeled back. To his right, the hooded signal officer pointed at him with his paddles. The cable was heard and felt as it was connected to the plane and pulled taut. Jimmie's thumb was in the air for a moment, and then he clapped as the signal officer began rapidly twirling a paddle over his head. David pulled his goggles down and advanced the throttle until the plane was fairly dancing, with the tail wheel climbing several inches off the wooden deck.

Now the paddle is held motionless above the signal officer's head. David braces his feet against the rudder pedals, wraps both hands around the stick, puts his head firmly back against the headrest, nods at the signal officer, and waits for the shock of the catapult.

In one quick and fluid motion, the signal officer turned and lunged into a lowered position with his arms and both paddles pointed straight out to sea. At nearly the same instant, David felt a tremendous jolt as *Macy's Magic* III accelerated rapidly down the deck.

He can feel his face sliding backward on his skull as the deck and superstructure of the carrier rush by in a blur. Soon the roughness of the deck and shaking of the airplane give way to smoothness, with nothing ahead but sky, that cursed island, and puffs of black smoke in the distance.

An aircraft carrier catapult launch was not something a pilot ever gets used to. The only thing more trying is a carrier landing, which he had yet to accomplish before his war was over. But the task, now, was to head towards Okinawa. There was little need for any great altitude as it was a short flight to the island and the low-level fire mission against dug-in Japanese gun emplacements and troops.

The enemy was raising hell with the Marines on the ground while taking potshots at landing craft and supply boats arriving on the beaches. He should be able to accurately expend his entire ordinance in no more than three passes over the target. Major Hansen's admonishment of making only two passes, echoed in his mind.

The target area was along a ridge and 400 yards long. The enemy was dug in and, when attacked from the air, would fall back into their vast tunnel system and wait. As they cowered in their dank, stinking holes, anti-aircraft crews would be heavily engaged in tossing deadly; exploding steel presents at the vulnerable aircraft.

These flak emplacements in the jungle were well camouflaged, making it difficult to find and shoot them. This was something every pilot, who usually had only one or two good opportunities to get away from that island unscathed, was rightly aware of. So, David would shoot up the ridge two times and head out to sea, just as Major Hansen ordered. Tarrying too long would only give him a greater chance of falling into the enemy gunner's sights.

Drawing closer, he could see multiple puffs from the deadly, black air bursts at several points surrounding the ridge. Explosions and smoke could be observed coming from the target area. With no pre-arranged pattern for making a run on the ridge, the planes attacked in the order of their arrival. David was near last in line.

The VMF–112 pilots would take turns diving in at 300 miles an hour, firing rockets and machine guns along the top of the ridge. The fighters would then pull up and make a long turn to port, out over the ocean, get in line, and do it again until they had nothing left with which to kill the enemy. If all went well and as planned, a significant number of the enemy would be dead or dying at the end of their attack. They would then head back and land on *Big Benn,* all, hopefully, safe and sound. Such are the rhythms and realities of war. A successful mission meant no empty places at the mess tables tonight.

The flight of Corsairs attacked the ridge at a slight angle, making it easier to get a better spread on the 1200 foot long target area. A couple of miles out, David toggled the switch to arm his eight rockets and fired a short burst from the .50 caliber guns in the wings, ensuring they were operational. A slight vibration and machine-gun bark told him he and *Macy's Magic III* were in business, ready to fly into battle and do severe damage to the Empire of Japan.

Banking slightly left, he lined up to make his pass from north to south. With wings leveled and ground targets aligned in the crosshairs, two rockets were fired, immediately followed by three long bursts of machine-gun fire. Rocks and dirt were thrown into the air from the impact and explosions of the rockets, striking fifty yards apart. Bullets peppered the area for 200 yards along the ridge top. David was satisfied with this and hoped some of that hot metal found its way into the tunnels and ripped enemy flesh.

He pulled up, applied full power, and began a climbing turn to come around once again. The second pass went much as the first. The remaining rockets were fired, with most of the machine gun ammunition also expended, tearing into the already torn skin of Okinawa. His active, gun-fighting career had come to a close.

From the corner of his eye, he noticed a flash of light on the ground as he passed over the ridgeline slope, just before turning and heading back to the *Bennington*. At first, he thought it to be nothing more than a glint of sunlight reflecting off some odd piece of metal, but seemed to have a frantic rhythm about it.

David Hamilton looked back.

He saw a Marine out in the open sunlight, waving something bright and shiny in his hand. The man was trying to get his attention with a mirror or something reflective. David throttled back and rocked his wings in acknowledgment, then he saw it. Less than a hundred yards ahead of the frantically waving Marine was a Japanese machine-gun nest. They were shooting at several men who were desperately scrambling for shelter against the attack by getting behind any rock or shattered tree stump that could be reached. He saw the signaling Marine collapse to the ground as bullets kicked up mud and stones around him.

With blood boiling, David pulled the throttle back more while pushing the stick forward and kicking the Corsair into a hard right, descending turn. Going back was a potentially dangerous decision, a risk, but it made no difference. This just became personal.

In seconds, he had lined up, leveled out, and was speeding

headlong towards the still firing machine-gun nest, a few hundred yards directly ahead. Jamming *Macy's Magic III* throttle full-forward, he yelled, "C'mon, old girl, let's get those bastards!"

With no rockets left, David would be hammering the enemy with all his remaining machine gun ammunition. One last gunfight at 300 mph, it would be. A long burst shook the plane. The nest and everything, for yards around, disappeared in an eruption of mud and sparks.

He pulled up sharply to make it over the line of torn trees on top of the ridge. A quick glance to the right saw several Marines standing and exuberantly waving their weapons. This would be a gratifying and memorable capping off of his final combat mission. It was a good feeling.

He could not see or know if the man who ran out into the open to get his attention, was one of the jubilant Mud Marines. *That guy had to be one brave son-of-a-bitch to expose himself like that, under fire,* he thought. *But the man helped save a lot of his buddy's lives.* David hoped the Marine he watched go down would survive this fight, this war, and make it home. He deserved it and deserved a medal for his courage.

Making a climbing left turn to get on course for the short return flight to the carrier, David was soon coming back over the ridge. He rocked the wings of the Corsair again, saluting the Marines who were, once more, waving their rifles high. With flak bursts ahead in the distance, he banked steeply to skirt the area where most of them seemed to be blossoming.

Suddenly, there was a flash of flame and a deafening boom. David was thrown violently forward, his body stretching the seatbelt harness. The open canopy of the Corsair slammed shut; he was momentarily dazed.

As his mind began to clear, he briefly wondered what was happening. Within a few seconds, he realized there was no longer any engine noise, only the sound of rattling and wind. To his left and below, the Marines were now standing, motionless.

Looking through the oil-streaked windscreen, he saw no blur of the huge, rotating, three-bladed propeller. There seemed to be but one short stub of a broken blade flailing in the wind, making the plane shake furiously. David Hamilton came to the gut-wrenching reality; an anti-aircraft shell had just hit *Macy's Magic III*, head-on.

"No, no, this can't be happening, not now! Not now!" he yelled out.

Oily black smoke began pouring out of the silent, wrecked engine, further obscuring his forward vision, but he could see the plane was in a nose-down attitude. Pulling back on the stick made little difference; all the controls were sluggish and loose. The altimeter showed just over 1500 feet. *Enough to bail out, but I have to go now!* When he attempted to open the canopy, it would not budge. Slowly, the plane began a turn to the left as smoke from the engine continued to increase.

"No, no! Got to get out now, please!" David screamed.

Unlatching his seatbelt harness, he tried to get a better angle in the cockpit and force the canopy open. As he leaned forward in the seat, trying to find something to grab on the canopy, there was a loud pop. The plane shuddered, and suddenly the cockpit became brighter. David saw oily flames streaking over the length of the canopy above him.

"Not fire! God, no, not fire!" he shouted in horror, over the wind noise and growing roar of the flames as the plane banked even steeper to the left and picked up speed. Desperate, pleading sounds were coming from David's mouth as he put his gloved hands flat on the plexiglass canopy, trying desperately to get a grip, to move or push it out.

He screamed in pain as the superheated canopy burned his

hands. Desperately, he began beating on the plexiglass until the tattered gloves fell off, exposing burnt and bleeding flesh. Rancid, oily smoke began to fill the cockpit; small licks of flames were poking through the floor near the rudder pedals.

As the spiraling of the plane became tighter, it was all he could do to push against the centrifugal force, pinning him to the right side of the cockpit as he struggled furiously to get out of the doomed fighter.

"God, don't let me die this way! Please, God!" David cried out. Briefly, his mind brought back the images and terror of watching Dan Owens die in a flaming Corsair.

Fingers of flames were beginning to come through the instrument panel. The floor of the cockpit was nearly covered in hot, smoky oil. David continued hitting, pushing, and scratching at the heat-softened plexiglas with his near useless hands while screaming in agony.

More loud cracking and popping sounds began as the plane spun violently; breathing was near impossible from the smoke and heat. He was now totally pinned against the side of the cockpit. Looking at the instrument panel, he saw the black and white photograph beginning to burn. Trying to reach out, he was unable to raise his arm.

As the violent shaking and noise of the failing airframe increased, David struggled to breathe. *Home, Lord, I only wanted to go home. I promised Macy. Please, let me go home again…* he pleaded; he prayed, waiting for impact with the Pacific Ocean. Inhaling as much foul air into his lungs that he could, David Hamilton shouted, with all his remaining strength,

"I promised!"

Darkness and silence closed in, then a blinding flash.

⇒⟨⟩⇐

SATURDAY

He was startled by the sound. Opening his eyes, David struggled to focus on the slowly rotating blades of a ceiling fan. Looking down, he observed a small, broken table and what appeared to be the body of a man lying on the floor. Confused, and after sitting up from a semi-reclined position, he found himself in a room, an office of some type, he thought. There was no longer any pain, and breathing came easily now. *What, what is this. Where am I? What just happened?*

Suddenly a door flew open; a woman stood in the doorway.

"Oh no, oh no," she said, while quickly walking towards him, stopped short, and knelt next to the man lying still on the floor.

"Sarah!" she yelled, looking over her shoulder towards the open door. "Call nine-one-one, Hurry!"

David, watching this unfold, said,

"Where am I? What's, what's going on here? Is this a hospital, or…Heaven?"

"Not now, not now, dammit!" the woman swore.

"But, am I… am I…" he stammered. "Dead?"

"Glaring at him, she shouted, "Not now, please! Sarah! Bring towels; his head is bleeding!"

Two more people came into the room.

"Oh my God, Evelyn, what happened?" one asked.

"I'm not sure, not sure, said he wasn't feeling well this morning when he came in," replied the woman, kneeling on the floor. "He must've passed out, hit his head on the table. I heard it from the outer office."

David stood up, feeling strange and dizzy. Glancing around the room, nothing was familiar. A large bookshelf, pictures, and other framed items adorned the walls. There was one large window, with curtains drawn. He thought, w*hat's going on here. I was in a burning plane; now I'm here, wherever here is. Is this actually Heaven? Is it, Hell? By the attitude of that angry lady on the floor, it might be.*

A girl came in carrying towels and handed them to the woman, who quickly put one under the man's head. She appeared to be dabbing blood with the other.

"Ma'am, I don't mean to intrude, but…."

"Not now, Mr. Haynes, not now," she replied, tersely, without raising her head.

"Haynes? Who is Mr. Haynes?" David asked.

The woman looked directly at him, with anger in her eyes, and shouted,

"Would someone escort Mr. Haynes out of here, please?"

A man kneeling on the floor, next to the woman, stood up. Taking a few steps over to David, he gently, but firmly, took him by the arm.

"Just come with me, Mr. Haynes," he said. "We have a situation here; best if you just go home now."

"But my name isn't Haynes, it's… and what do you mean, home? You know nothing about my home; who are you people, and where am I?"

"This way, sir," the man said as he briskly escorted David out and through another room, then into a hallway. "The elevators are to the right, Mr. Haynes."

"My goddamn name isn't Haynes, you stupid son-of-a-bitch. It's…"

Just then, several people in medical garb arrived, pushing their way past him and into the room. *Where is this place? What is happening! I need to leave and see if I can find out what's going on. These people are no help.*

Walking unsteadily down the hall, he wondered if this was a dream. But if he is dreaming, where is he at now? In his berth on the *Bennington*, dreaming, he got shot down and woke up in some strange place? It seems too real.

Moving to where the elevators were located, he raised a hand to push one of the buttons. Then put both hands in front of his face. *My hands were burnt and useless; now, they're fine. But, what is that ring?* Suddenly the elevator door opened, a young woman with short hair stared at him.

"Well, are you getting on or not?" she asked.

"Yes," he said and stepped into the elevator.

"Are you going down?"

"I, I suppose so."

As the elevator began to move, David took a quick look at his hands again, still amazed, then glanced over at the girl. It was difficult to tell how old she was. Very thin with a lot of eye makeup and odd, black lipstick. Her clothes were a strange mismatch of styles and colors. The girl's hair seemed to be both black and white, with streaks of blue. She had several tattoos, one on her neck and a great deal more, almost covering her left arm. Some sort of small, metal ball was fastened to one side of her nose, along with a thin ring in her lower lip. *She must be from some foreign country, speaks English well, though. Such a strange person.* He felt the elevator slowing.

"Miss, where am I?"

"On an elevator," she replied curtly, then walked out as the door opened.

Exiting the elevator, he found himself in a lobby where few people were present. Directly ahead was a large pane of glass in a steel door frame that opened, without being touched, when a man from outside walked up, then closed behind him. He assumed someone must be watching as people approached, then operated the door by remote control. When almost to the exit, it opened. David raised his hand and gave a small wave.

Outside was sunny and hot; it felt like Florida in the summer. Looking up and down the street, he saw palm trees. Many cars, trucks, and motorcycles were moving and parked; none were the least bit familiar. Everything seemed to be low and flat-sided, not a running board or whitewall tire in sight.

Some time ago, he'd read in a magazine what cars might evolve into in the future; none resembled what he remembered. *This is all very strange and out of place, almost, foreign.* The thought troubled him.

Most of the buildings appeared to be newer, very modern, with an abundance of glass. Some had doors with the remote control opening and closing system, just as the one he had encountered. Many were very tall, nothing like he remembered from his Marine flight training time in Florida a few years previous.

He began to take note of people on the street, many dressed, to him, strangely, some barely dressed at all. There were no men wearing business suits in view. The only hats seen seemed to be baseball-style caps, with some worn backward. *Why would they do that? It looks really stupid,* he thought. Many men needed haircuts, and a shave, except for a few who seemed to be younger yet completely bald. Not one woman was wearing a dress, only shorts or slacks, even denim jeans.

David looked at his hands, again noticing the ring on his left ring finger, and wondered how it got there. His wedding ring, which did not look like this one, was back on the *Bennington* and never worn for fear of becoming damaged or lost. He would begin wearing it again when he was home with Macy and Jenny. *Macy and Jenny, and home. I'm alive, didn't die in the middle of the Pacific, and now find myself back in America, maybe… Have to try and contact the Bennington, or at least the Navy or Marines; they should have some answers. Could be some sort of amnesia, or something, from the plane crash; I don't even remember hitting the water.*

There had been no thought or notice to his clothing, but it was obvious he was no longer wearing a flight suit. His shirt was short-sleeved with a multi-color, tropical pattern; the pants were denim with a leather belt. Footwear seemed to be some sort of fancy sneakers. It was odd to be wearing these athletic-type shoes out on the street, although he observed many others using similar styles.

What appeared to be a newspaper vending machine was a short distance away, in front of a store. Walking closer, he saw that it was. *This might help clear things up,* he thought, while approaching the yellow, steel, and glass box. The first thing noticed was the name displayed; *Fort Myers Florida Weekly.* David Hamilton was indeed, oddly and inexplicably, in Florida.

Fifty cents was the price to purchase a newspaper; he'd never paid more than a nickel or dime for a newspaper in his life. It might be a special edition, was his thought. Reaching into a pocket of the denim jeans, he found change and hurriedly picked out two quarters. After placing them in the slot, he opened the door and pulled out one paper. No attention was paid to the headlines or stories on the front page; his only interest was the date: Saturday, June first, 2019.

This can't be right… This can't be right! Frantically, he looked around as if searching for a way to confirm that what he had just discovered could not be possible. Q*uarters, the quarters I put in the machine. Coins have dates.* Jamming his hand back into the pocket and grabbing more change, he held each one up close to his face; one quarter was stamped 2010, another 2018. Two nickels were from 1999; various pennies and dimes showed similar dates. David lowered his hands and stared straight ahead in shock.

A large, plate-glass window behind the vending machine presented the image of a man standing, wearing denim jeans and a multi-colored tropical patterned shirt. He had an expression of great distress on his face. David moved his hand to put the change back into the pocket, then stopped. The image in the window did the same.

He stepped to the left, as did the man. David assumed this must be him, but the face was not his. Moving towards the glass made the image grow larger. He stared closely at the face, staring back at him, then put a hand to his forehead, as did the reflection.

He tried to reason this out; maybe the glass was dirty and causing distortion. Moving around to see if it would make a difference, didn't. Stepping yet closer to the glass, the reflection became larger and more clear. David Hamilton was staring at his own reflection, but it was a stranger's face.

The edges of his peripheral vision grew dark, and a feeling of weakness washed over him. The coins slipped from his hand, tinkling as they hit the sidewalk. *What's happening…* His knees began to buckle, and he felt himself going down; then, there was nothing but darkness and silence.

The cockpit filled with smoke and flames; he was trapped. No matter how violently he attacked the canopy, with his burned and bloodied hands, it would not budge.

"Derek."

"Oh no, no," David moaned. "This can't be happening."

"Derek, wake up, honey," a woman's voice said.

The roaring and shaking of the spiraling Corsair began to subside; then faded away, he felt someone holding his hand.

"It's okay, honey. I'm here now; you're going to be fine," the voice said.

Great relief and calmness came over him; it was almost heavenly. A smile began to cross his face.

"It was all just a dream, nothing but a bad dream. Macy? Is that you?" David said softly.

The hand suddenly pulled away.

"Who the hell is Macy?" the woman's voice asked angrily.

His eyes flickered open; he saw a man wearing a white lab coat standing at the foot of the bed in which he was lying.

"This is normal, Mrs. Haynes," the man said. "He's got a nasty blow to the head, and some confusion is not unusual."

"Well, that better be it," the woman said sharply.

David turned his head to the left; a woman he did not recognize was standing next to him. She looked upset.

"Who are you?" he asked. "You're not Macy."

The woman snapped her head, quickly, towards the man in the white coat.

"And maybe a bit of amnesia, be nice," he said.

The woman grasped David's hand again and smiled sweetly.

"It's me, Derek… Shelley, and this is Doctor Houston."

"Shelley? Shelley who?" David asked groggily.

"I'm your wife, of course."

"You're my… wife? And who's Derek?"

Shelley shot Doctor Houston a look.

"Be nice."

"How did I get here? Where am I?" David asked, glancing around the room.

"You collapsed on the sidewalk downtown, near the medical center building; you're in the hospital now," Shelly replied.

"We ran some tests and found nothing significant or serious," Doctor Houston added. "Might have been a combination of the heat and some dehydration, can't say for certain. What we do know is you have a bad bump, probably a mild concussion, and presumably a friend named Macy."

"Not funny, Doc," said Shelley, without looking up. "You were talking out of your head, Derek. Going on about smoke and fire, going home, even praying,"

"I remember... why do you keep calling me Derek?"

"That's your name, silly. Derek Haynes, surely you remember that much at least," Shelly replied, her voice rising.

People kept calling me Mr. Haynes when I was in that place, that office, David thought.

"They got your name and address off your driver's license when the ambulance brought you to the emergency room, then the hospital called me," replied Shelley. "And it's your birthday today, remember?"

"Yes, yes I do. Remembered this morning before...."

David thought it best not to share, with these strangers, what had happened earlier on this bizarre day.

"When will I be able to take him home?" Shelley asked Doctor Houston. "The kids are really concerned about him."

Derek began opening his mouth to ask, *what kids?* And then stopped.

"Let's give it a couple more hours," Doctor Houston replied. "We'll keep checking his vitals. If everything seems normal, he can go home. But take it easy for a few days, and come back in a week for a check-up. Sound good to you, Derek?"

After a moment, David said, "Yeah, sure. Sounds good."

"I'll be back in a while," Shelly said as she leaned down and kissed him gently, on the forehead, next to a large square bandage."

There are a few things I need to do before we get you home; your phone is right here next to the bed."

"My, my phone?" David asked, with confusion in his voice. "What phone?"

"Your cell phone, what else would it be?" Shelly said sharply.

He had no idea what she meant but replied,

"My cell phone, yes, of course."

She took something small, black, flat, and rectangular off the bedside stand and laid it alongside him on the bed.

"Call me if you need anything, okay?"

"Right, call you. With the, cell phone," he said to the woman and managed a smile.

Shelley and Doctor Houston left the room. A few minutes later, a nurse came in and asked how he was feeling.

"Okay, I guess, but I'm just really, really confused."

"That's common with head injuries, especially concussions," the nurse explained. "Things may be a little foggy for a few days, and then you should be able to go back to your regular life and schedule, hopefully."

David mumbled, "I'm not so sure about that."

"Excuse me?" she asked.

"Nothing, just, nothing."

After fluffing his pillow and tidying up the room, she began taking his blood pressure and temperature. Suddenly, he felt a strange vibration on his left side as someone yelled, "*Who let the dogs out! Who, who, who, who.*"

"Jezuzchrist, what the hell is that!" David said as he tried to kick himself away from the voice and buzzing sensation.

The nurse gave him a puzzled look and told him to calm down; it was just his phone. Reaching down, she picked it up and handed it to him. Taking it from her, it buzzed in his hand, and he dropped it on the bed.

"Aren't you going to answer it?"

David just stared at her.

She picked it up again, pushed something that made all the yelling and buzzing stop, then gave it to him. He held it in his hand until she motioned him to put it to his ear.

"Hello?" David said tentatively.

"I'm still in the parking lot. Hey, assuming you can come home later, what would you like for supper? We can have whatever you want."

He said nothing but realized it was that Shelley person on the other end, and this thing, they call a cell phone, has to be some sort of small radio device.

"Derek? Are you there?"

"Yes, I am here. Can you hear me?" he said loudly.

"Yes, I can hear you fine," replied Shelley. "Stop shouting. You want me to make your favorite meal?"

"Yes, yes, that would be nice, I guess. Over."

"Over? Over what?" she questioned.

"Oh, nothing, don't know what I was thinking."

"I'll see you later, honey. Get some rest," she replied and ended the call.

"Roger that, I mean, okay," said David and handed the phone back to the nurse.

"You must've got quite a bonk on the bean there, mister."

"That is the smallest damn radio I've ever seen," David said, with amazement in his voice.

"Well, that's because it's a cell phone," the nurse replied.

"So that's a cell phone, ain't that something. How does it work?"

The nurse shook her head, saying,

"I don't think anyone really knows," and walked out the door.

Seventy-four years, David did the math in his head. *Somehow it seems seventy-four years had elapsed since this morning when I flew off the deck of an aircraft carrier in the Pacific Ocean. Now I'm here, thousands of miles away, somehow, someway, all those years later. But I'm not me, not on the outside, anyway.*

Could I have died, and this is Heaven? If so, it seems to be located in Fort Myers, Florida, and populated by very peculiar angels. And I wouldn't think my head would hurt like it does, in this very odd kind of Heaven, he pondered while gently putting a hand on the bandage.

After a couple of hours, the nurse came in and told David he was being discharged. She helped get him out of bed and dressed, finishing about the time Shelley and an orderly, with a wheelchair, came through the door. They wheeled him down the hallway to a back entrance and outside, where he sat and waited while Shelley went to retrieve her car.

He had a few minutes to look around the parking lot and watch as the occasional automobile drove by. Still, nothing was familiar to him; but did notice some of the names on these vehicles. One passing by had a Mercedes badge on it, a German brand. He thought this odd and a bit disturbing but generally liked the futuristic style of the vehicles navigating the streets and roads in 2019.

It was good to see Chevys and Fords in the parking lot; nice to know they were still being manufactured, along with a few other familiar makes. Yet to make an appearance were any modern versions of Hudsons, Packards, or Studebakers, among others.

A white car pulled up and came to a stop. He could not see a brand name, and a chrome badge on the front made no sense but reminded him of a cowboy hat. He thought this to be a good sign.

Shelley walked around to open the door. As he slid into the front passenger seat, he was impressed by the interior's opulence. Everything was so detailed and modern, with many buttons, dials, and very comfortable seats. Shelley got in asked if he was ready to go; David nodded. She put her hand on a lever between the seats, pulled it back, and the car began to move.

"Oh, a hydra-matic transmission, no clutch pedal, nice," said David as they turned out of the hospital parking lot onto a side street.

"Hydra-matic? Clutch pedal? What's that all about?" Shelley asked, giving him a sideways glance. "We picked this car out together. I can understand you being a little confused, but you're acting and talking, really weird, Derek."

It was comfortably cool in the car, which seemed odd, being summer in Florida. Very few cars had air-conditioning back in his time. He thought of mentioning how well the newfangled air cooling system worked but decided to let it go, as most anything and everything he said was not being very well received. They drove away from the hospital and turned onto a road with two traffic lanes going in either direction and a grass strip in-between.

This was undoubtedly a different, changed Florida. He recalled, from his time spent here before, vast, open expanses, whereas here in Fort Myers, houses and places of business were now in abundance.

There was little talk during the ride, although Shelley asked if he had accomplished all the errands he had planned before being injured. David just shrugged his shoulders, saying he did not remember. What had happened to him earlier in his day was not something to share with this complete stranger, who obviously thought he was someone else.

"Your car," said Shelley. "I almost forgot about your car; we should go get it. Do you remember where it's parked?"

"I, I, uh," stammered David.

"Oh, never mind, you're probably in no shape to drive, anyway. Might get lost on the way home," chuckled Shelley. "We'll get it tonight or tomorrow sometime. Don't worry about it."

David replied that was a good idea and thought *because I have no damn idea what it looks like or where it would be.* And he also did not know how much longer this ruse could continue. Everyone believed him to be someone else, someone they knew. How could it be explained that he is not this person they call Derek Haynes, even if he looks like him, and there is no rational explanation why he is here, now, in their lives.

He noticed the word Corolla on the dash; it sounded Spanish and assumed it to be the brand name of the car. Who knows what has happened in the auto industry during the last seventy-four years. Approaching an intersection with stoplights, David had the feeling they were going to the left. Shelley put on the turn signal, and when the light turned green, she turned left.

After a few blocks, a right turn was made, and before long, they pulled into a driveway. The neighborhood looked to be a mixture of older two-story homes and one-story ranch houses, of which this was one. White letters on a black mailbox next to the street read, *The Haynes.*

"Well, we're home," he said, figuring this was probably a good bet and should not provoke any questioning looks or remarks.

As he stepped from the car, a boy and a girl ran out the front door towards them.

"Oh, Daddy, we were so worried about you!" the teenage girl said as she ran up and threw her arms around him. "How do you feel?"

"Fine, I guess. My head hurts, and I'm having some trouble remembering things..."

"You okay, Dad?" the boy interrupted. "When Mom called and told us what happened, and you were in the hospital, we were pretty scared."

He appeared to be nineteen or twenty, which would make him just two or three years younger than David. Taking a step towards him, he held out his hand. With a surprised look on his face, the boy shook it.

"Thank you for your concern, young man."

"Dad?" the boy said as they stood in the yard, shaking hands.

"Derek, what are you doing?" Shelley asked as she walked up.

"Oh, yeah, sorry," David said as he stopped shaking the boy's hand and gave him a quick, awkward hug. "I was, a, just shit'n ya', Son," then gave him a playful punch in the arm.

"Kids, your father is having a tough time with his memory, right now, as he said," Shelley spoke, shaking her head. "The doctors told us it might take a few days for it to clear up, so we're just going to have to put up with... I mean, help him. Karli, give me a hand with these groceries. Rob, would you put the car in the garage for me, please?"

Karli and Rob, right. Remember that, David thought.

The two women removed the groceries from the car, then the boy slid into the driver's seat and started the engine. As the three of them were walking up the sidewalk to the house, David saw the back of the car as it rolled forward, finally noticing the brand name. And it was not Corolla. *Toyota... Toyota? That's a Jap name! What is going on here!* David thought angrily, *a Jap car, in America!*

"Toyota," mumbled David gruffly under his breath.

"Did you say something?" Shelley asked, turning towards him.

"No, just got something caught in my throat and choked a little."

It was a nice house and cool inside. The last time he was in Florida, the only air-conditioned buildings were movie theaters and the occasional restaurant. *Derek Haynes must be doing pretty well to be able to afford all of this.* The living room was nicely furnished; David picked a comfortable-looking chair and sat down heavily. Shelley and Karli put away the groceries, and shortly, Rob returned from the garage.

"What's for supper?" he asked.

"Meatloaf, with mashed potatoes and gravy, apple pie for

dessert," Shelley answered. "Your dad's in bad need of his favorite comfort food."

David perked up upon hearing this; meatloaf and mashed potatoes were indeed one of his favorite meals. *What are the chances of this Derek person and me having the same favorite food? That's strange, very coincidental.*

"You want a beer, Dad?" Rob asked as he leaned on the chair.

"Yes, beer would be great. I haven't had one in a long time."

"Long time, like yesterday?" Rob said with a smile as he walked towards the kitchen.

"Yesterday was a long time ago," David quietly replied.

Rob brought him the beer, and David thanked him. The brand name was familiar, but on the bottle was the word, Lite. He wondered what that meant. Taking a drink, he savored the flavor. It was a good beer, no matter what the Lite thing was all about. There was no beer drinking onboard the *Bennington*.

Suddenly, a hand reached down and grabbed the bottle.

"Doc Houston said you probably have a mild concussion, so no beer for you, buddy," Shelley said, shaking her head as she scowled at Rob, who returned a grin and shoulder shrug.

Deciding he needed to find the bathroom, David walked down the hall off the living room, which had several doors. After turning into one of the rooms while automatically reaching left and flipping the light switch, he closed the door behind him. Instinctively, he knew the right door and the switch's location as soon as he started down the hall. It was strange, like knowing which way to turn at the stoplight.

Looking in the mirror above the sink, he got his first clear look at the face that was not his. There were similarities, and he was surprised by this, but it was not the face that stared back at him when last he looked into a mirror in his cabin on the carrier. Although, in truth, it did not seem much older. On the ship, he looked and felt more than his twenty-two years. This reflection showed a higher hairline, thinning on top, and slightly gray around the edges.

He pulled the wallet from the denim jeans; a Florida driver's license showed the name, Derek John Haynes. They were the same height, five-foot-nine, although Derek had at least thirty pounds on him, as could be verified by the reflection in the mirror and a slightly protruding belly. David's middle name was James. It occurred to him they had the same initials. Derek, too, was born on June first, but in 1967. David's mind began swimming with numbers.

This would make him, fifty-two years old. We both have the same birthday, but I'm twenty-two; at least I was this morning, born in 1923, so today, in 2019, makes me… ninety-six years old.

"This can't be real," David said softly to the image in the mirror. "Who are you? Why am I here? What's the purpose, what's, what's the reason for all, this? *If I'm now in 2019, what has become of Macy and Jenny?* he thought, although figuring the math for their current ages was not something he cared to reckon with.

After walking back to the living room, he sat down in a large, comfortable recliner. It reminded him somewhat of the overstuffed chairs in the ready room onboard ship. Shelley remarked from the kitchen that it was good to see him sitting in his usual place. David figured out how to make the chair recline and sat there quietly, trying to relax. Memories and sleep soon followed.

I'm going to miss you so much; so will Jenny," Macy said as she looked into David's eyes. "You have to take care of yourself and come back to us. Don't be a hero; you are already our hero."

It was a Sunday, and the last morning they would awake together in the yellow bungalow before he left for San Diego and back to war. They were lying in bed with Jenny between them; she made cooing sounds as they talked.

"I wish this awful war would be over," she continued.

"The Jap's are not going to give up, be another year, if not longer," David replied. "There's still the invasion of Japan itself, and it's going to be ugly, but I will likely be back here before that starts."

"Are you ever afraid when you're flying?" Macy asked. "You never say much about it in your letters."

"Oh sure, not so much afraid as nervous, mostly in the minutes before take-off. After getting strapped in and the engine running, it fades away, and I concentrate on what needs to be done."

"Once in a while, when you're gone, an uneasy feeling comes over me," said Macy. "Sometimes wonder if I'm feeling what you are, somehow, when you're getting ready to fly. Does that sound silly?"

"No, not silly, but you worry too much, Macy. Everything is going to be fine, really it is. I'll be back in a few months, and we'll be together again, forever and ever, the three of us, I promise, no matter what," David said and crossed his heart.

They both stared into each other's eyes, while Jenny now lay quietly gazing up at her parents.

"You come back to me, David Hamilton. No matter what, no matter what, no matter what...."

Macy's voice trailed off in his mind as David began to open his eyes; he wondered for a moment where he was. All thoughts and confusion of the day came rushing back like a torrent and made him weary. But something smelled real good, and he, or at least Derek Haynes's body, felt hungry, and technically, he had not eaten since breakfast in 1945.

"Suppers ready," Shelley said from the kitchen. "Come and get it!"

David roused himself from the chair, feeling very tired and sore. Karli asked if he had a nice nap.

"Yes, believe I did," he said, working up a smile.

The four sat down to a supper of homemade meatloaf, mashed potatoes, and gravy, with lots of butter; for dessert, there was apple pie. Shelley admitted the pie was store-bought, saying she did not have time to make one from scratch, as she usually did. David ate heartily, and perhaps it was his, or more correctly, Derek Haynes, rapidly filling stomach that made him feel more comfortable, more, at home. Without really knowing why he complemented Shelley on this being some of the best meatloaf she had ever made.

The meal progressed with minimal talk, other than the kids speaking of things David was unfamiliar with and how worried they had been about him. The boy and girl seemed like nice children. He thought Derek Haynes must be a good father.

Karli was a pretty and petite teenage girl. He guessed her to be sixteen or seventeen, with medium-length brunette hair, a beautiful smile, and an outgoing personality. She seemed to be quite fond of her dad, judging by the way she'd worried about his welfare after learning he'd been injured. Rob was perhaps an inch or two taller, with dark hair and an athletic, muscular build. He acted very mature for his age and was less talkative than his sister. David liked the kid right away.

Shelley appeared to be a good woman and mother, although a bit cranky at times, was kind and caring, very attractive, and had a sparkling smile when used. Her hair was short and blonde, her eyes blue. He got the impression she was strong and competent. *Wonder how strong she would be after finding out who I really am,* he thought.

Rob asked David if they were going downtown later to pick up his car. This was to be avoided, and he replied there was still some dizziness and would be best if he stayed home and rested.

"Keys?" said the boy.

"What? Oh yeah, keys, car keys," replied David, as he stuck his right hand into the front pocket of the pants.

Finding only a few coins, he felt in the left pocket and grabbed something he hoped were car keys. He pulled his hand out, found it was, then laid them on the table.

"That's them," said Rob. "Have any idea where it's parked?"

"Sorry, no, still kind of fuzzy, should be down around where I was at, somewhere."

"We'll find it, no problem," replied Rob.

Shelley suggested they all go together, perhaps stopping for ice cream on the way back. David begged off, saying he just needed to sit quietly, maybe sleep off the wonderful supper.

"You all just go along, maybe bring me back some chocolate ice cream."

"Don't you want your usual cookies and cream?" asked Shelley.

"Just chocolate ice cream would be fine."

"No, Daddy, cookies and cream, ice cream, like you always get. It's your favorite, remember?" Karli said.

"Oh, sure, yeah, just thought I'd maybe try chocolate for a change. That cookie creamy thing is my favorite, though; I'll have that."

He had never heard of it.

"You're just not yourself tonight, are you," said Shelley, with a frown, while cleaning off the table, as David retreated to the recliner.

Soon Shelley came over to let him know they were leaving; David expressed his appreciation for retrieving the car. After they were gone, he decided to explore the house.

Walking room to room, he found it fairly typical, although in some ways, to him, futuristic. He reasoned this was to be expected, from someone suddenly showing up in 2019, from 1945, and what an odd and outlandishly accurate thought to have.

Much of the furniture and accouterments seemed plain in comparison to other homes he had lived in and visited while growing up. Furniture and decorations, back then, seemed to have more lavish, ornate designs.

All three bedrooms had a large, black, rectangular, and flat, box-like item mounted on one wall, similar to a picture frame, with no picture. The same object, although much larger, was also present in the living room. He could not help but wonder about their purpose.

Notable and interesting were photos on the walls, family photos mostly, of the four of them. Looking at the display, David did not see himself pictured, only a family of strangers. Even though he looked like one of them, it was not his family. He thought back to Macy's picture wall in their home in Grand Rapids, wondering if it still may, somehow, exist.

A door in the kitchen led outside; in the backyard was a large, freestanding garage, the side entrance door unlocked. Flipping a switch just inside filled the interior with light. There were two empty parking spaces in front, plus a good-sized workshop area in the back. What looked to be a lawnmower someone could ride on, and a covered motorcycle, sat on the right-hand side, near a workbench.

Something tantalizing caught his attention on the left side of the shop. It was hidden under a form-fitting, light blue cover and was obviously an automobile. He approached the vehicle and picked up a corner of the cover, and much to his surprise, discovered a blue steel wheel, a whitewall tire, and a chrome hubcap with Ford on it.

"Now we're talking!" he said aloud as he reached out and touched the hubcap, then instantly pulled back his hand after feeling what seemed to be a mild electrical shock. *Well, that was weird,* he thought.

Rolling up the cover, front to the back, and removing it, revealed the unmistakable profile and design of a 1940's automobile.

He stepped back several feet to get a good look. It was a Navy Blue, two-door coupe. The color seemed a similar shade as *Macy's Magic III*; the newer replaced parts of it, anyway. *Finally, something I'm familiar with.* It appeared to be brand-new, and to him, wasn't that old of a vehicle. Opening the driver's-side door, he found a piece of paper lying on the seat. It was a color photo and a description of the car that appeared to have some connection to an automobile exhibition. 1941 Ford Super Deluxe Coupe, it read, along with other information.

I thought it might be a '41, the last redesign by Ford before the war. This thing is sharp and has had excellent care. Wonder what the story is; why does this family have a 1940s automobile in their garage?

He got in behind the large steering wheel, ran his hands around it, and fiddled with the buttons and switches on the dashboard. Then ran the shift lever on the steering column through its motions while depressing the clutch pedal, smiling all the while, happy to find something familiar in a sea of such unfamiliarity. Who would think an old car could accomplish so much, simply by existing. He felt an instant connection with the Ford; they both came from the same era.

The next several minutes were spent walking around the car, looking, touching, then sitting inside once more, for a time, enjoying the feeling, the normalcy of it. Again, he noticed the motorcycle parked near the workbench, some sort of cloth haphazardly tossed over it.

When he was younger, he had wanted either a Harley-Davidson or an Indian; he liked them both. His parents would not allow him to buy either, and once getting out on his own, he could not afford even a used one. Then he fell in love with Macy, joined the Marines, got married, had a little girl, and went to war, so it just never happened.

Getting out of the car, he walked over to the motorcycle,

curious to see what a Harley-Davidson, Indian, or whatever it might be, looked like in these modern times. Removing an old bedsheet, he searched for a name, bending over to get a better look at the wording on the gas tank. Straightening up abruptly, he said the word out loud,

"Kawasaki!" David Hamilton was stunned. Kawasaki was the name of a Japanese company that manufactured airplanes, war-planes. They built the fighter plane, which the American military referred to as a Tony. David had shot down two Tony's, killing the pilots. *What the hell is a motorcycle manufactured by a Japanese fighter plane company doing in an American family's garage!*

He disgustedly tossed the sheet back over the bike. So many of the good emotions he felt upon discovering the Ford Coupe faded away, replaced by increasing anxiety.

Stepping outside into the early evening sun, he watched a car pull into the neighboring driveway. A man stepped out, waved at him, and walked towards his house. David returned a tentative wave and then noticed the car's emblem, BMW, another German-made brand.

"Well, son-of-a-bitch."

He stared at it for several seconds before a sudden vibration and someone again yelling about dogs, came from his shirt pocket. It was the device everyone called a cell phone. On a glass screen were the words, *Shelley Calling*.

David had no idea what to do. Laying it on a picnic table nearby, he began walking down the driveway. Turning left onto a sidewalk, he set off at a brisk pace. There was a need to move, to get away.

All this has to be some sort of sick dream, a nightmare from which there was no awakening. He found himself in a nonsensi-cal and surreal future world while also trapped in another man's body, with no satisfactory explanation why, or how, for either.

After walking rapidly for two blocks, he began to tire and

slowed. A sudden, intense thirst gripped him, and somehow, he knew, just down the street, was a place where something to drink would be found. In near panic, he thought, *how could I know that? I've never been here before.* A block later, he came upon what looked to be some type of store and gas station. *There it is, and it seems familiar.* Walking past odd-looking gas pumps, he was surprised to see people filling their own vehicles, not a pump-jockey in sight.

Entering the store, David asked the foreign-appearing man behind the counter if they had any Coke. The man said nothing, only motioning with one finger to the rear of the store. He walked back to find another person opening a glass door and taking items out of what turned out to be large coolers mounted to the wall. Opening one of the doors, he picked up a bottle of Coke; it felt strange to his touch. It was not glass, as expected, but plastic. It also said Diet on the label. *Now, what the hell is Diet Coke? It sounds ridiculous.* Again pulling open a door on the cooler, he retrieved a bottle that only said Coke, leaving the other in its place.

"Two dola fiftin," the man said as David placed his purchase on the counter.

"What?" I can't understand you."

"Two dola, fiftin."

"Oh, two dollars… for a Coke?" he replied, surprised at the price.

"Coke, two dola, fiftin, you pay now," the man responded gruffly.

Pulling out Derek Haynes's wallet, he handed the man two dollars.

"Fiftin, you owe fiftin, you pay now," the man grunted.

David pulled a quarter from his front pocket and tossed it on the counter. *What a rude son-of-a-bitch,* he angrily thought and turned to leave.

He saw no bottle opener in the store or outside, but noticed someone in the parking lot twisting the cap off a bottle. Doing likewise, he took a swig. It seemed to taste fine, the same as always. *At least they haven't screwed that up.* After a couple of big swallows, he decided to return to the house simply because he had nowhere else to go and felt emotionally and physically drained.

As he passed through the parking lot, a small pickup truck pulled into a space directly ahead. Glancing at the back of the truck, as he took the last couple of swallows, he choked for a moment, threw the bottle onto the blacktop, then walked away, reluctantly headed back to the people who knew him as someone else, other than David Hamilton. Moving slowly, his head down, he lost track of time. Before long, someone touched his arm. It was Karli, and they were in front of the Haynes house.

"Daddy, are you alright?"

"I just needed to take a walk, trying to clear my head," replied David, in a low voice.

"We were worried when we didn't find you at home."

"Sorry, didn't mean to worry anyone."

"Let's go inside," Karli said as she put her arm around him.

"How are you feeling, Derek? You look so worn out; maybe you should have spent the night in the hospital," said Shelley as they walked into the house. "I tried calling to say we were on our way back, but it just kept ringing."

"I must have put it down, somewhere."

"It was on the picnic table," Rob spoke. "I see you took the cover off the Coupe, thinking of taking it for a spin when you're feeling better?"

"Just wanted to see… it's a nice car," said David tiredly.

"Sure is; we put a lot of time and work into it," replied Rob, with a grin.

David and his dad, too, used to work on cars together, in another time and place. Another world.

"Yes, a lot of work," he said, wearily easing into the recliner.

"Want to watch TV?" asked Karli.

"TV?" queried David.

"Yes, TV, you know, television?" Karli said as she glanced at her mom, who shook her head slowly.

"Okay, Karli, that might be interesting."

David knew little of television; it was in its infancy back in the late '30s and early '40s. Few people had one, and there was little programming to watch. He recalled viewing some minutes of a baseball game in a radio store when a freshman in college. Flickering black, white, and gray images on a tiny screen, no more than nine or ten inches wide. There was nothing of this sort in the house that he had come across. It was fascinating enough at the time, and the salesman in the store said it was the next *big thing*. Some people considered it a fad and would never replace radio.

"Want to watch the news?" Karli asked.

David did not think he could tolerate much more of this new world, this new reality. If indeed it was reality.

"No, not up for that."

"How about a movie? We could see what's playing on the old movie channel."

That might help ease his mind some, or make it worse. David thought, *at this point, what does it matter?*

"Sure, why not."

Karli picked up a small, black object lying on an end-table and pointed it towards the big dark, picture-frame-looking thing on the wall. Suddenly, a bright, colorful, and moving picture appeared in the frame, with sound. This made David sit up straight in his chair. *If this is television, it's come a long way; that screen must be five feet wide! And how did it just come on like that? Must have something to do with what's in Karli's hand.*

She pointed the device at the television again, and it quickly changed to a black and white movie. Within a few seconds, David realized he had watched this not long ago. It was *Going My Way*, with Bing Crosby and Barry Fitzgerald, one of the newer movies requisitioned by the Navy, for sailors and Marine aviators to watch, shipboard. The Mud Marines on bloody Okinawa, did not have such luxuries.

It was nearly over; a mortgage had been paid off, the choir was singing To-Ra-Loo-Ra-Loo-Ra. Playing Father O'Malley, Bing Crosby goes out the door and walks away in the snow; The End. It seemed odd to David, having this film on what they called the old movie channel. It was not that old, not to him.

Shelley asked from the kitchen if he would like to have ice cream. David had no appetite and told her maybe later but asked for something to drink; he was still very thirsty.

"Coke? Water?"

"Water would be fine, thank you."

He was expecting a glass, but Rob brought him a plastic bottle of cold water. *I guess everything comes in plastic bottles anymore, even water.*

Shortly, the introduction to another black and white movie appeared on the big, black, flat television stuck to the wall. The title on the screen announced, *Here Comes Mr. Jordan;* it was the film he and Macy had gone to see on their first date. As the opening credits scrolled by, his mind began to wander back, just a few years ago, to the late summer of 1941.

⇒+ +⇐

An incoming University of Michigan freshman, David arrived at Ann Arbor in late August. He would be sharing dorm lodging with another boy, and a few items for their room, along with required school supplies for his aeronautical engineering classes, needed to be purchased. Ann Arbor's Woolworths, a several blocks walk away, should provide everything on his list.

While sorting through a stack of notebooks in the store, he heard a female voice. A voice that sounded like music.

"Is there anything I can help you with?"

"I just need a few notebooks and things for school," said David, turning towards the voice.

He found himself gazing upon a beautiful girl with sparkling blue eyes and the most charming smile he'd ever seen. She appeared to be about his age.

"Then again, I could use some help," he replied, with a smile of his own.

"Are you going to school at UM?" she asked while stepping closer.

He caught the scent of her perfume; it wasn't familiar but somehow seemed to suit her perfectly.

"Yes, UM," he replied.

"I have a lot of friends going there. What classes are you taking, if you don't mind me asking?"

David looked at her for a moment before replying, taking time to enjoy her presence.

"Aeronautical engineering, you know, airplane stuff."

"That sounds so exciting! Do you fly?"

"No, I mean yes, will be; I'm enrolled in CPTP."

"I'm sorry, I don't know what that is," the girl said with a shake of her head.

"It stands for Civilian Pilot Training Program."

"That sounds interesting; tell me more."

"I've always loved airplanes and wanted to fly. The best part is the government pays for all my initial flight training. That's my reason for going to college, as they only take college students. We might be going to war someday, and the country will need a lot of pilots."

"Oh, I hope that never happens; I hate war," she spoke softly and frowned.

David could see this was upsetting to her.

"My name is David," he said, holding out his hand.

"I'm Macy, so glad to meet you, David," she said, smiling.

"So very glad to meet you, Macy."

The handshake was long and slow. It could have just been his imagination, or wishful thinking, as they looked at each other, but he felt something, something almost electrical. Maybe her touch, her scent. It was an odd, yet happy, feeling. He hoped, perhaps, a connection had somehow been made. It was a new experience for him; he brazenly wondered if she might ever feel the same. She was so beautiful.

Macy was shorter than David, with auburn hair neatly brushed and flowing almost to her shoulders. A clear complexion and that dazzling smile just seemed to emanate a glow about her. The dress she wore was pink, with a simple print pattern of small red flowers, roses, he thought. It fit her slender yet nicely curved body perfectly.

The two became instantly comfortable and chatted as if they had known one another for years. Macy helped him pick out additional items needed for his classes and dorm room. She suggested they walk around the store together; perhaps he may find other things that would be useful. David readily agreed, even though everything on his list was by now, checked off. To spend more time with her was all he wanted. And Macy was becoming enchanted by this young man, whom she noticed soon after he entered the store.

For the next half hour, they strolled the aisles, talking and pretending to shop, genuinely enjoying each other's company. After boldly asking if he could buy her a malt, she quickly accepted. Finding an open booth, Macy took a seat while David went to the luncheonette counter. After paying a quarter each for their re-freshments, he returned and asked,

"I love the perfume you're wearing; what's it called?"

"It's new, Chantilly, hasn't been out that long; is it too much?"

"Oh no, not at all," said David, looking into her eyes. "Can't quite figure out what it reminds me of."

"I bought it because there's more of a rose essence than others sampled. I love roses, any kind, but red is my favorite."

"She just loves red roses," said David slowly.

Macy crossed her legs, put an elbow on the table, and chin in her hand.

"Are you taking mental notes on me?"

"Maybe," he replied, grinning.

"So tell me," Macy said as she laid both hands flat on the table.

"Are you a Dave, a Davy, or just David?"

He so wanted to reach out his hands and touch hers.

"Always preferred David, but it's no big deal," he said, putting both hands on the table, a tantalizing few inches from hers.

"Then David, it shall be."

She so wanted to reach out her hands and touch his.

"How long have you worked here?" he asked.

"Since spring, right after graduation. I'm staying with my aunt here in town; home is too far away to travel daily," replied Macy.

She told the boy of her plans to work full-time for a year and then attend UM to become an elementary school teacher while working at the Woolworth store, part-time.

"What I truly love, though, is singing; some people say I have a nice voice," Macy said shyly. "I don't know if that's true, but…."

"Oh, you do, believe me, you do," David interrupted as he inched his hands forward and touched her fingertips. "When you first spoke, thought I heard music; I mean it."

Macy placed her hands on top of his, softly saying, "Flattery will get you everywhere."

When finally they moved to the checkout counter, David politely thanked her for all the extra time she had spent with him. The young girl said she was pleased to help. Very pleased. Not wanting to leave, he desperately tried to think of a way to ask if he could see her again. While still in thought, she gently put her hand on his arm,

"Please come back again, David."

"I will,"

Halfway back to the dorm came the realization that they had only exchanged first names, but he knew, for sure, there would be a return trip to the store. He had wanted to ask the girl out on a date but decided that may have been too forward for the short time they were together. In retrospect, when Macy put her hands on his, it would have been his opening to ask. *Next time*, he thought, *I'll ask for sure.* The idea of spending more time with this pretty and personable girl filled him with great anticipation, the likes of which he had never felt before.

School began, and David became busy familiarizing himself with the campus, classes, and studying. He was not able to return downtown for more than a week, and it made him anxious. Finally, there was a break during the day; taking advantage of the opportunity, he briskly made the trek to Woolworth's, assuming, hoping, Macy would be working. She had mentioned it was a full-time job. Although money was tight, he made a quick stop at a florist and bought a single red rose wrapped in white tissue paper.

Upon entering the store and not immediately spotting her, David roamed the aisles, searching anxiously for the girl named Macy. He was looking forward to picking up where they had left off, and more. After fifteen minutes, he became worried. Approaching a girl who was stocking shelves nearby, he asked,

"Miss, is Macy working today?"

"Who?"

"Macy, I don't know her last name; I was here sometime back, and...."

"I think I know the girl you're referring to."

"Great, where can I find her?"

"Oh, she doesn't work here anymore."

"What?" said David in disbelief.

"She just didn't come in one day; I don't know what happened to her—a nice girl, from what I've heard.

"Yes, a very nice girl. Would you know her last name?" he asked, hopefully.

"Haven't worked here that long myself; I'm her replacement. Never heard her last name mentioned, sorry."

"Do you think...would I be able to get that from the office, maybe a full name, address, a phone number?"

"They probably still have all that, I suppose, but won't give it out to strangers. I'm sure you understand."

"I understand," said David dejectedly. "Thanks for your time."

"Is there anything I can help you with?"

These were the first words he heard Macy say.

On the slow walk back to the dorm, he threw the rose in a garbage can. *If only I would've gotten her phone number.*

Weeks and months passed. On December 7th, the Japanese attacked Pearl Harbor, and the United States was plunged into World War II. David kept up his studies along with CPTP ground school classes and began flying J-3 Cubs when the Michigan weather permitted. In early 1942, the CPTP program became the War Training Service, WTS, to expressly qualify and train pilots for military placement. Those already enrolled or new candidates joining the program were required to sign a contract whereupon completing the WTS program, they would join the armed forces and become military aviators.

David gladly made the commitment, and in June 1942, having joined the Marines, was preparing to leave UM for basic training, followed by an advanced flight training in Florida. Never had he stopped thinking of Macy and wondering what became of her. By failing to secure a last name and a phone number, some way to contact the girl, an opportunity had been lost, and it gnawed at him. Many times he had ventured back to Woolworths, hoping perhaps, for another chance, but to no avail. *Okay, I'm giving it another shot before leaving Ann Arbor; who knows? It will just be the end of it if I can't find her, this one last try.*

Later in the morning, he dispiritedly made the familiar trip to the store and entered, feeling little to no hope. He had become resigned to it by now. After walking every aisle of the store, as so many times past, with the same disappointing outcome, he began making his way towards the door. A small group of people gathered ahead of him, blocking his exit; he waited for them to move.

Twenty feet away, two girls stood talking. He noticed the dress one of them was wearing; Macy wore something similar when they met. The girl briefly turned her head in his direction, then again to her companion. Almost immediately, she turned back his way.

Macy and David rushed together in just a few steps, touching each other, nearly embracing; both began speaking at once,

"You came back!"

"You weren't here."

"I'm sorry."

"What happened to you? Thought I'd never see you again!"

"I had to leave."

"So happy I found you!"

The girl Macy had been talking with walked over and pointed at David, "That's the guy."

"Yes, it is," said Macy as she looked at him. "Tell Mr. Potter I'm going to take my break now, would you, Bridget?"

Bridget said she would and suggested they go outside for a walk. While going out the door and onto the sidewalk, David asked what that was about.

"When I came back to work, Bridget said a boy had been looking for me and described you. I told her to keep her eyes peeled and let me know if he ever returned to the store again. It's been so long; I thought about you every day."

"What happened to you, Macy? Where did you go?" David asked as they walked.

"Two days after we met, my dad had a bad farm accident."

"Oh no, is he okay now?" David asked with concern.

"He's doing well now but was laid up for months. I needed to go home and help out, have only been back a couple of weeks. I was so afraid you'd gone off to war," Macy said, her voice trailing off.

Stoping, they grasped each other's hands and stood face to face.

"I was so stupid not to get your last name and number," said David.

"I should've written it down for you, but who knew what was going to happen. There was no way to get in touch. I kept hoping and praying you'd come back into the store and my life," Macy replied and threw her arms around his neck.

David put his arms around her waist, and they held that embrace, neither willing to let go. He was elated to hold this girl so close, at last.

As they parted, Macy spoke,

"My name is Macy McDonald, to whom, may I ask, do I have the pleasure of speaking with?"

"David Hamilton, and I am so pleased to make your acquaintance, Miss McDonald, finally and again."

"Likewise, I'm sure, Mr. Hamilton," replied Macy as they shook hands.

"I know this is a little brash, Miss McDonald, seeing as we have just met and all, but, would you care to accompany me on a date, this very evening?"

"Why, this is so sudden, Mr. Hamilton, I will have to give it careful and timely consideration…. Yes!"

They embraced again, then held hands while unhurriedly making their way back to the store. Pen and paper were quickly procured, and the pertinent contact information was exchanged, several wasted and precious, months late.

After agreeing to meet in front of the store at six o'clock that evening, David walked back to the dorm with a spring in his step and a head full of anticipation. After busying himself, again, with preparations to leave Ann Arbor for basic training in a few days, he then showered, shaved, and carefully picked out his wardrobe for the evening.

With no suit or sport coat taking up space in his meager closet offering, he settled on his best, and least shiny, pants, along with a light-blue, short-sleeved shirt. After a quick spit shine of his well-worn shoes, David gazed upon his image in the full-length mirror and declared the project a success, or at least adequate.

"First, okay, third, impressions are important," he said aloud to his reflection, then chuckled.

On his way back to the store, David dreaded the thought of having to tell Macy of his imminent departure for military training, but knew it had to happen. *Dammit, why couldn't we have gotten together sooner?* Now that they had found each other, again, he never wanted to let her go.

After one quick stop, a moment of anxiousness presented itself upon arrival in front of Woolworths and not finding Macy. Soon, she came into view, wearing a form-fitting, knee-length, white dress that fairly shimmered in the sunlight as she made her way down the sidewalk towards him. The fragrance of her perfume arrived a second after she walked up and took his hand, saying,

"Sorry, I'm a little late."

"It's fine, I know where you live, and I got your number. You're not getting away from me again, ever," said David, as he squeezed her hand.

"What are you hiding behind your back?" she asked, raising her eyebrows.

David brought his hand around and presented the girl with a single flower wrapped in white tissue paper.

"A red rose, you remembered," she said and kissed him on the cheek.

"This was going to be my gift to you when I came back the next time after we met; sorry it took so long."

"You shouldn't have spent the money, but thank you so, so much. This means a lot to me. Where are we going? I am yours for the evening, Mr. Hamilton."

"A couple of blocks down, there's a burger joint, and the State Theater is almost right across the street. I've never eaten at the place, but I've heard the food is good, and I do love good burgers," answered David. "Read in the paper that *Here Comes Mr. Jordan* is showing again. It's several months old, but they're not making many new ones anymore. Have you seen it?"

"No sir, haven't taken in a film at the State Theater yet, either. It's practically new, and I hear it's first-rate. Dinner and a movie sound wonderful!"

"I would be most pleased if you would accompany me, Miss McDonald," said David, as he held out his arm, which she readily accepted.

The couple chose a table near the restaurant's large front window. While watching people stroll by on a warm and pleasant

Michigan summer evening, they dined on burgers, fries, and chocolate malts.

"How do you like the food, good?" the girl asked.

"It's great, but the company even more so," replied David.

"You flatter me, sir," she said with a smile.

Taking a bite of his burger, he jumped slightly in his chair upon feeling Macy's foot rub gently against his leg.

"Why, Mister Hamilton, are you alright?"

"Never better, Miss McDonald, never better."

When the food was gone, they talked.

Macy was a farm girl from Fowlerville, a small town northwest of Ann Arbor, graduating high school just a year before, as had David. Her parents were second-generation farmers. The Great Depression had been hard on the farm and the family. The original plan of her working full-time for a year then part-time at the Woolworths while attending UM to be a teacher, had been put on hold. After missing several months of work while helping out at home, it would be another year, perhaps more, before she would be able to begin her studies.

"You know it just occurred to me, your last name is McDonald, and you live on a farm. Would that be, Old McDonald's Farm, by any chance?" David asked wryly.

"Why, as a matter of fact, yes it is," Macy shot back with a chuckle.

David cocked his head.

"Ever since I can remember, there's been a sign at the end of our long lane that says, *Welcome To Old McDonald's Farm*."

"Are you kidding me?" David said, laughing.

"True story," Macy replied, crossing her heart. "If someone were looking for Bob MacDonald's place, people would tell them to just look for the red sign with white lettering."

"I don't believe it."

"It's real; maybe you'll get to see it for yourself, someday."

"Maybe, someday. In the future." David replied, nodding. "You come from a large family?"

"I have a married, older sister in Chicago, and two younger brothers, still in grade school. My sister had a baby last year, so she couldn't help with the farm, and my brothers could only do so much. So it fell on me to go home."

"Understood. Family first, always, family first," said David, seriously.

"I feel the same way," Macy smiled, reached across the table, and took David's hand.

"Do you have any brothers, sisters?"

"Two older sisters, both with families, there's a nine, and eleven-year age difference between us. I was kind of my parent's afterthought, or maybe my mom just wanted to see if she could sneak in a boy, which made my dad very happy."

"What does he do?"

"Runs a garage back home in Cedar Springs, works on cars, trucks, and tractors. He's good at it and taught me a lot about mechanics. We rebuilt my first car together, a 1928 Model A Tudor sedan I'd bought for thirty dollars. We worked on it for almost a year; started driving it to high school when I was fifteen, then sold it before going off to college. Needed the money to get into MU, and my dad said it would be just another expense and distraction anyway."

"That is so great; you must be very close with your dad. I bet your car turned out nice. What color was it?"

"It was at least three different colors when we got it; looked like someone painted it with a broom," laughed David. "We found a nice color of blue, called Navy Blue No. 2."

"I didn't know there was more than one shade of Navy Blue," replied Macy.

"Neither did we, but it sure looked good on that old car. My mom's a teacher," David continued. "She helped me a lot with math. Math and I never got along, but she kept telling me that I'd need better math skills if I wanted to be a pilot. We spent a lot of long hours getting me up to speed on that subject."

"So, she's okay then, with you wanting to fly?"

"My parents taught my sisters and me to chase our dreams, although she probably wishes I was chasing some other kind of dream that kept my feet on the ground, but she is supportive. Originally, it was my dad's dream, you know, to be a flyer. He was in The Great War, World War I. Slogging around in those muddy, stinking trenches, he'd watch the biplanes flying and fighting overhead and became fascinated with them. Dad put in for a transfer to the air-corps to be a mechanic on the planes, with hopes of becoming a pilot. But a couple of days before transferring out, he was wounded in the leg. They sent him home and said his leg was so badly damaged; he'd never be able to fly. Spent three or four months in the hospital, still walks with a limp."

"That's terrible and so sad," said Macy.

"He bought me my first airplane ride, from a barnstormer traveling through our area; I was eight; put the hook in me right then and there, it's all I ever wanted to do, since."

"Are you going to be a pilot in this war?"

He could hear the tension in her voice.

"Well, about that," he began. "I've completed all the training available here; I enlisted in the Marines and will be leaving for basic training, then advanced military flight school in Florida, two days from now. I wish we had more time…."

Macy silently looked into his eyes. Then lowered her head.

"Do you have to go?"

"I signed an agreement. It's something I need and want to do."

"Alright then," Macy replied after a long pause.

Looking up at him, she tried to smile.

"We'll just have to make the most of the time; we have left together."

"I won't be gone forever, likely will get some leave time after advanced training is over. Then I'll come back to you, Macy McDonald; I will. I always will. Missing you already."

"Missing you too, David Hamilton," she replied.

"The movie starts at seven; we should get going," said David, looking at his wristwatch.

He hated to see her so sad.

The State Theater was nearby, so the walk was short and leisurely. After David paid forty cents each for their tickets, they made their way to the balcony. *Here Comes Mr. Jordan* was far from a first-run feature, so the theatre was not crowded. Young men and their dates, primarily.

They held hands during the newsreel, most of it about the war, with the Doolittle raid on Tokyo the previous April, still receiving much well-deserved coverage. It was one of the few bright spots boosting the spirits of Americans early in the war. The newsreel made him anxious to get on with his training and get into action.

David was younger, then, just nineteen. He had yet to experience the horrors of war in the Pacific, or watch friends fall out of the sky, on fire.

For Macy, it was bittersweet. She liked David, more than a lot and was so happy to be with him, to have found each other. Yet their time, together, would be limited to hours, and then David would be marching off into danger. She was already beginning to worry about the boy.

As the movie began, David put his arm around Macy; she put her head on his shoulder, simply treasuring each other's company. Every moment was precious.

After the show ended, and they walked out into the soft,

Michigan night, both became bathed in the warm color of the theaters, bright, neon lights.

They stopped and looked into each other's eyes. David took her in his arms; there was no turning back. Their first kiss was long and warm; they drank it in. At that moment, the connection was complete; for each, there would never be another, for eternity.

He took a few steps back from the girl; she gave him a curious look.

"Under these lights, you, your dress... Macy, you're glowing."

She cocked her head to one side, smiled, outstretched her arms, and slowly turned around, and around, and around again.

"I will always remember you, just like this," said David, mesmerized by the vision.

He again found himself watching the opening credits of their first date, first kiss, movie. This time, he was inexplicably, seventy-seven years into the future and surrounded by a family he did not know, while mirrors reflected the image of a stranger. The first, and only time he had seen the movie, was with Macy on a warm, June 1942 evening in Ann Arbor, Michigan.

He began to recall the storyline. A prizefighter named Joe was flying his private aircraft to his next bout but crashed along the way. He entered the afterlife and was informed he had been killed in the accident a. Upon looking in the *Book of Records*, it indicated he was supposed to live for another fifty years. The angel, in charge of his case, assumed he would die, so delivered his soul to the afterlife prematurely.

Joe demands of Mister Jordan, the angel's supervisor, to be returned to his body and finish the remainder of his life. Unfortunately, as his body was cremated, that would not be possible. He can be sent back to earth but will have to return in another person's body, someone recently deceased. Joe was none too pleased with this.

Although David had been weary from the day's happenings, he suddenly became more mindful while watching this old movie, realizing much of the plot was familiar. It was similar to his story and plight, in some measure, other than jumping into a dead man's body.

Suddenly the television went dark, and he heard people singing Happy Birthday. Rob carried a birthday cake, with candles lit, into the living room and placed it on a coffee table as he, Shelley, and Karli sang. When finished, Shelley said,

"I thought we should have your cake now before you fall asleep in the chair."

"Well, thank you all so much," he said and tried to smile.

The cake was cut and served with a scoop of ice cream. David still had little appetite but did his best to finish.

"Get Daddy's present, Rob," Karli told her brother.

Rob left the room and returned shortly with something brightly wrapped, which he handed to his father.

"Open it, Daddy, open it," Karli said. "We know you said not to get anything, but you'll like it, I'm sure. We went in on it together."

It was heavy, and after removing the paper, he found it to be a large book entitled, *The Definitive Guide to World War II.*

"Do you like it?" Rob asked.

David stared at it for several seconds before replying,

"Yes, it will be interesting to see what hap... I mean, to see what's in it. Might be something in those pages that I've missed. Thank you all so much."

"The kids thought it would be a nice addition to all the other things you have on the subject," said Shelley. "I'd think you'd have enough of that stuff by now, but that's what they wanted to get you."

He had no idea what she was talking about but thanked them

again and gently laid the book on the coffee table. Karli pointed the device at the television, making the movie appear once more, but there was little interest now, too much going through his mind.

"I'm just going to go sit outside for a while; enjoy the evening," he said, rising from the recliner, then headed towards the door.

"Are you okay, honey?" Shelley asked, with concern in her voice.

"Yeah, I'm alright."

But David Hamilton was not alright. He stood outside in the warm Florida evening, looking up at the sky, thinking of Macy and Jenny.

"Where are you now?" he questioned, softly, into the night.

Walking to the garage, he felt the need for something familiar. The 1941 Ford Coupe was still uncovered; he ran his fingers along a front fender. This was something from the '40s, as was he. There was a kinship with it, a feeling of familiarity. It was like an old friend, newly rediscovered after many years of absence; the machine filled a void. He liked the feel, the look; the color reminded him of his first car. Opening the driver's-side door, he slid in behind the wheel.

"This may be as close to home, to my time, as I am ever going to get," he said aloud and sadly.

The garage side door opened, Rob stepped in, closing it behind him. Scanning the garage and seeing his dad in the Coupe, he walked over, opened the passenger side door, and sat down.

"Dad," began Rob. "We're all really concerned. You had a pretty bad knock today, and, even though the doctor said it's not that serious, well, you've just not been acting like yourself."

David no longer could contain his emotions. The truth needed to be told. He grabbed the top of the steering wheel with both hands, put his forehead down on them, and began to sob as the boy sat motionless, saying nothing. Finally, David, wiping away tears, looked at Rob and said,

"I'm not who you think I am. It sounds like crazy talk, I know, and I can't make any sense of it myself, not one bit."

"I, I don't understand, Dad," stammered Rob.

"I'm not your dad; I'm not! I look like him, but, inside, I'm someone else."

Rob stared at his father for a moment, then got out of the car and walked over to the workbench.

"Dad, remember these?" he said as he returned, opening a photo album.

"But Rob…"

"These are pictures mom took of us, working on this car, together. For over two years, you and me," said Rob, as he tapped his finger on a photo of the two of them standing next to the unpainted car, dirty and smiling.

"You don't understand, Rob. I've been trying to figure out all day just what happened and why I'm here."

"You're here because you live here. You're Derek Haynes; you live in Fort Myers, Florida, you have a family. That's all there is to it. I know that head injury may have caused some confusion, but…."

"No, I'm David Hamilton, from Michigan. I have a wife and baby daughter."

"You're just talking crazy now, Dad!" Rob replied angrily. "Stop it, just stop it! Who the hell is this person supposed to be, anyway, this, this David?"

They both stared intently at each other; David turned his head forward, looking out over the blue hood of the car.

"Don't ask me to explain how or why because I just can't. This morning, I woke up on an aircraft carrier in the Pacific Ocean, off the island of Okinawa; it was 1945. I'm a twenty-two-year-old fighter pilot."

"Oh c'mon now, really? I know you've read a lot of books and watched a bunch of World War II videos and things," Rob returned. "But for you to come up with this bullshit story about actually being in, taking part in, World War II…."

David looked back at Rob, held up his hand, and cut him off.

There was a moment of tense silence before David again turned his head forward.

"Just hear me out," he said. "I need to tell someone. Sorry, it has to be you."

He turned back towards Rob, who crossed his arms and said, "I'm listening."

"This morning, I flew a Corsair off the deck of the aircraft carrier, USS *Bennington*. Today was my last combat mission as a fighter pilot. I'd made two passes on the island and was heading back to the ship. I saw a group of Marines, who were in trouble, pinned down by machine-gun fire on a ridge, and turned back to help. After killing the Jap gunners, an anti-aircraft shell exploded on the nose of the plane."

David looked down as these recent memories came flooding back into his consciousness. He took a moment to calm himself before continuing.

"The plane was going down; it started spinning. The canopy was jammed shut; I couldn't bail out," he took a deep breath.

"Smoke filled the cockpit, and there was fire; could barely breathe. I was going to die. A picture of my wife, me, and our little girl was taped to the instrument panel. I yelled, wished, prayed, to God, to be with them, again."

"You really believe this?" Rob asked.

David slowly nodded his head.

"It was real, it happened, and I was scared, angry. My last flight of the war, just one more and home, one more, but I didn't make it; I didn't goddamn make it!" he yelled and banged his hand on the steering wheel.

Rob could see his dad was genuinely, emotionally, upset. Whatever was in him, real or imagined, needed to be purged.

"But, but how did you, I mean, this, this David person, get here? Supposedly."

"You see, I just don't know," said David, shaking his head. "Everything went dark and quiet, then a flash. Thought I was dead, then heard a noise, and woke up in an office or something. A man was sprawled out on the floor, bleeding, had no idea where I was. Some people began coming into the room, and I was told to leave, to go home. They kept calling me Mr. Haynes. Outside, on the street, I saw things, things that made me believe I'd somehow jumped in time, to this time, your time. Saw my reflection in a window, but it wasn't me. Then I passed out and ended up in that hospital."

Rob stared at him with his mouth open.

"Well, that's quite a story," he finally said. "I have to tell you, Dad, or whoever you think you are; I'm having a tough time with this; you're going to have to prove it to me, seriously."

"Maybe we can look some of it up, like in history books or something, so I can prove what I'm saying is true," David said, exasperated. "Is there a library around here, somewhere?"

"Of course, there's a library; you know that."

"That's the point; I don't. Don't know what I'm doing here, and don't know why I'm not seeing me when I look in a damn mirror!" David said loudly.

"Don't need a library; we can look it up on the internet," Rob replied.

"What's internet?" asked David.

"Oh, good one, you're playing this up really well," Rob replied with a scowl.

"I have no idea what internet is, Rob. Can we drive there tonight or first thing in the morning?"

Rob stared at him and slowly said,

"No, we can use one of the computers in the house."

"I don't want Shelley and Karli to know anything about this, at least not until we can get everything sorted out. I need to trust you on this, Rob. Wait, you have a computer, in the house?"

"You know we do, more than one," said Rob, as he reached into his shirt pocket. "But we can look it up on my phone, too, right?"

"On your…oh, that cell phone thing? You can call somebody, and ask?"

"No, no, we can get on the internet and find information on almost anything. With a cell phone, a web search. On the internet? Remember? C'mon!"

David stared at him and shook his head.

"Cell phones are like mini-computers, you know this, you use one every day!" Rob said sharply.

"You mean to tell me that little thing in your hand, besides being some sort of radio, or phone, also houses a computer?"

"Yes," replied Rob, with a sigh.

"All the computers I've ever heard about took up an entire room. What planet am I on, Rob?"

"Jeezuz, Dad, just stop it! What's is it you say you were on?"

"Aircraft carrier, USS *Bennington*, and it was a ship, a damn big one."

"Whatever," said Rob disgustedly.

After a minute on the phone, he said, "Okay, so there was an aircraft carrier named the *Bennington*, and…."

"We called it *Big Benn*," David interrupted.

"Whatever," Rob repeated, giving him a sidelong glance. "And yes, it was involved during the invasion of Okinawa. It also had Corsairs onboard during that time. But you could've looked up all this in your research material and memorized it, doesn't mean you were there. That bump on the head today may have stirred it all up in your brain, your memory. Information like this could even be in that big book we gave you tonight; wouldn't surprise me a bit. I bet we could go back in the house right now and find most of this stuff you're telling me about."

"Don't think I could handle that," said David, looking down. "We lost the war; I realize that now. All of us thought we had it won and was just a matter of time until...."

Rob put his hand up.

"Whoa, wait... what? We didn't lose the war; what are you talking about?"

"I see Kraut and Jap vehicles all over the place. There's Mercedes, BMW's, a lot of other German stuff too, you know? Why, your mom drives a Jap car, made by Toyota! I'm seeing Nissan cars and a bunch more Jap brands, and sitting right over there is a damn Kawasaki motorcycle!" David thundered, pointing at the covered bike. "I shot down two fighters, built by Kawasaki! What are all those, things, doing in this country if we won the war? Is it even called the United States of America anymore?"

"Dad, wait..."

"Earlier, when I was at a gas station store, just down the street, some type of small truck pulled in that said Mitsubishi on it, Mitsubishi! They built the damn Zero fighter planes! After seeing all that, well, I just knew we had to have lost the war; it makes me so angry...."

"Dad, we did win the war, remember?" Rob interrupted. "Two atomic bombs were dropped on Japan in August 1945. They surrendered a few days later. You know this."

"What's an atomic bomb? It must've been damn big if they only needed two of 'em, as you say. What bullshit," David said in disbelief and crossed his arms.

"Just two, Dad, the first nuclear weapons in the world, each one killed thousands of Japanese in just two cities, mostly civilians. It was devastating. Scientists found a way to split atoms and basically harness the power of the sun, and, wait, why am I talking to you as if you don't know this?" Rob said loudly and gestured with his hands.

"Because I don't, but if it's true, and they killed thousands of Jap's, good! They deserved it," said David.

"Dad, please, it was a long time ago," Rob replied.

"Not for me," David quickly returned, glaring at the boy.

"Germany and Japan are our allies now, Russia and China, not so much," said Rob, trying to keep calm.

"What! Now you're just talking stupid shit, Rob. You're making it up."

"I can look it all up on here and show you," replied Rob, holding up his phone.

David stared at Rob for a moment before saying, "Never mind that, is the *Bennington* still around? We need to find some records that would show I was onboard and what happened."

Rob sighed and began working on his phone.

"It was decommissioned in 1970 and sold for scrap. Says here it also served during the Vietnam War. Oh, and was the recovery ship for the Apollo four space mission in 1967, the same year you were born."

"Viet… Vietnam Nam, war? Space mission? What are you talking about?"

"C'mon, Dad, you learned all this in school."

"Maybe Derek Haynes did, but I sure didn't. I'm telling you, this morning, I woke up in 1945, and now it is 2019. Last I knew about the world, and the war, ended seventy-four years ago, today.

I know nothing about any of these things you're telling me, and what's this about a space mission?"

"It was some unmanned test, two years before the moon landing."

"Moon? Who landed on the moon?"

"We did, Dad; Americans went to the moon, and back, in July 1969, and more times after. You can't have forgotten something like that."

"Space travel, a man on the moon. You're telling me this is true; it actually happened?"

"You know it did," said Rob, nodding his head. "There's even a space station with human beings on board, circling the earth now, right now, as we speak, remember?"

"Well, I'll be damned," said David. "When I was a kid, that was all just silly science fiction crap. Look, Son, I mean, Rob, you've got to believe me, you must. What else can you look up on that phone computer thing of yours?"

"Anything you want," said Rob, almost defiantly.

"VMF-112, look up VMF-112, 1945," David said quickly.

"What's that?"

"It's my Marine squadron, the Wolfpack. We flew Corsairs in 1944 and '45."

Rob worked on his phone before saying,

"I see there was a VMF-112, called the Wolfpack, and yes, they did take part in the invasion, of Okinawa."

"Just as I said," replied David.

"But, I mean, you know a lot about these things, especially aviation. You, you might have seen this somewhere, just remembered it, right?"

"Lived it, Rob; I lived it and watched good men die there, like Dan Owens, my wingman."

"Hang on; the battery is getting low," Rob said. "I'm gonna go in the house and get something else. We need to sort this out, now, tonight."

"Okay, just don't say anything to your mom or act suspiciously. You know she has a way of weaseling information out of, out of…."

David's voice trailed off.

"Yes, she does," said Rob, as he smiled, got out of the Coupe, and headed towards the door.

Stopping midway, he turned and walked back to the car. Bending over, he looked in at David,

"I know that, but if you are who you say you are, how would you?"

"I… I don't know, the thought just came into my mind, and I can't tell you why."

Rob stared at him for a moment, shook his head, and walked out of the garage. A few minutes later, he returned and sat back down in the car.

"Everything okay?" David asked.

"Yeah, I told mom we're looking to see if there's going to be any car shows nearby; it's all good."

"Now, what do you call that thing you have there, a big cell phone?"

"It's called a tablet," said Rob, turning it on. "It's kinda like a laptop, only smaller."

David gave him a stare.

Sighing, Rob said tiredly, "Never mind. What else do you want me to search for?"

"Try and look up records of combat missions flown off the *Bennington,*" David swallowed hard. "During June 1945."

"I'll try; it depends if they were ever placed online."

As Rob tapped on the device, David, nervously, wondered what he might be about to hear. It was inconceivable that kind of information could come from a small, shiny, black book-like device. He desperately needed to know what the record said about that day, this morning. Even though he already knew the answer.

After several minutes of working on the tablet, occasionally shaking his head, and mumbling, Rob said,

"This might be what we're looking for."

"What does it say?"

David could feel a lump forming in his throat.

"USS *Bennington, World War II, overseas losses, operational, and combat.* It has dates, types of aircraft, bureau numbers, squadrons, location, some but not all pilot names, and fate," said Rob, as he looked over at David. "And fate," he repeated.

Rob could not believe his father's story, that he was, somehow, a fighter pilot from World War II, who was shot down in the Pacific. Yet he knew, by the look in this man's eyes, a look that was both a mixture of dread and anticipation; for him, it was real. Rob scrolled to the listings from 1945.

"You said you had a friend, a friend who was killed?"

"Yes, Dan Owens, what've you found?"

"Do you remember the date?"

David went back in his mind, back to the plummeting fireball that was his friend and wingman, only five days before he took off for the final time.

"Would've been May twenty-six."

Rob looked down at the tablet and read slowly,

"May twenty-six, 1945. F4U–1D. Plane number 82325. VMF–112. Okinawa. Lieutenant Danon C. Owens."

"Fate, there's a D after his name," said David.

"Yes, D. Dead," Rob answered, almost in a whisper.

"Alright," David said and took a deep breath. "Now, June first."

Rob, reluctantly, looked back down at the tablet.

"There were three losses on that day."

"Corsairs?" David asked pensively.

"Yes, one," said Rob, without looking up.

"Read it to me."

"June first, 1945. F4U–1D," Rob began. Before he could continue, David interrupted,

"The planes bureau number is 82628, VMF–112, Okinawa,"

"That's right," Rob replied, barely audible.

"Name, and fate, Rob. I have to know."

Rob looked down at the tablet and cleared his throat.

"There is none."

"What do you mean, has to be!"

"It says at the top of the page here, all records may not be complete, that everything was compiled with the best knowledge at the time of the incident, and subsequently," replied Rob.

"Give me that," said David sharply.

Rob handed the tablet to him, pointing to the information at the end of the line; there was nothing but dashes as to the pilot's name and fate. Passing it back, he said,

"I can fill in those last two parts, Lieutenant David J. Hamilton, D."

"No, this can't be happening; it can't be," Rob said nervously. "I mean, you got the plane number right and everything, but how?"

"Because that was me this morning. I died on this date, in that plane; at least my body did, seventy-four years ago, today. Somehow, someway, my consciousness, spirit, soul, whatever, leaped into your dad's body, and I don't know why or what to do about it. I'm sorry, Rob."

"You're sorry? You're sorry?" Rob said, his voice rising. "If what you're saying is true, then, then where is my dad! Just get out, go somewhere else, go where you belong, I don't care where. Go to hell! Just let him come back!"

"If I only could, Rob," said David, shaking his head. "I just don't know why this is happening or how to stop it."

"Please, just let him come back…." Rob said, almost crying.

The side garage door opened, and Shelley stepped in. Rob quickly wiped the dampness from his eyes and turned off the tablet.

"You boys about done playing with your car stuff?" she asked while walking up to the Ford.

"We're done, for now, I guess," said Rob, trying desperately to gather his composure as he looked at the man in the driver's seat.

"Yeah, I guess so," added David.

"What are you guys up to?" Shelley questioned.

"Nothing," David and Rob said in unison.

"Car shows, just looking for car shows to go, too. You know how we like our car shows. Right, uh, Dad?"

David nodded his head in the affirmative.

"Uh-huh, right. So, you coming in soon?" she asked, still suspicious.

They both nodded. Shelley walked towards the door, then turned and looked at them, sitting in the old car. Placing hands on her hips, she said,

"You two *are* up to something, aren't you?"

Both men shook their heads. Shelley sighed and walked out of the garage.

"What now?" asked Rob.

"Don't know, but we're not done with this," replied David. "I truly appreciate what you're doing; it has to be tough on you."

"I still can't believe all this; it's just so, so…."

Rob was fumbling for the words.

"I know," was all David said.

Both returned to the house to find Shelley and Karli watching a color TV show, a comedy of some sort, and took a seat. David could not follow or understand most of the program; there was much on-screen laughter about things he did not comprehend, or find funny. Shelley, Karli, and even Rob, at times, were laughing, and it was nice to see.

He pondered what tomorrow would bring, or if there even would be a tomorrow, one that would be recognizable, familiar, anyway.

After the show ended, Shelley stood and announced she was going to bed and asked David if he was coming. He was exhausted and most definitely needed sleep, but this was not his wife; she was not Macy. He was married, and Shelley was another man's wife. David Hamilton could not go to bed with this woman. Suddenly, he became extremely uncomfortable. *I can't do this, just can't,* he thought.

"I, I think I'll be more comfortable out here," he said to Shelley.

"All night?" she asked. "Don't be silly; come to bed."

David bent over and picked up the large World War II book off the table.

"I'll just read some of this, for now, and, and come to bed later."

He knew this would not happen.

"Alright, whatever," Shelley said, as she shrugged her shoulders, turned, and walked down the hall.

"Well, I'm heading to bed, too," Rob added.

"Me too," echoed Karli, as she stood, yawned, then turned off the television.

"You going to be alright, by yourself, out here, D*ad*?" Rob asked sarcastically, emphasizing the last word.

"Yes, S*on*, I'll be just fine, thank you," replied David.

Karli kissed David on the forehead, avoiding the bandage, then switched on the reading lamp next to the recliner; she and Rob walked down the hall.

David had used the World War II book as an excuse not to go to bed with Shelley, but now, hesitantly, he began to turn the pages.

He read little of the text, mainly focusing on the numerous

photos and their captions. After more than two hours, he was near the end. The war with Japan had indeed ended swiftly and decisively following the bombing of Hiroshima and Nagasaki, using what was referred to as atomic bombs. The number of deaths caused by the bombing themselves, plus thousands who died later, was staggering.

"How could all that death and destruction happen, with just two bombs? My God…" he said softly to himself.

He thought *it's peculiar; the term, mushroom cloud, is used when describing photos of the immediate aftermath.* The words seemed so benign. Images showing the destruction of those two cities were incredibly appalling; he almost felt compassion for the Japanese people. Almost. The Empire of Japan had started the war with a sneak attack on America at Pearl Harbor. They fought viciously and killed many American fighting men, along with thousands of civilians, in other countries they overran.

They were responsible for my apparent dea… He did not want to even think of the word. *Accountable for this here and now. Whatever it is, or turns out to be.* He placed the huge volume back on the coffee table and turned off the reading lamp.

It was the end of a very long and unexplainable day. In the dark, he pushed the recliner back as far as it could go and tried to calm his mind, hoping to induce much-needed rest. Before long, an exhausted David Hamilton fell into a deep, image-filled sleep.

⟩⋅⟨

SUNDAY

"Get up, let's go, boy…." David said into Rob's ear as he shook him in his bed. "C'mon, we need to talk, plans to make, things to do."

"What, what's wrong?" Rob asked, not fully awake.

"Everything, still, but I know what needs to happen."

Rob stared at him for a moment, blinking rapidly.

"Oh, last night, in the garage. Was hoping I'd imagined all that."

Sitting up in bed, he looked at his clock radio.

"It's barely past seven, Dad, or whoever you are. What's going on?"

"Get dressed and meet me outside; we need to go somewhere and get breakfast. Gotta talk."

"Oh, okay, but it's Sunday. We all usually sleep in and have breakfast here, together. I guess you wouldn't know that," the boy replied.

"Just leave a note on the kitchen table or something; it'll be fine. Oh, and bring that book, tablet thing, whatever you had last night," David said and hurried out, grabbing a notepad and pen from the kitchen on the way before stepping outside.

By the time Rob had roused himself and gotten dressed, David already had the blue Ford idling in the driveway and was walking around the car, wiping it off with a soft cloth.

"Runs good, doesn't it," he commented as Rob stepped outside into the sultry, June morning.

He stood there for a moment, watching, yawning, and stretching, before speaking,

"Of course it does; we spent a lot of time on that thing… never mind," replied Rob, shaking his head as he moved towards the car.

David tossed the cloth on the picnic table and motioned the boy to get in.

"You should drive; I haven't driven in a long time, other than than a fighter plane at three or four hundred miles an hour," David said, opening the passenger side door.

Rob stepped into the driver's side, positioning himself behind the steering wheel, and closed the door.

"Pretty sure this doesn't go that fast."

"The color is similar to my Corsair, so maybe it will," said David, with a chuckle.

"Navy Blue No. 2," Rob spoke as he yawned.

"What did you say?"

"Navy Blue No. 2, remember? No, you wouldn't. Was a Ford color we found that my dad liked, so that's what we painted it."

"Well, isn't that something," said David. "My father and I painted my first car the same color. That has to be more than coincidental, right?"

"Don't know, and don't care. I'm hungry. Where we going for breakfast?" asked Rob.

"Haven't a clue; I'm not from around here. Is there some diner or greasy spoon that serves breakfast within a quick drive?"

"We can head over to Fort Myers Beach; it's not far," Rob replied. "There's a kind of old-time diner on San Carlos Boulevard you'd probably like, Pinks; I think it's called, they should be open by now. And just what in the hell is a greasy spoon?"

The trip to the diner did not take long. On the way, David commented on the four-lane highways and how well the Coupe seemed to run and drive.

"There weren't any highways like this back home in Michigan when I was growing up, or in Florida, during my Marine flight training. It might take some getting used to, on a long drive."

"They're easy to use, especially the interstates. You thinking of making a trip?" Rob asked.

"Actually, yes," said David, with a nod, as the boy flipped on the right turn signal.

Pinks was a simple, old-fashioned-style restaurant; a few cars were scattered about the gravel parking lot. As they were walking to the entrance, an older gentleman came out the door.

"Nice car," he said. "My dad had one a lot like it."

"Thanks, my son and I restored it together," said David, as he smiled and looked at Rob.

"Well, you both do good work. Keep it running; they don't make 'em like that anymore," the man said, then turned and walked to a Mazda Miata.

David watched for a moment as the man got into the car.

"No, they sure don't," he said, the smile leaving his face.

"Japan builds some of the best vehicles in the world now, but you just don't like anything, Japanese, do you."

"Nope, let's eat," David replied as he walked through the door. After finding an empty booth, they seated themselves.

Shortly, a waitress arrived to take their order. Both men quickly looked at the menu. David ordered ham and eggs with hash brown potatoes, while Rob chose a cheese omelet and a side of wheat toast. Both ordered coffee, with David adding a glass of orange juice. After the waitress turned and left, Rob spoke,

"There's something I need to say... here's the thing. I don't know what to call you, now, and it's bothering me."

"How do you mean?" pursued David.

"Well, I'm talking to you, but you're not my real dad, even though you, bodily, are. So, should I call you David, or what? Don't know what to do here, and you do call me Son, as you did with that guy outside."

"I get what you're saying," said David.

After a pause, he continued,

"I have a young daughter, well, a daughter, somewhere. The last time I saw her, she was too young to say, dad or daddy, or even talk at all. Having you and Karli call me dad was odd at first, but I like it, and I like calling you Son. For some reason, it seems natural. Does that sound strange, Son?"

"No, it doesn't, Dad," said Rob, with a smile. "My mom is already leery of what we're up to; I don't think calling you anything but Dad would help the situation. Let's just keep this father-son thing going."

"I'm good with that. Besides, your mom may be right about us being up to something."

"Oh boy, I hate even to ask," replied Rob, as he leaned back in the booth and crossed his arms.

"We, you and me, need to do some traveling," said David.

"Where and why?"

"You up for a road trip to Michigan, Son?"

"Michigan? What's in Michigan?"

"My past, my future, some sort of resolution," replied David, shaking his head slowly, side to side. "Answers, more questions, who knows. What I do know is; there are no answers to be found here. And the need to go back home to Michigan is pulling me like a magnet. That's why I asked you to bring that computer book. We need to look up some things before we leave."

"When are you thinking of leaving on this road trip? What's our time frame?"

"Leave tomorrow, hopefully."

"Tomorrow?" said Rob, uncrossing his arms and leaning forward. "And you want me to go along? What about Mom and Karli?"

"That's the problem; I don't know how much longer I can keep up this deception of being your dad. Your mom expects everything to be normal, but there's no normal for me in this time, your time. I'm living the life of an imposter, and I don't think it is going to end well, here, if it ends at all, and you're the only one I can talk to about it and rely on."

"I get it," said Rob.

"I had a dream last night, more of a vision, really," David began. "It… it was all jumbled up, saw things, strange things, it was confusing at times. But woke up this morning knowing this trip is necessary, imperative. You need to be my guide; I can't do it alone. This is literally a different world, and I'm not part of it. I know it's a lot to ask."

"How are we supposed to explain this sudden trip? I'm sure mom will be suspicious; well, she already is."

"We'll tell her this is something we've talked about doing and just decided to go. Hopefully, find some reason, some destination that will make sense, and she'll buy," David replied. "I hate to be deceitful with your mom, but…"

"Might work," Rob interrupted. "But as I said, she already figures we're up to something."

"There's nothing here for me. It will be the only way to get your dad back, I know it. As for what ultimately happens on my end, well, things can't go on the way they are, I have a destiny, and *we* need to find it. What's happening now is not fair to anyone."

"I suppose you're right; what's next?"

"We need to use your computing thing to look up people and places," David replied, just as the waitress brought their orders.

While eating, they talked, each asking the other questions about their lives. Rob was home from his sophomore year at the University of Florida in Gainesville. He was majoring in computer science and had secured a summer job at a large home improvement chain store. David was pleased to hear that the boy was not scheduled to start for another week, so there should be no issue with him needing time off for their travels.

David spoke of his younger days in Michigan, how he and his dad had rebuilt the 1928 Model A Ford, much as Rob and his dad, Derek, had rebuilt the 1941 Ford Coupe. And how odd the same obscure paint color had been chosen for both. They agreed it was a bizarre coincidence and wondered what, if anything, it might mean.

Rob recounted some of what he knew of his dad's life, mainly focusing on his keen interest, near obsession, with World War II history. His grandfather, Derek's dad, had been in the war, having joined the Marines as a teenager, in 1942, after the attack on Pearl Harbor. He was in his forties when Derek was born.

"Do you know what year your grandfather was born?"

"Not sure," Rob replied. I think my dad said he was nineteen when he joined in 1942, so that would be about, 1923, right?"

"Same year I was born, wouldn't know his birthday, would you?"

"No, I only saw the man a few times, never remember him smiling; he died when I was very young. Wait, you know, now that I think about it, my dad once mentioned that he and his dad had the same birthdates, which would've been yesterday. Weird, huh?" Rob said, then took a bite of his toast.

"My birthday was yesterday too, Rob."

"Are you serious?" Rob replied as he dropped the toast on his plate.

"Yes, and this is all tied together; it has to be. There's a reason, a message, and we need to figure it out."

"I can't disagree with that," the boy said.

Rob asked David what it was like, being a fighter pilot on an aircraft carrier. David was reluctant; there were too many recent and painful memories he did not care to revisit, not yet.

"Some other time. We need to focus on the present, the here and now. If you're finished with your breakfast, we should get going, make some plans. Is there someplace we can go and not be bothered?"

Rob suggested they head down San Carlos Boulevard to the pier.

"There are places to sit; it's a nice spot."

The waitress brought their check; Rob said he would pay for breakfast. After getting up from the booth, David left a quarter tip on the table.

"Dad, really? Sure you can afford that?"

"What should I leave? A quarter used to be plenty."

"In the 1940s, this is 2019; leave her at least three dollars, maybe four."

David pulled four dollar bills out of Derek Haynes's wallet, placing them on the table.

"Don't think I'll ever get used to your time. And hopefully, I won't have to for much damn longer."

After a short drive, the car was parked, soft drinks purchased, and a leisurely stroll to the end of the pier was made. David paused halfway out for a few minutes to look back at the beach that was just beginning to fill with sunbathers, swimmers, and waders. He remarked how everyone, young and old, seemed so happy, and what a nice beach area it was.

The temperature was already well into the eighties; tall, fluffy, cumulus clouds slowly rolled across a bright, blue sky. With only a light breeze, the Gulf waters were relatively still. When they reached the shelter at the end of the pier, a dozen people were milling about. Some fishing, others were taking photos of the peli-cans, who brazenly landed on the railing, looking for handouts.

"Usually don't see this many snowbirds in June," said Rob.

"Those are pelicans, Son."

Rob laughed out loud.

"No, Dad, some of the people feeding and taking pictures of the pelicans might be the snowbirds. That's what we call the people from up north, who come down and spend the winter months."

"Oh, they used just be called tourists," David replied.

Several sail and powerboats were turning and maneuvering out on the sparkling water. A pair of jet skis cavorting nearby caught David's attention; he asked Rob what they were. Two hundred yards out, a motorboat sped away, towing a single passenger parasail into the sky.

"Look, look!" David almost shouted while pointing at the para-chute as it climbed high behind the boat.

His attention quickly turned towards the beach as a woman windsurfer stood up on her board, caught the wind, and took off, briskly, across the gentle waves.

"Look at that thing!" David said excitedly. "It's some kind of a surfboard with a sail on it."

"Yeah, that's pretty much what it is; they do that a lot around here," Rob replied.

"Never seen such things. Between that parachute pulled be-hind a boat, and a sailing surfboard, you people know sure how to amuse yourselves. Ever do any of this stuff, Rob?"

"They have two-seat versions of the parasailing; Karli and I have gone up a couple of times; it was fun. You and mom, well, my dad and mom took a ride once."

David stared thoughtfully for several seconds at the parasail, drifting through the sky.

"I remember, we were…." he stopped. "No, no, I can't remem-ber that, right? Let's get to work."

"Yeah, I guess we should," said Rob quietly.

They found seats on one of the benches beneath the pier shelter roof, and Rob switched on the tablet.

"Where do you want to start? Should we search for car shows in Michigan?"

David gazed out over the water for a moment.

"We'll get to that. First, could you look up my name on that thing? Just to see what it might say. Put in David J.... no, make that David John Hamilton."

After a few minutes of working on the tablet, Rob looked up.

"There are several, from all over. Can you be more specific? Let's try your date of birth, and what is the name of the town you're from?"

"Try David John Hamilton, born June first, 1923; the town's name would be Cedar Springs, Michigan."

"Do you know the ZIP Code?" asked Rob.

David got a puzzled look on his face and was just opening his mouth to speak.

"Never mind," said Rob quickly. "I'll try what you gave me."

He looked carefully at the information that came up on the tablet, then told David there were no viable matches.

"Try putting in all that information again, but this time add World War II military record, something like that."

Rob tried again, but after a moment, he looked at David and shook his head.

"It's like I don't exist, never existed, a none-person. As if my entire life made no difference, at all."

"Don't get too upset, Dad; you can find a lot of things on the Internet, but it's not perfect. Information like this from so long ago probably is not going to be easy to find."

"Do one more for me, Macy McDonald Hamilton, try that."

Rob entered the name.

"There are a few, but all younger people. She would be quite a bit older now, right?"

"Ninety-six in May," replied David.

He was disheartened to hear this but knew planning for the upcoming trip now had to take precedence.

"You can look again, maybe some other time. Right now, we need to come up with a credible reason for a trip to Michigan. You said something about car shows; think your mom would believe we'd drive that far, just for something like that?"

"It might be a stretch, as there are plenty around here; she would question why such a long drive," replied Rob as he tapped on the tablet. "You know, I just got to thinking about museums, searching now for something that might work."

"Like what?"

"Car museums, antique cars, specifically. World War II, and aircraft museums. Maybe air shows where they might have World War II aircraft, which she knows we would enjoy seeing and be willing to travel that far. Okay, here we go, write these down."

"There's an old car museum near Kalamazoo, the Henry Ford Museum in Dearborn, and an aircraft and space museum, past Lansing. Also, a big air show at Battle Creek, starting this week that might work for us. Where are we headed, specifically?"

"I'd like to go where we lived last, Grand Rapids. Made a promise to my wife that I'd come home, no matter what, and that was home. It's as good a place as any to start."

"Understood," acknowledged Rob.

"Maybe there's closure waiting for me. Or at least a clue, for you too, Rob. For everyone."

They spent nearly an hour looking for and at information on the tablet, with David making notes of places and events they might, supposedly, want to visit in Michigan. Their cover story would be a father and son road trip, a getaway to visit areas of interest to both.

When finished, they leaned on the railing and looked out over the water. After a few minutes, David spoke,

"The Coupe, do you think it would be able, to make this trip?"

"Are you thinking of taking it that far?" Rob questioned. "I assumed we'd use one of the newer cars. It would be more comfortable and easier to drive on such a long trip."

"No, it has to be made in that car, if you think it'll make it. I feel it's a needed connection, and I'm not setting foot in anything Japanese. Besides, that car was part of the dream I had."

"How's that?"

"I had visions of looking out over that blue hood, saw wide highways, small towns, and winding, hilly, two-lane, country roads. There was some guy, just a voice, a foreign voice, directing us where to go, I think. And a sign, of some sort, on a country road. I couldn't make out what it said, but it was brightly colored. Also saw the house where Macy, Jenny, and I lived in Grand Rapids, but it was the wrong color for some reason. And there was a Ferris wheel, with big balloons flying over it. That was really an odd one."

"Dad, there's pictures of the air show at Battle Creek; it also has a hot air balloon festival, looks like a carnival, too, with a Ferris wheel."

"No kidding?"

He showed David images on the tablet.

"This has to be a sign we're supposed to go there, Rob."

Rob slowly nodded his head in agreement.

"That blue car was in the dream, in the vision, Son. It's important we take it, what say you?"

"Nothing wrong with it that I'm aware of. Almost good as new and has always run and driven fine. We've never gone more than a hundred miles or so to a car show, but if we take our time, don't press it too much, and bring along some tools and parts, it should be fine," answered the boy.

"Then we'll do it," replied David, with a smile.

Rob gathered the notes, glanced at them, then did a double-take.

"This isn't your... my dad's handwriting," he said, pointing at the yellow notepad.

"No, don't imagine it would be, would it," David replied as he turned to leave. "Guess we better go talk to your mom."

Rob, further stunned by evidence this man he was talking to was not his father, nodded, then both walked back to the car. On the drive home, they made sure their stories were aligned. It would be essential to give the best presentation and explanation as to why they were, suddenly, taking a near 1400 mile road trip to the state of Michigan.

"This day, this Sunday morning, is the beginning," said David.

"Beginning of what?"

"Of doing whatever it takes to figure this out and set things right, for everyone."

"Michigan? You two are leaving for Michigan, tomorrow? Is this why you snuck off this morning, to plan this?" Shelley asked, using relatively high decibels.

"Well, we've been thinking about it for a while now," replied Rob to his mother.

"Yeah, awhile now," repeated David.

"Seems all very sudden to me," Shelley replied as she crossed her arms and leaned against the kitchen counter.

"Really, Mom. We've been searching and found some cool car, airplane, and World War II museums, and an air show. We both thought it would be a great getaway for just the two of us; before I start work, it'll be fun guy stuff. Oh, and educational, too. Only be gone for a few days, right, Dad? Probably not even a week, I'd imagine," said Rob while glancing over at David as both nervously sat at the kitchen table.

"Yeah, places like that, a few days, fun. I made notes," David responded.

"Let me see that," said Shelley, as she reached for the notepad lying on the table.

Rob grabbed it first and quickly began reading off some of the destinations David had written down. His mom did not need to see handwriting; she would not recognize as her husbands.

"I'm not so sure about this," Shelley said as she looked at David. "Just yesterday, you were in the hospital. Do you think you're well enough to travel? Been acting pretty goofy since the fall."

"Yeah, yeah, feeling fine now, hardly have a bump anymore, and it doesn't hurt at all," said David, as he reached up and touched the bandage on his forehead, then tried not to grimace because it still hurt.

"Why don't we all go? It might be a fun family trip!" Karli said enthusiastically.

"I can't get off work on this short notice; besides, pretty sure they want a guy-only trip," replied Shelley, tapping her foot.

"Yeah, Rob and I would just kinda like to get away by ourselves, you know, maybe do some bonding," said David as he took a drink of iced tea.

"You were in the delivery room and watched him being born; how much more bonding do you need?" Shelly replied with a grin.

David had a quick mental image of this woman, he did not know until yesterday, giving birth, and promptly choked on his tea until it came out his nose.

"Are you alright, Daddy?" Karli asked as she came over and began patting him on the back.

"Yeah, I'm fine," David said hoarsely and cleared his throat. "Swallowed wrong."

"Which car would you take?" Shelley asked.

"Oh, we're going to take the Coupe, kinda fits our theme," replied Rob.

"You sure that's a good idea? It's an old car; I don't want you two to get stranded in the middle of nowhere."

"It'll be fine," said David, with a gravelly voice, while giving a thumbs-up.

"Good, then I can use your car while you're gone, okay? Karli asked.

David nodded his head and gave another thumbs-up.

"Well, heaven forbid I'd come between two boys and their big blue toy. Rob, you need to do most, if not all, of the driving; I still don't think he seems like himself."

"Oh, don't I know it," said Rob, trying to keep a straight face.

"What's that?" asked Shelley.

"Nothing, I'll keep a close eye on him; it'll be fine. Should be a very, interesting trip."

"When are you planning to leave?" queried Shelley.

"In the morning, no AC in the Coupe, so might as well head out before it gets too hot," responded Rob.

David cleared his throat and nodded.

The rest of the day consisted of packing bags and loading the old car with items they might need, using a list put together while driving back from the pier at Fort Myers Beach. A selection of tools and spare parts was chosen and packed in the trunk. David asked about maps; Rob replied they would not be needed, as he would bring along a portable GPS unit. David gave him the now-familiar, stare of bewilderment.

"I'll show you how it works once we're on the road."

In the garage, they found an old road atlas to take along. David was pleased with this, saying it would be helpful for him to track their progress. A trip was made to fill the car with gas, then a supermarket stop for sandwiches, assorted snack foods, drinks, and ice for the cooler they would be using. It was beginning to sprinkle by the time everything was loaded in the car; Karli suggested they order delivery pizza for supper.

As they sat eating at the kitchen table, Rob showed Shelley and Karli information he'd printed out on places they planned to visit. The truth was they might never see any of them, save for the air show. The information on David's aircraft carrier, and its combat records printed out the night before, were already stashed in the glove box.

Around ten o'clock, after watching another old black and white movie on television, *It's Great to Be Alive*, from 1933, Shelley suggested everyone turn in, as the boys had to get up early the following day.

A wave of panic washed over David; he could not get away with spending another night in the recliner. There would be no chance, this time, of not going to bed with Shelley. Rob could see the uneasy look on his face. He knew David was highly concerned about spending much time alone with his mom. What should be any normal conversation between them may bring up suspicions and difficulty answering accompanying questions. He wondered how any of this could, eventually, ever be fully explained to his mother.

While Shelley was still in their bathroom, David got into bed wearing only a T-shirt and underwear after considering going to bed fully clothed. He then gave thought to faking immediate sleep. Before long, she slid into bed next to him, wearing a light nightgown; he hurriedly turned on his side, away from her.

"Aren't you going to wear your usual sleep shirt?" she asked while turning off the light on the nightstand. "I can get it for you?"

"No, this is fine, thanks. Wow, I'm really tired, and tomorrow is going to be a long day. Sure hope I can get to sleep quickly. Yep, sure need my sleep," he said nervously.

"Missed you last night. You know how I hate sleeping alone," Shelley said, snuggling up behind him.

She leaned up on one elbow while pushing her body against his and putting her hand on his arm.

"Don't I get a good night kiss?"

David Hamilton was feeling very, very uneasy. She was another man's wife, he was not her husband, but she did not know it. Arousing any suspicions, or any other kind of arousal, most definitely needed to be avoided.

"Okay, I guess…" he said and turned back towards her.

She giggled at his response.

Macy was the last woman he kissed before shipping out on the *Bennington* and a long time, even before that. The short kiss with Shelley was soft and pleasant; he enjoyed it; in a guilty kind of way. It was familiar to him, and when it was over, they looked at each other in the darkness and kissed again.

This time he felt no guilt; something stirred inside him. It seemed as if he belonged there. Suddenly and strangely, he felt very relaxed and at home. He put his arm around her shoulder. She placed her head on his chest, and they listened to the steady rain on the roof as both fell asleep.

MONDAY

David slept well, so well he did not notice when Shelley got out of bed, to make breakfast.

"Get up, lazy ass, don't you hear Michigan calling?" she said, walking into the room, then sitting on the edge of the bed.

He gradually began to wake and opened his eyes to see her smiling face.

"What's that?" he asked, then yawned.

"Michigan, you and your son are starting on your road trip to Michigan today, duh."

"Michigan?" he asked and yawned again while stretching his arms. "What's in Michigan, Shell?"

"Quit being weird; breakfast is almost ready, come on, get moving," she said, stood up, clapped her hands twice, and headed towards the door, then stopped and turned.

"You haven't called me Shell since you came home from the hospital," and walked on down the hall.

Suddenly, dizzy and confused, David sat up in the bed and looked around; nothing was familiar. *Where am I? What is this place?*

For a few seconds, he could not remember who he was, and then the reality, the unreality of it all, came back upon him so hard and heavy, he could almost, physically, feel and hear it. He flopped heavily, back down onto the bed, saying aloud, "When will all this end?"

"I made blueberry waffles with blueberry syrup, might as well send you off with a good breakfast," said Shelley as he walked into the kitchen.

Karli and Rob were already seated at the table. David thanked her for making one of his, or at least Derek's, favorites, even though he didn't know if it was, but liked it enough to have two servings, plus orange juice and coffee.

Rob finished up his breakfast before David, went to the garage, and pulled the car out onto the driveway. Shelley busied herself making leftover meatloaf sandwiches for them to take. Before long, breakfast was finished, and the cooler had been packed with food. It was time for goodbyes.

As both men stood next to the car, Shelley raised her cell phone to take a photo. David asked what she was doing.

"Need a picture for the album you guys keep of that damned old car, of course," she replied, grinning.

"Right, and she's taking it with a phone. Makes all the sense in the world, your world, anyway," David said quietly to Rob out the side of his mouth, as he slowly shook his head and smiled.

"One more, say cheese!" Karli said, demonstrating a large smile.

Both of them said cheese in unison while Shelley clicked away.

"Hey, Gary!" Shelley yelled to their next-door neighbor, who had just walked down his sidewalk to the mailbox. "Can you get a picture of the four of us, please?"

David recognized him as the driver of the BMW.

"Sure, glad to," he said and walked over, carrying his mail. "Where you guys headed?"

"Destination, Michigan. Road trip for a man and his son," replied Rob, as he looked at David.

"Sounds great," said Gary, taking the phone from Shelley. "Heading north, huh? Isn't it something, what's happening up around Gainesville? Saw on the news there's still no trace of the girl who disappeared near Archer a couple of weeks ago. The cops are almost certain it's related to the other girls who've gone missing. Something real ugly going on up there."

"How many is that now?" Shelley asked.

"Six, in the last six months," replied Gary.

"A lot of girls were afraid to be out by themselves at school, hope they find the son-of-a-bitch, and fry him," said Rob angrily.

"Me too," added Karli, with a frown. "What kind of a psycho would do things like that?"

"Okay, all you folks stand over there by that pretty car, and I'll snap a few," Gary said.

As they stood arm-in-arm, Gary took their picture. David glanced around at the three people he'd come to know over the last few days.

This is a nice place, a nice neighborhood, and these are good people. Derek Haynes is one lucky guy, he thought. There was a feeling of envy. He hoped Derek could get back to his family soon but knew what that was going to take, even if he didn't know what would become of him when it happened. There was some sadness in leaving, but he did not belong here.

There was hugging and admonishments to drive carefully and stay safe, with assurances given. Shelley and David hugged last, along with a quick kiss. For a moment, there was a thought of not going. Suddenly, it seemed, almost, like the wrong thing to do. He felt the urge to stay here with this family, and he could not understand why. But the thought of *his* family, Macy, and Jenny, brought him back. Soon, Rob was driving down the street away from the house, with much waving back at the two people standing in the driveway.

"Here we go; I guess we need to get this done," said Rob.

"Yep, it's not done until it's done," was the reply.

"I see you took off that big bandage; it still looks pretty rosy."

"It'll be fine, will heal faster this way," was David's response. After a few blocks, he asked,

"What was all that back there, the missing girls?"

"Since before last Christmas, young girls, teenage and early twenties, have disappeared around the Gainesville area. Everyone assumes they've been kidnapped and murdered, but no trace of them has been found, at least not yet. Police, to this point, don't have much to go on. There's a lot of scared people up that way. The monsters who do these things are called serial killers."

"So, girls around Karli's age then?" David asked, and Rob nodded.

"Monsters like that need to be put down, no mercy," said David.

Soon they were on US 41 North, then blended into the traffic stream on Interstate 75 North, Michigan bound.

"This was in my dream, remember, I told you? Looking out over the hood of this car, on wide roads, and they sure are wide," said David. "I've flown off runways that were narrower than this."

"Modern interstate roadway systems, Dad, they're all over the country. Four lanes, and more, can get you just about anywhere, easy and fairly quick."

"When I was growing up, we were lucky to have gravel roads; a lot of them were just dirt, Rob. Not a lot of long stretches of two-lane paved highways, back then, especially in rural areas."

The sun, rising in the nearly cloudless sky, promised a warm and humid day. All windows were down and brought a scent of lush Florida vegetation.

"Too hot for you, Dad?"

"No, I like warm weather, always loved summer in Michigan. Most of my time with the Marines was in the Pacific. I'm used to hot. The islands, you know, some places were good, nice, all tropical and pretty, like you'd see in the movies. Others, not so much. Many were infested with sand crabs the size of small dogs. A lot of them had been shelled and bombed by us, or the Japs, or both. They all smelled like death and destruction.

Rob sensed this was a dark place; David did not want to go.

"How was everything with mom last night? You looked awfully nervous."

"Went well, very well, your mom was great," David said, with a smile on his face.

Rob, inadvertently, swerved the Coupe over the centerline.

"Wait, what? Define great," he said with a scowl.

"What do you mean?" David replied, then paused. "Oh, no, not that. Jeezuz Rob, I meant there wasn't much talking."

"Not much talking, huh? What was there, then?" Rob asked, still scowling.

"I meant, we barely talked at all, so I never said anything stupid to get her stirred up and suspicious, that's all. We basically just said good night and went to sleep."

"Oh, good. Sounded like you, well, you know," said Rob, as the scowl left his face. "She could have easily been fooled, under the circumstances. Glad that didn't happen, so thanks for that; it would've creeped me out."

"I most certainly understand where you're coming from. But wow, your mom, she was great, I mean, really, really great," said David, with his head down, trying not to smile.

Rob snapped his head sideways, grinned, and punched him in the arm.

"You are one sick bastard."

"Meet me tonight in dreamland,
Under the silv'ry moon.
Meet me tonight in dreamland,
Where loves sweet roses bloom.
Come with the love light gleaming,
in your dear eyes of blue."

Macy sang along softly, with the song playing on the radio in the hall. Jenny smiled and cooed as she watched and listened to her mother while being bathed.

"Meet me in dreamland,
Sweet, dreamy dreamland,
There let my dreams come true.
Meet me tonight in dreamland,
Under the silv'ry moon."

Jenny kicked and splashed with delight.

"Under the silv'ry moon.
"Meet me tonight in dreamland,
Where loves sweet roses bloom."

While lifting the baby out of the bathtub, the doorbell rang.

"I'll be right there," she yelled while quickly wrapping her in a large, soft towel, assuming it must be her neighbor and landlady, who had mentioned possibly stopping by for coffee and a visit.

Betty and her husband, Tom, had rented the bungalow to Macy and David in 1943. Betty was several years older and enjoyed having a baby next door; their only child, a daughter, was away in college. The two women had become close friends.

She carried Jenny to the door, turning down the radio along

the way. Betty was standing on the other side of the screen, but she was not alone.

The Western Union messenger wore a black patch over his left eye; and no expression on his face. Betty's expression was one of deep concern. With their men off to war, seldom were telegrams a welcome part of servicemen's families, lives.

"Ma'am, I have a telegram here for you; it's from the...."

"I'll take it," interrupted Betty.

"Somebody will have to sign," the messenger said quietly.

Betty grabbed the telegram, along with his clipboard, and quickly scribbled her name, then looked in her purse for change to tip the man. He held up his hand and said in a low voice,

"No need, ma'am, no need."

Macy was beginning to tremble; she felt her knees going weak. Betty quickly stepped inside and took the baby. Macy looked at the messenger, for several seconds, before managing to say,

"I know these things are not easy for you."

"Ma'am, I, I know it may not help much," he began. "But I was wounded early on in the war; that's where I got this patch. Lost my eye in the Philippines, still have a hunk of shrapnel in my hip, too. My folks got a telegram saying I was wounded but was going to be okay, and, I guess, what I'm trying to say, ma'am, is, a telegram's not a visit from a couple of officers and a pastor, in one of those big, long, government cars, with a star on the side."

Macy nodded, her eyes beginning to tear.

"Yes, I know. I'm so sorry you were wounded."

"Hope everything works out for you and your little one. God bless ya' ma'am," he said, turned, and walked towards the open gate in the white fence. He had a noticeable limp.

Barely discernible, from a few steps away, Macy heard the words,

"I hate this goddamn job."

⟞⟝

"I can't believe how fast people drive on this highway," said David.

"Interstates are the way to go if you want to get there quicker," replied Rob.

"But everybody on this road is passing us; how fast we going, Rob?"

"Barely sixty, you, my dad, always said that was fast enough for this old car. Most of the time, the speed limit is seventy, but people usually go faster."

"That's good, whatever he thought was best," David replied, sitting in the passenger seat and watching the scenery go by at a distance.

"But there's something wrong," said Rob, with concern in his voice.

"What do you mean, what's up?"

"It's like, there's no power," Rob returned. "For the last several miles, it's been getting worse, pretty much since we got on the interstate. The motor doesn't seem to be missing, but I have to keep my foot down all the way, just to get close to sixty, and that's not right, not right at all. It isn't steering well, either, as if all the tires were half flat, just wallowing around. This has never happened before; I don't know what to make of it, was fine yesterday and when we started out."

"Maybe it just needs to warm up more; let's give it a few miles and see what happens," suggested David.

Twenty miles later, as they approached Punta Gorda, a semi-tractor-trailer rapidly passed them, generating considerable noise and wind.

"Feels like a damn racetrack out here, Rob."

"Yeah, and we're losing," was his reply. "The car's no better. It's slow and a handful to drive."

David looked out the side window, at palm trees and wooded areas, offset from the interstate, and said,

"Do we have to stay on this road?"

"Not really, but it is the best way," replied Rob, as he turned to look at David.

"This isn't right, Rob, I have the feeling this big wide highway won't take us where we need to go, if that makes any sense, and the car does not fit this type of travel."

"I think the car agrees with you," Rob scowled.

David stared straight ahead for a moment.

"Let's get off here, take some back roads," he said, pointing at the upcoming Punta Gorda exit ramp.

"We need to stop anyway and see if we can find what's making the car run and drive like an old garbage truck. It's gonna be slow going on two-lanes through a bunch of small towns and rural areas, though, assuming it keeps running, was Rob's reply."

"I'm sure it'll be slower, but the car's not liking this route, and neither am I."

"So, the car's speaking to you, now?" Rob said as he put on the right turn signal. "If you intend to go the entire way, not using interstates, and assuming we can find out what the trouble is, it'll take longer, a lot longer. Probably tack on a day or two; I figured you'd be in more of a rush."

"This will be the way to go; I can feel it."

"It's your trip; I'm just your guide and traveling companion," said Rob, with a half-smile. "Whatever you feel we need to do, I'm good with."

After exiting Interstate 75, Rob pulled into the parking area of a gas station. Raising the hood, he began looking for any obvious problems, finding none. David checked the tire pressure on all four wheels; they were acceptable.

"Well, I can't see a damn thing wrong under the hood, and the tires are fine. I don't know what to tell ya," Rob said, exasperated. "All we can do is try these two-lane highways and see if, for some reason, it makes any difference. But I can't imagine why it would; maybe just going a little slower will help. If not, we'll have to turn back and get a different car. I'll need to hook up the GPS now; it'll help us find the right roads and turnoffs out here in the wilderness."

Rob reached into the back seat, grabbed a small box, and took out the contents.

"Hate even to ask, but what is a GPS?" David said.

"Global Positioning System, it uses satellites in space to show where you're at, where you're going, and how to get there."

"Satellites, you say, in space? So, then they actually don't make roadmaps anymore?"

"Yeah, they're still available, and we have that old Atlas, along with Florida roadmaps in the glove box, but this is much better," said Rob.

He attached the GPS unit to the windshield with a suction cup holder, then plugged the power cord into a cigarette lighter on the Coupe's dashboard.

"I should be able to program it to keep us on secondary roads," he said while tapping on the device. As the Coupe began to roll across the parking lot towards the highway, a voice with a distinctly British accent came out of the car radio speaker,

"Please turn left."

David smiled and shook his head.

"Well, ain't that something, it talks, through the damn radio. Ya' know, that voice seems familiar, for some reason."

He flinched upon feeling and hearing the cell phone in his pocket. Rob, grinning, looked over at him.

"You gonna answer it?"

"What for? The only people I know in this century are you, your mom, and Karli. And why does some idiot keep yelling about letting dogs out? I don't care about his damn dogs."

Rob laughed and said, "Might be one of them; check the display."

David pulled the phone out and looked at the small screen.

"It's some name I don't know. Not going to take it, just somebody expecting your dad to answer."

"Just as well," replied Rob. "There's a small switch at the top on the left-hand side of your phone; just slide that down, and that mean man and his dogs will go away. But it will still vibrate."

"Please turn right," the GPS voice, with the British accent, said.

"Will do, Henry," responded Rob.

"Who's Henry?" asked David as he flipped the small switch.

"It's the name we gave the GPS voice; he's not from around here."

Two-lane highways suited David. He felt more at ease traveling through the countryside than the rapid-paced and impersonal interstate highway. It felt more natural and comfortable, and part of what he had seen in his dream, his vision.

After turning onto another two-lane road, as directed by Henry, Rob worked his way up through the three gears on the steering column, pegging the speed at sixty miles an hour.

"Seems fine now," he said, with some bewilderment, as he moved the steering wheel smoothly back and forth.

"Well, that's good," said David. "Told you this old machine didn't like that four-lane crap. This's the path we were always meant to be on, for whatever reason."

"The big roads never bothered it before; feels quite perky now; let's give it a little test," Rob replied, flooring the gas pedal.

The car began to accelerate rapidly.

"Holy shit!" he exclaimed. "All of a sudden, it's like we have an extra hundred horsepower, and it steers like a sports car! What the hell is going on?"

"I think it feels more at home; we both do," said David, as he watched the green scenery rapidly flashing by.

After more than three hours on the road, they arrived in a small town, where another element of David's dream came into view. Two blocks down the road was a large sign that read, McDonald's.

"Rob, we need to stop there," he said, pointing. "Looks like it might be a restaurant. You hungry?"

"Well yeah, I guess so."

"I feel like it's burger time. Think they have burgers?"

"Yeah, I bet they just might," chuckled Rob. "Why do you want to stop there?"

"It's the name, McDonald; Macy's maiden name. A big, bright sign with that name on it showed up in my dream. Figure we're on the right road now; I mean, how many restaurants named McDonald's could there be?"

"Umm, well…" said Rob hesitantly.

"I feel good about this, and kind of hungry. Pull in and park, Rob, and let's see if they can fry us up a couple of burgers."

"What kind of a restaurant is this?" David said upon walking through the doors.

"It's called fast food, not like the restaurant we went to yester-day. You place an order at the counter, then take it to a table or booth, yourself, usually a couple of minutes or so later."

"They cook it that fast?"

"Most times, and it's always good."

"How do they do that?"

"Just the way it's done, in places like this, in our modern, non-patient world."

They stood in line a few minutes before placing their order. David was impressed by the signage, showing all the different choices of food combinations.

"That reminded me of standing in the chow lines during basic training," said David, as they carried their trays to a booth near a window.

"But there wasn't much of a variety. Way too often, we were served what was often not so fondly called, shit-on-a-shingle, creamed chipped beef on toast."

"Thanks for sharing," was Rob's reply.

"So, what's your verdict, any good?" he asked David after they had eaten for a few minutes.

"Yeah, real good, and has a lot of stuff on it I didn't even ask for. I like these French fries; they're kind of skinny, though."

"Good, glad you like it. We seldom eat at places like this, but it's a nice treat every once in a while."

"Too bad we won't be able to find another place like this, this, McDonald's restaurant; I'd like to eat here again," remarked David.

"Oh, I wouldn't worry about that," said Rob, as he put a couple of skinny fries in his mouth.

"Maybe they ought to start a chain of these, you know, open up the same type of restaurant in different locations, with this fast-food thing," David said, through a mouthful of burger.

"Nah, it would never catch on," said Rob, trying to deadpan his expression.

Once back on the road, Rob asked David if he'd like to listen to some music.

"What kind of stations can you get?"

"I have some of the CDs my dad likes, with 1940s music on it, might make you feel more at home, so to speak."

"What's a CD?"

"Compact disc, it's like a vinyl record that holds a lot of music. I brought a player we can plug into the radio, look in the glove box."

"Sounds good; let's see what kind of music your old man likes."

He pulled out the portable CD player; Rob directed him how to hook it into the radio. A button was pushed, and the sound of "Little Brown Jug" by Glenn Miller filled the car, making David smile.

"I always liked Glenn Miller; he was my favorite bandleader. Did they ever find him?"

"Find him?" Rob asked.

"He was being flown across the English Channel in December of 1944 and never arrived. Just wondering if there was ever any conclusion."

"Oh yeah, my dad and I read about that. "Nope, he just vanished with no official word on what happened. Kind of like what happened to you...."

Rob stopped talking, leaving only the sound of road noise and Glenn Miller's music.

"Dad, David, I'm so sorry, didn't think before opening my stupid mouth."

"It's all right," replied David. "Happened a lot back where, and when I came from. War does that, people disappearing, an' all. Many questions and few answers. Yeah, happened to me, it seems."

Turning his gaze out the side window, he repeated, "Happened to me."

⟞⟝

The red light was flickering on the answering machine when they returned home from running a few errands and lunch.

"See who that is," Shelley told Karli as she began sorting through the mail.

The recorded voice from the other room was not familiar, nor could she make out much of what was being spoken, but the words, *extremely important,* were clear.

"Mom, it was some woman; I didn't recognize her name," said Karli, as she walked into the kitchen, looking upset. "She asked for Dad and left a number; I wrote it down, said it's important someone return her call as soon as possible, didn't say why. It's scaring me."

"Well, I'll give her a call right now and see what's up," replied Shelley, trying to use an upbeat tone in her voice, hoping to lessen her daughters concern. "Might be someone from the hospital, I'm sure it's probably nothing… well, you know, not nothing, but, but, I guess we'll just have to call and find out," she said and tried to smile.

Karli nervously leaned against the couch in the living room where her mother sat, and dialed the number.

"This is Mrs. Derek Haynes; who am I speaking with?"

"Yes, Evelyn, I'm Shelley; what is this in regards to?"

"Evelyn who?" Karli asked.

She made a stop motion with her hand towards Karli.

"No, he's not here; Derek and our son went on a car trip to Michigan, not sure where they would be right now. Is this about the fall he had on Saturday?"

"Oh, you didn't know? He fell and hit his head on a sidewalk, was in the hospital for a few hours, then released. He seems to be fine now. Well, maybe a little forgetful, perhaps."

"Yes, I believe that was the street."

There was a long silence as she listened intently to the woman on the other end of the line.

"What! I didn't know anything about that, just that he had some errands to run, and…."

"Very confused, that's right, and didn't seem to be himself. It was as if he didn't recognize me, or our kids, at first anyway."

"Right, we all assumed it was from the fall and bumping his head, maybe a mild concussion. The doctor at the hospital said he might be a little confused for a time. What exactly are you trying to tell me?"

Shelley sat quietly as the woman spoke.

"That's absurd, simply ridiculous. I can't see how that is even possible. So what are we supposed to do about it!" she asked, almost shouting, then leaned forward on the couch and placed a hand across her forehead.

"I'm, I'm just not understanding any of this. Derek never mentioned it before. I'm going call him right now and get this straightened out."

"What do you mean, I shouldn't?"

"Dangerous? What could happen?"

"So, you've already tried to call him, not surprised he never answered. It seemed almost as if he'd never used a cell phone before."

"Okay, our son's name is Rob; do you think he knows what's happened? Both of them were acting suspiciously before they left. Should I call him and find out what he knows? Is he in any way at risk?"

"Doctor who? Let me write that down," said Shelley, picking up a pen. "Will he be contacting Rob?"

"Alright, if you think that's best…."

"Yes, we'll have to trust you both; that's all we can do, for now, I guess."

"I just want my husband back."

She slowly hung up the phone and began to cry.

"The Western Union man was right," said Betty, sitting on the couch with Macy.

In her arms, Jenny was beginning to fuss; gently, she bounced her up and down. But for a few birds singing outside and the big clock ticking in the hallway, it was quiet.

"I know," said Macy, as she dried her eyes with a white handkerchief. "He meant well, but everything has changed now."

She looked down at the telegram, lying between them, and in a soft, trembling voice, spoke the words, "Missing in action."

"I know honey, I know, it could be a lot of things," replied Betty. "Doesn't necessarily mean…" her voice trailed off. "Who knows, there might be another telegram on the way right this very moment, with good news."

"I'm just so scared and don't know what I'll do…." Macy said, barely above a whisper. "He promised he would come back."

She took Jenny from Betty and rocked her in her lap.

"Meet me tonight in dreamland,
under the silv'ry moon."

As she softly sang, Macy became aware of the chirping birds outside.

"Meet me tonight in dreamland,
Where loves sweet roses bloom."

"Oh, you look so much like your daddy," she said in a hushed voice.

Jenny gazed up at her mother and smiled, then yawned. Tears were, again, trickling down Macy's cheeks.

"Betty, could you put Jenny in her sleeper, then in the crib for a nap?"

"Sure, honey, why don't you lie down for a spell. I'll take care of the baby for as long as you need. When she's settled in, I'll make us some sandwiches."

"I'm not hungry," said Macy, as she handed Jenny to Betty and tried to blink back the tears.

"His birthday," she said.

"What was that, dear?"

"His birthday, I remember… all day long I felt uneasy, and don't know why. I wonder if…."

"Try not to think about that now, Macy; you just get some rest."

"I appreciate you being here and your help; I really do," she replied.

As Betty carried Jenny down the hall to the nursery, Macy sat, listening to the birds outside and the clock rhythmically ticking. After a few minutes, she arose and walked a few steps to the wall, where an arrangement of framed photographs was mounted. She had begun the collection soon after they moved in, starting with only a few. Now, numerous prints were on display, both before and after they were married, and the three of them, along with pictures of David and the planes he flew.

In the center of the collection was a hand-colored, 8x10 print taken at their small wedding; a fleeting smile brushed over her face. One photo that David had taken of her, while noticeably pregnant, brought back the memory of peoples reaction when shown this for the first time. Such pictures just simply were not taken or displayed. It was considered too personal, too crass. She always thought this to be funny and never failed to point this image out to visitors, just to see the reaction and expression on their faces.

There were many individual photos of Jenny, from newborn up to a month ago. Betty's husband, Tom, was a photography buff and had taken most of them. Her favorite was the three of them, outside, in the yard, with the tree swing. She had an 8x10 made for the wall and sent David a 5x7, along with a wallet-size print. In the last letter she had received, he had mentioned the larger one was in his cabin onboard the carrier, the smaller one in his plane.

He considered them his good luck charm and would talk to the photos every day.

Tom would often save the last frame or two of film in his camera, and offer to snap a picture of Jenny, sometimes of both mother and daughter. He was a good photographer, and there was never any cost for Macy. This helped with expenses, as being a military wife, money was often tight.

She focused on a 5x7, not far from the colored wedding picture; it was the first photo taken of the three of them, as a family, standing next to their car, right before leaving the hospital with Jenny, at four days old. Fondly, she remembered the wonderful surprise David had for her when they returned home that day.

Further away was the last photo of the little family, taken at a park in San Diego, California. They asked a passerby to take their picture with a camera she had borrowed from Tom. It was the final time they were all together. David had wired money for train fare, so she and Jenny could make the trip west to be with him before shipping out for his final combat tour.

"It was such a good day," she whispered, then reached out and touched the photo.

"When will I see you again?" Macy asked.

They had taken Jenny for a walk in her stroller on a brilliantly clear day. After stopping to buy sandwiches and soft drinks, they made their way to a park overlooking the San Diego Bay harbor, not far from where they were staying. A blanket was spread on the ground, and as the baby napped, they sat and ate, then spoke of their future together.

"Depends on how things play out this last time, but I'll be back here, training pilots before the invasion of Japan begins; that's a certainty. Then we'll all be together, for good," replied David.

"I hope and pray for that every day and hate watching you leave, again."

"We've talked about this, Macy, you know I...."

"It's what you do, understood, but I worry so much and don't know what I'd do if you... didn't come back."

"Hey now, you're clouding up a really nice day here," said David, moving next to her and placing an arm around his wife. "I've said all along, nothing is going to keep us apart, one way or the other; I'll find my way back to my girls."

"And I'll wait for you, for as long as it takes," said Macy, staring intensely into David's eyes. David kissed her, then little Jenny, sleeping quietly in her stroller.

"I love flying but am sick of war. This will end, it will, and we'll find ourselves back in Grand Rapids, working on a little brother, or sister, for this pumpkin right here."

"Just one? I know you want a son."

"I do, maybe a couple."

He smiled and kissed her cheek.

It was a warm day; just the hint of a sea breeze carried the fragrance of freshly mown grass, children were running and laughing in a nearby playground. The rippling bay waters sparkled in the sun. Ships seemed in no hurry to go anywhere; their horns could be heard signaling arrivals and departures. It was a mournful sound. The brutal war in the Pacific seemed a million miles away.

"These roads aren't too busy, and the towns are mostly small and easy to pass through. You feel like driving for a bit?" Rob asked of David as he turned down the radio.

"Sure, if you don't mind."

"Great," replied Rob. "Might be good for you."

After pulling onto the shoulder, they exchanged seats. Rob began to explain some of the subtle nuances of piloting a vintage

1941 Ford Coupe. David sat quietly looking at Rob; a smile came to his face,

"I can handle this."

"Yeah, I suppose you can," said Rob sheepishly. "Just stay on this highway, and Henry, the GPS guy, will tell us when and where to turn next."

"Roger that, I guess this makes you my copilot now," said David.

He put the transmission in first gear, let out the clutch, then slowly steered back onto the highway; two more shifts brought the car up to just over fifty-five miles an hour.

"How does it feel?" Rob asked.

"It's about the only remotely normal thing I've done in a while."

He turned the volume up just as Glenn Miller's "Moonlight Serenade" began to play.

"This one brings back a lot of memories, your mom and I… I mean, my wife Macy loved dancing to this."

"It's one of my dad's favorites too. He'd always mention the beat of the song, reminded him of soldiers marching. Sounds odd, but I can imagine it too."

"Not odd at all, Rob. I've always thought the same thing since the first time I heard it."

The two men stared at each other for a moment before David returned his attention to the road.

"Does it bother you, the song, I mean? I can put in a different disc," asked Rob.

"No, it's fine, brings back good memories," David smiled as he spoke.

"My dad likes 1940s music the most. He told me it's always been comfortable and familiar to him. He's a real World War II buff, so when we began searching for a car to restore, instead of something from the 1960s or 1970s as originally planned, we ended up getting this one."

"Your dad has good taste in music and cars. Though having recently been a participant in that war, can't say I'm a fan."

"I can imagine," replied Rob. "Sounds strange, but several times my dad told me of an odd sensation, that, that he'd been in the war, said he could, feel things."

"Really," said David with surprise.

"Mom would give him a hard time about it, saying she was not surprised, after all the World War II books, videos, and such that he had. Transference, she called it. That seemed to bother him; he took it seriously. Last year he quit mentioning it to her or even saying much about the subject when she was around."

"That does explain her remark the other night when you gave me that book."

"You don't have to answer or talk about it at all, but, well… what was it like flying in combat off an aircraft carrier?" Rob asked. "At car shows, or wherever we'd meet them, Dad would ask World War II vets about their experiences. Not many of those who were actually in combat wanted to say much about it, so I'll understand if you don't."

David wasn't sure if he wanted to talk about it, either. Everything was still fresh in his mind, including his horrifying last flight, but he liked this boy. He reached out and turned down the music.

"It was dangerous as hell, all of it. It's unnatural, you know, flying. If God wanted us to fly, he would have attached wings to our sorry asses. That's what my CPTP instructor often said, not quite sure what point he was trying to make, but he was most definitely a colorful fellow."

"CPTP?" queried Rob.

"Civilian Pilot Training Program I was enrolled in, at college, kind of a government-sponsored flying club. This guy taught me and a bunch of other rookies the basics of flying. I soloed under him. Elmo Zimmer was his name. He was short but tough."

"Must have been fun," said Rob.

"Yeah, and scary, at first anyway. We flew the Piper J–3 Cub, a two-place tandem aircraft, a damn fine trainer for us virgins. As I recall, it was a Saturday morning, an almost perfect day for flying, hardly any wind, blue skies, sunshine. Soloing that plane seems like only yesterday."

"What year?"

"1942."

"That was a long time ago, I mean, you know, from now," replied Rob.

"Not much more than three years for me, Son."

"Still hard for me to believe."

David turned his head to look at him.

"Imagine it from my side."

"I can't. So your solo went okay, then?"

"I made probably a half dozen takeoffs and landings with him, and when we pulled up in front of the hangar, he suddenly folded down the door of the Cub and hopped out. Zimmer said it was time to take it up on my own; I asked him if he was sure."

"Kid, I'm putting a fifteen hundred dollar aircraft in your care," he replied. "Yelling back at him through the noise of the running engine, I said, 'Screw your airplane, what about my ass!' He just laughed, folded up the door, and waved me off. I didn't say it to be funny."

"I bet!" laughed Rob.

"So I taxied into position, did a quick check of the controls, and pushed the throttle full-forward. The tail came up quick, and it wasn't long before the Cub and I were airborne and climbing heavenward. I took a quick glance at the back seat, and of course, no Zimmer. That's when it dawned on me, somebody's gonna have to land this crate, sooner or later, and I'm the only one up here."

"So, did you crash?" Rob asked sarcastically.

"No, smart ass, I didn't, and we called it a crackup, not a crash. My first landing went fine, then did two more after that, no problem. What a fantastic feeling of freedom; it was exhilarating, and I thought I was pretty hot stuff and had this flying thing all figured out. After taxiing back to the hangar, there was a small, informal ceremony with Zimmer, me, and a couple of other student pilots who were there. The tradition with newly soloed pilots is to cut a small strip off the back of their shirt, have the instructor sign and date it, then nail it to a wall inside the hangar. I politely asked Zimmer to cut an extra small strip if he would; as being a college student, I didn't have many decent shirts to begin with. Bastard thought that was funny, cut off an extra-large chunk, hardly ever wore that shirt again, if I bent over too far, the crack of my ass would show."

"So, this is what you meant by a crackup?" Rob said, barely able to contain himself.

David gave him a look.

"Funny guy."

"He sounds like quite a character, this Zimmer," chuckled Rob.

"Oh yeah, he'd sit in the back seat of the Cub during lessons, always had a clipboard with him; at first, I figured it was for taking notes but seldom saw anything clipped to it."

"Why'd he have it?"

"Didn't take long to find out. If, or more correctly, when, one of his students did something while flying the Cub he deemed improper or risky, to the point of being dangerous, he'd real quick like, smack 'em on the back of the head with that clipboard, to get their attention, you know. Then he'd holler at the top of his lungs, 'Jesus H. Christ, maybe you wanna die, but I don't!' It was quite the little attention-getter."

Rob was convulsed with laughter.

"He'd then explain, in colorful language, how the government was spending a crapload-load of money and time to train new pilots for the war effort. And, that he would personally take offense in having to replace dead pilots and instructors, along with perfectly good airplanes that some dumb ass student pilot flew into a barn, or water tower."

"Did you ever get smacked?"

"I'll admit to once," David said, holding up a finger. "That's all it took to get the message; I'm a quick learner. But there was a method to his madness. Almost all students got smacked, sooner or later. How they responded told volumes about their attitude, aptitude, and character for flying. A few students, after getting clipboarded, just fell apart. Some panicked and locked up on the controls or wet themselves, or both, which did not bode well for them being in any sort of wartime or combat situation. If they responded badly after a smack in the back of the head, with a clipboard, what are they going to do when bullets start flying through the cockpit, or an engine conks out?"

"Wow, that makes a lot of sense. What became of those guys, the ones who couldn't hack it?" Rob asked.

"They were thanked for their efforts, then politely, and firmly, told perhaps they'd be better off joining the crocheting club, as it more closely suited their temperament, but probably ought to change their underwear first," replied David with a straight face.

Rob doubled over with laughter. After finally regaining his composure, he asked David how long did he plan to travel today.

"I suppose another couple hours or more, or until we're hungry again, then find a tourist court or hotel if we can, assuming they still exist."

"They're called motels now, Dad. Came from the term, motor hotel, I guess, and there's plenty around, shouldn't be an issue."

"Snappy name," replied David. "What's your dad like, Rob? Tell me more about him; I know it's probably awkward for you."

Rob rolled the word over in his mind. Yes, it would be awkward telling a person who appears physically to be his dad, but isn't, about himself. But then, just another absurd moment, in an absurd and inexplicable few days.

"You already know his birthday, same as yours, June first, but in 1967. He's from a small town in Missouri."

"What's he do for a living?"

"High school history teacher, not surprisingly, and does photography part-time, mostly in the summer months. Family pictures, high school seniors, things like that, he's good at it. After graduating high school in 1985, I believe it was, he arrived here and went to the University of Florida in Gainesville, where I'm going now. Mom is a native Floridian. Dad stayed in Florida to teach after graduating; they met in 1994, got married in 1996. I came along in 1999; Karli's two years younger. You already know he likes working on old cars."

"But, what's he like?" pressed David.

"I don't know; he's great, he really is."

Rob felt uncomfortable, awkward, and paused for a moment before continuing.

"My dad, he, well, his dad… I guess they weren't very close. His name was Frank, and he was a Marine in the Pacific, had a tough time of it, from what I understand."

"Yeah, we all did, those damn Japs…."

David managed to stop himself before going into a ranting rage.

"Was he a Mud Marine?"

"Yeah, infantry, ground pounder, did some island hopping, saw a lot of horrible things he struggled with for years. That's what my dad told me anyway."

"Do you know what islands? I could have flown over the area he was in, maybe provided air support for whatever unit he was with. Like I said the other night, I helped those Marines who were pinned down by killing all the Jap gunners, 'cause this one Mud Marine was on the ground who… Anyway, go on."

"Dad hardly says anything about him; I don't think Frank talked much about the war, either, only saw him twice. I remember he was tall."

David nodded.

"He spent a couple of months in a VA hospital, after the war, had wounds that bothered him the rest of his life, other issues too. Dad said it made him mean and drink too much, and when he drank, he got meaner. His wife, my grandmother, who died before I was born, was at least his second, maybe third wife, not sure. Frank was in his forties when my dad was born. He didn't talk much about my grandfather, so his life is a little cloudy.

"Dad's an intelligent and interesting guy. He's easy-going but does have a temper that comes out every once in a while. I always thought he was intimidated and frustrated by his father. I guess Frank had enough belligerence in him for two or three men. After college, dad seldom went back to Missouri, especially after his mom died."

"What's behind him being so interested in World War II?" David asked.

"Being a history teacher, maybe he figured studying World War II would help him understand his dad better, you know, the way he was, what he went through, something like that."

"Think it did?"

"I couldn't say, but he has become very attached to the World War II era, almost obsessed. As I said, it gets on my mom's nerves; Karli is good with it, and I think it's great. We rebuilt this old WW II era car together…" Rob's words trailed off.

David knew this was upsetting to the boy. Derek, his real dad, had gone missing, suddenly, and he had to feel cheated and frustrated. The cell phone vibrated in his pocket; pulling it out and seeing it was the same name and number as earlier, he tossed it over his shoulder into the back seat.

"Be nice to your phone; it might help save your life someday," Rob said.

⭇ ⭆

"How's my big girl?" Macy asked as she walked through the door.

"Mommy, mommy!" Jenny said as she ran to her.

Macy bent down and scooped the child up off the floor, giving her a big kiss and a long hug.

"Oh, she's just fine," said Betty, stepping from the kitchen while drying her hands on a towel. "No problems, as usual, and even ate all of her applesauce for lunch."

"You're such a good girl for Aunt Betty, Jenny!" Macy said with a smile.

It was 1946, September; the war had been over for a year. Macy had remained in the house in Grand Rapids and began working in a dress shop downtown. It kept her busy, along with paying the bills. Betty and Tom took care of Jenny while she was working. The last correspondence, two months earlier, from the War Department, stated David continued to be officially listed as missing in action, although presumed deceased. She had not given up hope that somehow, someway, he would return to her and Jenny. Though after more than a year, she had made a decision.

"Please stay for supper, it's just leftovers, but you're more than welcome," said Betty.

"I appreciate it, as always, but we need to go."

Macy paused for a moment.

"I have plans to make, things to do."

"Plans?" asked Betty.

"I've decided to move back home."

"Oh, I'm so sorry to hear that, child. You, and this precious little girl, have become such a welcomed and important part of our lives."

"And you've both been wonderful, simply wonderful; I can't thank you enough," replied Macy. "I thought, hoped, prayed when David came back, he'd come right here, to our home, to Jenny and me, and everything would be fine. So often I've imagined him walking down the sidewalk and opening the gate…."

She paused again.

"I just feel it's time to go home to my family now."

Tom walked into the room and greeted Macy. Betty told him she and Jenny were moving back to Fowlerville.

"Well, that's too bad," said Tom, frowning. "Though I certainly understand why you'd want to be with your people. If there's anything we can do, anything at all, we'll be more than happy to help. How are you traveling?"

"I'm selling the car, so will be taking the bus; there are a few things I'll send home; the rest I'll carry with us on the trip. Maybe you could help me pack the things that need to be mailed, Tom, and get them to the post office if you don't mind?"

"Not at all, not at all, you just let me know when you need me. There are boxes in the basement you are more than welcome to have."

Macy thanked him profusely and said they planned to leave within a week. She put the baby bag over her shoulder, told Jenny to wave bye-bye to Betty and Tom, then walked out holding Jenny's hand, closing the door behind her.

"I feel so bad for that poor girl," said Betty. "She has tried to keep busy since David went missing and keeps up a good front, but inside she is so sad, just so, so sad, and lost."

Tom put his arm around his wife.

"She needs to be with her family now."

"Without her knowing if David is dead or alive… It would make it easier to move on if she only knew he was, gone," she sadly replied.

"Nothing easy about any of this," replied Tom. "The girl is always going to have a hole in her heart, for that boy. I hope she'll be alright."

"Just so sad," Betty said as she leaned against Tom.

The next day Macy told Sally, her employer, she would be leaving at the end of the week and thanked her for the opportunity to work in the shop. Sally said that she would be genuinely missed, wished her all the best, then asked if there was anything new on David. Macy shook her head, no.

In the evenings, after work, she set about collecting items to be sent to Fowlerville; clothing, a few household items, and most of Jenny's toys. They had rented the house furnished, so there was no concern over furniture or the few appliances.

Tom and Betty came over on a Friday evening to help her box up everything that needed to be mailed. Previously, Tom had collected negatives from all the photos he had taken of the family and presented them to her. The last things Macy packed were the photographs displayed on the wall. One by one, they were placed in two boxes with care and sadness. She had purposely left this task for last, reluctant to take them down, as doing so seemed to signal an ending.

An end of so much that was good. An end of a time that was sweet, with the promise of an even sweeter, brighter future. An end to a young girl's dreams and plans for a lifetime with someone she loved and would grow old with. Truly, David was her soul mate, for all time.

Wrapping each framed photo carefully in newspaper pages and placing them gently in the boxes, Macy wondered if she was also packing away the remainder of her hope.

Jenny, who had been playing with toys not yet packed, came over to her mom, carefully picked up a framed photo of David standing next to his Corsair, then gently placed it into the box, saying,

"Daddy's plane."

"That's right, Jenny, that's right," then gave her daughter a long hug.

Saturday morning, Tom drove Macy and Jenny to the post office, left off the boxes, then made their way to the bus station. Betty had said her goodbyes earlier, at the house, after giving Macy sandwiches, drinks, and treats in a paper bag for the bus ride. Along with smiles, and the wishing of good luck, there was deep and underlying heartache.

At 9:31 a.m., Macy and Jenny Hamilton boarded the idling Greyhound bus that would take them from Grand Rapids to Fowlerville. Jenny became restless, so Macy reached into the paper bag to find a treat and touched something solid. Pulling it out, she found it to be a small, framed needlepoint piece Betty always had hanging in her kitchen. The few carefully stitched words gave her a measure of comfort, hope, and yet, sadness.

At 9:35 a.m., Tom heard the bus rev up, with an accompanying puff of diesel smoke from the exhaust; he watched as it slowly began to pull away. In little more than a minute, it was out of sight.

⟞⟨⟩⟞

It had been another fitful night. Any amount of time spent on Okinawa was more than enough to bend a man's senses and warp reality. Few things could be relied upon to relieve the tension and dread. Sleep was a luxury, simple comfort, only a fond remembrance.

The Tall Marine, and his company, had spent the night in a

relatively secure position below the ridge. With darkness retreating, the torn landscape became more defined in the gray and hazy light. Before long, it would be time to advance back up that ridge, again, but not yet and then not all the way. First, there would be a flight of fighters arriving to attack the enemy points of entrenchment using a lethal combination of lead, steel, and fire. The Mud Marines much welcomed this.

The weather had been atrociously wet, but a forecasted clearing had presented an opportunity to request the Navy and Marine aviators attack the Japanese troops, solidly dug in on Horseshoe Ridge. He and other members of the 1st Marine Division were to ascend a short way up the ridge, wait until the aircraft had dealt destruction upon the enemy, then quickly make their way to the top and attempt to finish off whatever miserable souls who might be left alive.

Only an hour, perhaps two, had the Tall Marine slept, lying covered under half a pup tent panel. The struggle to keep mist and rain from soaking through to the bone was the nightly drill. It had not worked well, as usual, but was preferable to being in the open, barely. Everyone went to sleep in the mud and woke up in the mud. A perpetual stench of rotting vegetation, unburied bodies, and body parts only added to the surreal ugliness of the nightmare.

Their sergeant came down the line of men, some not yet stirring in the semi-darkness, passing out ammunition and K-rations. He advised there would be no fresh water until later in the day, if they were lucky.

The Tall Marine packed away the ammo, then pulled out a small, round, shaving mirror. He stared into it for a moment, hardly recognizing the muddy, beard-stubbled face looking back. Tucking it away, he then sat and stared at the K-ration package, trying to decide whether or not even to bother.

"Ya' gonna eat thet there shit, or jest stare at it 'til it turns ta steak n' eggs?" his buddy Duke asked as he walked over and sat down beside to him. They had been friends since boot camp, on Parris Island, in 1942.

"Don't bother me, hillbilly; this is an important decision," the Tall Marine replied. "The wrong breakfast selection could ruin your entire damn day."

"Well hell, yer on Okinawa, thousands of Japs be try'n ta kill ya', how much worse could yer day git, ol' buddy," said Duke, slapping him on the back.

Instant coffee was included in the package, but little water to make it and no time for a fire. Hot coffee was considered a luxury in the jungle. With the perpetual smell of rot and death, the thought of having any canned meat was out of the question. Nor did the Tall Marine care to expend needed energy trying to chew on the hardtack biscuits, deciding finally upon the combination of a fruit bar, dried apricots, a few salted peanuts, and a piece of hard candy for dessert.

"Damn fine choice," said Duke, while facetiously clapping his hands.

"I done partook of all ma Spam, if'n ya' don't be want'n yers, I'll be a'take'n it."

The Tall Marine handed it to him, saying,

"You coal miners are a hardy bunch, ain't ya. Stupid, but hardy. Bet yer wish'n ya could be back in that mine, right about now."

"Ya' bet yer sweet ass, sonny. Ain't no Japs a'roam'n ta hills of Kentucky, a'shoot'n at poor dumb bastards like us," replied Duke.

After eating, the Tall Marine placed the remaining K-ration in his rucksack and shook the canteen attached to his belt. Deciding it was more than half-full, he took a big swig of water then popped the hard candy in his mouth.

Word came down the line to make sure their weapons were

clean, clear, and functional. The two buddies had performed this the night before but unloaded their .30 carbines and again gave them a good going over. Nothing left to do now, but wait for word that the fighters were inbound, then head out.

⊨⊨ ⊫⊨

Having traveled two-lane highways for the majority of the day, David and Rob had not covered an abundance of ground. It had been a pleasant drive in the old Ford, with ample daylight left in the day. Rob had taken over driving duties again after fifty miles, with David saying he was becoming uncomfortably tired.

"I know the Gainesville area well; what say we plan on spending the night there, then hit it hard again tomorrow," suggested Rob.

David said that sounded fine. A few miles out of Gainesville, he pointed to a billboard just off the highway.

"Rob, look at that, look at that! There's another restaurant named McDonald's ahead, like the one we ate at before. What are the odds? Now I know we have to be on the right track!"

"Odds are pretty good. There are four of them in Gainesville, two on either end of University Avenue."

David looked at Rob incredulously and said,

"What are you talking about?"

"Remember when you said someone ought to open up a chain of restaurants, like McDonald's? Well, someone did a long time ago; they're all over the country. All over the world, actually."

"Seriously? Ain't that something," laughed David. "Being as it was Macy's maiden name, and I saw it in the dream, figured it was a good sign. But, if they're all over, maybe it's not."

"I think the fact they are all over *is* a good sign," Rob replied.

"Maybe so; I like the way you think, boy."

Before long, they had made their way to the McDonald's, on

the eastern end of University Avenue. As much as Rob enjoyed the occasional visit to fast food eateries, he hoped David would soon get over his fascination with them. While eating, he checked on his phone for nearby motels, finding a reasonably priced one just east off Interstate 75, and reserved a double. It was June; most students were gone for the summer, fewer tourists were traveling into the state, making accommodations more readily available. After registering and putting their things in the room, they made a leisurely two-block walk to an ice cream shop they had spotted while driving to the motel.

"Dad," began Rob as they sat outside, eating their dessert. "You getting nervous about what we'll find, or what'll happen, in Grand Rapids?"

David shook his head and replied,

"I don't know what to expect, just know we have to go there."

"This is all something you saw in the dream?"

"Yes, this trip is something you know has to be done, even if you don't know why. It made no sense to stay in Fort Myers; nothing was going to happen there. My fate only moves in one direction, as I see it."

"What else do you recall about that dream."

"It was so brilliant, so real," began David. "Made sense at the time, and I had the feeling things would be okay if we made this trip. Some of it has, well, not faded exactly, but sort of softened on what I remember, mixed in with other things, things I shouldn't be remembering."

"Go on."

"I was flying across the water, looking out over the long nose of the blue Corsair, but the ocean turned into a road, a two-lane highway, but I was still looking out over something blue. Soon realized, it was the hood of that car sitting back at the motel."

"Quite a transition," commented Rob.

"You were with me; at least I think it was you, don't know who else it would be. Ya know, I just thought of something; there was that voice with a foreign accent I mentioned before; I didn't know where it was coming from, but it just kept saying, "*Go home. Go home, now.*" I'm wondering if it wasn't that GSP thing we're using, Henry, his voice."

"GPS," Rob corrected.

"Yeah, whatever, almost forgot about it, that foreign voice."

"Quite a coincidence, maybe," replied Rob suspiciously.

"Yeah, so it would seem. Remember music too, like we were listening to earlier, from the '40s, my time, playing in the background. Strange."

"Been nothing but strange lately," Rob responded. "Anything else?"

"As I said, so much of it has begun to fade or get all jumbled up. There was the sign I told you about; I think red and white, bet we run into that further down the road; I'll know it when I see it. And the big hot air balloons, with a Ferris wheel. Those exist, in Michigan, by what you showed me."

David frowned, then said in a serious voice,

"I remember, remember in back, something... something behind me, us... it made me uncomfortable and angry. I sensed danger, evil. I got some of that same feeling when you all were talking about those missing girls."

Rob felt uneasy upon hearing this.

"I'd look in the rearview mirror, and it was dark, ahead it was bright. I had the sense of running away from something, something shadowy and dark, that was following, stalking us," said David, staring straight ahead. "It was very disturbing."

"And trees, trees, and other things were going by, in a blur, close to the road. I knew that was right, and this is the right way to go. I guess that's where the uncomfortable feeling came from, being on that four-lane. It wasn't our road to take; even that old car knew it, I swear.

"And, I remember clearly, seeing Macy, in a room, a dark room, with other people around, and the smell of roses. I saw her; she was real and alive. This trip's just as much about the journey as the destination. I'm sure of that now."

"Beginning to look like it," agreed Rob.

"You know, you're a pretty sharp fellow for a young punk," said David, with a smile.

"Correct me if I'm wrong, old man; my dad may have turned fifty-two a few days ago, but I'm only twenty, and you, sir, just turned twenty-two. Just saying, from one young punk to another," said Rob, with a grin.

"Where I came from, you got old pretty quick or died young," replied David, with little emotion.

"You're right. I can't even imagine," Rob said, nodding soberly.

"My head's getting a little fuzzy, Son. We should head back to the room, get some sack time, probably have at least another three days or more traveling in front of us, the way we're going. Oh, and by the way, I'm sure gonna miss your mom tonight, again," David said with a sideways glance.

"Bastard," said Rob, with half a grin.

On the way back to the motel, the street lights were beginning to glow as it was nearing sundown. It was comfortably warm, yet not too humid. Their last day in Florida ended with a gentle evening.

Rob suggested they leave the television off; he was concerned most of what David, the fighter pilot from 1945, might observe, especially news programs, would prove too overwhelming for this tortured soul and impossibly difficult to explain. This entity inside his father's body was fragile enough without sorting through world history for the last seventy-four years. No good would come from further confusing an already confused situation. David approved of the suggestion, saying he was too tired anyway and needed to sleep. Tomorrow, the highway north calls.

≈ ≈

A haze settled over the dank, musty body of water in the hours after midnight. It was the middle of May, and amidst the night sounds of crickets, frogs, and katydids, came four voices out of the darkness. Three men excited, mocking, and laughing—a girl, panicked, with muffled, pleading, and desperate cries for help. Streetlamp's soft illumination glowed from a small, nearby town, but only pale moonlight exposed the unfolding horror taking place.

This night, there would be no help forthcoming, no salvation. No heroes. Soon, the anguished cries were silenced.

Stolen off the street, the girl had been reduced to nothing more than brutal, murderous amusement. The click of a cigarette lighter briefly cast dark, flickering shadows upon the gruesome scene as she was dragged to the water's edge. There was a splash, followed by laughter. Another innocent life tacked onto their maniacal score.

The three men walked leisurely through the tall grass towards a silver-colored vehicle. With headlights off, the car slowly pulled away, turned onto a gravel road, and disappeared into the night.

≈ ≈

TUESDAY

R ob's cell phone alarm clock went off at 5:45 a.m. David suggested they get cleaned up and go to McDonald's. The boy shook his head, stating they had brought enough food along to provide their own breakfast.

Although he had been looking forward to one of their egg and muffin meals, David reluctantly conceded. Soon, they were both fed and prepared to get back on the road north. It was overcast and damp, with a mist hanging in the air. As they walked out of the ground-floor motel room door, someone spoke,

"Where you guys headed?" asked a female voice.

At first, neither could see from whom or where the voice was emanating. In the dim light, one room away, was a figure sitting on a backpack and leaning against the wall, a cell phone to an ear. Next to the person was a bright yellow tote bag with a cartoon parrot on the side.

"Where you guys headed?" she repeated, lowering the phone.

Warily, Rob moved closer. It was a young girl, her long, dark hair in a ponytail. She appeared to be about his age, with an athletic build, and very attractive. He smiled and said,

"North."

"How far north?"

"Long ways north," said Rob, still smiling.

"And that would be…" she said while raising her palms in a questioning manner.

Rob turned and looked at David, a few steps behind. He was vehemently shaking his head, no.

"Michigan, going to… going to look up some distant relatives," said Rob, turning back to the girl.

"Perfect," she said while getting up and grabbing her backpack. "Would you guys mind terribly if I tag along? I'll pay my own way and have money for gas."

David stepped closer for a better look at the girl, who could not be more than five feet and a couple of inches tall.

"Miss, I don't think that would be a good idea," he said, stepping yet closer. "My son and I are on this trip, and, well, it's complicated, we…."

He abruptly stopped talking and turned to Rob.

"Can I speak to you for a moment?" he said, putting a hand on his shoulder.

As the girl put the phone back up to her ear, Rob overheard,

"It's nobody you know; maybe I'll see you later, maybe not."

They walked several steps away, and with their backs turned, David said, quietly,

"Rob, that girl is Oriental; I think, she's Japanese."

"Oriental? Who uses that word anymore? And so what, she could be Irish, for all we know," replied Rob.

"Did you hear me? I think, she's Japanese," David said in a quiet, almost pleading voice.

"Yes, I heard you; she's all alone on a dreary morning and seems to need a ride. What's the big deal?"

"Well, she…" David said as he looked down at his shoes, then back at Rob. "She's Japanese."

"We should find out her story, alright?" said Rob, tiredly.

"I, I'm not so sure about this, Rob; it makes me uneasy, having one of them around."

"Really? She's not much more than five feet tall and something over a hundred pounds, maybe. I think we can both handle her if she goes berserk and pulls out a samurai sword or something. If it makes you feel better, I'll frisk her," said Rob, with a smirk.

"You smart-ass son-of-a-bitch, this shit ain't funny, boy."

Rob walked back to the girl, now standing under the light of the motel overhang.

"You know I can hear you, right?" she said, matter-of-factly.

"Right, so what are you doing out here, all by yourself? It could be dangerous, considering what's been happening."

"Yeah, and thanks for reminding me," the girl replied. "I'm a student at the University of Florida, trying to get back home to Michigan, a town East of Lansing."

"Me too, a student, I mean," replied Rob. "What year?"

"Junior, this fall, taking psychology classes."

"So am I, Junior, computer science, probably passed each other in the halls, or on-campus somewhere," said Rob. "So, how did you come to be sitting here today, alone, on this lovely morning?"

"My boyfriend and I had made plans to drive me back home to Michigan; that was him on the phone just now. It was going to be a surprise; I haven't told my parents when I would be back."

"So, what happened?"

"He's gotten really strange lately, to the point of scaring me; I suggested we needed to take a break. On the phone last night, he was very insistent about coming to my apartment, said we needed to talk. I told him that wasn't a good idea. He got pretty pissed off and threatening."

"Sorry to hear that," replied Rob.

"I just knew he was going to come over anyway, so I packed up my things and left. It was late, and I was walking. Didn't want to spend money on a room for just a few hours, so decided to park out here for the night. At this point, I was planning on taking a bus headed towards Michigan."

"Can your parents help you out?"

"Oh sure, but they, especially my dad, were not big on me going so far away to school in the first place. He wanted me to stay in Michigan. Call me stubborn, but I have to prove I can get by on my own, away from home. It's complicated, but you know how strict those Oriental parents can be," she replied, raising her voice enough to be sure David could hear.

Rob chuckled, looked at David, then said,

"Oh, I'm very familiar with complicated when it comes to parental issues."

"The boyfriend apologized on the phone, was sorry for being such a jerk, and still wanted to take me home. I told him no thanks, but he could drive me to the bus station. Said he'd be right over. Now wish I wouldn't have told him where I'm at."

"He sounds like a pervert," said Rob.

"How can I be sure you two aren't perverts?" she asked, cocking her head to one side.

"You can't," said David as he stepped closer.

"Don't know what possessed me to ask where you were going, just blurted it out, and I never do anything like that. Just had a feeling it was, well, alright, the right thing to do."

Rob stared into the early morning gloom and suddenly sensed he could not leave this girl here, alone. It was a heavy, uncomfortable feeling, bordering on dread. A possibly unsavory character, at this moment, might be on his way to pick her up. And considering the ugliness that had been occurring in the area, he knew what had to happen.

"We can help you out if you're not in a big hurry. We're traveling mostly back roads on our way to Michigan; Miss, I'm sorry, I don't know your name. Should I call you stubborn, as you requested? I'm Rob Haynes."

"Omora, Sunni Omora, no big rush getting home," she laughed and reached out to shake his hand.

"I knew it, I knew it," said David, looking down and shaking his head. "Dad!"

"Omora is not an Irish name, Son."

"Jeezuz, Dad, cool it!"

"What's his problem?" Sunni asked.

"He has issues," answered Rob.

"No kidding," she replied.

"Anyway, this is my dad, Derek, David… Derek Haynes."

"Sounds like you're not sure," said Sunni, with a smirk.

"It's complicated."

He picked up her backpack and began walking towards the Coupe, a few parking spaces away; Sunni texted something on her phone, then placed it in her pocket.

"This your car?" she asked.

"Yeah, why? You got a problem with that?" David said sharply as he opened the trunk lid.

"Looks pretty old; you sure it'll get to Michigan? What year is it, looks like maybe a forty-one?"

"Yes, forty-one, it'll be fine, young lady; it's only four years old," snapped David.

"Four years?" Sunni questioned.

"Since we rebuilt it, my dad and I, we finished rebuilding this car four years ago," Rob interrupted, giving David a quick glare. "That's what you meant, right, Dad?"

"Yeah, whatever," said David as he grabbed the girl's backpack from him and unceremoniously tossed it into the trunk. "Wait, how would you know what year it is?"

"My dad is into old cars; he has a couple of his own. Is this the Standard or Deluxe?

"Super Deluxe Coupe," said David curtly.

"Sweet! I like the color, Navy blue?" Sunni questioned.

"Navy Blue," replied David, slamming the trunk lid shut. "No. 2."

"I bet you're a real expert on Toyotas," David said under his breath as he turned away.

"What was that? Didn't quite catch it," Sunni asked, cupping her hand behind an ear.

"Nothing," he replied.

"You driving, or me?" Rob asked.

"I think you'd better," David said as he walked around to the passenger side door, where Sunni was now standing.

He stopped, stared at her for a moment, then opened the door and folded the front seat forward.

"Thank you, sir," said Sunni as she climbed into the back seat with her tote bag.

"Oh, you're welcome, so glad to have you along," he said, with more than a hint of sarcasm.

David got in and closed the door. Rob, who was already behind the wheel, gave him a little punch in the arm.

"Be nice, old man."

"Yeah, be nice, old man," repeated Sunni, then laughed.

Giving Rob a half-smile, half glaring look, he said. "Old man, I'll give you old man, you little shit, guess you've forgotten who you're dealing with here."

"If only I could," laughed Rob as he turned the key then pushed the starter button.

Not long after they had entered the street bordering the motel, Rob's phone rang; it was his mother. He hoped she was calling simply to see how the trip was progressing.

"Hi mom, can't talk long; I'm driving; what's up?"

"About the same, I guess; why?"

"From who?"

It was several seconds before he spoke again.

"I see."

"Yeah."

"That's quite something, huh."

"Okay, we'll be careful. I need to get off the phone now; I'll try and call you later. Yes, love you too, say hi to Karli, bye."

"Your mom, huh?" asked David, after taking a quick glance into the back seat.

"Yep."

"You don't think she suspe... knows anything about..." said David quietly before being interrupted by Sunni.

"You two guys bank robbers or something?"

"Why, what have you heard?" said Rob, as he turned and smiled at the girl, who chuckled at his response.

"Really, Rob, you think she...."

Rob cut him off.

"It's fine, Dad. We're fine."

Less than a minute following their departure from the motel grounds, a car drove hurriedly into the parking lot and lurched to a stop. A blonde-haired man exited the vehicle and began frantically walking up and down the length of the building. After lighting a cigarette, he got back into the silver Mercedes sedan and drove away.

"What did he say?" Karli asked.

"Couldn't talk much, but I'm sure he knows."

"I agree," returned Karli. "It was very odd the way they came up with this trip, all of a sudden."

"And both acted the suspiciously the night before when I went into the garage," replied Shelley. "It's all kind of adding up now, isn't it?"

"It is, Mom, if what that woman, Evelyn, said is true. How soon do you think we should leave?"

"We need to talk with Rob again first and tell him about the doctor and what he and Evelyn need to do, but probably should start packing."

"Will they be traveling with us?"

"No, she says he is still recovering and not yet ready to travel. They'll have to meet us whenever, and wherever, the right time and place can be found."

"That's going to take some planning," replied Karli.

"And little time to get it done," added Shelley. "This doctor says if not carried out promptly, he's afraid there's a chance your dad may be... lost for good. We'll need to get on the road soon."

"Mom, is there anything, anything at all we could've done differently, you know, so this wouldn't have happened?"

"No, honey, we had no way of knowing; even the doctor says he cannot understand the how or why. He's never even heard of such a thing in all his experience. Unprecedented, Evelyn said."

"Why did it have to happen to dad, Mom, to us?"

"We may never know, Karli. We may never know. But we have to be there, for your father."

Sunni could not rationalize her compulsion to ask these two strangers' destination, and then to discover it was Michigan; it seemed such a strange, uncanny coincidence. Was it fate, luck, providence? Rob's dad seemed odd, troubled, and was not the least bit friendly towards her for reasons unknown. Nevertheless, she felt safe with them, safe and relaxed, especially with Rob. Sunni realized she had almost instantly become more comfortable with these two strangers than with the, hopefully, gone for good boyfriend, Carlos.

They had only been together for two months. At first, he was likable, and they got on quite well, though lately, he had turned pushy and mean, to the point she was afraid to be alone with the man. Sunni was sure she wasn't going to miss him. *Out of my life, forever,* was her thought and hope.

"Where you guys from?" she asked.

"Fort Myers," replied Rob. "Ever been there?"

"No, never been further south than Gainesville, yet. School takes up too much time, and I'm not much of a traveler."

"So, never been to Japan, huh?" David asked.

Sunni considered, for a moment, asking if he had an issue with people of Japanese descent, but thought better of it. She had just met these men who were doing her a favor; it was too early in the trip to risk ruffling any feathers.

"Nope, never have."

"Your parents come from there?" David continued.

"Just stop it," said Rob gruffly.

"No, in fact, my grandfather was born in a Japanese internment camp, in California, during the second world war."

"Is that right," replied David. "I don't know much about those; I was out of the country a lot when that was going on."

"Really?" Sunni asked sarcastically. "Just how old are you?"

"You'll have to excuse my dad's rudeness, Sunni; he hasn't been himself lately, and gets confused and cranky, very easily. And often," said Rob while looking over at David. "Believe me; he used to be a lot nicer guy."

"Considering the times, it was probably a good idea, you know, those camps," said David matter-of-factly.

It took Sunni a great deal of restraint, and force of will, to keep from leaning forward and yelling in his ear. A good time to change the subject.

"So tell me about the car. It's a cool ride; where'd you find it?"

Rob began recounting the story of how they saw an online ad about a large auction of vintage and classic cars in Missouri.

"That was in 2010; I was eleven. My dad was looking for an early muscle car, like a '67 or '68 Camaro, maybe a Mustang, something like that. We drove up to Missouri with a trailer, fully expecting to bring something back."

"How'd you go from a '60s muscle car to an early 1940s Ford?" the girl asked.

"That's the odd thing, as we wandered around the grounds where the cars were parked, before the auction began, we just kept coming back to this scruffy old Ford. Dad said it reminded him of the one his dad and a friend owned together for a time. I remember he'd showed me an old picture of them and the car."

"Was it Navy Blue?"

"Couldn't say, it was a black-and-white print, but he thinks it might have been; it was a darker color. We often just refer to this car now as Navy Blue No. 2. So, at the auction, he'd walk around this car, look inside, and then walk around it again. First, he'd smile a little, then frown, shake his head, and we'd go look at something else. But we'd be back, half an hour later. I thought he was nuts."

David sat quietly, listening to Rob.

"So when the cars were going up on the block in the big tent, he let some of the others we'd looked at and considered go through without a bid," continued Rob. "After a couple of hours, they drove this car into the tent; I heard him say, 'at least the damn thing runs.' Well, the bidding started slow, and after a few bids, he raised his paddle. Two minutes later, they hammered it sold. Dad seemed more relaxed after that. 'Looks as if we have ourselves a project car, Son,' he said to me, all smiles."

"It was quite a surprise, as he'd never mentioned anything about wanting something like this. After getting my license, I was looking forward to having a hot Camaro, Mustang, or something, to drive. But I'm not disappointed. We had a ball restoring this thing together, and it's still a neat car.

"As we were putting it on the trailer, I asked why he went with this one and not one of the other cars we looked at. He shook his head and said, 'The car has personality, Rob; it spoke to me.' Being eleven, this seemed pretty lame, but as we worked on it and I got older, it did seem as if this car, this mechanical thing, has a personality."

"And a purpose," spoke David.

Rob looked over at the man.

"Maybe so," he replied.

As Rob continued telling Sunni the details of restoring the Coupe, and she asked the occasional question, David seemed to be paying close attention while periodically nodding his head. Then, curiously, as the story of the car's restoration, and their adventures with it, continued into the morning hours of the still gloomy Florida day, he would speak up and say he remembered different things.

Rob was happy to talk with Sunni and tell her of their experiences with the Ford and other car stories. She liked cars and seemed to be knowledgeable of them. He spoke of how well the project had progressed, how few problems or issues they had.

"It was almost as if the car was helping us get it back on the road. Does that sound strange?" he mentioned at one point.

Telling Sunni of the work done on the old car was also a good way to keep David from talking much, as he knew nothing of the twenty-first century. There was tenseness between Sunni and David; that needed to be quelled.

He was much taken aback when David seemed to recall a few

details on the car project. Perhaps it was just an attempt to inject enough fake knowledge into the story to make it sound as if he and Rob did this together, and if so, it was quite convincing. Or perhaps it was something else.

⇒+ +⇐

The rain had stopped by the time his squad moved out onto the muddy trail. Word had come down that the fighters were marshaling on the carrier's decks, preparing to launch. It would not be long now. Lieutenant Watts gave the order to move into their positions, halfway up the side of Horseshoe Ridge, earlier than planned. Once in place, it would allow the Marines needed rest and preparation time before their rapid assault began, after the carrier planes had completed their carnage.

Men moved slowly and steadily along the rubble-strewn path. The repugnant odor of death grew increasingly more distinct as they approached the base of the ridge.

The Tall Marine began to notice something not seen in the last several days. Shadows were becoming more and more visible, cast from the remains of trees cut in half from artillery shelling and previous air attacks. Few words were spoken; they were trying to move forward quietly. Some looked at each other, gave a thumbs-up, or pointed to the sky and grinned.

Shadows on the ruined landscape meant the fighters would be inbound, and soon. The clearing weather will provide a more effective and accurate delivery of ordinance to help make the Marines' job easier, if anything could be easy, on Okinawa. It also meant the much-feared Japanese anti-aircraft emplacements would be more likely to get a more accurate bead on the flyboys.

The Tall Marine had witnessed several Marine and Navy aircraft shot out of the sky, and it made him angry. Those emplacements were well hidden and frequently moved, making it difficult for the fighters and artillery to find and kill them. And they needed to be killed.

As it often did, his mind wandered to thoughts of home, with the same overriding notion; would he ever see it again. The heat on this miserable island was brutal. Coming from a small, rural, Midwestern town, summertime would find him bailing hay for farmers; he and a crew of friends did this for years. It could be sweltering and uncomfortable work, but nothing like this constant heat and humidity.

Back home, no one was actively and intensely seeking to kill you. No dead bodies were lying in the hay fields, stinking up the place. No potential for death just around the bend or over the next hill. The calmness and safety of that world seemed so distant. In truth, it was less than two years, and now he found it difficult even to imagine or recall. What he wouldn't give to be back, shirt-less on a hayrack, stacking bales, and joking with his friends, in-stead of being shot at by enemy soldiers, on some Pacific Ocean island he had never heard of until some weeks ago.

Hay bailing usually began in June. *It's May now,* he thought; *if I were home, it wouldn't be long before we would start, or is it June?* He stopped, turned, and quietly said to the Marine behind him,

"Nick, Nick, what day is it?"

"Just another goddamn day, in paradise," replied Nick, and kept walking.

"Duke, hey Duke," the Tall Marine said to his buddy. "What's today, the date?"

"I'm a' go'n with Nick's answer," he replied.

"No, really, you know what the date is? I've lost all track of time in this shithole."

Duke stopped for a moment.

"Let's see, secn't of June be ma dear old momma's birthday;

I always 'member it, an' thet be tomorrow, so today, be the first, June one. Thet gonna work for 'ya, big fella?"

"Yeah, thanks," the Tall Marine replied.

"Glad to hep out ya'll, an' yer feeble mind."

"Hey Duke, wish your momma happy birthday next time you write her, and when you get back to Kentucky, give her a big, wet, sloppy kiss from me, right on the mouth."

"Yeah, yeah," said Duke as he walked away, prominently displaying his middle finger.

June first, shit, it's my birthday; I almost forgot.

The Tall Marine was twenty-two years old.

David was hungry, as were his two fellow travelers. For the past hour, they had successfully fended off David's suggestion to search out the nearest McDonald's, as they plied the winding rural roads and watched the red clay hills of the Georgia countryside pass by.

"It's beginning to feel like I'm traveling with Bonnie and Clyde," chuckled Sunni. "Nothing but back roads; seems as if we're on the run and sneaking around. You guys sure you're not looking for a bank to rob?"

"The less you know, the better off you are, little girl," said Rob, in his best, fake, sinister voice, then softened his tone. "Love that movie; I've watched it several times."

"Me too, kind of hokey and not all that accurate, but the '60s had some great flicks," replied Sunni.

"What movie?" David questioned.

"Bonnie and Clyde, we've watched it before, Dad, from 1967. You know, the year, you were born?"

"Oh yeah, them," replied David.

"Nasty bastards; I was almost ten when they got killed, and they deserved it."

"You remember seeing the movie for the first time when you were ten, right? You told me that," Rob spoke up quickly while giving David a pointed glance.

"That's right, ten when I saw the movie," said David looking back at Rob and slightly shrugging his shoulders. "So when we going to stop and eat, I'm getting pretty hungry."

"We'll see what's in the next town; work for you, Bonnie?" Rob asked Sunni.

"Sure, maybe we can find a bank to stick up on the way out of town, Clyde."

"Funny girl, right, Dad?"

"Hilarious," replied David, without smiling.

Driving into the small town of Abbeville, they spotted a place called the Country Kitchen; after parking in the restaurant lot, they entered.

"Nice menu, good variety," said Sunni, after the waitress had seated them.

"Think I'll have a burger," David said, predictably.

"Try something different, lots of other choices here," said Rob, pointing at the menu. "They have meatloaf, mashed potatoes."

"So they do. Sounds good, meatloaf it is," David replied as he folded his menu and laid it on the table.

Sunni ordered fried shrimp with fries and coleslaw, while Rob chose roast beef, baked potato, and a salad. As they ate, he said,

"It's not McDonald's, but pretty good, don't you think, Dad?"

"Yeah, makes me think of home."

If Sunni had not been sitting at the table, Rob would've asked, *which home?*

After they had finished, Sunni excused herself to use the restroom, leaving David and Rob alone.

"Dad, you're going to have to watch what you say around Sunni."

"Right, it's just that I got used to it being only the two of us and never wanted her to come along in the first place, you know that. And remember when I was telling you about my dream? How something was behind us making me feel uncomfortable and angry? Well, I'm pretty sure it's that little Japanese girl in the back seat," said David as he jerked his thumb backward, over his shoulder.

"Or it might be your own anger towards anyone and anything Japanese," Rob replied, looking straight into David's eyes.

"Damn straight, but you can see where I'm coming from, right? I've been at war with those people,"

David paused for a moment and looked down at the table.

"And I'm stuck here, now, for some reason, screwing up your family's life. Sorry if I get pissed off, but...."

"That was a long time ago, not for you, but in history," interrupted Rob. "And Sunni had nothing to do with it."

"Exactly right, not long ago, for me," replied David, clearly upset.

Sunni walked up and, while putting cash on the table, asked, "Ready to go? This is for gas and my part of dinner."

David stared at the girl, then told her to keep it; they had everything covered.

"You sure? I've got the money," she countered.

"It's fine, Sunni; hang onto it for now. We're happy just to help you get home," said Rob. "We better get moving."

"I'll drive for a while if that's okay," David said after returning to the car.

"You sure?" Rob questioned.

"I'm fine," David said as he opened the driver's door and got in.

After Rob and Sunni had taken their seats, David turned the

ignition key and pushed the starter button. The engine turned over slowly; after a few seconds, it fired and settled into an idle.

"We probably need to change out that battery soon," suggested Rob.

David sat very still, staring out over the hood of the car, before saying in an oddly strained voice,

"Right, it's over, it's over… three years old, now…."

Suddenly he stiffened and began to rock forward and back, nearly striking his head on the steering wheel, while saying,

"No, no…no!"

"Dad! Are you all right? Dad!" Rob said excitedly.

David slowly stopped rocking.

"I don't know… I don't know what just happened," replied David, shaking his head.

"I better drive," said Rob quietly.

"Yes, you should. I'm sorry, Son."

Sunni felt uneasy. When Rob got out to change seats with David, she also exited and pulled him aside.

"What's going on? What's wrong with your dad? This is scaring me."

"I can hardly begin to explain," sighed Rob. "But, he's been having a tough time the last few days. Fell and bumped his head, and, well, it's more than just that. A lot more."

"Is he going to be alright? Maybe I should stay here and call my folks."

"And I wouldn't blame you, Sunni. My dad; see, he needs help. It's important that we get to Michigan; I'm hoping everything will be all right then."

"Anything to do with the distant relatives you mentioned?"

"Everything. I don't know how it's all going to turn out for him, for my family," he replied to the girl.

"I should just let you guys go on alone and work this all out."

He gently put his hands on her shoulders.

"You need to come with us; can't explain why, I just know you do."

Sunni looked up at Rob for several seconds.

"For some reason, I trust you. Let's go to Michigan, but maybe you shouldn't let your dad drive."

"Probably a good idea," said Rob, then walked her to the driver's side of the car. After opening the door and folding the seat forward, she stepped in and sat down.

"Everything's going to be all right," spoke Rob.

The rest of the afternoon passed calmly. David, for the most part, sat quietly in the front seat, seeming to sleep occasionally. Rob noticed it did not appear to be a restful sleep. Once, he roused himself enough to say it was a good idea to take the longer, more rural route around Atlanta, mentioning the traffic through that city around rush hour was always bad. Then fell back to sleep. Rob and his father, Derek, knew this, but he wondered how David, the man from 1945, would.

Sunni and Rob made small talk, the girl leaning forward and resting her crossed arms on the back of the front seat. Mostly the conversation revolved around school and classes, avoiding any mention of Rob's dad. By the time they had made their way past Atlanta, the sun was sinking low in the Western sky. Shortly, they began searching for a place to spend the night, settling on a motel in Cleveland, Georgia. Sunni paid for her own room, as they all agreed the three of them having one together, would be very awkward.

With no restaurant in the budget motel, they chose one just across the street. After a good meal, they all returned to their respective rooms, as everyone was tired. Saying he felt stiff and sore from driving and thought a short walk would help loosen him up,

Rob left the room. He needed to contact his mother. Outside, he found a bench in a landscaped area on the motel grounds and made the call. It was an emotional and confusing conversation.

Rob recounted the strange and unbelievable story that had been related to him, with all the detail he thought she could absorb and process. While also stressing David's desperate need to travel to Michigan.

"It's where he left his family, a wife, and child. The man needs to try and find them, Mom, if that is even somehow possible."

He explained he didn't know what they could hope to accomplish after all these years since 1945, but there was no other choice than to help find whatever destiny lay before David, and somehow get his dad back. Shelley shared the information she learned from the phone calls with Evelyn and how the doctor she worked for could not rationalize what was happening or why. She explained the doctors' urgent need to meet with his dad, or more correctly, David, personally, in the next few days. He felt it was the only chance to set things right. Both were drained by the end of the exchange.

Rob did not tell his mom about Sunni; it would be difficult to explain why he felt; somehow, she was part of this. Besides, he liked her and figured Shelley would not be approving of another person becoming involved. Especially someone who was essentially a hitchhiker. He would call again and let her know where they were and how things were going, and yes, it would be a good idea for Shelley and Karli to head north as soon as possible.

Upon returning to the room, Rob found David asleep. After setting the alarm on his cell phone, he quietly undressed, slipped into bed, and quickly fell asleep.

He awoke to someone shaking him.

"Rob, Son, wake up! Wake up! Where are we?"

David was kneeling on his bed next to him and speaking frantically.

"What's going on? What is this place? How did we get here?"

"Dad, what's wrong?" Rob asked as he slowly sat up.

"I... I don't know, Rob. Something happened, I don't know what, something, and now, I'm here. Where are we?"

"We're in Georgia, Dad, remember? On our way to Michigan?" Rob said, drowsily.

"Georgia? Michigan? Why would we be going to Michigan?"

"To try and find your wife and daughter."

"Shelley and Karli? What are they doing in Michigan?"

"No, no, you were shot down, in the Pacific, World War II. Okinawa, remember?"

"Shot down?"

"You had a wife, Macy, and a daughter, Jenny. We're driving to Grand Rapids, where you lived," said Rob slowly.

"Macy... Michigan? I don't know any....."

"David? David?" Rob said tentatively.

"Who's David?" said the man, his voice sounding odd and confused, then suddenly placed both hands on either side of his head. There was a look of pain on his face; the sound of low moaning seemed to come from deep within him.

"Yes, Macy and Jenny," said David calmly. Lowering his hands, he slowly stood up and moved back to his bed. "Had a bad dream, I guess. Sorry I bothered you."

David climbed back into bed and pulled the covers over his shoulders, and said, "G'night, Rob."

The boy slumped down and leaned on one elbow while looking at the man in the darkness. *What just happened here? It's almost as if...*

The thought tortured him.

He turned and beat his fist on the pillow, then sat up, hands covering his face. *Almost as if my dad was back, trying to get back. My dad, Derek, was trying to escape the grip this man David has on him.*

"He was here. He was here, and I chased him away," he whispered into his hands.

The boy's moist eyes made his palms damp.

There was a chance, maybe, to end all this, right here. But I was half asleep and didn't see it. With this thought, he lay back in bed, but sleep came sparingly. All too soon, the light of a new day began softly filtering through the drawn curtains. Glancing at his cell phone, he saw the alarm would go off in less than half an hour. The decision was made to get up and shower.

⇥ ⇤

WEDNESDAY

Sunni was awakened by the sound of her cell phone ringing. Rousing herself, she saw it was nearly 3:30 a.m.

"What do you want, Carlos?"

"I want you, baby; you weren't, weren't at the motel yesterday when I got there; I miss you," he replied.

"It's better this way, Carlos."

"C'mon, Sunni I, I've been real good to you, give you, gave you nice stuff, and everything. You know, like that pretty yellow bag I give ya 'couple of weeks ago, still got it?"

"Yeah, taking it home with me, to Michigan," replied Sunni curtly.

"Still have it, huh? Look, tell me where you're at, and I'll, I'll pick you up. We can drive ta Michigan t'gether; it'll be fun. My heart just broke when you texted, say'n, saying you'd found somebody else ta dri, drive you home, I love you, yer, my girl," Carlos slurred.

"You don't love anyone but yourself, and I'm not your goddamn girl. I've already left Florida, and I suggest you sober up, grow up, and get a life. Leave me the hell alone, please."

"You, you on your way to Michigan, now? Who you with, Sunni, anybody I know? Where you at, girl?"

"I told you before; it's nobody you know. Nice kid my age, and his dad, from Fort Myers, and it's none of your business!"

"Oh, oh yeah, well, yer my girl now, and I'm making it my business! Who are these guys? I'll beat the shit out of 'em, and you too, or, or worse! Now, now tell me, tell me where you're at, goddammit!"

"I'm not your girl, so leave me alone, Carlos. Get out of my life. I don't ever want to see, or hear from you again, understand? And what's your obsession with that yellow bag? You lose your mind?"

"Listen, girlie, you, you stop talking to me like, like that! If, if you know what's good fer you. You better tell me where you're at, or I'll...."

"You'll what?" Sunni yelled into the phone. "Stay away from me, loser, you... you psycho bastard, or I'll call the cops!"

"You're just an unappreciative slut, and I swear you try, try'n leave me, an' it'll be the biggest mistake of your short, little life, sweetheart, I, I promise you that. You hear me!"

Sunni ended the call, turned off the phone, and threw it across the room onto a chair.

When Rob came out of the bathroom, he found David standing by the large motel window, curtains drawn open, staring outside.

"I had the strangest dream last night; they've been getting more and more jumbled up," said David, as he made a twirling motion with his finger. "But this one was like; I couldn't remember where we were going and why. I was confused and starting to panic. It's fine, now, though. How'd you sleep?"

"Oh, just great," Rob lied.

It would not be a good idea to bring up what happened a few hours earlier. The situation may be getting too precarious and out of balance.

He tried calling Sunni to see if she was awake, no answer. After dressing and walking down the hall, he gently knocked on her door; shortly, it cracked open, and she looked out, leaving the chain lock on.

"Oh, it's you, come in," she said, removing the chain.

Rob noticed she looked haggard.

"Rough night?"

"The asshole ex-boyfriend called me in the middle of the night, is all," she said, running her hand through long, dark hair.

"Why?"

"Wants to get back together. I said we were done and to leave me alone, which really got him mad. Didn't get much sleep after that."

"Anything I can do?"

"Yeah, you can beat the shit out of him, for me… No, I'm sorry, it's just that, he's nuts, crazy. Gonna stay far away from him when I get back to school. Sorry I didn't get up sooner; we doing breakfast?"

"My dad hasn't cleaned up yet, figured we'd have the motel's continental breakfast. Will be faster than stopping someplace, so we can get on the road sooner."

"Fine with me; I'll take a quick shower and meet you in the lobby."

After finishing breakfast and loading their belongings in the trunk, they gassed up the old car. While Rob was filling the tank, Sunni asked David if he felt better and had slept well.

"Yeah, I guess," he said gruffly.

"Yeah, you're feeling better, or yeah, you slept well?" Sunni pressed, then thought perhaps she should not have even spoken to him at all.

After a moment, David replied, "Feeling better, I'm feeling better. I don't know what happened yesterday. It was as if I, I couldn't control my mind, was having weird thoughts, remembering strange things."

"Glad you're feeling better; I was worried about you, Mr. Haynes," said Sunni, leaning forward and gently touching his shoulder.

The touch surprised David.

"You can call me Da... Derek. Wait, you were worried, about me, Sunni?"

She suddenly realized this was the first time the man had spoken her name.

"Thanks, I guess," continued David. "Didn't sleep well, bad dream, what I remember of it."

"I hope everything goes well once you get where you're going; I just want to thank you again for taking me along," she said and sat back in the seat.

For a moment, David was going to respond by saying he wasn't the one who invited her, but didn't.

"You're welcome," he said stiffly.

After paying for the fill-up, Rob got in and closed the door.

"Did you put in premium, Rob? You know the old girl likes her premium gas," said David, matter-of-factly.

"Yes, yes I did, just like always," Rob replied, thinking, this again, is not necessarily something David, the fighter pilot, who has invaded his life, would know.

"You guys up for a road trip?" Carlos asked of his two companions."

"Road trip, where?" Rico asked.

Rico was the shorter of the two men sitting on a couch, drinking beer, smoking marijuana, and playing video games on a large flat-screen television. He is stocky, with a shaved head, a small goatee, and two swastika tattoos on either side of his neck.

"Michigan, someplace in Michigan," replied Carlos.

"What the hell is in Michigan?" RayBob, the taller man, asked.

Wiry yet muscular, his dark hair flows almost to his shoulders; he and Carlos have been friends for several years. They, along with Rico, who has been with them for a few months, share the same dark desires and secrets. All three are in their mid-twenties.

"I've got some unfinished business that needs to be taken care of, and I think you know what I mean," Carlos replied. "She's with another guy, maybe two, so you both are gonna have to come along."

"That Asian girl you were trying to make it with?" Rico asked.

"Thought you were just gonna dump her," RayBob added.

"Never could get her to put out, just a little, do-nothing, goody-two-shoes," Carlos replied. "We talked about me driving her home to her parent's place in Michigan. I wasn't up for that kinda shit but would've been a good opportunity during the trip to nail her. That's all I wanted anyway, but she made it clear I wasn't gonna get lucky on that drive or anywhere. I don't need that kind of dis-respect, so told her I wasn't interested. No sir, she wasn't gonna get a free ride all the way up there without me get'n any benefits."

"I don't get it; what's the point in chasing her up there now? Rico queried. "Why not just let her go?"

Carlos looked at the two men and began to explain,

"That bag, the one from, well, you know who I mean, a couple of weeks ago? The last girlie, from Archer? She had the yellow tote bag with the bird on it. Well, I gave it to Sunni, see, thought she'd like it, but...."

RayBob quickly and loudly interrupted.

"You what! Stupid bastard, you were supposed to take it out of the trunk and burn it along with the rest of her stuff!"

"Yeah, that's the problem, RayBob, now if you'd let me talk! We were watching TV the other night, and she saw the bag in a news story about the girl… they showed a picture, you know, a snapshot thing, of her, holding it. Sunni said it looked just like the one I gave her."

"That's just great," RayBob said disgustedly. "Now we gotta drive all the way up there and get it back, right, genius?"

"I blew it off, said I was sure they make a lot of 'em," Carlos angrily replied.

"Did she buy it?" Rico asked, with nervousness in his voice.

"I don't know, but we can't take any chances. Told her I'd changed my mind about us going to Michigan, but she blew me off. Then tried getting her in my car by offering a ride to the bus terminal, that didn't work either. Too bad, otherwise we wouldn't have to do this trip. So, we'll go up there, find her, take care of business, then get the hell back here, quick."

"Perfect, nothing to it, doesn't sound the least bit risky. What an idiot," RayBob said.

"Yeah, yeah. She got pissed off last time I called, said to leave her alone, or she'd sic the cops on me."

"And so we go to Michigan," replied RayBob, tossing his hands in the air.

"Because of a stupid bag, you were supposed to get rid of. All we need is for her to walk into a cop station around here, carrying that goddamn thing. So what's gonna happen, to her, after we get it back?"

Carlos looked RayBob directly in the eye and coldly said,

"You know *exactly* what's gonna happen."

"Yeah, you're gonna need a new tattoo," replied RayBob, shaking his head.

"Rob said they were taking back roads?" Karli asked her mom as she carried a suitcase to the white Toyota.

"He said your dad… this David person, was more comfortable traveling that way, for some reason. So we'll take interstates, should be able to get to wherever they're heading, about the same time, I guess that's one good thing," replied Shelley as she pulled a cell phone from her purse.

"You calling Evelyn?"

"Yes, she wants to know when we were leaving."

"Evelyn? This is Shelley Haynes, my daughter and I are just getting ready to take off. How is the doctor doing?"

"Good, glad to hear he's better. So, you should both be able to meet up with us in Michigan?"

"Okay, okay, that should work fine. I'll keep in touch with Rob to see how things are progressing and if there's any change."

"No, for now, it's better if I communicate with Rob directly, not the doctor, and I'm not surprised this David person never answered Derek's phone."

"All right, I'll get in touch when I know more."

"I'm happy the doctor is that confident. Okay, bye for now."

With everything packed in the car, and the house locked, Shelley said to Karli after they both were in the front seat, heading down the driveway,

"This sure is not how I expected to spend my summer."

"Who could ever imagine…." Karli replied. "What's the reason you gave for taking time off from work?"

"Family emergency," Shelley spoke, staring straight ahead.

Within a few minutes, they had turned onto the entrance ramp to Interstate 75 North. Windows were rolled up, and the air conditioning switched on. Soft rock music turned down low, played on the radio, the cruise control was set just over the speed limit. Both settled in for the long drive. Neither felt like talking.

⊶ ⊷

Nearing a supermarket on their way out of town, Sunni suggested it would be a good idea to refresh the cooler with more meal-like food they could eat while traveling, fewer snacks.

"Wouldn't have as many restaurant stops," she explained. "So we can get more miles behind us in a day."

"You in a rush?" David queried.

"Not at all, just thinking it would be more efficient and cheaper," she replied.

"I'm with her," said Rob, pointing his thumb in the back seat while turning into the supermarket parking lot.

A variety of ready-to-eat, road trip type food, and drinks items were bought, along with two fresh bags of ice for the cooler; they then made their way back to the blue Ford. As he approached the car, Rob noticed something different about the left rear fender.

"Dammit!" he said, pointing at the back of the car. "Someone must've bumped into it, in the motel parking lot last night or while it was parked here."

Bending over, he ran his hand across the deep and distinct dent.

"That really sucks. Whoever it was, had to have known they hit something," Sunni said. "People are jerks."

"Fixing it is no big deal once we get back home; it just pisses me off," Rob replied.

"That's too bad, at least it's still drivable, so we can keep going," said David, sounding tired.

"Dad, how about we have Sunni sit up front with me. You'll be more comfortable in the back seat, maybe lie down for a while, stretch out."

"Sounds like a good idea, Rob. Not feeling like myself today."

Oh boy, that doesn't sound good, Rob thought, *or does it?*

"You won't mind sitting in the front seat with this goofy kid, would you…Sunni?"

"Not at all," said the girl, smiling as she heard him voice her name again.

After exiting the parking lot, David asked,

"How long do you think it will take before we get to Grand Rapids?"

Rob studied the GPS display for a moment.

"Probably couple more nights lodging, then part of the next day. You know, we can try the interstate again; it would be much, much quicker, shave off a crapload of time. Just saying."

"Let me think on it," replied David.

"I feel so important now, sitting in the front seat; it's like, a promotion," said Sunni, with a grin.

"Just thought my dad needed a little back seat time, more comfortable. He's getting old, ya' know."

"I heard that," came a voice from the back seat. "I'm not that old, but this body sure as shit is."

"Yeah, whatever that means," Rob said as he looked in the rearview mirror at the man.

"Well, I'm not dead," David said, paused, then added, "Yet."

Rob decided to let that one go.

"So, Rob, you have a girlfriend back in Florida?" Sunni asked, turning her head towards him.

"No, not really, do you?" he replied, looking back at her with a straight face.

Sunni's face went blank, then her eyes became wide, and her

mouth opened in surprise; she began laughing and gave him a playful slap on the arm.

"You're too funny. No, just a creepy ex-boyfriend named Carlos, who I hope never to see again."

"Yeah, he sounds like a bad dude. The guy won't be trying to get back at you, will he?" Rob asked.

"Nah, don't think so, but he's gotta temper. He hangs with a couple of guys that are bad news, for sure. Only met one of them once, totally creepy, bad vibes. So glad I didn't agree to have him drive me home. Dammit, now that I think about it, he does have my parent's address; I can't see it being a problem, though."

"We could do a quick detour over towards Lansing, leave you off, and…" spoke Rob before David interrupted,

"No, we can't, sorry. Gotta get to Grand Rapids, we, or you, can drive this girl where she needs to go, after that."

"Sorry, Sunni, he's just kind of obsessed."

"It's fine; doesn't matter when I get home. My folks don't even know I'm headed that way."

"You sure?" Rob asked.

Sunni smiled and nodded.

"So, does he go to school in Gainesville, this nut-case ex?"

"No, he's a few years older than me, a spoiled rich kid, works for his daddy, who owns a couple of car dealerships. Carlos was a real charmer at first and a good-looking guy. He keeps in shape, something over six feet tall, with kind of short, blonde hair, probably dyed. He started getting pushy and weird, said we needed to, well, you know. I explicitly told him I wasn't ready to, *you know*, but the bastard never stopped pestering me."

"For guys like that, no means yes, or at least a maybe," said Rob.

"Not where I come from, wasn't raised that way," she said firmly. "He started to really tick me off, and kept pushing for me to get some tats, said he pay for 'em. At least half of his right arm is covered with skulls, real death-head kinda stuff. It seemed like every couple of weeks or so; he was adding a new one. Not about to get into that kind of thing, no telling what I'd end up with, or where. Even just being alone in the car with him, anymore, was getting too scary."

"Couldn't you have given him a dose or two of some Japanese Judo shit or something?" David said while making slashing motions with his hands. "Maybe borrow your daddy's samurai sword?"

"Hey, in the back seat!" Rob said loudly. "You're supposed to be resting, remember?"

"Whatever," said David, while crossing his arms and slumping against the back cushion.

"What is wrong with him?" Sunni said softly to Rob.

The boy shook his head.

"Long story, maybe I'll be able to tell you someday."

"I'm a psychology major, and that guy certainly seems to me to have some serious, deep-seated issues with anyone, or anything, Asian," she replied with a frown.

"Oh, you don't know the half of it, girl," said Rob, nodding.

"Heard that," spoke David.

"How far today?" Sunni asked of the boy.

"Without stopping for meals, just fuel and bathroom breaks, hopefully, we can get into Indiana by dark. It depends on how many of these damn little towns we have to slow down and crawl through, because someone insists on it, even though he also seems to be in a rush."

"Heard that, too," came the voice from the back seat.

"We're gonna cross over I-75 within an hour or so, Dad. Could hop right on and cruise easy, maybe, if the car lets us."

David thought for a moment, then replied,

"Nope, not yet; just keep going the way we are."

"Okay," sighed Rob. "You're the captain of this ship or plane, or whatever."

"Steady the course, copilot," said David, pointing his hand forward.

"You like airplanes, Derek?" Sunni asked.

David took a deep breath and said,

"I've had some recent experience."

For a better part of the day, there was a bright overcast, with the occasional burst of sunshine. The partial cloud cover aided in keeping the temperature palatable inside the Coupe. Windows rolled halfway down provided adequate cooling and comfort without being too windy for easy conversation between Sunni and Rob. David made the occasional comment but was, for the most part, silent.

Making their way through Tennessee was uneventful and passed quickly, considering the back roads being traveled. An opportunity to merge onto Interstate 75 came and went, without a word from David. Rolling hills along with wooded and green rural areas made it easy on the eyes. The air was fragrant with the scent of pine, and occasional wood smoke, as they motored into Kentucky.

With relatively little traffic, the old Ford Coupe was in its element. Briefly, the road paralleled a set of railroad tracks. David watched as the diesel locomotive of a freight train caught them, then slowly pulled ahead before rounding a gentle curve and disappearing into the distance. *I wonder if they still use steam locomotives in this century,* he thought.

The smell of oily steam, and coal smoke, seemed to be everywhere as he, Macy, and Jenny hurriedly made their way down the line of waiting locomotives in San Diego's Union Station. With his leave nearly over, their treasured few days together as a family was coming to an end. Soon, he would be heading back to the war. They had taken a taxi to the station and were rushing to find the assigned train platform for Macy and the baby's journey back to Grand Rapids.

"All aboard!" the conductor shouted.

David wrapped his arms around both of his girls, kissing them hurriedly before the conductor helped Macy step up into the Pullman car. Before long, a window opened.

"David, David, over here!" Macy called out.

He ran to the window, reached up, and grabbed her hand.

"I wish we had more time," she said fervently as the train shuddered and began to move.

"We'll have a lifetime when I come back. Take good care of our little girl, and yourself!" David replied, now walking quickly alongside the railroad car.

"And you be careful, don't be a hero," said Macy, her voice pleading. "Come back to us."

He was beginning to run; the station platform was coming to an end, only yards ahead. Their hands slipped apart as David came to a stop and sadly watched the train carrying his young family rumble off into the distance in a smokey haze.

No, he thought, *I don't suppose any steam engines are left in this whole confusing and modern world.*

Near midday, fresh sandwiches, drinks, and chips were distributed in the car as the trek continued through Kentucky. Sometime later, as they approached the outskirts of Frankfort, Henry, the GPS voice, instructed a left turn just ahead. Rob made the turn, and after a couple of miles, Sunni looked at the small screen for a moment, then remarked,

"Does this seem right to you? It looks like we should've gone further north then probably ended up on Route 421, but I can't see much of the map on the screen, to be sure."

"It should be alright; Henry has gotten us this far pretty accurately, but I suppose there could be a few glitches on a long trip like this," Rob replied. "There's a road atlas under the seat if you want to get a better look at the area."

Pulling out the tattered book, Sunni turned to the Kentucky map page.

"See here, Rob," she said, holding it up and pointing, "Jogging to the west takes us out of our way, as I see it. I think we should have gone straight."

"I hate to start second-guessing GPS now, but we can turn around and find Route 421 if you like, but we'll be backtracking," Rob said.

"It's probably no big deal," Sunni replied. "Just stay on here for a while, then turn right onto Route 55. That will get us back on what looks like the best course, to me, anyway."

"Roger that, navigator," Rob said with a smile and a salute.

"Better do it; no telling what might happen if we cross her..." came a voice from behind them.

Sunni briefly looked at Rob and scowled, folded her arms, then stared straight ahead.

Several miles down the road, Henry's voice told them to make a right turn, placing the travelers on Route 55 and heading north-ward once again.

"See," Rob began. "We were going to be turning here anyway. I think Henry knows exactly where to take us."

"Yeah, I suppose so; it just seemed like we were going out of our way, for some reason," Sunni replied.

It was getting towards evening as they drew nearer to the Indiana-Kentucky border. In less than an hour, they would be in the Hoosier State.

Navy Blue No. 2, had other plans.

⇒⇔⇐

"Listen," the Tall Marine said in a hushed voice as he pointed his finger skyward.

"Yeah, buddy, I done hears it," whispered Duke. "Love'n me the sound of them radial engines, in the morn'n."

"Corsairs," said the Tall Marine. "The sweethearts of Okinawa. It won't be long now. We best hustle and get in position, don't want to miss the big show."

The group of Marines picked up the pace at the urging of their Sergeant and quickly drew within a hundred yards of their jumping-off point. It wasn't long before they heard the sound of rockets being fired and explosions, above them, along with the near-constant chatter of .50 caliber machine guns, strafing the top of Horseshoe Ridge. Through the uproar, a Marine shouted,

"Breakfast is served, you sumbitches!"

Rounding a bend in the trail that funneled into a small clearing, a machine gun opened fire. But this was not from any aircraft, and it was close. The man walking five yards ahead of the Tall Marine suddenly spun around and pitched violently onto the muddy ground, his upper torso riddled with bullets. He never cried out, never made a sound.

The Tall Marine, and Duke, realized immediately what they had stumbled into. Less than a hundred yards directly ahead of their position and hidden in the hillside rubble, a Japanese machine-gun nest was intent on wreaking havoc among the Marines. They dashed for what little cover could be found on the hillside, both managing to reach shelter from the hailstorm of bullets behind a tall, shattered stump and a downed tree.

Both returned fire in the direction of the machine gun, as did the other Marines who were not hit, though the firing continued unabated from the Japanese-held position. Even with the cacophonous sounds of gunfire all around, the Tall Marine could hear the roaring and distinctive whistling of a fast-moving Corsair above. It was getting louder and closer. He quickly threw off his pack and began frantically searching through it.

"What y'all do'n?" Duke yelled above the din.

"Have to get that guy's attention; it's our only chance!" the Tall Marine shouted back. "Gotta get him to look down here and take out that gun, or we're dead!"

Pulling out the small mirror, he frantically began trying to signal the onrushing Corsair that was rapidly growing larger in the sky, but in the shadow of the tall stump and hillside, no direct sunlight was reaching the glass.

"He cain't see it! Not 'nuff reflection!" Duke shouted.

Both looked at each other for a moment, and then, the Tall Marine began to stand up.

"No, no, don't! Don't!" Duke screamed.

"God help me," said the Tall Marine as he spotted a large patch of bright, sunlit ground several yards ahead.

He ran out into the open, firing the carbine in his right hand while frantically waving the mirror with his left. He could not know if the sun was hitting the glass at an effective angle or if the pilot was even looking his way. In desperation, he would shoot, run a few steps, stop, and shoot again, all the while frantically trying to get the pilot's attention, as bullets kicked up mud all around him, with many tearing at his already tattered uniform.

"Hey, hey, he's done slow'd down!" Duke yelled at the man.

"I think he wiggled 'is wings. He's a'turn'n! He's a'turn'n! Thet beautiful blue sweetheart is a'coming back!"

The Tall Marine stopped and looked skyward, then at Duke, who was now frantically yelling and waving for him to retreat to the relative safety of the fallen tree. He watched in horror as his friend turned, took a few steps in his direction, then became engulfed in a hail of Japanese machinegun bullets. Through the massive amount of mud splatter, Duke saw the man's clothing ripple with multiple body strikes before he made a half-turn, stumble, fall, and lie motionless. Seconds later, the sound of a roaring engine and whistling wings made him look up to see the Corsair coming in low and fast, firing one long burst into the machine gun nest.

"Get 'em, kill 'em! Kill 'em all!" Duke screamed.

After the Corsair ceased firing, it pulled up sharply to hop over the ridge top. Marines leaped to their feet, cheering while waving their weapons in the air. It was apparent the machine gun emplacement had been destroyed. After all the noise and violence of the last few minutes, the sudden stillness as the howl of the blue fighter rapidly faded, seemed a strange and almost surreal sensation. Many quick, and sincere prayers, were answered, on that day.

Duke's exuberance quickly faded as he forlornly returned his gaze to the Tall Marine, lying on the ground, several yards away. Then he saw movement, just barely at first, soon the man's head lifted, and he began struggling to get up on his knees.

"Frankie! Frankie!" Duke yelled as he vaulted over the downed tree and ran towards his friend.

"Frankie, are ya' hit? Where are ya' hit?" Duke asked as he slid to a stop next to him.

"I, I don't know," Frankie breathlessly choked out through mud-covered lips.

"Everything went dark; then, then, there was a, bright flash. Thought I was dead... the Corsair, did he get the Japs?"

"Oh yeah, pounded the liv'n shit out of 'em, let 'em have it good, he did."

"Thank God, thank God. That pilot saved our asses, and I want to shake his hand someday when all this is over," said Frankie as he pointed towards the sky and managed a brief smile.

Duke quickly began checking him for injuries. Frankie's uniform had been ripped to shreds, but there was no blood. His shirt fell apart when he tried to remove it from his shaken friend. Miraculously, no wounds could be found on his body.

"I, I jest cain't unerstan' it, I done saw them Jap bullets hit'n y'all over, but ya' ain't hit nowhere's on yer sorry body," spoke Duke, shaking his head in disbelief.

Just then, the Corsair came roaring back over the ridge; Marines, once again, raised their weapons and yelled at the top of their lungs. Duke helped Frankie to his feet; he waved feebly as the plane flew overhead and, with a final dip of the wings, headed out to sea.

"We owe him our lives," Frankie said with great emotion.

"Lotta men here will be a'gree'n with ya'," said Duke, over the rapidly diminishing sound of the fighter plane.

Before long, the Marines heard rapid-fire booming in the distance.

"Flak," Frankie said, then yelled in the direction of the speeding plane, "Flak! Watch out for the...."

The sound of an explosion ripped through the air as the nose of the Corsair erupted in flames, then went silent; a trail of oily, black smoke formed behind the plane as it began to sink out of the sky. All the Marines stood motionless, staring at the stricken aircraft.

"No, no, no, don't let this happen!" Frankie screamed out.

Duke tried to hold up his shaking friend, but he collapsed to his knees on the ground.

"You bastards, you bastards! C'mon, this is not right! This is not right!" Frankie yelled while picking up a handful of mud and throwing it across the bullet-riddled landscape.

As the plane continued its descent, it began a slow turn to the left, the black smoke growing in intensity. Frankie tried to get to his feet.

"Get out! Get out of that plane!" He screamed as he collapsed back onto his knees. "Lord, save this man...." he was nearly weeping.

The spiral began to tighten as the speed of the plummeting Corsair increased; soon, it was over water and spun out of sight, behind a hill. No one saw a parachute. Duke and the others did not observe or hear the final moments, of the unknown Marine pilot, in his falling, burning fighter.

"It's my fault," said Frankie, after a long silence.

"What ya' mean, what's yer fault?" Duke asked.

"I signaled him with the mirror," Frankie replied. "He was heading back to his boat, but I turned him around. Now he's dead, sure as hell."

"Frankie," began Duke, "Don't be a'beat'n yerself up. Ya' did what ya' felt had ta be done. Took a damn bushel of balls, ta be a'jump'n out there in the open under fire like thet. Batshit crazy, man, cain't believe y'all still breathe'n."

Frankie pointed a shaking, muddy finger towards the water.

"That pilot, he had people. Family, friends, wife, kids maybe, never gonna see 'em again, and they never gonna see him. He's not going home, and it's on me."

"No, Frankie, no, it ain't yer fault. He wuz jest a'do'n what he had ta do, jest like you wuz," said Duke, struggling in vain to comfort his friend.

"Because he came back, those Japs had time to zero in on him, Duke. I got that man killed."

Shortly before sunset, as they were driving in light rain on Route 55 through the town of Eminence, Kentucky, the Ford flathead V-8 went silent. Throwing in the clutch, Rob tried to restart the motor with no success. As the car slowed, he saw a sign ahead, *Bentley*

Auto Repair. After turning into the driveway, they coasted to a stop in front of a large garage door. A *Closed* sign hung on the glass entrance door next to it, although lights were visible inside.

"What's the problem?" David, who had been dozing, asked sleepily.

"The motor quit running, but I assume you already figured that out, Dad."

"Yeah, I noticed, Rob."

"Can't fool you."

"This place open? Lights are on," said David.

"Says closed; I'll knock and see if anyone's around. We've got tools and some spare parts, but it's dark, raining, and I have no idea where to start looking for the problem."

Rob got out of the Coupe and knocked on the glass. A man appearing to be in his sixties soon walked over, unlocked, and opened the door.

"May I help you?"

"Sure hope so," replied Rob. "We have a problem with our car."

The man looked past him at the Coupe, wet and sitting silently in the driveway, softly illuminated by a streetlight.

"That's quite an oldie," said the man.

"1941 Ford, 221 flathead V-8, Super Deluxe Coupe," replied Rob. "I hate to ask, but is there any way you could check it out? The thing just quit running. Thinking, well, hoping, it'll be something fairly simple and obvious."

The man looked at the Coupe again.

"Interesting. Sure, I'm here working on my own projects and was about ready to head home, but no problem, I'll check it out for ya. What happened there?" The man asked, pointing at the dented fender.

"Got bumped last night at the motel or in a grocery store parking lot this morning. It looks like we'll have to revive our body and fender work skills, again," said Rob.

"Well, that is just a shame; glad it wasn't worse. I'll get the door; then we can push it in."

Rob thanked the man. As he walked back to the Coupe, the large garage door began to open behind him.

"Nice guy, he's gonna take a look at it," he said to David and Sunni.

Navy Blue No. 2 was pushed into the garage, and the man lifted the hood.

"You just don't see these much anymore, not with the original type engine, anyway. So many guys, just hotrod 'em. You know, put in big, modern motors and all, along with fancy wheels and tires. This looks to be very original."

"It is; we bought it as a project car; my dad and I did all the work ourselves," replied Rob.

"Looks great. I'm Mike, Mike Bentley," the man said, shaking hands with Rob.

"I'm Rob; this is my dad, Derek, and our friend Sunni. We're on our way to Michigan, coming from Florida."

"That's quite a trip for this old fella; what's in Michigan?" Mike Bentley asked.

"Oh, something yet to be determined," David spoke up.

"My dad would love to see this car, would you mind?" asked Mike.

"No, that's fine; we love showing it off," Rob replied.

"He's in the office. This building used to be a Ford dealership years ago; it opened around 1915 or so. He worked here as a mechanic for a long time until the dealership closed and the building came up for sale. We went in together, bought it, and opened this shop more than thirty years ago now. I'll go fetch him."

After he walked away, Rob said,

"This might be our lucky day; if his dad is an old Ford mechanic, he may be able to help Mike find the problem quick and easy."

Shortly, Mike and an elderly man with a cane slowly made their way into the garage area. Thin, frail, and slightly bent over, he took a few steps, raised his head, and stopped.

"Anything wrong, Dad?" Mike asked.

The old man stood and stared, then, almost hesitantly, began moving towards the car, stopping again, ten feet away from the vehicle.

"Oh my, my…brings back memories…" he said, in a low and tired voice. "Lottsa memories."

"Guys, this is my dad, Don, but everyone calls him Duke. Dad, this is Rob, Derek, and Sunni," said Mike, pointing them out in turn. Duke continued staring at the car until finally saying,

"This here is like see'n 'n ol' friend, again. It be perfect, rat down to them big, wide, whitewall tires. Takes me back, 'long time, fersher."

"Let's see if we can get this beauty back on the road," Mike said as he rolled a toolbox over to the car.

"I think the old gentleman likes your car," Sunni whispered to Rob.

"Sure seems to," he replied. "He has to be in his nineties; chances are he's worked on cars just like this, over the years. But this seems more personal."

As Mike began going over the engine with his test equipment, Duke slowly walked around the car, taking in every little detail and running his hands along the still wet fenders. It reminded David of what he did when first discovering the vehicle back in Fort Myers. After opening the driver's-side door, the old man peered in, looked around the interior, nodded his head, then smiled without saying a word.

"Your dad seems to be bonding with the Coupe," said David to Mike as he watched him work.

"Takes him back to his youth, I'd imagine."

"I know the feeling," said David.

After several minutes of scrutiny, Duke began to speak,

"Used ta have an automobile zackly like this one, rat here, years and years ago, after the war. Well, me 'n a friend, we'd done owned it t'gether. T'wuz the only way, either one of us could afford the thang. Same color, or pretty close. Looks ta be the same inside, or pretty close. Same motor, them big wide whitewalls, t'wuz a beautiful thang, jest like this'n here."

"The one your Marine buddy and you had when ya'll was dig'n coal? Isn't there a picture around somewhere, with you two and the car?" Mike asked.

"Yeah, somewheres. My buddy, he wuz a tall fella ya' know, me, not s'much. We'd be a'need'n ta move thet front seat forward n' back, every dang time we's done changed off a'drive'n," said Duke, with a chuckle.

"You were Marines?" David interrupted. "Where were you deployed?"

"The Pacific, of course," Duke replied.

"Where in the Pacific?" David pressed.

Duke looked at David, scowling, and replied,

"All over thet damnable ocean. Jest about every stink'n hellhole you'd ever, or never heard of. Probably would'a marched rat in'ta Tokyo, if'n I didn't git kilt first, 'cept they dropped them big bombs, an' ended the whole shebang."

"Yeah, I heard about that," David responded.

Duke cocked his head as he stared at David. Before he could get out another word, David continued to press,

"Okinawa, were you at Okinawa? Mud Marine?"

"We wuz there, ya' bet yer ass sonny, my buddy, he done got pretty messed up," said Duke, lowering his gaze.

"I know, tough time for all of us...." David began and then stopped.

"Yer kind'a n' odd sorta fella, ain't ya,' sonny," Duke responded.

"I mean, tough time for all you guys, all you Marines on the ground, and aviators too, I've heard."

"Sure wuz," Duke said with a far-off look, as if remembering something from long ago. Something painful.

"Yeah, well, anyhow," Duke continued while tapping his cane on the floor. "We got outta the service late in '45; I convinced 'im ta come back here ta live after he done left thet hospital he wuz in fer a spell. Said I'd hep 'im git a job, in the mines, ya' know. Don't reckon he wuz right keen on thet, but done took me up on it. Only worked t'gether, fer like two years or so, before he up'n left. Moved 'imself on back ta home.

"The work here done kept 'im occupied, 'n the pay weren't too awful. T'was a nasty, dirty job though. He'd be a' bitching 'n a' moan'n 'bout being in the mine, ya' see, so, I'd jest remind 'im there weren't no damn Japs a'taking potshots at us, no more."

He stopped and looked at Sunni.

"Sorry, miss, don't know if yer... well, didn't mean to o'fend. Jest the way we talked, back then. I done give up hate'n, a'long time ago."

"I'm third generation, American-born Japanese. It was wartime, it's history," replied Sunni, with an understanding nod, while thinking it would be nice to hear this from Rob's father on such matters.

Duke nodded back.

"Rented a small house, jest on the edge of town here, we did, my buddy an' me. He did'n have no vehicle of 'is own. Me, I had 'n ol' Model T jalopy from a'for the war. Worked well 'nuff, if'n it be pointed downhill, 'lest y'all had ta try'n stop the dang thang. So one day whilst we wuz in this here garage, wait'n to have sump'n fixed on thet ol' heap, we done saw this here purty automobile, sit'n out on the lot. Well, not this'n, but ya' know, one jest like it. Jest like it." Duke said while gently touching the Coupe.

"Wuz in real fine shape, it wuz, not much fer miles on the clock, as people did'n drive a bunch during the war, gas ration'n 'n all thet. Only be five years ol' at the time, it done been bought from this here dealership, bran spank'n new, in 1941. Guess ya' could say this here garage, be its spiritual home. It would show up an' git all refreshed an' healed up when it wuz a-hurt'n. The both of us, we jest done fell in love with thet thang. Made a deal rat on the spot with a sales fella, who was his sef a vet, ta be a'make'n payments on it. Told im' jest keep thet there old rat trap jalopy. But I do b'lieve they done give us twenty bucks trade-in fer it, though. I let 'em know they'd have to be a'provide'n their own hills.

"Every week we'd both be a'take'n some cash out'n our pay, 'n be a'pay'n the dealership here. I'd usually be the one ta bring it in, so on them days, I'd jest kinda hang 'round, watch'n the mechanics work'n, an' ask'n questions 'n such. Bout the time we done paid it off, the owner of the dealership went 'n offered me a job, turn'n wrenches. Say'n if'n I wuz gonna be here so dang much, might jest as well git paid fer it. Didn't pay no more than shovel'n coal all damn day, but cleaner, an' safer, fersher, so I jest came rat out an' tol 'im, well hell yeah! My buddy tolt me if'n we's weren't gonna be a'working together no more, he'd be a'move'n on, but wanted thet blue car.

"Cain't blame the fella. He done had some money put a'way, what he did'n drink up, an' paid me ma half. Tolt 'im I sure wuz gonna miss thet purty blue thang, 'n all the times we done had in it, the good times, anyways. Figure'd he fersher needed thet car more'n me. It done saved both our fool lives once, wuz a damn miracle, I tell ya! But thet's a story for 'nother time. With'n all the troubles in thet boy's life, he wuz gonna be a'need'n as much safe keep'n, thet could be a'conjured up.

"After he went an' moved back ta where'n he'd come from; a'for the war, we sorta lost tetch after a spell. He done got himself hitched a few times, I heard. Had a bunch a'problems with thet sorta thang. Don't know whatever 'come of 'im, prob'ly gone by now; I'd 'magine. Guess'n he had 'im some kids, 'least a son, fersher, anyways, I heard. Sure would like ta talk ta thet boy, someday, sure would. I'd tell 'im 'bout his daddy. Tell 'im, what a great guy he wuz, 'n a brave sumbitch, too.

"He should'a gotta a damn medal fer some of them thangs he done, out there in thet big dang ocean. Wuz'a shame, jest a dang shame, he never wuz a very happy fella, after we got back t'home, drank too much. Shit, we both did, I reckon. He was a'carry'n a lot of guilt, n' tried to drink it away."

"Guilt? Over what?" asked David.

Duke hesitated for a moment.

"There wuz this time, this, one time, when we wuz on Okinawa, 'n a bunch of us done got pinned down, this pi...."

"There it is, right there," interrupted Mike.

Everyone's attention turned to the front of the car, where he had been quietly searching for the source of the breakdown.

"Hotwire to the coil, burnt in half, right in the middle. That's kinda an odd spot for that to happen."

Duke shuffled over to take a look, then commented,

"Well, looky thet. Thet be the 'riginal type of coil what came on them cars when they wuz new. Think'n '41 wuz the last year they put 'em on. Thet's a Niehoff, ain't it, Mike? Sorta odd-shaped thang, reddish-brown color?"

"Right you are, Dad. Still remember this stuff, huh?"

"That's what came on it when we bought the car in Missouri," said Rob. "The motor ran fine, so we left it, trying to keep everything as original as possible. But we do have a modern one in the trunk, as a spare, should I get it?"

"Hang on," replied Mike. "I'll replace this wire and see if it'll start and run. Would be nice to keep it."

"Missoura? Ya, ya bought this here vehicle, in Missoura?" Duke asked.

"Yes sir, Missouri, at an auction in 2010. I can't recall the name of the town right off hand; I was only eleven at the time," Rob answered.

"My Marine buddy wuz from Missoura, mighty odd."

"What's odd?" asked Mike.

"The day my buddy wuz a'leave'n for Missoura, he done stopped in here when I wuz work'n, ta say, g'bye n'all. When he gots ready ta head out, motor'd spin over but it weren't a'start'n. Well, I checked it over fer 'im 'course, thought it might be the coil, the Niehoff coil. Took it off, I did, came back here 'n checked it, rat on thet there bench, as a matter a'fact," said Duke, pointing to a corner of the garage.

"Sure nuff, it weren't no good, so went 'n grabbed a new one from the parts bin. Told 'em in the office, I'd be a'paying fer it, kind of a going-away present. The boy didn't have much money after a'paying me my half, ya' know. On my ways back ta put it in the car, I grabs me a small, white paint pen, 'n writes, *From DB* on top of thet thang. He asked what the repair wuz a'gonna cost, so I shows 'im thet coil an' said it be all taken care of. He wuz mighty appreciative; 'n thanked me several times. I puts the coil on an' gots the thang a'going. We shook hands, 'n he drove off. I never saw the boy, again. Why you a-look'n at me like thet, Mike?"

"There's some writing, in white, on top of this coil, Dad."

"No, what ya' try'n to say?" Duke asked incredulously.

"It's faded and worn, hard to read, but the last two letters sure looked like DB, to me," replied Mike, with a grin.

"That's right," Rob spoke up. "Saw that when we were working on the car. I thought it was just a paint smudge at first and was going to clean it off with solvent, but it looked like writing of some sort, so decided to leave it. Somebody wrote that on there for a reason; it was part of the car's history; remember, Dad?"

Soon as Rob said this, he knew he should not have. David stared at Rob for a moment, then played along,

"That's right, Son. I said just leave it alone. Meant something to someone, right?"

"Right," said Rob, with relief.

"Ya' means ta tell me, right here 'n now, ya' thinks this might be the same 'zack car we done had, back then?" asked Duke, his eyes growing wider.

"Unless serial numbers could be found in some old records to match up with this vehicle, would be hard to say for certain. But what are the odds of finding what seems to be your writing on this old part, on this old car, exactly like the one you had?" Mike replied with a smile. "This might be the same one; I'm bet'n it is."

"Oh my, my, my, wish'n it was so. Hope'n it be so," said Duke as he, once again, tenderly ran his hand over the blue fender of the Ford Coupe, remembering a still unexplainable happening that occurred in a dense Kentucky forest, seventy-three long years past.

"How ya' do'n, ol' fella," he said, barely above a whisper, his eyes becoming moist.

"This is amazing!" said Sunni, with exuberance. "Last time you saw this car, it was heading back to Missouri. Rob and his dad found it there, your initials and everything; what a wonderful story. What an amazing coincidence! And to think, if we'd taken the route I thought was the best way, this town and garage would've been missed entirely. I guess Henry knew what he was doing all along."

That jog to the left, those extra turns, did take us out of our way. They brought us here, for a reason. This thought made Rob uncomfortable but not surprised.

"This, this here done had ta happen, fer a reason, right?" Duke asked of no one in particular as he brushed a tear from a furrowed cheek.

"Who's to say," replied Mike, putting a hand on his father's shoulder. "Just enjoy it, Dad. Believe. It's not a bad thing."

"I know, I know. Jest, thet it brings back such memories, such memories," said Duke as he shook his head.

"Let's get a picture of Duke and the car!" Sunni said excitedly.

"That would be great," replied Mike. "Let me change this wire first and get it fired up."

Within a few minutes, the wire had been replaced, the flathead V-8 started on the first try and ran perfectly. Mike's toolbox was rolled away, and Duke was positioned alongside the Coupe. Cell phone photos were taken as the old man, his hair nearly as white as the sidewalls on the tires, tried to smile. It was hard to hide his emotion. When finished, he gently patted the old car as a person would pat an old friend on the back, then, turning slowly, made his way towards the office, with Mike at his side.

"Well, time to go. Gotta go, gotta get moving," said David, as he clapped his hands together.

"Okay, you pull the car out on the driveway; I'll go take care of the bill," Rob replied.

Upon entering the office, he noticed Duke looking through the drawers of a small filing cabinet next to a desk.

"What do we owe you, Mike? We really appreciate you doing this for us."

"Was easy enough to find, even easier to fix. If it had been daylight, you'd have spotted the problem right away, likely. Glad you folks stopped by; it's been quite an interesting evening. The same car my dad and his buddy used to own…. It's simply unbelievable how it somehow found its way back here, after all these years."

Rob stared at Mike for a moment before saying,

"Yeah, a person has to wonder…."

"You don't owe me a thing," said Mike, smiling as he reached out.

"Seriously?" Rob replied as they slowly shook hands. "We certainly don't expect you to do this, for nothing."

"My pleasure, our pleasure," Mike said, holding up both hands. "Gonna have a great story to tell for years to come."

"Here t'is," a feeble voice said from behind Rob. "Knew it be 'round here, somewheres."

Rob turned to find Duke holding out a small, black-and-white photograph.

"This here be the one I wuz a'tell'n y'all 'bout, me'n Frankie, an' our car. Yer car now, t'wuz took some time in '46."

"Frankie?" Rob asked as he gently took the photograph from the old man's wrinkled hand.

"Frankie, my Marine buddy, I bin tell'n ya' 'bout. Guess'n I never did a'mention 'is name to y'all."

Rob viewed the image in stunned silence. It was the same photograph his father Derek had shown him, years ago, of his father and his fellow Marine friend, with their Ford Coupe back in the '40s. It was easy to tell the men apart. Duke still had the same smile; the other man was taller, with no smile at all.

"This can't be," said Rob softly.

"Sorry, did'n quite ketch thet," replied Duke, cupping a hand behind his ear.

"Frankie, your friend, here in the picture. What was his last name, his full name?"

He already knew the answer.

"Frank, we called 'im Frankie, Frankie Haynes."

Rob could only stare in disbelief at Duke, then back at the photo.

"We wuz best friends soon as we met up at Marine basic train'n, 'n all through the war. Ya' can see jest how tall he wuz in thet picture. He were a much more jovial fella back then, 'til we gots in ta combat, 'specially after Okinawa. Messed 'im up bad, guess I told ya' thet. Did'n gets a chance ta tell ya' the rest of the story, 'bout what happened on thet stink'n island."

Rob stood silently, transfixed.

"Ya' see, the group, Frankie 'n me, wuz in, done got pinned down by a machine gun nest. Some mighty good fellas had already bin hit before, well, this Corsair fighter had jest made a run on thet island, shoot'n up the place with rockets 'n .50 cal's, 'n wuz a-head'n back out to sea, to his boat, justa fly'n by, almost right over us. Frankie, he grabs his shave'n mirror, see, 'n like a damn fool, runs out in the open, a'shoot'n his carbine at the machine gun an' a'wave'n the mirror 'round, trying ta signal thet Corsair driver, ta git his attention, ya' know. We needed hep...." Duke lowered his head.

"He did, too, but them Japanese machine-gun bullets done kicked up mud all 'round, an' on 'im, 'n Frankie went down. I jest knew he wuz dead. So thet pilot, see, he done makes a sharp turn an' sure 'nuff done comes rat back 'round with guns a-blaze'n, rat in ta thet nest of machine gunners, then pulled up 'n flew over the top of the ridge we wuz at. Not 'nother round came from them Japanese boys.

"Most all of us wuz saved by thet guy an' his blue airplane; we sure wuz. An' ya' know, by some miracle, Frankie wuz alive, he wuz! Nary a scratch on 'im. After a bit, thet pilot came back over the ridge. Course we'z all jump'n up 'n down, holler'n, a'wave'n at 'im. Man, we loved thet guy thet day, first day of June, never gonna forget thet date."

Rob Haynes knew how this story ended. Duke took a deep breath before continuing.

"This guy, this guy, 'im an' his airplane, well he be a-head'n back out to sea... it weren't long... damn, I can still see it in my mind. Well, thet airplane got hit right smack in the nose by flak. His motor quit run'n right off, 'n he started a-smoke'n real bad, 'n then turn'n real tight, spin'n as he wuz a'go'n down. He never got outta thet die'n airplane. We did'n see no chute. Lost track of 'im, disappeared behind a hill, wuz right a'fore he hit the water, I reckon.

"Frankie, well he kinda went berserk, yell'n, cuss'n, blame'n 'is sef for thet pilot get'n kilt, an' all. I tried ta tell the boy what he did, run'n out there in the open, flash'n thet mirror, saved a lot of Marines, 'n he wuz lucky jest ta be alive. Poor soul, he never could come ta grips with 'im live'n, 'n thet pilot, die'n. Felt guilty 'bout thet all the rest of 'is days, I 'spect. We'd all seen people die; lotta people we know'd, an' wuz friendly with. But this here stranger, get'n kilt hep'n our sorry asses.... It, well, real serious like, messed up poor ol' Frankie, it did.

"We never found out noth'n about thet brave boy wuz, fly'n thet airplane. Those kinda thangs, well, jest get lost sometimes. Frankie had a powerful need ta know thet man. His folks n'all, needed ta find out what happened ta 'im, all the lives he done saved. T'was only fit'n, Frankie'd say. Oh, we got 'holt of the Navy 'n Marines, trying ta find out about 'im, never heard one dang word back. There was some talk 'bout Frankie get'n a medal for what he did, thet day at the ridge, almost get'n 'imself kilt n'all, signal'n thet pilot. Nothing ever came of it. In war, stuff gets pushed back, ya know, 'till it jest disappears altogether. People, they die; 'n people, well, they fergit. Frankie said he did'n want no goddamn medal, no how; thet dead pilot deserved it more than he did. He wuz jest the one who got 'im kilt. He'd talk 'bout that fly-boy a lot when we wuz together, mostly when a-drink'n. Won'erd where he come from, if'n he be married, had kids, ya' know, all thet. Nope, never did find out 'bout 'im. Damn shame."

Feeling lightheaded, Rob handed the photo back to Duke.

"You alright, Rob? You're look'n a little peaked," asked Mike.

"I'm fine. Just putting a face to the story makes me... Well, anyway, we need to head out. Would like to get a few more miles in before stopping for the night. Again, my dad, Sunni, and I want to thank you for all your hospitality and help. It was great to meet you both, and, everything."

"Was good to meet you too, Rob; stop in on your way back, if you can. I know a ton of people who'd like to meet y'all and see dad's old car; we'll make a day of it. Gotta agree with Sunni; what an amazing coincidence."

Feeling a touch on his shoulder, Rob turned.

"Jest got ta think'n, never did git yer last name," said Duke.

There is no way I can tell them our last name is Haynes, Rob thought. *It's all getting too complicated, too bizarre. Too much to try and explain, too much!* He blurted out the only name that came to mind.

"Hamilton, our last name is Hamilton."

Walking out to the running car through the increasing early evening drizzle, Rob had but one overwhelming conclusion. *Mike is wrong; there are no coincidences.*

He stopped several feet from the Coupe. A streetlight highlighted small rivulets of water moving continuously across the dark surface of the car, making it seem animated, alive. And something was different.

Leaning down, he ran his hand over the rear fender. The dent, discovered in the morning, was gone. Rob straightened and took a step backward. He turned to look at the old building for a moment, then focused again on the car, saying out loud,

"What are you? And how, and why, is this all happening?"

＝÷＝÷＝

"Did you pack that stuff away good, so it won't be found if we get stopped and searched?" Carlos asked as he loaded two pieces of luggage into the silver Mercedes' trunk.

"Don't worry about it," replied Rico.

"That shit better be hid right; we don't need no grief from cops," RayBob said as he walked out of the house.

"I said don't worry about it. We do this kind of thing for fun and profit, remember?" Rico returned.

"And you'd better do a damn good job," said Carlos. "If I get busted for weed, or anything else, one more time, my old man says the car is gone."

"He says that all the time... hasn't happened yet," Rico replied." What excuse did you give him for taking time off work?"

"Said I was driving a friend home from college, who lives out of state. Didn't mention a name or the state; I doubt he cares, and we don't want anyone knowing about this trip anyway," said Carlos as he slipped behind the wheel of the Mercedes C- Class sedan.

Rico climbed into the back seat while RayBob settled in the front.

"Here," Carlos said to RayBob, handing him a black, semi-auto handgun. "Put this in the glove box; it's damn uncomfortable sitting with this thing stuck in my belt."

"Think you're gonna have a use for that, cowboy?" Rico asked from the back seat.

"Some people might need extra persuading, but we got our blades, like always. Should be able to finish this nice and quiet, without any loud noises, no gunfire if we can help it. But if it hits the fan..." replied Carlos.

"Done it quiet, every time, except for the last one. But there was nobody around to hear," Rico coldly added.

"Got any idea where we're going, in Michigan?" asked RayBob.

"That stupid girlie gave me her parent's address when she thought we were heading up there together. I figured we just show up, then hang around and watch for her and the two guys she's with. It's not a very big town, around three thousand people, then grab her when we can and have some fun before we finish up."

"What's the name of this berg?" Rico asked.

"Got it here," Carlos said as he fished a piece of paper out of his shirt pocket. "It's east of Lansing, some hick town called Fowlerville."

⚊⟨ ⟩⚊

"Ya' know, he won't be celebrating Christmas this year, again," said Frankie, staring at the glass as he turned it in his hand.

"I know, I know," sighed Duke.

"Didn't last year, ain't gonna do it this year, ain't gonna, ever again. Been dead more than a year and a half now," Frankie continued as he tilted the glass and downed the remaining whiskey in three swallows.

It was two days before Christmas, 1946. Frankie Haynes and Duke Bentley had arrived at the Blue Goose, one of their regular Kentucky drinking hangouts, two hours previous. Payday at the mine earlier in the afternoon allowed the alcohol to flow copiously. Being a holiday made Frankie more morose than usual, which often spelled trouble for the two vets. Duke had the feeling this would likely end up being one of those times.

"What's a guy gotta do to get a drink around this joint!" Frankie yelled while slamming the empty glass down on the table.

"Easy boy, easy. We don't be want'n no trouble, this here be'n one of the few places in the whole damn county thet'll still allow our sorry asses in the door," Duke quietly said to his already inebriated friend.

"I don't care," said Frankie, swinging his open hand side to side in front of him. "Come on, dammit, I need a refill. What kinda chicken shit outfit is this, anyway?"

Shortly, the heavyset bartender walked over, put both hands on the table, and leaned in.

"Come on, guys, keep it down. We're all trying to have a good time here. It's almost Christmas; lighten up."

"Did you, you bring me another drink?" Frankie asked, pointing a finger at the man called Sarge.

"Yeah, I'll get another drink for ya', but keep it down here, Frankie, okay? I know you guys was combat vets; like a lot of us, y'all lucky just to be alive, more'n likely. Lotta people never made it back. One more drink, then maybe go home and, you know, spend some time with your people, your families," he said, with an easy smile.

Duke knew what was coming next. Frankie staggered, awkwardly, to his feet, knocking the chair over, then leaned closer to Sarge and stuck a finger in his chest.

"What... what the hell ya mean... by that?"

The burly man grabbed his hand while saying in a low voice,

"Look, I don't want no trouble. Just say'n, maybe y'all need to be with your families; it's that time of year."

"What ya know... what do ya know 'bout people n' their families?" Frankie slurred as he yanked his hand out of the man's grip. "I know, I know lotta guys who never, never got home to their families... ever again! Many of 'em, still over there, a-rot'n in some cold, forgotten, grave, somewhere. Some, some a'lying at the bottom of the ocean, in'a wrecked, goddamn airplane."

"I know, Frankie, I know the story," Sarge said, putting a hand gently on his shoulder.

Frankie abruptly knocked it away.

"You don't know noth'n, noth'n! Ya don't even know his name; nobody knows his goddamn name!" Frankie yelled, then violently shoved the man with both hands.

Sarge stumbled backward, nearly falling, then lunged at Frankie.

"That's it; you're both outta here!"

Duke got to his feet, intending to step between the two men. Sarge pushed him aside with one huge arm, knocking him to the floor; then grabbed Frankie and slammed him against the wall. Two men quickly stepped over to Duke, picked him up off the floor, and began carrying him towards the door, as Frankie vainly tried to fight the angry bartender, who outweighed him by a good seventy-five pounds. To the loud taunts of other bar patrons, both soon found themselves outside in the December chill of a Kentucky evening, sprawled on the ground.

Duke rose first, brushed himself off, and slowly began walking towards the five-year-old, blue car in the parking lot, pulling the keys from his coat pocket as he moved. Frankie struggled to his feet, all the while shouting obscenities at the small crowd of people now standing outside. He staggered to the car and grabbed the keys from Duke's hand.

"I'll drive this... sumbitch."

"Yer too damn drunk ta walk, ya' ignorant fool, much less drive," was Duke's angry retort.

"Just, just get in and shut up, and thanks a lot for not backing me up, ya' lil' weasel."

"I ain't no weasel, 'n the man's gone," shouted Duke at his frenzied friend. "It wuz war; people get kilt in wars. Ya' gotta let it go; it's eat'n y'all up inside, man!"

"I don't give a shit no more, Duke, I just don't give a shit. Get in, ya weasel."

"Yer gonna be a'get'n us both kilt one of these here days," replied Duke, as he stepped into the front passenger seat, then slammed the door shut. "An' I ain't no damn weasel!"

The crowd of people heard the flathead Ford V8 start. After a few seconds of gunning the motor, it shot out of the parking lot, tires spewing a torrent of flying gravel behind. As the car reached the blacktop country road, headlight beams were observed illuminating trees along either side of a densely wooded area lining the roadway as they sped away, swerving from lane to lane. It was evident to all the car was picking up speed as they watched the taillights disappear over a slight rise in the road.

"Them boys gonna get hurt or killed tonight if that stupid bastard drive'n don't get his shit wired together," said a woman standing in the group.

"Crazy man. Just plain ass crazy," another patron commented between sips of beer.

"Hope somebody's watching over them guys tonight," said another, solemnly.

⟞⟞ ⟝⟝

"That was quite something, this old car belonging to Duke and his friend, back in the '40s, small world, huh," said Sunni from the back seat, as they motored north out of Eminence, on a wet and shiny, two-lane highway.

"Yeah, beyond amazing," Rob said. "Almost magical."

"Wish we could have got a look at the old picture he was talking about," Sunni continued, "That would have been interesting, could have compared then, and now."

"I'd liked to have seen that myself," replied David.

"Wouldn't have made any difference, nothing or nobody you would've recognized, other than the car," Rob spoke.

"True, and it's just a car, not like it's a living thing," David said.

"Sometimes I wonder," replied Rob.

"What?" David asked.

"Nothing," was Rob's short answer.

"Whatever. How much did Mike charge us for the repair?"

"Not a thing, even though I insisted. It was a simple fix, and he and his dad were glad we happened...." Rob hesitated before continuing. "Happened, to stop in. It was quite an interesting experience for both of them. That's what he told me."

"Was nice of him," said Sunni.

"Sure was," David joined. "I would've liked to hear more about his Marine buddy, the tall guy. Wonder what the rest of the story was. Sounds like it had something to do with being pinned down, maybe by a machine gun...."

Suddenly, for an agonizing moment, David was back in *Macy's Magic III*, firing six .50 caliber guns into a Japanese machine gun emplacement. He felt the vibrations through the stick, heard the sound of gunfire melding into the howling roar of the Corsairs radial engine. Bullets were impacting all around the enemy, sparks and mud flying high in the air. Once again, he felt the anger, the hatred, the bloodlust.

Kill 'em, kill 'em all, he thought as his jaw clenched tight, reliving what happened only a few days previous. The Marines were waving their rifles in salute as he came back over the crest of the ridge; he dipped his wings, banked into a turn, and pointed the plane towards the sea before....

"Dad? Dad, you all right?" Rob asked as he gently placed a hand on his shoulder.

David's head snapped left; a shudder went through his body; Rob felt it.

"Dad, you okay?"

"Yeah, yeah. Just had a bad moment, you know what I mean," he replied, looking into Rob's eyes.

Rob nodded.

"Is everything all right, Derek?" Sunni asked, leaning forward from the back seat. "You seemed not to be here for a moment."

"Fine now. Could you get me a bottle of water from the cooler, please? I'm suddenly very thirsty."

She handed him a cold bottle; after taking several long swallows, he said,

"Thank you, and thanks for your concern."

This made Sunni smile.

It wasn't long before the trio crossed into Indiana. As the misty rain had stopped, the decision was made to drive somewhat longer into the night. An hour later, before finding a suitable motel near Interstate 65 at Columbus, Rob filled the gas tank in preparation for getting an early start the following morning. Their goal being to get through Indiana and into Michigan well before sunset.

After a quick and light meal, they headed to their rooms, with Rob saying he first wanted to check the car over as to oil, coolant, and such, before going to bed. He didn't tell them there was also a phone call to be made.

"Mom, we're in Columbus, Indiana. By this time tomorrow, we should be well into Michigan," said Rob, as he leaned against the Coupe, sitting in the parking lot.

After a moment, Shelley replied,

"Then what?"

"I think we're heading to where he used to live. Where are you two?"

"Some ways into Kentucky. Just got to sleep when you called."

"Sorry, had some car trouble, so we stayed on the road longer. Told him and Sunni I needed to check the car out before we left tomorrow morning so that I could call you."

"Sunni? Who or what is a Sunni, Rob?"

Shit, he thought.

"Umm, it's a girl. I mean, she's a girl. You see, she needed a ride to Michigan, from Gainesville, she goes to school there, you know, and well, we were headed that way and, well, she's very nice, and my age. You and Karli will like her, I'm sure. I think."

"With all that's going on, you pick up a damn hitchhiker. What am I going to do with you, Rob? What were you thinking?"

"It's all good, Mom. She's nice, and we all get along fine," he lied. "Just trying to help her out."

"I don't think that should be your main focus of attention right now, Son. Does she know the situation?"

"No, Mom, she doesn't. How could I even begin to explain that?"

"If you didn't pick up strangers along the highway, there'd be no need to worry about it, now would there."

"Right, right, yeah. It'll be fine; we'll be leaving her off near Lansing sometime, I guess."

"Sometime? You guess? We are going to have to have a long talk, boy."

"Not to change the subject," Rob began, desperate to change the subject. "But I feel it would be in my best interest to do so, are the doctor and this Evelyn person on their way to Michigan, now?"

"No, not yet. Evelyn said it would be best to find a convergence point, hopefully, the day before, and then they'll fly out. Would you have any idea, yet, where and when that might be?"

"On our list of things to see or do on this trip, such as car and airshows…."

"That you both lied about," interrupted Shelley.

"But it was a list of real things and places, Mom. There's a week-long airshow at Battle Creek running now, and it's on the way to where we're heading. I'll ask tomorrow if he wants to stop there. I'd think he might; I can let you know as soon as possible."

"If you believe that would work," replied Shelley.

"Let Evelyn know about all this so she and the doctor can make plans to head this way. It would be a good idea if you and Karli try and get a little closer behind us, in case this all comes down in a hurry. We're still traveling on primarily two-lane roads, so if you are doing interstates, it should work out okay."

"I don't understand his insistence on taking back roads, Rob."

"He says it's more comfortable, feels it's the right way to go. I have to tell you, Mom, there have been some interesting, unexplainable things happening on those back roads. It all seems tied to this trip. Almost like, it was, meant to be."

"How do you mean?"

"Would be better to tell you and Karli, in person, when we meet up."

"Okay, just be careful. You said there was car trouble. Is everything good now?

"Yeah, it was a simple thing. Working fine, running almost as if it knows where we're going."

"We can talk later, Rob, when this is… this is all over and done. And by the grace of God, it will be over, and everything will be sane and normal again. We all need to get some sleep now; keep us informed, you hear?"

"I hear. Love you, and tell Karli I love her; good night, Mom."

Rounding the corner of the hallway just off the parking lot on the way back to the room, he nearly ran into Sunni, leaning against the wall with her arms crossed and a perturbed expression on her face.

"You were right, Rob. Sunni doesn't know, and just what *should* she know? What's going on with you and your dad, and what have you gotten me into? I have a whack-job ex-boyfriend to worry about, but feel safe with you two. Well, I did anyway."

"So you heard," said the boy, as he leaned against the wall next to her.

"Heard enough. I'd come down to help you with the car, spend some time together, talk. I like you, like you a lot. Then heard you on the phone and didn't want to interrupt, but jeezuz, what's going on?"

Rob stared down at his feet for a moment.

"It's my dad; I can't give you all the details; hell, I don't even have all the details. But he's, he's having, I guess what you'd call, an identity crisis. When I told you he's not himself right now, I meant it. He's literally is not himself; thinks he's someone else. Truly believes it."

He was not prepared to tell her the entire story, not yet.

"That's just crazy; did he have an accident, a head injury? I've noticed what looks like a recent scratch or bump on his forehead," she asked.

"Yeah, he fell, hit his head on a sidewalk a few days ago, and now, somehow, he knows things, things that he shouldn't or can't know, but does."

"Shouldn't he be in a hospital, or resting, and not taking a long road trip?"

"Physically, he's fine and insists on going to Michigan, looking for people from his past, his family, he says. He couldn't do it alone, so I had to come with him. Some people will be meeting up with us in Michigan to see if this can all be straightened out and get him back to being my dad. I know; it's hard to believe."

"So your mom is heading this way, too?"

"Yes, she and my sister Karli are traveling behind us. The two other people you heard me talk about are the ones we'll be meeting. I don't know them, but they're key to all this. We have to find a place to join up."

"The air show you were talking about?"

"It's a possibility if I can make it happen."

"I feel so sorry for your dad, your whole family," Sunni said as she put her hand on Rob's shoulder. "I just didn't know what to think… that phone call scared me."

"Believe me; you're in no danger…."

Rob paused, thinking back to the gloomy morning they met, and he wasn't so sure.

"Don't ask me why, but for some reason, you're supposed to be here. On this trip, on these roads, with us."

Sunni looked up at Rob and asked,"Why?"

"I told you not to ask me that," replied Rob, smiling. "There's a reason why we're all together. It can't be just chance or coincidence. I felt very protective of you right after we met. You need to be with us."

He turned towards the girl and looked into her eyes.

"Fate, do you believe in it, Sunni?"

"I believe we make our own fate, Rob."

"I've been rolling it around, over and over in my head the last few days," he began. "Everything happens for a reason. Good, bad, or indifferent. Things happen, and we may never know why, at first, anyway. If something is fated to happen, it will—no changing it or second-guessing. Whatever turns a person takes, or decision they make, it was fated to happen. It's like a big damn cosmic script; that we can't figure out or change."

"Sounds deep, and kind of depressing," said Sunni, making a face.

"We can't change the past, can't predict the future," Rob replied. "We can only do the best we can in the present. It is what it is, I guess."

"The Rob Haynes theory of; *it is what it is,* got a nice ring to it," Sunni said, with a smile. "Let's print up a bunch of T-shirts; we'll make millions."

"I like that," Rob said as he put his arm around her waist and gently pulled her closer. She did not resist.

Sunni put her arms around Rob, looked up into his eyes, and quietly said, "Is *this* fate?"

"Has to be," he replied softly.

⟫⟪

THURSDAY

"That old bucket of bolts ready to go?" David asked Rob. "I'd like to be in Michigan before dark."

Sunrise was still nearly an hour away. They had risen early and were breakfasting on the motel's selection of fruits, pastries, coffee, and juice.

"It's fine, don't see any problems ahead, with the car, I mean," replied Rob, as he peeled the paper from a muffin.

"I didn't fall asleep right away last night; it seemed like you were out there a long time. Thought there might be a problem."

"Nope, it was all good. In fact, very good," repeated Rob, looking at a smiling Sunni across the table.

Biting into the muffin, he jerked slightly in his chair as he felt Sunni's foot rub against his leg.

"You okay, Rob?" Sunni asked as her smile grew.

"Never better," Rob replied and slowly nodded his head. "Never better."

David sipped his coffee while watching the two young people, recalling a June evening in 1942.

"Alright then, we need to finish up here; gotta get some miles behind us before the sun comes up. I mean, if you two are finished playing footsie and all."

Both Sunni and Rob's heads snapped towards David, who said as he rose from his chair,

"Wasn't born yesterday; I know how this works," and walked towards the door.

Sunni began giggling as she and Rob placed the leftovers from breakfast into a paper, carry-out bag.

"Busted," said Rob, with a grin.

While the flathead V-8 warmed up, they settled in, with David occupying the back seat, Sunni in the front, and Rob stationed behind the wheel. It was comfortably warm, with the forecast calling for clear skies through Indiana. Although still dark, it was a pleasant start to the day. With windows down, the traffic noise on Interstate 65 could easily be heard. Rob was fiddling with the GPS, plotting a course through Indiana via their usual, two-lane, and blacktop roads.

"Rob, forget the two lanes," David said from the back. "Let's get on that four-lane over there and make some time."

"You sure, Dad?"

"I'm sure. That portion of the trip is over now; we've got to finish the mission. You good with that, young lady?"

"Absolutely!" Sunni replied.

"Okay then," Rob said as he tapped *City Center, Grand Rapids, MI,* into the GPS, pulled the headlight knob on the dashboard, and guided the car out onto the highway leading to Interstate 65 North.

Though pleased to finally travel on the interstates, he knew his mom and Karli might not be able to catch up as quickly as hoped and needed. He would try to sneak in a text when he could, notifying them of the change.

Before long, they were driving down the ramp that poured onto the interstate and heading towards Indianapolis. He cautiously edged the car up to nearly sixty-five miles an hour, half expecting the mysterious problems from the first part of the journey to make themselves known, once again. But the old Ford continued to run strong and steer straight.

"How's it feel?" asked David.

"Great; seems it has decided to get with the program."

Rob looked in the rearview mirror to see David giving a thumbs-up.

Sunni and Rob picked at the leftover breakfast in darkness as the car glided along at a leisurely sixty. Hopefully, this would help allow his mother and sister to close up the distance. Flirtatious glances and quiet comments moved comfortably between the two young people as the rising sun began to brighten the car's interior.

David spoke from the back seat,

"You're from Lansing, right, young lady… Sunni? I think we should take you home before we head up to Grand Rapids. It's not that far out of our way; I'm sure you're anxious to see your folks."

Although he had become somewhat cordial to the young Japanese-American girl, he was still anxious to have her gone.

"Changed your mind, huh, Dad? I think she should stay with us for longer than that," said Rob.

"Yeah, I bet you do," David shot back.

"Well, I don't live in Lansing. It's some ways east of there, down I- 96, small town."

"I've spent some time in Michigan, might know it. What's it called?" David asked.

"Fowlerville," she answered. "Has a population of around 3000 and…."

"Fowlerville?" David loudly interrupted as he grabbed the front seat and abruptly pulled himself forward. "Fowlerville? You're kidding me!"

"I guess you've heard of it," she replied.

"Fowlerville," he repeated.

"How do you know Fowlerville?" Rob asked over his shoulder.

"That's Macy's hometown, Son."

"Oh…Macy, yes, Macy," said Rob, thinking quickly. "The girl you told me about that you used to know, right? You never mentioned where she's from."

"Right, Macy from Fowlerville. The girl I used to know, from long ago and far away," said David as he slowly sat back into the seat.

"She must have been very special to you," Sunni said, glancing over at Rob, who nodded.

"Yes, still is," David replied.

Sunni could see David was distressed over the memory of this woman named Macy. She decided to change the subject.

"That's the name of a song from the '40s, right? "Long ago and far away," I remember hearing a woman sing it. My dad likes music from that era, so I'm kinda familiar with a lot of the tunes."

"Jo Stafford sang it; that was my favorite version. Others did it too," replied David quietly. "I remember when it came out in 1944."

"You remember, from 1944?" Sunni questioned, looking at Rob again. "But you can't be that old, how could you remem…"

Rob reached over, gently touching her on the shoulder, and shook his head. She recalled the previous night's conversation.

"Anyway, it's a beautiful song. The '40s had a lot of great music," she said while giving Rob an understanding glance and nod.

Fowlerville, Rob thought, *Sunni is from Fowlerville, now I find out so was Macy, David's wife. No coincidences.*

Few things on this trip surprised him anymore.

"It's a text from Rob," Shelley said as she handed Karli her phone. "What's he say?"

"They're traveling on the interstates now, no more two-lane roads," her daughter answered."

"Oh great, where are they now?"

"Heading to Indianapolis on I-65, but not going very fast. You want me to text him back?"

"Just reply, *okay*. Anything else?"

"Only; speed up, tell others."

"There's a rest area just ahead," said Shelley. "We can make a quick stop, and I'll call Evelyn."

Duke began to stir when he heard the sound of tapping. While blinking his eyes open from a dead sleep and looking out over the hood of the Ford, he saw long soft shadows cast from tall trees. There was another tapping, and a voice,

"Hey, hey y'all okay in there?"

Turning to his left, he saw a Kentucky Highway Patrolman bent over and tapping his nightstick on the car's driver's side window. Frankie was sitting very still, chin on his chest. Reaching over, Duke grabbed his coat and shook him.

"What… what, I'm here, ready to go, sir, let's get 'em," he said, raising his head and looking around, finally focusing on Duke.

"What's going on, man, where, where are we?"

"Don't rightly know where we be, but we's got us a visitor," Duke replied with a hoarse voice while pointing at the side window.

Frankie turned his head and came face-to-face with the Patrolman, just as the man tapped the window again.

"Y'all wanna roll down this window, so I don't have to shout no more?" The officer requested.

Frankie lowered the window.

"Howdy, officer, what's up?"

"Just check'n to see if you boys ain't dead or something. We got a couple of calls before the sun come up from people driving by on the road. Said there was a vehicle gone off and sit'n in the woods. They could see taillights glow'n."

"Powerful nice, folks be'n so concerned, 'n all," said Duke politely. "What time do it be, officer?"

"Bout six thirty or so. Why don't you two fellas step out here so's I can get a good look at ya'," the officer said as he opened the driver-side door.

After both had exited the vehicle, Duke walked around and stood next to Frankie, sleepily leaning, on the front fender.

"Considering the circumstances, I suppose you boys, been drink'n, can I assume that?" the officer began.

The two friends looked at each other for a moment before Duke replied,

"Ain't gonna lie to ya', yes sir we have, well, we did. But thet wuz some time ago, last night. Not rightly sure how we got in these here woods."

"Where was you boys at, an' where was you head'n?"

"We stopped and tossed back a few at the Blue Goose, just a few miles out of town, was head'n home to sleep it off, sorta had a rough night," replied Frankie.

"The Blue Goose, ya' say? What town was y'all heading back to?"

"Why, Eminence, of course, we cain't be too fer away from there. Musta pulled over and dozed off, a'for we gots ta town," replied Duke to the man.

"Eminence is forty miles from here, son; you're in a different county now. You boys musta turned the wrong way."

"What the hell, Frankie," said Duke loudly. "You done went the wrong damn way! Knew'd I should'a drove."

"Coulda swore I was going in the right direction, Duke," Frankie replied.

"Well, the way y'all went tear ass'n outta thet parking lot, we be lucky not end'n up in them trees 'cross the road, rat then and there," Duke angrily shot back. "We wuz a'wobble'n all over the damn place."

"I can see ya take'n the wrong turn, but what I can't see is how y'all ended up sit'n in these woods like this," spoke the officer.

"Truthfully, sir, I don't remember. Suppose'n I just pulled off and drove a ways into these woods, parked it and fell asleep. Is this some kind of log'n road we're on, or someth'n?" asked Frankie.

"This ain't no kind of road t'all, an' you're at least fifty damn yards from the highway, parked in the middle of a thick patch of big trees. How, in the hell, did you two get here without bang'n up your vehicle, or even touch'n any trees? And how in the hell, are y'all gonna move this car, with trees right directly in front and back of ya'?" asked the officer as he moved to the rear of the Ford.

"I don't have no recollection of git'n here, must'a dropped off right quick, like whilst we wuz on the road," offered Duke. "One thing I does 'member, fersher, is this tall dumb ass here a'call'n me a lil'weasel before we done got in this here automobile. Called me thet twice, he did. Anyways, guess'n we can just foller our tracks out the same way we done came in till we get's ta the road."

"I didn't call you no weasel," said Frankie curtly.

"Sure as shit did, boy, two damn times. Done called me a lil' weasel for not hep'n ya out with thet big bartender. Well, I wuz gonna try, but....."

"Guys," interrupted the officer.

"I did not call you a weasel, little or otherwise."

"Did too, I wuz there, 'n heard it with my own two jug ears."

"Guys," the officer repeated, putting his hands on his hips.

"Ya must'a been dream'n, Duke."

"It weren't no dream, ya' called me a lil' weasel, hurt my feeling's, ya' did, an'...."

"Hey!" yelled the cop. "If'n you two idiots are done with your lover's quarrel, I'd like ya'll to come back here and see something."

They both walked to the back of the Coupe where the highway patrolman was standing. After glancing around, Duke asked,

"What we look'n fer?"

"Tracks, tire tracks through the grass and weeds, leading up to your vehicle," the Patrolman said, holding both hands out in front of him.

Frankie and Duke looked around behind the car, in silence, for a few moments.

"Well, officer, I don't see a danged thang," Duke finally spoke.

"Exactly!" said the Patrolman, with annoyance as he held up a clenched fist. "I cain't see no bent over grass or weeds, no broken twigs or branches on the ground behind the car, or anywhere else. No tracks in the dirt, noth'n. And yet, there are big trees not more than 2 feet from the bumpers on either end of your vehicle and not a scratch in the paint. It seems this blue car just up and magically goddamn appeared here, out of proverbial nowhere. Y'all got any kind of explanation for that kind of shit?"

"No sir," the two men replied in unison.

"We surely don't," added Duke.

"Well, if this ain't one for the books, and maybe for some kind of citation, 'cept I don't know what I could write ya' a ticket for. Ya ain't drunk, now, and I didn't see ya' driving when ya' was. Y'all went off the road into the woods and didn't hurt a damn thing, including the woods! It's like something or someone, just miracled this car and yer two dumb asses here, and I ain't about to write up no report, or ticket, with the word miracle in it. They'd laugh me outta the cop shop."

Now, here's what's gonna happen, and pay attention. I'm

walk'n back to my cruiser, parked over there on the highway, which I couldn't drive back here 'cause there is no damn way *to* drive, here," the Patrolman said, gruffly, while pointing both hands at the ground. "Then I'm gonna go get me some breakfast, and when I come back here in an hour, I expect y'all and this, this, miracle machine, to be gone. Y'all hear what I'm say'n to ya'?"

"Yes sir," again, was the unison response.

They watched as the man walked off through the woods muttering to himself, turned and looked at each other, then at the Ford, sitting sedately and unmolested in the middle of thick, Kentucky woods.

"How did we get here without get'n killed?" Frankie spoke. "We've both been to funerals for people who done something similar and didn't live to tell the tale."

"Don't I know it," replied Duke. "I got noth'n, other than we sure is lucky, or somebody be a'look'n out for a couple of losers like us."

"Guess we weren't meant to die last night," said Frankie soberly.

"Cain't argue thet, buddy, cain't argue thet. Jest like when I done saw ya git'n hit by them Jap bullets, an' ya pitched over in the mud. I jest knew ya'all was dead, but ya warn't, somehow, ya jest warn't," said Duke. "But I be a'tell'n ya one damn thang fersher, my tall an' lanky friend. If'n ya' ever, ever try an' drive thet drunked up again; I'm a'gonna smack ya'll up 'longside yer stupid head with a tire iron. I'm as serious as a preacher in a whore house."

"Wouldn't blame ya' one damn bit, if ya' did," agreed Frankie, then added, "I doubt we'll ever get this lucky, or charmed, again,"

Duke gently ran his hand over the fender of the 1941 Ford Super Deluxe Coupe, saying quietly,

"I don't know how ya' did it or why, but I surely am appreciative, ol' fella."

After starting the engine, Frankie began the long, arduous task of turning the steering wheel entirely from one side to the other while moving the vehicle forward and back, inches at a time, until finally freeing the car from its original resting place between the tall trees. With Duke walking alongside the slowly maneuvering automobile, guiding their progress, they awkwardly worked their way through the dense stand of trees, reaching the highway a few minutes short of an hour later.

"You drive this sumbitch," Frankie said, breathlessly, to Duke. "I can't lift my arms no more or push in that damn clutch pedal."

Within an hour, they entered the town of Eminence, Kentucky, grateful to be alive, yet unable to understand, or reconcile, the mysterious turn of events from the previous night and this morning. There was no comprehending how the blue car, inexplicably, kept them from harm. And why.

⇒+ +⇐

"C'mon man, pull in here; I need a break," said RayBob, from the back seat.

"Yeah, I gotta take a leak and stretch. This shit is get'n old," Rico joined.

"Yer just a couple of pussies," scowled Carlos as he slowed for the rest area exit. "Make it quick."

The parking lot was near empty, stopping one space away from a white car; they all exited the silver Mercedes.

"I'll stay here till you two get back," Carlos said as he lit up a cigarette. "Don't need anybody snooping around."

He watched his two companions enter the men's restroom just as a woman and teenage girl left the concession area, walking quickly towards him. As they passed by, headed towards the white Toyota, he spoke,

"Hey, ladies, how you doing today?"

This remark, from the tattooed, blonde-haired stranger, both startled and irritated Shelley. She stared at him for a moment, feeling extremely uneasy.

"Fine, just fine," was the reply, as she fumbled nervously for the car keys in her purse.

Turning and looking at the front of the Toyota, she said,

"Stay right there, Karli."

The purse slipped from her hands and fell to the pavement, most of its contents spilling. She quickly knelt down to retrieve the scattered items.

"Let me help you with that," said Carlos as he moved closer to Shelley.

Kneeling in front of her, he reached out a heavily tattooed arm.

"Mom?" Karli said as she began walking towards the two of them.

"Stay there!" Shelley shouted, looking at the girl.

When she turned back, Carlos held the car keys between two fingers, his face a few inches from hers. She could smell cigarettes on his breath; his eyes were dark and menacing.

"Well, that must be Karli," said Carlos, in a voice that sent chills through the woman's body. "So, what's your name? Both are mighty pretty; you two could be sisters."

Standing up, slowly, she began to tremble; Shelley took one step backward and said, in the firmest voice she could manage,

"Give me those keys."

"Say please," Carlos said mockingly as he stood and stepped nearer.

"Give me my keys, please," taking another step backward, she bumped into the car; no further retreat would be possible.

"Say, pretty please," Carlos replied as he held out the keys in front of him, swinging them back and forth on a finger.

"Give me those goddamn keys, you son-of-a-bitch!"

"Whoa, feisty. I like feisty; it gets me excited," he replied, with a leer, and moved closer.

"Who's your sexy friends?" RayBob asked as he and Rico walked up.

"This tasty young morsel here is Karli," said Carlos, pointing at the girl. "Don't know this one's name, yet, but if she wants her car keys back, she needs to be more friendly, real friendly. Both these girlies do."

He looked towards a secluded wooded area behind the rest stop building. An ugly smirk crossed his face.

"Yeah, I think these girlies need to earn their keys back; what ya' think, guys?"

"And maybe learn not to be so rude to their fellow travelers," added RayBob, coldly.

"I'd like to get real friendly with this young one here," Rico said as he stepped towards Karli, then reached for her.

Karli, nearly in tears, quickly stepped back from his approach.

"Get away from her, you bastard!" Shelley shouted. "Or I'll...."

"You'll what? I'll tell you what you're gonna do from now on," Carlos said threateningly. "Me and my two friends would like...."

"Is there a problem here, folks?"

All eyes turned towards the Kentucky Highway Patrol car that had quietly slipped up behind their vehicles and stopped. The officer behind the wheel repeated slowly, "Is there a problem?"

Karli, still fighting back tears, began to speak; Shelley cut her off.

"No, officer. My purse spilled, and I accidentally kicked the keys under our car. These, these, gentlemen, helped us to retrieve them. I was just saying thanks."

"Thought I heard yelling," the officer responded.

"No, nobody yelling here, right guys?" Carlos said, looking at his friends, who both, nervously, shook their heads, no.

"You people are a long ways from Florida, aren't ya'? Give her the keys, now," the officer said sternly.

Carlos took a step back and extended the keys to Shelley, who immediately grabbed them from his hand. She quickly gathered up the remainder of the spilled items and motioned Karli to get in the car as she unlocked the doors.

"Y'all have a nice day, ma'am," the officer said as he slowly backed up to allow Shelley to pull the car out onto the rest stop roadway, all the while keeping his eye on the three men.

As they drove towards the entrance ramp to Interstate 75, Karli began to cry.

"That man, who tried to grab me, there were swastikas tattooed on his neck; he just looked evil… Mom, I was so scared! What would have happened if that cop wasn't there!"

"I know, honey, I know. It's okay now, everything's fine, but we can't tell the boys about this. Not till everything's over," Shelley said as she watched, through misty eyes, the patrol car and silver Mercedes grow smaller in the rearview mirror.

⚒ ⚒

By late morning, the old car and its three passengers had made their way around Indianapolis and merged onto Interstate 69 North. Following a stop in Gas City to refuel and treat themselves with a quick meal at a local McDonald's, per Davids's annoyingly constant urging, they were again droning along at the usual, sedate, sixty miles an hour, heading towards Fort Wayne. Even with the slow pace, they expected to cross into Michigan by mid-to-late afternoon.

"Can't this crate go any faster?" David asked Rob.

"I suppose, but we agreed to take it easy and not beat up on the car, remember?"

It had been driven at interstate speeds on various excursions with no ill effects to the now seventy-eight-year-old vehicle. That the others would not be able to catch up was Rob's concern.

"Should be well into Michigan before dark, Derek," Sunni added. "There's plenty of time."

"Not so sure about that," replied David from the back seat.

She had no reply. Derek was a troubled man, and she felt for him, even if he could be, more often than not, overbearing and rude. Overhearing Rob's conversation with his mother was disturbing, but Rob's bizarre explanation piqued her interest. She was glad to ride along with them to Grand Rapids and observe what might unfold.

This was a significant destination, for whatever reason. Perhaps there would be answers to questions not yet asked. Turning towards Rob, found him looking at her. He was a nice boy, and she liked him a great deal, such a contrast to the frightening person she had, unfortunately, been involved with. Sunni shuddered at the thought of his last words. *'I'll hurt ya; I swear you try and leave me, and it will be the biggest mistake of your short, little life. You hear me!'* They echoed in her mind and made her shiver.

It had been an early start to the day, and David was tired. He regretted not being able to help Rob with the driving duties but was concerned it would be too much of a sensory overload, given his state of mind, during the latter part of this journey. He could not help feeling that time was short and slipping away, which greatly obstructed his thinking and perception.

It was warm yet comfortable, even with the windows rolled partway down. Having filled up on yet another McDonald's burger, he felt drowsy. Half reclined in the corner of the back seat, David hoped for much-needed rest and perhaps a clearer mind. Before long, they would arrive in he and Macy's home state.

Drowsiness became overwhelming; the road and wind noise lulled him further, then seemed to drift away. Strange thoughts and unfamiliar remembrances began to form, delivering discomforting images.

"And what are you going to do when you get there?" It was a woman's voice.

"What are you going to do when you get there? The voice repeated.

There was darkness in what appeared to be a long hallway, or tunnel, with only a glimmer of light, in the far distance.

"What are you going to do, David?" Are you going to finish?"

"What… finish what?" David asked of the voice.

"What do you intend to do when you find the end of your road?"

The voice was closer now and more familiar.

"Her, them, both of them. They're my family. I have to find out what happened, where they are. Promised I would come home," he replied to the phantom voice.

"I know David, but that was a long time ago, and Derek has a family too. You have taken him from us."

The light in the distance became brighter; the figure grew closer, yet hard to discern. But he knew it was Shelley.

More memories invaded his confused and conflicted mind, all at once. They were sitting together in a darkened movie theater; in 1994, watching a movie entitled *Forrest Gump*.

Upon graduating from the University of Florida, in 1989, Derek never returned to live in Missouri, instead accepting a teaching position in a Fort Myers school district. He had dated a few girls in the nearly five years he'd been teaching, with nothing serious developing. In his mind, there was no hurry entering into marriage. Perhaps a cautious remnant of his father's failed marriages.

Shelley worked in a camera store he frequented, after taking up photography, as a hobby. Many long conversations ensued whenever he came in to have film processed, primarily involving the images he created. He would show her his photos and explain them all in detail. A close friendship soon developed.

She was genuinely interested in his growing photographic skills and always commented on his efforts. Before long, Derek worked up the courage to ask her out on a date. Shelley gladly accepted the invitation. She wore her blond hair longer then and had recently moved into her own apartment. A relatively shy girl, she felt relaxed and comfortable around Derek.

"So, what are your plans for the future?" she asked of Derek, across the table in a restaurant, while waiting for their meals. It was their second date.

Derek, surprised by the question, answered,

"I, I don't know, not sure. Why do you ask?"

"Oh, no reason. Ever plan on settling down?"

"Settle down? Not much to settle down from. My life hasn't been exactly what you'd call exciting since I moved to Florida." Derek chuckled, then quickly added. "Until I met you, of course."

"Good catch," she replied with a smile.

Later that evening, in the theater, they held hands. A connection was being formed between two people who both thought, *this might be the one.*

Slowly, the theater became engulfed in thick, heavy darkness, only the light and images from the screen being visible. No longer could Shelley's hand be felt in his. The character Forrest Gump was sitting on a park bench, talking to a stranger. His words now difficult to hear, or understand, until,

"*My momma always said,*" he turned his head and stared out of the screen into the blackness of the theatre. "*What do you intend to do when you find the end of your road, David?*"

He awoke from his semi-sleep with such a jolt it nearly knocked him onto the floor of the car.

"Dad, what's wrong?"

David was confused, momentarily caught up in the twilight memory of the thoughts and images.

"Had a strange dream, or something, about your mom and me, before we were married, a date."

"You mean *my* mom, Shelley, right? My mom Shelley, right, Dad?"

There was silence from the back seat.

"No, no, wait, that's not right, can't be. Who is Forrest Gump, Rob?"

"Dammit! Rob said as he pounded his hand on the steering wheel.

"What's wrong?" asked Sunni.

"Almost, almost."

"Almost what, Rob?" David asked.

Rob looked over at the girl and shook his head,

"Almost to Fort Wayne, Dad. Almost to Fort Wayne."

Within two hours, Rob pointed out the window.

"Here we are, and there's the sign, Welcome to Pure Michigan."

"Good to be back home," said Sunni.

"I've never been to Michigan," Rob replied.

"Just been a few years for me, only since nineteen for… well, it's been a while, I guess," David said, from the back seat.

Sunni looked at Rob. He shrugged his shoulders and quietly told her it was okay.

"How far is Grand Rapids from here?" asked David.

"I'll have to check it on the GPS. You know, that airshow we looked at on the computer is just up ahead. We could spend the night at Battle Creek and then go to the airport in the morning, maybe. I'm sure they'll have some World War II planes, you know what I mean?"

He was trying to formulate a plan, whereas the doctor could meet up with and confront David. But he needed to find a place, a perfect location. If he could convince this disjointed fighter pilot to spend the coming night at Battle Creek, there may be an opportunity to bring this to a conclusion tomorrow. And he desperately needed to contact his mom to find where they were and how soon she and the others could arrive, if David agreed to his proposal.

"No, we need to go on to Grand Rapids, running out of...." David replied, "We just need to get there."

Rob sighed and said, okay. Another opportunity would need to be found or created.

It was getting dark as they neared Battle Creek. Driving past the airport where the airshow was being held, aircraft of various shapes and sizes could be seen in the fading light, parked on the tarmac and grassy areas. David sat quietly, staring out the window.

"You say they have World War II aircraft at this show, fighters?"

"That's what I read," replied Rob.

"Suppose, suppose they have a Corsair?"

"They might, Dad, they just might."

"Maybe stop when we come back through. If we come back through…" spoke David softly.

Suddenly, Rob had the makings of a plan.

It was past 9 p.m. when the three weary travelers stopped at a motel, not far off Route 131, near Kalamazoo. After a quick, light meal, everyone turned in for the evening; it had been a long day. Tomorrow they will reach Grand Rapids.

⇥ ⇤

Fort Wayne was gray and damp when the three men left the motel room and got into the Mercedes. The sun had not yet risen.

"How come we had to get up so damn early? And I'm hungry," said RayBob as he settled in behind the steering wheel.

"Don't sweat it; we'll stop at a drive-through on the way out of town, eat in the car," Carlos snapped back.

"Yeah, I'm hungry too," chimed in Rico from the back. "What's the rush? Michigan isn't going anywhere."

"We gotta keep moving, no telling how far those three are ahead of us," Carlos replied, clicking the seatbelt together. "Just stop at the first fast food place that's open, and we'll get something to go."

"Why don't we just forget all this and go home. We're lucky that state cop in Kentucky told us to just be on our way and didn't search the car. I don't think…." Rico said before he was cut short by an angry Carlos, who turned in the seat and pointed at him, menacingly.

"I don't give a shit what you think. We need to get that bag back and make sure little miss Sunni never talks to the cops or does anything else that'll put us on death r… well, you know what could happen. And that goes for anyone who gets in our way. So shut your trap."

"Yeah, yeah, whatever," replied Rico. "But you're starting to scare the shit out of me, ya psycho bastard."

"Don't you ever call me that again!" Carlos shouted. "It's the last thing that girlie said to me, and she's gonna regret it. Come on, let's go." He then turned forward and angrily slapped his hand on the dashboard.

⚒ ⚒

"Battle Creek, that's right. Try to find a place to stay in, or as near to town as possible, then wait for us," Rob told his mom on the phone.

He had gotten up early and drove to a gas station across the street from the motel to top off the tank and make a much-needed call to Shelley.

"Sorry I couldn't call earlier, Mom. No chance to last night, got to Kalamazoo late, I was never alone. Had a quick meal and went right to bed; we were all pretty tired."

"Why Battle Creek?" she questioned. "Shouldn't we just keep trying to catch up?"

"I don't think that will work now. We still have someplace to go, a lot of driving yet. It makes no sense for you to chase us; you need to be ready, be in place. We will bring him to you unless something else happens. I have an idea for a location around Battle Creek; it's not that far from Angola, where you're at now. Might be the perfect situation where the doctor can finally end this."

"We'll have to trust your judgment," Shelly replied. "How's he doing? Can you see any difference, any change?"

Rob wanted to tell her of the dream David told him about, his dad and her together on a date but was afraid it might cause false hope and make her too anxious. At this point, it would just not be fair.

"Oh, he's tired and still confused about a lot of things. I'm praying tomorrow when we get to Grand Rapids, it will, somehow, be over right then and there, and we can all go home."

"So are we, Rob. We'll be checking out in less than an hour and then will head up to Battle Creek. Once we find a place to stay, I'll call Evelyn and let her know what's up so that they can join us. Be careful, honey; Karli and I are praying for you all."

"I'll call when I know more, Mom. Get settled in, and rest. Love you both."

FRIDAY

It was overcast when they left the motel and headed north on Route 131 towards Grand Rapids. David watched the Michigan summer greenery roll by from the back seat. Little, overall, seemed changed from what he remembered of the Michigan countryside. *Maybe grayer, probably just the dreary morning,* he thought. A person tends to remember sunshine and good times when searching for happy, fond memories.

It was late spring of 1944 when he spent his last days in Michigan, and the final time he set eyes upon the yellow bungalow with the white fence on Sitka Trail, where he, Macy, and Jenny lived. It seems so long ago now; it had been a long road to....

Suddenly, remembering something he had heard recently made him uneasy. And he didn't know why, but it was a question that needed to be answered. *What do you intend to do when you find the end of your road?*

As they drew nearer to the city, it began to sprinkle. A few taller buildings could be seen in the cloudy distance.

"It's all so different from last the time I was here," remarked David of the skyline.

"It's had a lot of growth over the years," Sunni spoke up. "It's a nice little city. Do you have the address to where we're going?"

"960 Sitka Trail. Would you have any idea how to get there from here, by any chance?" David asked of Sunni. "I don't think I can find my way around anymore; so much has changed."

"No, sorry, I'm not that familiar with Grand Rapids. Did you live there?" the girl asked.

"Many years ago," replied David.

"Sunni, could you punch that into the GPS for me?" asked Rob After Sunni had entered the address, she said to David,

"Do you still have family living there?"

"I don't know," was David's pensive reply."

"That's why we're here, to at least find out what happened to them if we can. Dad, you want to stop for a while, maybe get something to eat first?"

"No, Rob, let's get this done."

Navy Blue No. 2 turned onto Sitka Trail in the 600th block. Rob drove slowly while the trio checked out numbers on the houses as the blocks ticked past.

"Doesn't look the same as it did; it sure doesn't. Seems like newer houses that weren't here before, and some empty lots," David remarked.

"The place might not even exist anymore; it could be a different house there now, or, nothing at all," replied Rob.

"I know, Rob, I know. But I have this feeling if we… wait, stop here, pull over!"

As the car rolled to a stop, David stared across the street at a small house, numbered 960.

"Is that it?" Rob asked quietly.

The bungalow, now dull white, with a sagging roof over the small front porch, looked tired and run-down. Many pickets on the wooden fence were weathered and gray, some missing; the gate appeared to be stuck open, eternally inviting visitors to enter. A patchwork of grass and dirt covered most of the small yard; the big tree and swing were gone. Crookedly taped on the drab, blue-green door was a faded, orange and white, *For Sale* sign.

"It's a different color now; it was yellow before," David began. "Used to be a tree off the corner of the house, with a swing. Macy would sit there on nice days, holding Jenny and rocking back and forth. Helped put her to sleep, she said, in her letters. There was a picture taken of the three of us, right there, by a neighbor. I had a copy in my cabin on the carrier and a smaller one in the plane."

"Wait, Macy? Carrier? I don't understand," Sunni spoke up.

Rob put a finger to his lips, and she became silent. He opened the door, stepped out, and folded the front seat forward. David stood in the sprinkling rain, staring at the house for a moment, then slowly began to walk forward.

The siding became a brighter yellow with every step; the front door once again red. Quickly, the yard filled in with green grass. Near a corner of the house, a tree materialized with an empty swing, slowly moving back and forth in a gentle, warm breeze. The sky became a brilliant blue. He could feel the sun's warmth on his face. When he reached the sidewalk, the fence was whole again, and white. The front door opened, and David saw what he had so often dreamt. Macy stepped out onto the front porch, holding Jenny. For a moment, time stood still as they both paused, then quickly began moving towards each other; David's mind was screaming with pure joy, *I'm home! Dear God, thank you, I am home!*

"May I help you?" a woman's voice asked.

David stopped halfway down the sidewalk and once again saw the old, worn, white house with the faded *For Sale* sign. Bowing his head, he felt the raindrops and cool dampness in the air.

"May I help you?"

David looked to his left, where an older woman, wearing a

scarf, was standing in the yard next door. She began walking towards him.

"I saw you looking at my rental house while you were sitting in that old car; thought you might be interested in buying it."

David slowly shuffled towards the woman.

"I used to live here, I mean, knew people who did, back in the '40s. During the war."

"Oh, a lot of people have lived here over the years," she replied. "It's a nice little bungalow, built in the '30s sometime, not sure what year, you know. I can take you inside if you'd like to look around. Belonged to my grandparents originally, they rented it out for years. Helped with their income, especially as they got older, you know. It's really a nice place; needs some fix'n up, though. Be just the thing for one person, or two, maybe a young family. Not very big, you know. Been a few people who've looked at it, mostly young people. It needs some work, but it's a good, easy fixer-upper."

David stood quietly, nodding.

"But these young people nowadays, well, you know, they just don't want to work for much of anything, anymore. They just want to have it all done and ready to go, with no pride in accomplishment at all. My grandparents, well, they passed it on to my mom, who passed it to me. My husband and I are getting too old to do much work on it ourselves and keep it up. And I don't want to pay someone to do any repair work, you know. So just decided to sell it. I can take you inside if you'd like? That porch roof, it can be fixed pretty easily, and the whole place needs painting, of course. It wouldn't take much work. And I'm sure it could use some modernizing, you know. Would you like me to show you the inside? It's a lovely little house."

"I know," said David, wearily. "About the people I knew, who lived here, do you…."

"Oh, nobody's lived here for two, maybe three years now. They were a nice couple, a guy, a real nice fella, and his wife. At least I think it was his wife, can't say for sure, always wondered. It made no difference to me, none of my business, you know, and they had a small dog; he was never any trouble, the dog, I mean. Always paid their rent on time, I was sorry to see them move away. Believe they went to Texas; no, maybe it was Oklahoma. You know, I'm not really sure where they…."

"Ma'am," David interrupted.

He was exasperated, and the emotions of the last few minutes had drained him mentally, and Derek's body physically.

"You said your grandparents owned it?"

"Yes sir, they did, really nice people, been gone for some years now. A lot of people rented this little house. Guess I mentioned that, didn't I?"

"Yes, ma'am, you did."

"Would you like to take a look around, inside?" she asked again.

"Sure, why not," said David tiredly.

He was reluctant to go inside after having seen the rundown condition of the bungalow. But the conversation was exhausting him, and he was getting nowhere. Might as well take the tour, perhaps press her more on the previous residents and what became of them. They walked onto the small porch, where the woman unlocked the door, pushing it twice before it opened.

"Sometimes it sticks," she said. "But it can be easily fixed, you know."

With all the shades drawn, the light inside was subdued. It had the musty smell one would expect of an old, closed-up house. She flipped a switch, and an overhead light fixture dimly illuminated the living room. David remembered it, the same one from before, not that long ago, to him. The room was bare, save for a reading lamp in a corner, and one old, steel, folding chair. They walked down the short hall to the back rooms, one being Jenny's nursery, the other, he and Macy's bedroom, both now empty and dank.

While standing in the nursery, as the woman babbled on about the house, David began to remember details of the rooms he'd left, in his world, barely more than a year before. He could clearly recall where Jenny's crib, with the changing table beside it, had stood, given to them by Tom and Betty. They had no need for it; their only child, a daughter, was in college. An old dresser they had bought from a neighbor across the street for a dollar would have been in a far corner. It wasn't fancy but worked well enough for storing Jenny's clothes and other items.

A warm remembrance came to mind, it seemed not so long ago, before Macy and their newborn daughter came home from the hospital. He had surprised his wife by painting the entire nursery pink. She was delighted and immediately set about decorating the room with photos of flowers, roses mostly, and landscapes cut from magazines, then pasting them to the walls. All gone now. Slowly taking in a breath, he could still recall the lingering scent of fresh paint and baby powder.

A switch just inside the bedroom doorway on the right brought to life an overhead light fixture in the middle of the ceiling, as an attached fan, with drooping blades, hummed and slowly began to rotate.

The closed blinds on a corner window faded in David Hamilton's mind, replaced by white curtains, gently moving in a breeze as sunlight streamed in.

Tiptoeing over to the bed where Macy lay, he quietly slipped in beside her,
    then leaning over his sleeping wife, gently kissed her lips. Awaking, she turned towards him and, blinking the drowsiness from her blue eyes, said,
    "I want you to always wake me, just like this... Sleep well?"
    "Yes, I did. And you?"

"Of course, whenever you're here. Oh, look," Macy said, glancing at the alarm clock on the nightstand.

She sat up and began throwing off the covers.

"It's past Jenny's feeding time."

"You just lay back down, young lady," said David as he pulled the covers back over her. "That little girl is fed and changed. It's Sunday morning, and you just relax."

"You're so good to me," Macy said, wrapping her arms around him.

"You're more than worth it, and I think maybe mom and dad need some... alone time," he said softly, pulling her closer.

"Oh yes, I love alone time," Macy said and gave him a long, soft kiss.

"Figured I'd make us breakfast, you know, later, after..." said David as they both lay back in bed.

She turned, propped her head upon her hand, looked into his eyes, and giggled.

"You, make breakfast?"

"Are you questioning my culinary expertise?"

"No, of course not," she laughed. "I was just wondering if you knew where to find the...."

"Kitchen," a voice said.

David turned towards the sound.

"What?"

"Kitchen, I said, would you like to see the kitchen?" asked the woman.

He somberly looked back into the quiet, empty bedroom with the slowly rotating fan and closed blinds.

"All these appliances are less than ten years old, you know. They all work just fine, and everything's electric. Even have a nice little microwave," she said as they walked into the small kitchen.

"What's a microwave?"

"You know, a microwave oven? You put food in it, and it heats it in a minute or so?"

"Yes, yes, of course, a microwave, oven," replied David, while nodding his head, oblivious to what this woman was talking about.

Walking back into the living room and over to the now bare wall, where Macy had her photo collection, he reached out and touched it.

"This used to be wallpaper, kind of a beige, and small flowers with thin leaves," he said to the woman, without looking at her.

"Why yes, it did. My mother had the wood paneling put on back in the '70s, I believe. It still looks pretty good, though, don't you think?"

"Yes, looks fine," David said and turned towards the woman. "Do you know if your grandparents, or your mother, did they ever talk about people who lived here, from 1943 to1945, maybe later? Would've been a young couple in their early twenties, with a small child, a baby girl?"

"Oh, I wouldn't remember anything like that. So many people have lived here, and I wasn't even born until after the war, you know. Well, the rain is starting to pick up; I'd better get back to my place if you're not interested in the house. But maybe you can come back and see it again, on a nicer day," the woman said as she turned and headed towards the door. "It's a nice little place; sorry I wasn't any help with the people you're asking about."

"Thank you, ma'am; I'm sorry too… I was hoping, well, thanks for talking with me and showing the house," said David as they both stepped outside onto the porch.

"Oh, you're quite welcome, and I hope you find who you're looking for," the woman replied as she closed and locked the front door, then quickly made her way through the rain, back to the neighboring house. She walked up the steps of the covered porch and was reaching for the doorknob.

"Tom and Betty."

She jumped and turned around to find David, standing a few feet away.

"Tom and Betty, that was your grandparent's names," David said calmly. "They lived here, in this house."

"Oh my word, you scared the daylights out of me," she replied breathlessly. "Why, that's right. How did you know that?"

"I remember them, remember hearing about them. Ma'am, again, did your grandparents ever say anything about, talk about people who lived here, named David and Macy?"

It was his last chance.

"David and Macy," the woman repeated. "Don't recall them speaking of anyone by those names, right offhand. I wish I could help."

David lowered his head, nodded, and turned to walk down the steps, feeling suddenly very heavy and tired.

"Macy, Macy, wait a minute, wait just one minute," the woman said while tapping a finger on her chin.

David stopped and turned back, staring intently at the woman.

"You know, it was a long time ago, I was pretty young, but I do recall now that you mention that name. Tom and Betty did, once that I remember, say something about a woman with a baby who lived next door. I think my mom had asked if they ever heard from Mary or Macy; no, I'm sure it was Macy."

"Yes, yes, what happened to her?" David asked, his voice rising.

"I think they said her husband was in the war, a flyer, I think, yes. I guess the poor boy never came home. That's so sad, isn't it?"

David nodded his head slowly.

"What else can you tell me, please?"

A large man dressed in jeans, and a T-shirt, stepped out of the door and onto the porch.

"Everything okay? I heard loud talking; you alright, Eve?"

"Oh heavens yes, this nice young man was just asking about some people who lived in the bungalow, back in the '40s, you know. I was telling him about the young mother who I believe lived there. Do you remember my grandparents, or my mom mentioning anything about that, Blake? It would have been a Macy and her poor husband who never came home from the war. Oh, I'm so sorry; where are my manners. This is my husband, Blake; I'm Eve. Don't believe I caught your name."

"It's David, David Hamilton."

"David, same first name as the man you're asking about. Well, isn't that a coincidence," she replied.

"Yes, a coincidence. Please, Eve, what else can you tell me?"

"I remember your grandpa mentioning something about them a couple of times, I think, years back," said Blake. "The guy, the husband, whatever his name was, disappeared somewhere in the Pacific, fighter pilot."

"Yes, I believe that's right," added Eve.

"Do you know what happened to her? Where did she go?" David asked tensely.

"Oh, she left, she went away, went away, not sure where or when. Do you remember anything about that, honey?" Eve asked Blake.

"Most likely sometime after the war was over, 1946 probably," Blake replied. "I guess she stayed and waited for her husband to come back, or least word of what happened to him. Nothing ever came of it, I'd imagine. Tom said he took them to the bus station, this Macy, and the little girl. Never saw them again. I believe she and your grandma may have corresponded back and forth for a time, though."

"Did he say where they went?" David asked.

"Said she went home, wherever that was. I don't remember the name of the town," replied Blake.

"Fowlerville," said David, almost in a whisper.

"What's that?" Blake asked, leaning in closer as David cleared his throat.

"Fowlerville, I said Fowlerville."

"Could be, I don't remember," Blake replied, shrugging his shoulders.

Stepping forward, David took his hand and shook it vigorously; he hugged Eve.

"I can't thank you both enough. Thank you, just, thank you." He then walked briskly down the steps and into the increasing rainfall.

"David!" Eve called out as he crossed the yard of the old bungalow, heading towards the street. "Did you say your last name was Hamilton?"

He stopped and turned back towards the woman.

"Yes, ma'am, Hamilton."

"You know, the more I think about it, I'm almost certain the last name of the other David and his wife, was Hamilton also. That's quite another coincidence, isn't it?" Eve said, with a bemused look on her face.

"If you say so," David said, loud enough to be heard over the rain.

"Hey, you never mentioned where you're from," shouted Blake.

As David looked at the old bungalow, he once again saw the home as he left it in 1944. Spreading his arms wide, he yelled,

"Here!" then sprinted towards the Coupe.

He climbed into the back seat shivering from excitement and chill of the rain.

"How'd it go?" Rob asked. "Find out anything?"

"Not at first, but it turns out the lady is a granddaughter of our landlords when we lived there. The house has been in their family for a long time, and I did find out where Macy and Jenny went; they…."

David looked at Sunni, watching intently from the front seat.

"That's, that's the people, I knew, years ago that, well, I've, that I've, been trying to find, and…." David stammered, attempting to keep up the ruse.

"She knows," Rob replied, looking over at Sunni. "I told her the whole story."

Sunni looked at the man in the back seat; she had been calling Derek.

"It sounds crazy but explains a lot. I'm good with it, even if I don't understand how any of this is even remotely possible,"

"Imagine how I feel," replied David.

"I'll be here to help you, all that I can, David." She reached into the back seat and touched his hand.

"Thank you, Sunni, he said softly."

"Where to now?" Rob asked.

"Blake and Eve, the couple over there, told me Macy went home," said David as he pointed towards the two people, still standing on the porch. "Which means they went to Fowlerville."

"Fowlerville, my hometown?" said Sunni with surprise. "Another happy coincidence!"

Rob slowly shook his head and said nothing.

"We can leave you off at your home, then Rob and I can…."

"Oh hell no!" she interrupted. "I'm in this to the finish, whatever that might be. You guys are not going to get rid of me that easy, not now."

With the headlight knob pulled, and windshield wipers rhythmically slapping back-and-forth, Navy Blue No. 2 slowly pulled away from the curb and motored down the watery street.

"What an unusual man," Blake said to Eve as they watched the red taillights disappear into the grayness of falling rain. "Strange, him having the same name as the people he was looking for, then said he was from, here?"

"Yes, very strange. He seemed to be, such an, old soul," Eve replied slowly.

"They're driving away, in a 1940s car, looking for people, from the 1940s," Blake said, then looked at his wife, "You don't think...."

"Makes you wonder, you know? It just makes you wonder," she said.

＝← →＝

Shortly past noon, they turned onto the entrance ramp to Interstate 96, heading towards Lansing and Fowlerville, Michigan. David had no realistic expectations of finding Macy and Jenny still residing in their old house in Grand Rapids. Too much time had passed in this new reality that had been forced upon, or chosen, for him. The best he could have hoped for was a clue to their whereabouts. And by the grace of God, or some strange and continuing surreal providence, he received just that, from the people living next door to the little bungalow on Sitka Trail. Now it was on to Macy's hometown.

There has to be a reason; there has to be an explanation, David thought, still trying to make sense of it all; *what could, and would be the end?* Occupying Derek Haynes's body could not last forever; he knew that, and likely not even for much longer. With every passing day, every passing hour, he felt the presence of this man trying to make his way back, back to his family, just as David Hamilton was trying to find to his.

It was easier, now, for them to talk. No longer a need, or reason, to hide the strangeness and mystery of the circumstance from Sunni. Although baffled by Rob's explanation of how this journey came to be and how it may end, she did not feel uncomfortable and was accepting of the events which had unfolded in their lives over the past several days. Being a psychology major, there was much curiosity about the phenomena just revealed to her, and she was eager for answers.

The young girl had no reason to suspect the growing menace that awaited.

Rob still carried most of the conversation with Sunni; they had an obvious and growing connection. David, at times, felt an inclination to be more accepting towards the girl of Japanese descent. But the military warrior in him still had a vivid and painful memory in his disjointed mind from only a few days past that he could not, or would not, let go.

War feeds hatred; hatred feeds war. Any healing and forgiveness, by the grace of God, would take a significant amount of time. The old fellow at the garage in Kentucky told Sunni his hatred had quieted over the years. He had the luxury of time. David Hamilton had, not yet, a week.

⇒⊹⇐

"You sure this is the right address?" Rico asked of Carlos.

It was nearly 6:30 p.m. The three men from Florida had parked near the end of a sparsely populated street on the northwest side of Fowlerville. The early evening sun caused the shade from trees surrounding a two-story brick and wood home to extend further across the yard. The silver Mercedes was sitting almost a block away.

"I saw the number when we cruised by; this is the place, alright. She wrote it on this piece of paper," replied Carlos, holding it up for RayBob and Rico to see.

"There's no car in that or any other driveway, or parked on the street, with Florida plates," said RayBob.

"I know, it could be in the garage, or just not here right now. We need to find out if anybody's home. Rico, you go knock on the door," Carlos said.

"Then what?" Rico asked.

"See who answers; they should be Asian. Just ask if so-and-so lives there."

"Who is so-and-so?" Replied Rico, with a confused look on his face.

"I don't know, just make up something. Joe Blow, Mr. and Mrs. Smith, I don't care. We just need to see if anyone's in there," said Carlos, with exasperation.

"Why don't you go knock on the door, Carlos? You're the one looking for her," Rico came back.

"You simple, stupid son-of-a-bitch, suppose Sunni answers the door, then what? Should I just politely ask if she would like to come out and go for a ride, so three guys can take turns, then waste her?"

"Yeah, guess that ain't a good idea," admitted Rico.

"Just go knock on the damn door; she's never seen you," RayBob said from the back seat. Just make up a name to give them, and if somebody answers the door, just say you're sorry to have bothered them and walk away."

"Okay, pull up closer, so I don't have to walk so far."

Carlos reached over and slapped Rico on the back of the head.

"She doesn't know you, but she knows my car, you dumb-ass! This is supposed to be a surprise party for the girlie, remember? You want me to pull in the driveway and honk the horn? Get out!"

"Okay! Alright! I'm going; I'm going!" Rico said as he opened the door.

"Don't screw this up," Carlos said, pointing at Rico.

"Man, he is dumb," said RayBob as he and Carlos watched Rico cross the street and walk towards the house.

"Dumber than dead weeds," Carlos replied with a grin.

"Dumber than a box of rocks," RayBob said, chuckling.

"Dumber than, dumber than, he's just dumber than shit!" Carlos said loudly.

"He would have to take night classes and study real hard, to work his way *up* to being dumber than shit!" RayBob said, laughing.

The laughing stopped when Rico turned and walked up the sidewalk leading to the house.

"So, getting edgy?" RayBob asked.

"Yeah, you could say that."

"Been a while since Archer," said RayBob.

Carlos looked in the back seat at his friend, lit up a cigarette, and took a drag.

"Don't suppose there's a handy lake or pond around here with some gators in it, do you?"

After stopping at a Lansing truck stop off Interstate 96 to refuel, the journey to Fowlerville continued. Now less than an hour away from Sunni's parent's house, there was both a feeling of relief and uncertainty. Rob looked at Henry; the GPS stuck to the windshield.

"We should be there right around six thirty. Think it would be a good idea to call your folks now, and let them know we're coming?"

"Would be way too much explaining to do on the phone, Rob. Even just the parts I could tell them. We're so close now; it'll be better to show up, introduce you both, and take it from there. Once home and safe, I don't think there'll be any issues, and my dad is really going to dig this car."

"What does he do for a living?" David asked, trying to make polite conversation with the girl.

"He works for a company that provides IT and other services for businesses."

"You've lost me already. What is an IT?"

"Information technology, Dad. It means they do work with

computers and other kinds of technology. That'll be much of what I'll be doing after graduation," Rob replied.

"We used to live in Detroit; my dad worked for GM," Sunni continued. "It was getting so dangerous to live there, we moved to Fowlerville in 2003, when the company he works for first started up. I wasn't very old and don't remember much about living in the city."

"You think this IT stuff might help us find anything about my wife and daughter when we get to town?" David asked.

"We didn't find anything when planning the trip, remember? But we can try and do a more detailed search," Rob said."

"Is there a town hall or something like that, in Fowlerville, that maybe we can search through some records?" David asked of Sunni.

She thought for a moment before replying,

"Yes, there is, but I just had an idea. What was Macy's maiden name?"

"McDonald. Like the restaurant."

"Why don't we apply some low technology. Let's look in the phone book for Hamiltons and McDonalds. I'd think, or hope anyway, there may still be some family connections around who might be able to help."

Rob softly slapped his hand on the steering wheel.

"Damn, girl, that is a great idea, don't think I'd ever have come up with that. I'm too much in the habit of doing everything online with computers."

"Sometimes simple is best, well, we'll see, anyway," said Sunni, with a smile.

"I'd heard you oriental types, could be pretty clever, some- times," spoke David from the back seat.

The girl snapped her head around and glared.

"That was meant to be a compliment, right? Right?"

"Sure, what the hell did you think it was? Jeezuz, give me a break," replied David, a bit put off by her reaction.

"He *is* over 95 years old," Rob said, trying to smooth things over. "Well, kind of, I mean, depends on how you look at it."

Sunni turned forward, crossed her arms, and murmured,

"Ignorance has no age."

Scant conversation followed after the exchange until Rob steered onto the exit ramp towards Fowlerville.

"Henry says 2.4 miles from here; hope your folks won't be too upset when we just pull into their driveway.

"It'll be fine," replied Sunni. "You two guys have gotten me home in fine shape; I hate to think what this trip might have been like, with crazy Carlos."

⇒⇐

"There was nobody home," said Rico as he climbed back into the car. "I rang the doorbell several times, and knocked, didn't see or hear any movement, nothing."

"Where the hell is everybody?" Carlos said angrily.

"Might've just gone out for supper, who knows," responded RayBob. "We can come back later and check it out, but for now, let's go find a place to stay and get something to eat. We really shouldn't be sitting here for too long anyway; some neighbors might become suspicious."

"They left well before we did, so should be around somewhere," said Carlos as he started the Mercedes.

"We don't even know what kind of car they're driving," added Rico.

"You two keep your eyes open for anything with Florida plates, you hear?" Carlos said as he turned the car around in the middle of the street and headed east.

After almost two blocks, he flipped on the left turn signal.

"Hey, that's a cool old car," Rico said, pointing.

"Where?" RayBob asked as he leaned forward from the back seat.

"Just ahead, 'bout half a block up, kind of a Navy blue. Looks like something from the '30s or '40s, maybe," Rico said, now pointing out the side window as the Mercedes began to turn.

"I doubt the people we're looking for would drive an old clunker like that up from Florida. And we didn't come here to look at old cars." Carlos replied.

"Still cool," said Rico as he stuck his hand out the window, waved, and gave a thumbs-up.

⊫· ·⊨

"Just up here two blocks, on the left," Sunni said while looking out the side window as they motored past houses and yards.

"Hey, some guy down the street just gave us a thumbs-up; he must like old cars," said David.

"Yeah, I saw that, probably jealous of such a fine, vintage machinery," replied Rob.

"Turn in at the next driveway," Sunni said a few seconds later, pointing out the window. "Well, fellas, we made it, been quite an adventure. And unless I miss my guess, it's not over yet."

Parking the Coupe in the driveway, they all exited and made their way up the sidewalk to the front door.

"Hello! Anyone home?" Sunni yelled while ringing the doorbell.

After a short wait and no response, she pulled a set of keys from her yellow tote bag, unlocked and opened the door.

"Mom, dad, anybody home?"

"Doesn't seem like it," said Rob.

"Suppose I better call," she said while pulling out her cell phone.

"Just make yourself at home; the bathroom is just down the hall, on the left."

David went to find the bathroom while Rob sat down on the couch next to Sunni.

"Mom, where are you? I just walked in the front door to find an abandoned house."

"Yes, just a little while ago."

"Umm, a couple of Florida friends gave me a lift home."

"No, you don't know them; yes, they're good people."

"It's fine, mom, so where are you?"

"California? What for?"

"Oh no, how's he doing?"

Sunni continued the conversation with her mother, making the occasional comment or asking a question. Rob thought it a good time to retrieve their luggage and other items from the car, appears this will be their base of operations, hopefully, for only a short period of time. He considered it a benefit that Sunni's parents were not home; it would have been additional people to deal with, more made-up stories and explanations to try and keep straight.

Returning to the house, he found Sunni telling David that her parents had flown to California to be with an uncle, her dad's brother, who had been in a car accident and hospitalized.

"Is it serious?" Rob asked.

"At this point, not life-threatening," Sunni replied. "But he's pretty banged up. My folks said they would stay there for at least a few more days, so I guess we have the house all to ourselves."

"Sorry to hear that, I mean about your uncle," replied Rob.

"Yeah, me too. Where's your phone book?" David asked abruptly.

"Cool your jets, dude. We're not even settled in yet, and you're *my* guests now. Don't make me regret taking up with you, two," said Sunni, as she looked at David.

"She's right, Dad; we'll get to it just as soon as we can. Let's relax a little first; been a long trip."

"How long is this relaxing thing going to take?" David shot back.

Sunni stared at the man while deciding whether to respond. But let it drop.

"Who's hungry?" she said, trying to smile. "I'm starving and have eaten enough road trip food to last me the rest of the year. Let's go downtown and have a nice relaxing meal, my treat."

She stepped over to David and put a hand on his arm.

"We'll go through the phone book when we get back; I promise, and make a list of numbers to call tomorrow morning."

David gave a tired sigh and agreed.

It was decided the Coupe needed a break, so it was pulled into the two-car garage, next to a black, five-year-old Mitsubishi Outlander. As Sunni walked around to the driver's side, David said quietly to Rob,

"Feels like I'm conspiring with the enemy."

"Okay, Dad, keep your voice down, please."

"Mitsubishi built the Zero fighter's, you know," replied David as he opened the rear passenger door of the SUV. "We called them Zekes."

"Who's Zeke?" Sunni asked as she stepped into the vehicle.

"Somebody he knew during the war," replied Rob, with exasperation in his voice.

She backed the Outlander down the driveway and onto the street, then headed east towards downtown Fowlerville. After a few blocks, they neared a Chinese restaurant on Van Riper Road. She could not help herself.

"Feel like a little Oriental dining tonight, David?"

"Very funny," he replied.

Rob just shook his head.

A popular grill was chosen on Grand River Avenue. David had suggested the McDonald's they had passed but was outvoted.

"I came here often with my parents; never had a bad meal," Sunni said as they walked a short distance down the sidewalk.

"Don't suppose the drinking age in Michigan is any different than Florida," said Rob.

"Nope," replied Sunni. "No alcohol here for us two, but we can have something at the house later when we get back, if you like."

"I'm not drink'n no goddamn sake," spoke David gruffly.

"Ahhhh!" Sunni said while shaking her hands in front of her face.

As they walked into the restaurant's entryway, a silver Mercedes with a Florida license plate passed slowly by.

⊷ ⊷

"I want to thank you again for supper; it was delicious," said Rob upon returning to Sunni's parent's home.

"You're more than welcome, both of you," was Sunni's reply. "Should be beer in the frig; grab one for me, please."

"Sounds good, Dad; you want a beer?"

"Sure, where's the phone book?" David replied, quickly, his anticipation growing and his patience shrinking.

"Should be one in my dad's home office; I'll go get it; there's a pad and pen in the kitchen. Let's just sit at the table."

Within a short time of searching the Fowlerville-area phone listings for Hamiltons and McDonalds, they had accumulated less than fifteen names and phone numbers.

"I thought there might've been more," said Sunni.

"So many people only use cell phones now and have dropped their landlines. Can't say I'm surprised," added Rob.

"So what does this mean? Will it be harder to find any relatives?" David asked.

"Hopefully not," replied Rob. "We can ask everyone we do contact if they know any others to call, the ones with just the cell phones, whatever leads they can give us."

"That's what I was thinking; we'll do what we can," Sunni said.

"Sunni should do the calling. You're from the area, and it might seem less like an outsider calling and asking for personal information," Rob suggested.

"Right, lived here most of my life, and I do vaguely recall going to school with a couple of kids whose last name was McDonald, so there are or were, some around at one time," she replied.

"Can we start calling now?" David asked anxiously. "Will be seven days tomorrow since we planned and began this search."

"I know, Dad, but it's after ten; we don't want to be bothering people this late. They might be less friendly and helpful, and I wouldn't blame them."

"That's true, and tomorrow's Saturday, so should be more people around on the weekend, anyway," Sunni added. "You can spend the night in my room, David. I'll show you where it's at."

After walking upstairs, she got him situated. David was quiet; the only word spoken, barely above a whisper, was *thanks* as Sunni went out the door.

Returning to the living room, she found Rob sitting on the couch sipping his beer.

"I feel terrible for what your dad, well, David, is going through, Rob, I truly do. But that man can sometimes just drive me crazy!"

"I know the feeling. He's not my dad, not the one I knew just a week ago, anyway. David was, until last Saturday, fighting in World War II. Even saying it out loud, it's still hard to believe."

"So his hatred for the Japanese people is disturbing, but understandable, sadly, being wartime and what the man has gone through. I get it," said Sunni as she sat down beside him. "I have to keep reminding myself of that. He's hurting for the family left behind, but you and your family are hurting too. It has to be almost intolerable for everyone."

"Something significant is gonna have to happen before he, well, moves on," Rob said softly.

Turning toward Sunni, he continued.

"He's in there, my dad, fighting to get out, I know it. There's been a few times he was almost back, just for a moment, but.... David can be very insulting and annoying, but he's really just a war-hardened kid, only a couple years older than me, and completely lost here, in our time. My dad, Derek, well, he's not like that at all, actually very friendly and open. I think you would've liked him; I mean, you *will* like him... This Carlos guy, now there's somebody who doesn't sound very pleasant."

"After a while, there was something about him that made me uncomfortable," Sunni began. "I just chalked it up to new relationship jitters, but then it got even spookier."

"How so?"

"You know that tote bag I carry?"

"Yeah, yellow, with the parrot."

"Around the time that the last girl, the eighteen-year-old from Archer, disappeared, the middle of May, Carlos gave it to me. Said he thought I'd like it, and I do. He mentioned it came from a thrift shop, and that's why it looked a little worn. Like that rich bastard ever set foot in a secondhand store in his life. I told him it was fine, even with the few small stains."

"Stains?"

"Yeah, I tried washing them out, but it didn't help much. So a few days later, we were watching TV at his place when they showed some pictures on the news, you know, cell phone pics, of the girl, Moni Torres. In one of them, she held a bag like mine. After I told him it looked exactly like the one he gave me, Carlos suddenly got real nervous and said they probably sell a lot of those in Florida. He told me if I didn't like it, he'd just take it back."

"That is kinda weird," said Rob, with growing concern.

"I know, right? Told him that didn't mean I wasn't happy with it, only commented about the bag looking like the missing girl's, that it was just a spooky coincidence."

"Then what?"

"He changed the channel and sat there, hardly saying a word or paying any attention to me, just smoking a damn cigarette. So I left; he was getting really annoying. A few days later, he shows up with a new tote, saying he thought I'd like it better than the yellow one. He offered to throw it away for me."

"That is beyond suspicious, Sunni," Rob said with a frown.

"It wasn't long after that he changed his mind and offered to drive me back here. Said we could surprise my folks, and I shouldn't call them in advance to tell them we were coming. I was no longer comfortable around him, so whenever he'd call and want to get together, I'd always come up with an excuse not to; I just didn't want to be alone with him. But he kept bugging me about the trip, said he wanted to help. The more I think about it; it may not have been such a good idea if I'd gotten in the car with him for a ride to the bus station that morning we met. Sure glad you guys were there."

"Damn Sunni, this guy just sounds dangerous. Glad you decide to stay away from him."

"Last time we talked was Wednesday, middle of the night. He called, was drunk or drugged up, probably both, and threatening. I told him if he didn't leave me alone, I'd call the cops on him, which made him scream'n angry."

"When you get back to school, and if he is still lurking around, you do need to call the cops on him; he's not right in the head," Rob said earnestly.

"I'm planning on it. He's a long way from here, though, so I'll just try and enjoy the summer and deal with it when I get back to Gainesville. Maybe he'll have given up by that time and leave me all alone. Probably has a new girl already, poor thing."

"Please make sure and be careful, Sunni, okay? Might be a long day tomorrow; suppose we better get some sleep," suggested Rob as he stretched his arms out at his side.

"You can stay in the guest room at the end of the hall; I'll sleep in my folks' room."

"Sounds like a plan," Rob said, standing up.

Sunni grabbed his arm and pulled him back down on the couch.

"What, no goodnight kiss?" she asked.

"Oh, I suppose, if you insist," Rob said, smiling. "How many?"

Sunni moved closer, her face only inches from Rob's, then softly said, "I'll let you know when you're done."

SATURDAY

"You ready for this?" Rob asked David.

"Let's do all Hamiltons first; there's not that many," he replied.

They had all slept in. Not having to wake up and be on the road was both refreshing and relaxing. Sunni prepared omelets, and by the time they had finished their breakfast, it was nearly ten; David Hamilton was getting anxious.

Sunni put her phone on speaker, laid it on the kitchen table, and tapped in the first number. It was no longer in service.

"Probably had it shut off and just using their cell," she said.

"Lot of good that does us. Cross it off," spoke David.

Sunni entered the next number on the list, a man answered.

"Hello."

"Hi, this is Sunni Omora; I live here in Fowlerville and have friends visiting who used to have relatives in the area. Would you have any knowledge of a lady, she would be quite elderly now, by the name of Macy Hamilton? Her maiden name would have been McDonald."

"No, that name is not familiar," the man politely answered.

"She had a daughter; her name was Jenny, Jenny Hamilton; she would be in her middle seventies. Does that ring a bell?"

"Not at all. We moved to Fowlerville in 2013; I don't think we'd be able to help you, sorry."

"That's okay; we're just going through the phone book to see if we can make a connection. I appreciate you taking the time to speak with me," Sunni politely replied.

"Cross it off," David said.

The following three calls were similar, people who were not native to the area and could offer no help. The last Hamilton on the list was another not-in-service recording.

"Cross it off."

"We may have better luck with McDonald's anyway," said Rob. "Being Macy's family name, you'd think there'd be a more of a chance of finding people who would know some history of the family."

"You'd think," David said.

"Hello, McDonald's," it was a woman's voice.

Sunni gave her the explanation for calling, and the woman replied,

"My family has been here since sometime in the sixties, but I don't recall anyone by those two names right offhand. Did you try calling any Hamilton's?"

"Yes ma'am, all that could be found in the book. Unfortunately, we didn't have any luck."

"Oh, that's too bad. There were some McDonalds I went to school with; my kids did too. But I can't remember their first names now and don't believe I ever knew or met their parents. If using the phone book doesn't help in locating the women you're looking for, maybe you can find some old school records. That might be useful; you never know."

"Yes ma'am, that's a good idea, and thank you so much for speaking with me!"Sunni replied enthusiastically.

"Well, that is something to try if we can't make any progress this way," said Rob as he looked at David.

The next several calls were a combination of phone numbers not in service, sorry can't help, and one, *please leave a message*, which Sunni did. Only one number remained.

"Did they live on a farm?" the man on the other end of the line asked.

David sat up straight and nodded.

"Yes, yes they did," Sunni replied.

"Don't know if this will help, but when I was very young, my parents and I, along with my little brother, would happen to drive past a place in the country. I'm not sure where it was now, but I do remember a red and white sign at the end of a long lane. We just thought it was hilarious. It said, *Welcome To Old McDonald's Farm*, you know, like the little kid's song they used to sing in school."

David jumped out of his chair.

"Yes, Macy told me about that on our first date! Ask him if he knows how to get there."

"I heard the question and have no idea where it was," the man replied. "Not even sure what side of town it might be on; probably doesn't even exist anymore. So many of those old farmhouses and buildings have been torn down over the years. Sorry I can't be of more help."

"Oh, you've been quite helpful, and thank you so very, very much," replied Sunni.

"That was the last number, but the farm Macy grew up on was a real place; it existed and is around here, somewhere," said David. "What do we do now?"

"We could try to find some old school records, as that lady

suggested, and maybe do a record search at the town hall," Sunni suggested.

"Alright then, let's do that," said David as he took a step towards the door.

"But it's Saturday, David," replied Sunni. "The town hall won't be open. We could try on Monday, but the schools are closed for the summer; we'd have to find a principal or superintendent who could give us access to old records if they even have any going back that far. Don't think there's any more we can do today; I'm so sorry."

"Dammit!" David said angrily.

"Or we could drive aimlessly around, all over the countryside, looking for a place that may no longer exist," spoke Rob.

"Let's do it!" David said loudly.

Rob had made the comment in jest, but he could tell David was getting desperate, as was he. It is Saturday, the last day of the air show in Battle Creek, is Sunday. Somehow he has to get this man there and meet up with the doctor from Fort Myers, and the others, by tomorrow.

"It was a joke, Dad. I don't think it would be worth the time and effort," he replied cautiously.

"Joke or not, it's worth a try. We have to keep on trying," David replied.

"Dad, I just think it would be a waste of...."

"Sunni, can't you... can't you make some more calls to someone who might know something? Someone who could help? God, I am so tired..." said David as he slumped back into his chair.

Leaning forward with his arms crossed on the table, he put his head down.

"I suppose there might be some contact information on the internet. We could at least get some phone numbers for the town hall and schools," Sunni said as she looked at Rob questioningly. "I still don't think we can do anything until Monday."

Everyone sat quietly. Was this the end of a long journey and the attempt to heal this person's tortured soul? All the pushing, driving, striving to get to this point, only to reach a dead-end? The coincidences that had led them here were surely no coincidences at all, and yet, seemed to be for naught. Time is a cruel master, and time is running short. Spirits were low.

And then the phone rang.

"Omora residence, this is Sunni,"

"Yes, you called a little while ago; and left a message asking about some McDonalds who lived in the area? I can help you with that," a man's voice said.

David's head immediately came off the table.

"That is fantastic!" Sunni excitedly replied.

"I'm a realtor in Fowlerville and handled the sale of the McDonald property. In fact, Bob McDonald was my great-uncle who farmed the land for a long time. My name is Jack McDonald, by the way."

"So, the place, the home, still exists?" Sunni asked.

"Oh yes, yes. Not many original outbuildings left, but the house is still there. Most of the farmland has been sold off over the years, so not a real working farm anymore. I think there might be some horses out there now. It's on Pine Ridge Road."

"Anyone living in the house?" Sunni asked as she looked at David, who was now leaning intently towards the cell phone, still lying on the kitchen table.

"Yes, nice family by the name of Baker; they've lived there for several years. You should contact them."

"We're looking for relatives of the McDonald family from many years ago, as in the 1940s."

"That's why I called you back, Sunni. The Bakers are a direct relation to the Bob McDonald family. I'd think they would be able to answer at least some of your questions."

For a moment, there was silence as the three people stared at each other.

"Hello, is anyone there?" Jack McDonald asked.

"Yes, sorry. Do you have a phone number we could call?" Sunni queried.

"Yes, and I wish you luck finding what you're looking for."

Sunni wrote down the phone number and thanked Jack McDonald profusely.

"Well, I think this is it," said Rob.

"Make the call," David replied, with a tremble in his voice.

Sunni keyed in the number on her cell phone. It rang three times.

"Hello," a woman's pleasant voice answered.

"Is this the Baker residence?" Sunni asked as calmly as possible.

"Yes, this is Rose Baker. May I help you?"

"I hope so," began Sunni. "I'm calling from Fowlerville, and it's a long story, a really, long story, but I have a person here who is, or may be related to, someone we hope you might know or know of."

"Yes, go on," Rose Baker replied.

"We were told a girl by the name of Macy McDonald grew up where you live and was married during World War II to a man whose last name was Hamilton. They lived in Grand Rapids for a time. We also heard Macy moved back to Fowlerville after the war with her young daughter, Jenny. Would you perhaps have any information on them?" Sunni asked, nervously tapping her fingers on the table.

"Why yes, of course," replied Rose Baker, with a soft laugh. "Jenny is my mom."

David Hamilton's mind exploded in a myriad of memories and visions. Of the first time he met Macy, their first date, the first kiss. The day Jenny was born, and he cradled her in his arms. A vision of walking through the white fence gate towards the little yellow bungalow they called home and seeing his wife and daughter on the porch, waiting to greet him. A vision that only existed in his most desperate and wishful dreams.

He became aware of someone touching his hand. It was Sunni; her other hand covered the phone.

"David, what do you want to do?" she asked in a hushed tone.

"We need to go there," he said, almost breathlessly. "We need to go there, now."

"Ma'am," spoke Sunni into the phone. "Would you mind terribly if we came to your house to see you, and maybe talk some more, in person?"

"You mean, now?" Rose Baker asked.

"Yes, if that is at all possible, there are three of us. We won't take up too much of your time."

"Oh, I suppose that would be alright; we can give you the tour; there are a few horses here if you like horses. Don't believe I caught your name?"

"Sunni, Sunni Omora, I live in Fowlerville with my parents. My two friends who will be coming along are Rob and his, his father…. David; they've come from Florida."

"David was my grandfather's name; I never knew him," replied Rose Baker. "He was lost in World War II. I'll give you the address and directions to get here."

"Thank you so much, ma'am. You don't know how much this means to my friends," Sunni said as she looked at David.

"I have a granddaughter… I have a granddaughter," he repeated after Sunni ended the call. "Wait, we don't know if Jenny is still alive, and Macy… we didn't ask!"

"Well, we can't call her back again, now, but we'll find out soon enough, Dad, we'll find out soon enough," Rob said. "Let's take the Coupe."

Driving to the McDonald farm, a few miles out of Fowlerville, would take little less than ten minutes. To David Hamilton, it seemed an eternity. He had a granddaughter to meet and questions to be answered about the fate of his wife and daughter.

"So, what's our story?" Rob asked.

"How about you are distant relatives of the Hamilton family and have heard about David's family for years, but nobody ever knew what became of them," suggested Sunni.

"That'll work as well as anything, I guess," replied David.

"We'll just have to make it up as we go, but let's not get stupid," added Rob. "And Dad, you have to be careful not to let too much out of the bag. I can't imagine how emotional this is going to be for you."

As they turned onto Pine Ridge Road, David said, "Just look for the sign at the end of a long lane."

"You don't think it will still be there, do you?" Rob asked.

"In the dream… There was a sign on a country road; it was red with white letters. Couldn't make out the wording, then, but it was there, in the dream. You'll see it."

"But, after all these years?" the boy replied.

"Look for the sign," said David, confidently.

After a couple of miles, Rob slowed the car as he looked to the left.

"Well, I'll be damned."

It was aged, both the red and white paint were somewhat faded. It hung slightly crooked, on a post not far from a mailbox with the name *Baker,* on it. The words were still legible; *Welcome to Old McDonald's Farm.*

"Told you so," said David.

The Coupe slowly made its way up the near hundred yard long gravel lane, with green cornfields on either side. A large, two-story white farmhouse with red trim and shutters sat to the left at the top of the lane; on the front was a roofed porch extending the length of the house. In the back was a red barn, trimmed in white.

As they got closer, David noticed a rose garden just across from the house. It made him think back to the flower bed at their home in Grand Rapids.

A newer, brown, steel building sat to the left, at the end of the lane. Next to it, an old rusty windmill turned lazily in the breeze. Between the steel building and the barn were half a dozen horses, surrounded by a white, board corral.

"We never got here," David began. "People didn't travel much during the war, gas rationing and all. We were going to bring Jenny for a visit after I got back; Macy showed me pictures; I recognize the house and the barn, there were other buildings too, gone now. Was long ago, in your time, anyway."

"You need to keep calm, Dad, no matter what," said Rob, seriously. "We're gonna have to play this by ear, and ease into it, understand?"

A woman and young boy walked out onto the large porch as the car rolled to a stop on the driveway in front of the house. She was middle-aged, attractive, had short brunette hair, and wore white jeans with a sleeveless, red and white striped top. The boy appeared to be seven or eight; he was wearing shorts and a worn T-shirt, with the picture of a horse on the front. As they walked down the porch steps, a man stepped out of the house and followed them. He was tall and burly, with slightly graying hair. His faded jeans and denim work shirt spoke to country and farm living in the Midwest.

"You must be Sunni," the woman said as the three exited the car. "I'm Rose Baker."

She reached out to shake the girl's hand.

"These two handsome gentlemen are my husband Wayne and our grandson, Liam."

"My traveling companions are Rob Haynes and his dad, Derek... David," Sunni returned.

"Sounds like you're not sure," Rose said with a smile.

"Well, he'll answer to either," Sunni replied.

"If he answers at all," Rob added, with a nervous laugh.

David laughed too, but it was not without effort. He was fixated on his granddaughter, a woman who appeared to be Derek Haynes's age. There was so much he had to ask, so much he needed to know, but Rob was right. He can't just blurt out he was her grandfather and ask what happened to Macy and Jenny. They would likely call the cops. *Keep calm*, he thought; *you've been led here by forces you cannot understand. Just let it unfold.*

After all the proper handshaking was complete, Wayne spoke, as he strolled around the Ford,

"That's quite a fine old car you've got here, early forties?"

"1941, found it in Missouri some years ago, needed work, but we kept it as original as possible. My dad and I did the restoration ourselves," answered Rob.

"Nice. Holy cow, Florida plates!" Wayne said when he reached the back of the car. "You didn't drive this old-timer all the way up here from Florida, did you?"

"Yes sir, we did, and it's been quite an adventure, right Rob, Sunni?" David said as he looked at them.

"Certainly has, almost unbelievable," Rob said.

"I bet. Any problems along the way?" Wayne inquired.

"Not too much; we took mostly two-lane highways for a good part of the trip. It was like traveling cross-country used to be, back in the 1930s and 1940s, I'd imagine," added Rob.

"I bet that was fun, like traveling back in time," said Wayne.

"Something like that," replied David, straight-faced.

Sunni stood at the back of the car, staring. She opened her mouth to speak and then stopped.

"My daddy is gonna love this car!" Liam said excitedly.

"That would be our son, David, named after my grandfather,

the one I told you about on the phone, Sunni; he was a pilot in the war," said Rose. "But we've always called him Davy."

David had a strange tingling sensation and thought; *if she only knew.*

"He's over at the air show in Battle Creek now, helping out, works for a charter service at the airport, fly's corporate turbo-props, and jets, all over. He's quite the pilot; we always figured he got that from his great-grandpa."

"Keeping it in the family," commented David, nodding.

"We always spend at least one day at the air show, haven't made it there yet this year, but plan on going tomorrow morning," said Wayne. "Perhaps you folks would like to join us if you're not doing anything else, I mean. It is always a great show, and Davy would love to check out your vehicle."

"And they have a carnival with rides, and games, and every-thing!" Liam added.

"That would be a great idea, right, Dad?" Rob said, feeling some needed relief. "That's one of the reasons we came up here."

"Yes, it is," David replied. "Rob says there will be World War II fighter planes there?"

"Oh, absolutely," Wayne confirmed.

"Let's show 'em the horses! Liam said excitedly and took off, running towards the corral.

Sunni nudged Rob as they walked together, several feet behind the others.

"Am I losing my mind, or is that dent in the car fender, gone?" she whispered.

"It's gone," he said softly.

"How, when? This is getting way beyond strange, Rob."

The boy shrugged his shoulders, shook his head, and said,

"Just something else we'll probably never fully understand, but it happened at the garage in Eminence, that I'm sure of. Duke did say he thought it was the car's spiritual home and returned when it needed fixing. I'm just as surprised and confused as you are," he quietly replied.

"But, for it to have traveled, almost randomly, all those miles," Sunni spoke in a hushed tone. "And then just quit running, right in front of that garage, can't be a coincide...."

"Liam loves horses; we let him ride the more docile ones," said Rose as they neared the barn.

Rob leaned in closer to the girl and said, "There's nothing random about any of this."

"You raise horses?" Sunni asked as she looked away from Rob.

"Not raise them, exactly; these are all rescue horses. Our daughter-in-law, Corina, got us into it," Wayne responded. "She works at a veterinary clinic in town as an assistant, loves animals, big and small. Sometimes a horse will become available for adoption, but the clinic has no place to keep them until new homes can be found. So they're boarded here for a time."

"They're hardly any bother at all. Corina does most of the chores and any training," added Rose. "The vet clinic pays all the expenses along with any medical needs, and the boy likes helping his mom with their care."

Liam was already standing on the wooden fence boards, watching the horses milling about.

"They have names, and I know every one," he said with a wide grin.

"All of them arrived named, but sometimes we just change them as we get to know their personalities," said Wayne. "The horses don't seem to mind."

"This black one right here we call Midnight because, you know, he's really dark, like night. That one with the spots, I wanted to call Spot, but my grandpa said it sounded too much like a dog's name," Liam said with a laugh. "So we call him Charger; he's always prancing and running around. My mommy won't let me ride him. That one right there by the barn is Indian Joe because he's smaller than the rest and kinda looks like an Indian pony, don't you think? This one here, that's mostly white, is Buttercup and is really gentle. I get to ride her sometimes. She's kind of dirty now and needs a bath. Over there, next to Buttercup, we call him Rebel. My mommy says he's a trouble-maker and hard to train because he just won't listen! In the corner is the one we call Nelson; he's my favorite and the best horse ever!"

"So, what's your connection to the McDonald family?" Rose asked.

David took a deep breath. *Here we go.*

"Well, uh… the Haynes, we're relatives, way back, of the Hamiltons, and we had a family reunion, I guess it was last sum-mer, and David and his family were brought up. We all got curious about whatever happened to his wife and daughter after David… didn't come home from the war."

"That's still just so sad," said Rose, in a soft voice.

David paused for a moment.

"Yes, it is," he replied and took another deep breath. "Nobody knew anything except she went to some little town in Michigan called Fowlerville, where she was from. So when Rob and I planned on coming up to Michigan, for, you know, the air show and stuff, just thought we'd see what could be found out, then let the others know. That's it."

Rob gave him a quick, approving nod.

"That's such a nice thing to do, trying to find some closure for David's family, about his family," said Rose.

"Closure, yes closure," David said nervously.

"There never was any with my grandpa. No one ever heard a thing about what happened to him, at least anything we were ever informed of," Rose began. "But I think my mom would be the one to fill you in best concerning her and her mom, Macy."

"Jenny... Jenny is still, around?" David said as he heard the sound of a vehicle coming up the gravel lane.

"Oh yes, she lived here until we moved in seven years ago; that's her and our daughter-in-law Corina, who just drove in," returned Rose.

David suddenly felt weak. Leaning against the wooden fence and steadying himself with one hand, he said,

"She, she, must be much older now, in her seventies?"

"She turned seventy-six this year, I believe, didn't she, Rose?" Wayne asked his wife, who nodded.

"How about that," said David, his voice cracking slightly.

"I'm sure she'd be happy to answer any questions you might have for your family," said Rose, as she waved at the two women now getting out of the car.

Corina, the driver, wearing blue jeans and a black T-shirt bearing the name of a veterinary clinic, was young, in her early thirties, athletic with short blonde hair.

Jenny was about the same height as David and wearing white slacks and a light blue blouse. Wisps of gray highlighted her auburn hair. She wore her age well.

Though now a woman of advanced years, he could easily recognize many of Macy's features in her face and the way she moved. She was beautiful.

My daughter, my daughter, was all David could think. He struggled not to say it aloud as he saw this grown woman, who he never had a chance to watch mature into adulthood, walk up to the small group. His feelings and emotions were the same as when he first set eyes upon her, the day she was born.

Liam jumped off the fence and ran over to his mother.

"I told these people the names of all the horses, Mommy, and how I get to ride Buttercup sometimes."

"Did you now?" Corina said. "Well, wasn't that nice of you."

"Jenny, Corina, this is David, or Derek, as the case may be, Haynes, his son Rob, and their friend, Sunni. Sunni is from Fowlerville," said Rose. "Derek and Rob came all the way from Florida."

David managed to take the few steps towards them, then reached out to shake Corina's hand.

"We wondered whose old car that was. Nice to meet you," said Corina as she grasped his hand.

As David stepped towards Jenny, Rose spoke,

"The Haynes are relatives of your dad's family."

"Really!" Jenny responded, extending her hand.

"I'm David," he said and reached for it.

"That's very interesting; I'd like to hear about...."

As their hands came together, she felt a sudden jolt.

"Oh, oh my! What was that? Did you feel it, David?"

David did feel it, and for a moment, he saw her as a young child, again.

"Yes, I felt it too, Jenny."

"Wonder what would cause that, static electricity, maybe?" Jenny questioned.

"Too warm and humid for that," answered Wayne.

"What... what a strange feeling," Jenny said, with wonder in her voice. "For a moment, I... oh never mind."

At the same time, both realized their hands were still touching. Slowly, they slipped apart, and Jenny spoke,

"Have we met before? I feel as if I should know you."

There was no correct answer for him to return.

"I don't believe we have," was the reluctant reply.

The other answer could not be spoken, not now.

"Oh, okay then," said Jenny, but she wasn't so sure.

Wayne suggested they all retire to the porch and get out of the hot sun. As they settled into chairs and a porch swing, Rose went into the kitchen to get everyone cold drinks. Sunni joined her to help.

"So, you came all the way here from Florida; I'm so glad you could stop in and visit with us," Jenny said. "I don't really know much about my father's family. After mom and I moved here in 1946, there wasn't much contact, between the families, I mean."

"That's a shame; people should get to know their relatives," said David. "Jenny, do you remember your dad, at all?

"Unfortunately, no. I wasn't much more than a year old when the three of us were together for the last time."

There was sadness in her voice. Sadness for a man she had no memory of, except for old photographs and memories her mother shared over the years. It is possible to deeply miss someone, you never really knew.

I'm here now; everything is going to be all right, David thought. If only he could say it out loud. Being the father of a daughter was still fresh to him, and it ached immensely not being able to speak these words and comfort his child, even though she was now an adult. He wanted to reach out and touch her, to hug her.

"I'm sorry you both had to live with that loss," was all he could say.

As they conversed, David had to be cautious with his questions and remarks. Derek Haynes was born many years after the war ended. Too much familiarity with Jenny, and her mother's younger life, would not be in the realm of believability.

Rob was helpful, occasionally adding details that helped with the cover story. He was also happy for David, finally hearing some of the history of the little family he left behind. The necessity of the trip and all its travail seemed to be working; it was coming together. Now perhaps, soon, there would be an ending. David could be set free, and his father would return.

After finishing his drink, Wayne excused himself, saying he

and Liam had horses that needed tending. Sunni and Rose were talking on the far end of the porch.

Jenny remembered nothing of living in Grand Rapids but told of her childhood, a happy one, growing up in Fowlerville. Macy had rented a house in town until Jenny was in eighth grade, and then they moved into the farmhouse with her parents, who were getting older and needed help. Jenny spoke of other children she went to school with over the years, who also lost fathers and other family members during the war; it was sadly familiar in those times.

Within two years of graduating high school, she had married a man named Thomas Burden. They met while attending a local junior college. Rose was born in 1965.

"He was a good man, such a good man, and he did so love Rose," said Jenny and then fell silent.

David knew the quiet sound of sorrow and loss.

"Tom joined the Army in the spring of 1967, went to war, to Vietnam. He was killed in action, July 1968."

David lowered his head. Little of this war was known to him, but he did know war. Although choked with emotion, he said,

"I am so sorry, Jenny, so, so sorry. I didn't know."

"Well, how could you. At least we know what happened, and Tom was sent home to us. There was closure. He's buried in Greenwood Cemetery. Mom never had the luxury of knowing what happened to my dad, just a missing in action telegram from the government, and, well, she never gave up hope, never."

David could see Sunni and Rose had heard the last part of the conversation; Rose came over and sat down next to Jenny, putting an arm around her. She, too, had lost a father to war at a young age. Sunni stepped behind Rob.

"Well anyway," said Jenny as she sat up straight, trying to compose herself. "Some years later, I married again. He was a decent fellow, younger than me, and had moved from Illinois to work for

Chrysler in Detroit. He made a good living, and we had a good life until the layoffs in 2001. He lost his job, then seemed to lose interest in everything except drinking. He had a few part-time or short-lived jobs around here, but just never recovered."

"He was a good stepdad to me for as long as I lived here, a nice guy," Rose added.

"Then Wayne and I were married and started a family of our own, but it was easy to see mom was unhappy."

"So, what happened to him?" David asked.

"Both of us agreed it wasn't working. I was not going to put up with the drinking, and he couldn't, or wouldn't stop, so we divorced, and he left. No great drama, was just gone, haven't heard from him in years, but I do pray he's well and happy."

"That was also around the time my grandma, Macy, was requiring more care," began Rose. "She lived alone in town by then but was getting older, so it freed up time for mom to focus on her care. Wayne and I bought the farmstead here, so she could buy Macy's home and stay with her full-time. But she's gone now, in a much better place."

David felt a wave of emotion rise upon hearing these last few, yet definitive, words. He allowed them to sink in for a moment. There was a feeling of closure, at last, to the fate of his family. As promised, he had returned, at least his spirit, his soul, and was grateful to whatever power, to whatever entity, that provided this strange journey to meet his grown daughter and get to know her and learn of her life.

Jenny had become a fine woman, mother, and grandmother who had experienced her own tragedies and loss but remained strong. She began her own family, a family by all indications, had turned out well.

He had not been granted the opportunity to return home after the war ended, to enjoy and participate in his daughter's growth into womanhood. But for less than two years, he had missed her entire life. To grow old with Macy, the only woman he ever loved, had been denied. And now she's gone. The three of them uniting, in life, once more, was not to be.

Age, death, and destiny pay little heed to the passions and wishes of mortal men and women. The ending had come; there was a peaceful feeling. All that could be done has been done. He sensed his journey was nearing an end. With a calm voice, David quietly asked his daughter,

"Jenny, your mom, when did she, pass?"

"Pass?" Jenny returned.

"When did she... pass on?" David said.

It was painful to speak the words.

"Oh, she hasn't passed on," Rose answered.

"But, but, you said she was gone, and in a better place," David replied with great surprise.

"Well, she is. Macy's gone from her house and moved into a nursing home. A nice place just outside of town," Rose said.

David Hamilton's mouth dropped open.

"Mom began deteriorating rapidly a couple of years ago; I could no longer care for her myself, at home," said Jenny. "So we decided to place her where she would get the proper care; it's the best thing we could do. Why are you so surprised?"

"But, but she was born in May of 1923, which would make her... ninety-six years old!"

"Yes, ninety-six," replied Rose. "How do you know she was born in May of 1923?"

"How is she?" David asked, ignoring the question. "Is she doing well?"

"No, not very well," said Jenny, sadly. "My mom has been bed-ridden for several months; her eyesight was getting worse; we don't think she can see now at all, hardly opens her eyes and recently stopped talking. Though lately, she inexplicably smiles every once in a while for a short time. Heaven knows why. Almost every day, I go and talk to her, even read to her, with little response. So sad to watch, but she keeps hanging on, just won't let go."

"That's wonderful," said David, trying to keep down his excitement over this incredible revelation.

"Not so wonderful, David," replied Jenny, troubled by his response. "You couldn't know this, but she never married again. I kept trying to tell her it was okay. Okay, to start over, find someone to share her life with. But mom always said she and my father were still married. Married in the eyes of God and in her mind and heart, so that was not going to happen. 'Till death do us part,' she would tell me, 'those words were in our wedding vows. There has never been any official indication or confirmation that your father has died. For all I know, he's still out there somewhere, trying to get home.' Finally, I just quit bringing it up. She was content with the memories of my dad, and that was that."

David looked over at Rob and Sunni; their smiles spoke volumes. Rob nodded; he knew what had to happen next.

"I'm sorry Jenny, it's just that, that after all this time... it's simply amazing," said David. "Is there any way... we could go see her?"

"Oh, I don't know about that," Jenny began. "Pardon me for not understanding why you would want... she's doesn't seem to be aware anyone is even in the room, hasn't uttered a word, in a week. And you don't even know her."

"I think my dad might like a picture taken with you and your mom, Jenny," Rob chimed in calmly. "You know, to send out to other members of the family, letting them know what we found out about David's long-lost wife and daughter."

David reached over and grasped his daughter's hand. Jenny's eyes widened for a moment. After staring at him for several seconds, she said,

"We are going to visit mom. We all need to go see her, now."

"I'm not so sure about these people, the Haynes," Rose Baker said, with some trepidation. "They seem friendly enough, but doesn't it seem strange they showed up out of nowhere, asking questions about Macy and you, Mom? It appears to me that David may know more than he is letting on."

Along with Jenny, Corina, and Liam, she and Wayne were in their crew-cab pickup, leading the way to the nursing home, with David, Rob, and Sunni behind them in the Coupe.

"He did, at times, seem to know quite a bit, but that could also mean he is a legitimate relative of the Hamiltons and just curious," replied Wayne. "Makes sense to me; I don't think there's anything nefarious going on here."

"I really like their car, and so will my daddy," Liam spoke up. "Do you think they will go to the air show with us tomorrow, Grandpa, so my daddy can see it?"

"They might, Liam, I hope so. It sounds like David has an interest in World War II aviation. He'd enjoy it, I'm sure. We'll have to wait and see."

"I suppose they're probably alright. Sunni's nice, and she's local. Probably getting all worked up over nothing," said Rose. "Mom, you're awful quiet."

"I have a feeling that I know David from somewhere, in the past," Jenny answered quietly as she gazed out the window. Then thought, *but I can't tell you why, or who.*

"I think we're close, Rob. Close to the end of the road, well, my road anyway," David said as they followed the Baker's truck.

"What do you intend to do when you find the end of your road, David?" Sunni asked from the back seat.

The hauntingly familiar words reverberated through his mind. This question has been posed before, in half-dreams, by shadowy visions. How strange to hear them spoken now by a young girl who had intruded herself upon their journey only a few days earlier.

"I think it's already been determined, just by us being here," he replied.

Bringing the girl along on their trip was not something he approved of or ever warmed up to. Only days before, Japanese soldiers had blasted him out of the sky. Sunni was not to blame, of course, though people, who looked like her, were. And David Hamilton knew it was irrational to feel this way. Still, he did not have the luxury of time to forgive his enemies, nor necessarily anyone who reminded him of them. But he felt the end of the quest was near, and this Japanese girl, this Japanese-American girl, had been accommodating and kind to him since they met and had begun traveling together. Amends were in order.

"Sunni, I just want to say, well, I'm sorry if I've been rude and unkind to you these past several days. Please understand where I was coming from; you had nothing to do with what happened to me. It was war, and...."

"I understand," Sunni interrupted as she reached forward from the back seat and touched him.

These were welcoming words to the young girl. After Rob had recounted the bizarre details of what had transpired, she felt great compassion for this displaced soul. Although his demeanor and comments directed at her were often unpleasant and misguided, she could not imagine the loss and confusion he must be enduring. Sunni also felt David knew his possession of Derek Haynes's physical body was nearing an end, and it would be time to, move on.

"After being together with my wife and child, today, finally, I don't know what's going to happen next, my fate," said David. "But I have the feeling you'll get your dad back very soon, Rob. So, I just want to thank you both, now, while there's still time, while we're alone. I've not always been easy to be around, but none of this would've been possible without your help. You made it happen, and I'll be eternally grateful and happy to have spent this time together. Eternally, quite the word, considering the situation at hand, isn't it?"

"I hope you find the peace you're searching for," said Rob calmly, looking over at the man. He felt the weeklong emotional burden, perhaps, at last, beginning to lift.

A few minutes later, both vehicles pulled into the nursing home parking lot. Upon entering the facility, Jenny informed the woman in the reception area that they had come to see her mother, Macy Hamilton. The receptionist took a quick count and said they usually do not allow more than four people at a time to visit, and they were seven. Jenny explained it was a special occasion, as distant relatives from Florida had come to see her, and it was extremely important.

"Okay, I don't see what harm it would be, but just for a few minutes, now, folks," the receptionist admonished. "Enjoy your visit."

As they made their way down the long corridor to Macy's room, Rose reminded Liam that he needed to be very quiet. David was last to enter; it was dimly lit by one fixture at the head of a bed where Macy lay. Little more than a couch, chair, and dresser took up space in the small quarters. Mounted on a wall was a framed, antique needlepoint piece in the center of several photos, many of them from the little house in Grand Rapids. The words were prophetic.

> *"Those who love,*
> *And are loved,*
> *Shall always, from afar,*
> *Make their way home."*

Several more photographs of Jenny and Rose, as they grew from infants to adulthood, along with their family photos, were located on another wall. A nearby nightstand held a vase holding six red roses.

"It always smells so nice in here," Liam said quietly.

"We have flowers delivered at least three times a week or bring them in ourselves from the garden at the farm," Corina spoke softly. "Macy loves roses and had a rose garden wherever she lived. It always made her happy."

Jenny moved to the far side of the bed as David slowly approached the woman, lying motionless in the subdued light. Seventy-five years of her life have gone by since David had been with the woman, the girl he married, though only months in his memory. Yet, he knew it was Macy merely by being in her presence. Leaning over the bed and touching his wife's now silver hair, he took her hand in his as Jenny grasped the other.

In his mind, the elderly woman transformed into the twenty-one-year-old girl he'd left behind, with hair once again auburn, her skin young and smooth. He closed his eyes, gently kissed her lips, and for a brief moment, glimpsed the image of a girl slowly turning and glowing under the bright neon lights of a theater in 1942.

"Macy," spoke David.

"What is going on here?" an increasingly concerned Rose whispered to Rob.

"Wait," he quietly replied.

Macy's eyelids, gently, began to flutter and then open. She turned her head and smiled.

"David," her soft voice again, sounding like music to her husband.

"Jenny is here too; we all are," he responded.

"Jenny," said Macy, as she turned towards her daughter. "Your father has come back to us, as I knew he would."

"It's been a long time," replied Jenny, knowingly looking at David.

With the three of them together, again, Jenny confirmed the instant connection; the electric feeling and visions in her mind experienced earlier, had been real and true.

Rose grabbed Wayne's arm and said softly in a shaky voice,

"This can't be happening; he's only my age. It isn't possible."

"Mommy," Liam said as he took his mother's hand, "what's wrong with that light?"

"I promised to come back but was shot down. Things went black, black, and quiet. Then, somehow, woke up in the body of this boy's father," said David, looking at Rob. "But we're together again; that's what's important now."

"On your birthday, I felt something terrible happened," Macy said softly.

"It was my birthday," David replied, nodding.

"You came back to us; I always knew it would happen," said Macy as she squeezed his hand.

"I've traveled a long way to get here," replied David. "In miles and time."

"The three of you… I've watched your journey; it made me smile. Been saving my strength for this moment, and I have missed you so."

"We thought you were leaving us, Mom," said Jenny, as she began to tear up.

"No honey, but… there's so little time left…" she wearily replied.

"I'm sorry it's been so long," said David, gently stroking her hair.

"It was meant to be this way. You're so close now, David, so very close. But you must go on, you must."

Slowly, she reached up and put her hand on the side of his face, then, barely above a whisper, said,

"We will be together again, soon."

Macy's expression grew serious as she peered at the others, now gathered at the end of the bed, her tired eyes searching.

"The girl... the girl," she struggled to speak. "There's, danger...."

Sunni could feel Macy's eyes on her.

"The girl, who is with us?" David asked with concern.

Macy nodded weakly, then said,

"Blue door, David, blue, twenty-eight...."

It made no sense. The only thing any of it would seem related to was the color and number of his plane. He leaned in closer to be able to understand his wife's increasingly faint words.

"Save her. Save her, and be free," she said so weakly only David could hear; before closing her eyes.

Macy was quickly fading back into unconsciousness.

"I love you," she spoke in a whisper and was silent.

David and Jenny put their heads next to Macy's ears, each saying quietly, "I love you," then he softly kissed his wife on the forehead, barely feeling the squeeze of her hand.

A nurse entered and told everyone they needed to leave the room. David and Jenny lingered after the others exited and watched as Macy's vital signs were taken.

"There's no real change in her condition," the nurse said as she removed the stethoscope from her ears.

"She was talking just a short time ago," Jenny told the woman.

"Really?" the nurse said with surprise. "She hasn't spoken a word, or barely moved, in a week; was she able to communicate coherently?"

"Yes, but only briefly. She even opened her eyes and knew, well, appeared to recognize us," replied Jenny, as she looked at her father.

"Macy seemed to know we were coming; and told us she'd followed our trip here from Florida, and I believe her," David added.

"Sir, are you an immediate relation to Mrs. Hamilton?" the nurse asked. "If not, you'll have to leave."

David looked at Jenny, who replied,

"Yes, very much so. He stays."

"How long does she have?" asked David, somberly.

"Only God knows. Amazingly, she has hung on this long. Her body is slowly shutting down; there is no other easy way to say it," replied the nurse, lowering her voice. "It's simply amazing she was awake and talking; I am so happy for you all."

"Words needed to be said," Jenny replied to the woman. "Towards the end, she seemed to be saying things… things that made no sense, something about a door, and a number. Then closed her eyes, and went away again."

"The brain does some very odd things, especially in the elderly. It may be long forgotten memories and thoughts, momentarily coming back," the nurse began. "Random synapses firing off, and recalling experiences from years, decades ago. It's not uncommon, and unfortunately, so many things they speak of are just nonsensical to everyone but them. Again, I'm so glad for your family that you could talk with her; it may never happen again. It's best that you all go home now. We'll call if there's any change."

After joining the others, Rob suggested moving outside into the courtyard-like visiting area in the complex center.

"Rob, I need to be alone, now," said David, upon entering the enclosure that was lush with flowers, shrubbery, and trees. "I think it might, be time."

Rob nodded as he looked at the man, who was his father, in appearance only. After a week in his presence, this strange journey may be approaching a conclusion. The fate of David's soul, his consciousness, would never be known to Rob, but he was happy for him, to move on, if that was indeed at hand, complete his purpose for being here and be, finally, at rest.

And he was anxious to get his father back, to resume their normal lives, if anything could be normal, ever again. At last, perhaps, he would be able to call his mother and sister and tell them, it's over. Now, after Davids's much-desired reunion with his wife and daughter, there should be no immediate and desperate need to meet with Evelyn and the doctor. Finally, he should be set free from Derek's body.

Rob believed this was about to happen. He and David shook hands, then embraced.

"I think you owe these good people an explanation," said David.

"Where do I start?" Rob replied, with a catch in his throat.

"I'll leave that up to you, Son."

David looked at everyone, smiled, then turned and walked the path between flower gardens towards a small picnic table, several yards away, in the shade of a tree. The group quietly watched as he calmly took a seat.

"What in the world?" Rose said as she watched the strange man who had so suddenly entered and disrupted their lives, sitting alone at the picnic table.

"He's my father," said Jenny.

Rose began to speak; Jenny held up her hand.

"Not bodily, I know, but his soul, spirit, whatever, is my father. Mom knew it; that's why she awoke, and Macy knew he was coming. What happened in her room just now; was a miracle."

"My dad, Derek Haynes, went to downtown Fort Myers, Florida, last Saturday," Rob began, "and came back with a bump on the head and a different personality, a different entity, existing inside him. With what seemed to be several strange coincidences, a promise has been kept, and I don't believe in coincidences anymore."

He walked over to Sunni.

"Meeting this girl on the way here was no coincidence. She was meant to be with us, for reasons we may not even know yet," he said while looking at her.

For most of an hour, Rob told of the previous week's extraordinary events. No mention was made of the four people who would be waiting for them in Battle Creek. He hoped and prayed; there would be no need.

Everyone kept a watchful eye on David, still sitting quietly and often staring at the garden's scenery or looking up into the sky. Rob excused himself; there was a phone call to make.

"Mom, I think it might be over."

"What do you mean, over? Is your dad back?" she asked excitedly.

"Not yet, but might be close."

"For God's sake, tell me what's going on!"

"We found David's wife and daughter, and they're both still alive. The three of them were together again, as he so desperately needed, at a nursing home in Fowlerville. David is off by himself now; I think everything is going to be alright."

"Oh, Rob, we are so happy to hear you say this," Shelley said through tears.

"The doctor and Evelyn are here in Battle Creek with us now; what should I tell them?"

"Just wait, Mom, until we know for sure. They'll still need to talk with dad, at some point, to explain what's happened, or try too..."

David clasped his hands together on the table and slowly lowered his head down upon them.

"Hold on, Mom; something may be happening. I'll get back to you." Rob said and ended the call.

Everyone stood transfixed, wondering, and waiting.

"What's going to happen now?" Rose asked in a whisper.

Rob leaned over to her and quietly said,

"Hope I'm about to get my dad back."

Several more minutes went by with no change in David's position or demeanor.

"Is that man okay?" Liam asked. "He's not moving anymore."

"I don't know, Liam," replied Wayne. "Rob, you should go see if, you know, he's alright and if anything's changed."

Rob did not know what to expect, or what to do. He was hoping, even assuming, this man at the table would simply stand up; and be his father again.

"You need to go over there," echoed Sunni.

After watching for another minute, Rob slowly walked to the picnic table.

Standing next to the man, who was noticeably breathing, he said, tentatively,

"Dad? Dad?" Are you, okay?"

The man slowly raised his right hand in the air, made a fist, and then abruptly slammed it down on the table.

"Dammit, goddammit!" he swore and sat up, looking directly at Rob.

"Nothing is okay, and nothing has changed. Not a damn thing, I'm still in your world, and your dad isn't. What is going on? This should've been over. Macy said I had to go, and I'm ready!"

"David," said Rob, tiredly. "I'm so sorry."

"Nobody's sorrier about it than I am," replied David dejectedly. "If those damn Jap gunners hadn't blown me out of the sky, none of this would be happening!"

"I know; please keep your voice down," Rob said quietly.

"Don't care, I just don't care, Rob. If I hadn't turned back to help the Marines, those bastards wouldn't have killed me. That's what they did; killed me. But I had to go back, had to. I hate 'em, hate 'em all, God forgive me, I do," David said as he stood up and looked towards where Sunni was standing.

The boy was crushed. All the high hopes of this coming to an end, at this moment in time, had just evaporated. Nothing had changed. His father was still lost, and David Hamilton was more infuriated than ever at everything, and everyone, Japanese. He'd helped this man, put up with him for a week, apparently to no good end. Rob felt cheated and was not looking forward to making the next phone call to his mother, waiting in Battle Creek, for good news.

Waiting, in Battle Creek. He rolled the words over in his mind, and suddenly it became obvious. This was *not* going to end here; it was never going to end here. For whatever reason or cosmic plan unknown, it needs to end, in Battle Creek.

"You know how you always say; it's not done until it's done, Dad?"

David angrily replied, "Yeah, so much for that shit. This should be done, but it's not."

"Then apparently, we have to keep going. There has to be more to all this than we thought," Rob snapped back.

"Like what!" David said sharply.

"How do I know? How does anyone know! We need to move on, Dad, or do you want just to hang around this place, soaking up the scenery?"

"Move on? To where? The whole purpose of this was to get here, to find my wife and daughter and be with them again."

"Then I guess we're not done and need to head back."

"Back? Back where, Florida? There's nothing in Florida for me," said David, lowering his voice.

"Unless you have a better idea? We'll stop at Battle Creek, the air show. Maybe, somehow, that will help; who's to say?" Rob said calmly. "All of what we thought, hoped was going to happen by now, well, it hasn't. So here I stand, arguing with a stubborn twenty-two-year-old World War II fighter jock. And Macy said you had to go on, not go."

David was quiet.

"Fine, we'll go *on* to the damn air show. Maybe I can swipe a Corsair and fly off into the sunset," he said, glancing at Sunni.

"Not with my dad's body, you're not, dumb ass," replied Rob, as he gently poked David in the chest.

As they walked back to the group, Sunni knew by the scowl on David Hamilton's face, not to say a word; she had heard the entire conversation.

Everyone expressed their sympathy and disappointment that it had not gone as hoped or expected. It was agreed they would meet at the McDonald farm the following morning for the journey to Battle Creek.

It was a quiet return drive to Sunni's parent's house; the tension in the air was palpable. Upon arriving, the dreaded phone call to Shelley was placed. She and Karli were profoundly disappointed but agreed that at least one more act, clearly, needed to be played out, something that had been inevitable from the beginning.

Shelley reported the four of them had attended the air show that morning, and the doctor had found the optimal way, time, and place to meet face-to-face and with David. He was confident this strange experience, which had so disordered all their lives, could quickly be brought to a successful conclusion.

Sunni left the house, hoping to perhaps ease some of David's renewed wrath by driving to the downtown Fowlerville McDonald's and picking up carryout orders for all. And she needed the time alone.

"That's her; I'm almost positive it is!" Carlos said, pointing.

"Where?" RayBob asked, swiveling his head.

"Right there, that black Outlander," replied Carlos, pointing again. "Just turned into the McDonald's drive-through."

They had a good view while sitting on the terrace of a bar, just across the street.

"Yeah, I see her," chimed in Rico.

Since arriving in Fowlerville, their time had alternated between visiting various drinking establishments and driving by Sunni's parent's house, looking for signs of their target's presence. With no sure success in detecting anyone staying in the home, they were beginning to think she may not have returned to Fowlerville after all, which was disturbing. But the three of them were determined to wait until she showed up, as far too much was at stake. And now they had eyes on their prey.

Likely, the yellow tote bag was still in her possession. The fear she may begin piecing together their involvement with the latest missing girl in the Gainesville area, along with the others, was growing. Florida still has the death penalty, and this was a dark reality in all of their minds, but they did not speak of it. The evidence had to disappear, and so did Sunni Omora.

"I think you're right; what now?" RayBob asked.

"We're going to quickly finish our drinks, get in the car and tail her. If she drives to the house, then we'll know for sure," replied Carlos as he lifted his glass. "Then we wait."

After Sunni returned home, they sat quietly in the living room, eating their meal while watching an old movie, *The Walking Dead* with Boris Karloff, from 1936, on television.

"I pray to God tomorrow will be my last ride in that old car, anywhere," said David before heading to his room.

The other two had no response but held the same sentiment. All had retired by ten o'clock, but not before Rob called Rose and filled in the remainder of the details surrounding David's story. He explained what would happen at the air show, the why, and the how, and suggested she call her son Davy and brief him on the situation. She agreed, although stating he was not going to believe it.

⊨‹ ›⊨

SUNDAY

As the sun rose, summer humidity created a bright haziness. Across the dewy lawns of the neighborhood, faint shadows slowly became increasingly defined as the morning grew brighter. By the time Navy Blue No. 2 backed down the driveway and headed out of town, the dew was gone. Moments later and a block to the west, the engine of the silver Mercedes came to life. Slowly it began to pull away, keeping the blue Ford in view while maintaining a discrete distance.

As the car drove up the long dusty lane, Wayne was just finishing packing a cooler and lawn chairs into the crew-cab pickup.

"Looks like a fine day for an air show, or any other happening someone might have in mind," he said.

Rob nodded in agreement.

"Hope we get to watch the balloons fly; they're really pretty!" Liam said excitedly.

"If it's not too windy in the early evening, I'm sure we'll get to watch them take off," replied Corina. "Don't forget your hat, Liam. It's going to be very sunny today."

Wayne told Rob to follow along. Two-lane highways would be

taken cross-country to avoid driving to Lansing and getting on Interstate 69 to Battle Creek. It would be a more direct and shorter route. After reaching the end of the long driveway, they turned right and headed southward on the blacktop that was Pine Ridge Road. One hundred yards away to the north, the silver Mercedes pulled out onto the blacktop from behind an old, run-down barn.

"Don't get too close," said RayBob. "Might spook 'em."

"Yeah, but we don't have any idea where they're headed, so can't lose sight either," replied Carlos.

"Son-of-a-bitch, I'm tired," said Rico from the back seat as he rubbed his eyes.

"What's your problem? You could at least lie down back there," replied RayBob. "We had to spend the night watching the house and couldn't even wake your lazy ass up to help."

"Hey, I bet that's the old car we saw Friday, coming down the street when we first got here," Rico said, pointing at the blue Ford car in the distance. "Sure looks like it, and I waved at 'em. Too bad we didn't get a look at the license plate."

"That would've been nice, can't do anything about it now," said Carlos.

"I still say we should have gone in their last night and finished it," said RayBob, nervously. "How do we know we're even going to get a chance to get close to her?"

"Look, we don't know how many people were in there, or if they have a security system with cameras, maybe an alarm that goes right to the cops," stated Carlos. "Would have been too risky, and we are a long way from home, in unfamiliar territory, RayBob. No, we will try and snag her when she is by herself. Just have to find the right opportunity is all."

"I wonder if they're heading back to Florida," remarked Rico from the back seat.

"Don't know, maybe," replied Carlos.

"Maybe we should just head back to Florida, ourselves, and deal with her there, after she gets back," RayBob said as he stared straight ahead.

"You know we can't do that, man," said Carlos, looking over at him. "We need to get that bag and take care of little Miss Omora, quick. Then beat it out of this state."

"Why in the hell did you have to go and give her that nice little piece of evidence in the first place?" RayBob asked angrily. "That was crazy, just stupid crazy. Do you know how much risk you put us all in, do you? And probably made her more suspicious by trying so hard to get the damn thing back."

"I know, I know, I screwed up, get off my ass! That bag and her will both be disposed of, don't worry about it," Carlos snapped back. "First chance we get, and maybe we can have some fun with the girlie. It's not like she's going to be able to tell anyone afterward."

"Mom, when did you know, or suspect, he was your father?" Rose asked.

She had spoken little since the previous day's bizarre events, and they knew she was apprehensive about Macy's condition. Jenny was a strong woman, but all realized her emotions must surely be overwhelming and confusing.

Initially, Liam had many questions that had too many complicated answers for a young boy to try and comprehend. For the most part, they explained that David was his great-great-grandfather, who had been lost for a long time and finally found his way back home. It was the truth, after all. He seemed satisfied with that, then spoke mainly about the air show, the planes they would see, and how he wanted blue cotton candy at the carnival.

After a moment, Jenny said,

"Yesterday in the yard, when we met, and he touched my hand;

it was like… electricity. David was suddenly, and strangely, familiar, someone I should know. In that instant, my mind filled with pictures of my mom, dad, and me, when I was a baby. It was an eerie sensation. When he wanted to see Macy at the nursing home, I knew it was the right thing to do after touching my hand the second time. There was no doubt in my mind."

"I was amazed when you said we needed to go," Rose said. "Here's this total stranger wanting to go see an elderly woman he'd never met. To me, it was troubling and more than a little creepy."

"That's understandable, Rose, but I knew this man had a connection to us, almost right away, more than what they were saying. Never in a million years could I have imagined he would be my dad. Oh, I know he is not my father physically; he would be the same age as mom, but inside, he is. It's almost magic. From Rob's explanation last night, when he called, it's a strange turn of events how all this came about and just what it's going take to end it. When the three of us were touching yesterday, it was so evidently him. And even if I could not imagine how, I accepted it."

"Your daughter was freaking out in the nursing home when Macy opened her eyes and started talking," said Wayne.

"I wasn't surprised; I really wasn't," began Jenny. "It just seemed like the most natural thing. Almost like we had never been apart. As if more than seventy years just melted away. We were a family again, if only for a moment, and it was the most wonderful, complete feeling. There was an energy to it."

"I knew something strange was happening," said Rose. "And when the light began to grow brighter, I almost lost it."

"Light, what light?" Jenny asked.

"The only light that was on, at the head of the bed, Liam noticed it first. Soon as the three of you were together, it began to grow brighter and brighter. Don't tell me you didn't notice that, Mom."

"No, I didn't," said Jenny, with a smile. "Magic."

"What do you think Macy meant when she said danger?" Sunni asked Rob, looking over at him in the front seat.

David was asleep in the back, and these were some of the first words she had uttered since leaving the house.

"I don't know, towards the end, she was getting incoherent, probably meant nothing," the boy replied.

"I could feel her eyes on me, Rob. It was scary and uncomfortable."

"Can't imagine what danger that could be or how she'd know. Your psycho ex-boyfriend's back in Florida, more than a thousand miles away."

"I suppose you're right," Sunni said as she reached for sunglasses in her bag.

"This bag, I told you how weird he got over this, and wanted it back, then got mad when I wouldn't give it to him?"

"Yeah, I remember, but still, it's doubtful he'd drive all the way up here just to get some tote bag, right? It makes no sense. But really, you need to stay away from him when you get back," replied Rob, seriously.

"All that weirdness started after seeing the news story about the missing girl from Archer, who was holding a bag like this one."

Sunni suddenly felt a chill ripple through her body.

"You don't... you don't think he had something to do with that..." Rob asked nervously.

"I don't know, but just now had a chill thinking about it. I got a very, very bad feeling after what Macy said. Like it was some sort of warning. And those stains on the bag, Rob, I'm scared!"

Rob knew she was genuinely upset. Even though they'd been together only a few days, he had come to know her well.

"When you get a chance Sunni, you need to call the Gainesville police and talk to them about this. Likely nothing will come of it, but why take the risk? I'm sure they're checking out all kinds of tips and leads. Do it anonymously, say you'll send them the bag if they want to check it out; Carlos never has to know. You'll have the whole summer here, away from him. They should be able to check him out and determine that he was not involved, or...."

"It's the *or* that's scaring me to death," Sunni interrupted, trying to keep her voice down.

"To think of what he might have done... I can't stop shaking."

Rob reached over, put his arm around Sunni, and pulled her close.

"Don't worry; you're perfectly safe now. Here, and now."

The two lanes of cars, leading into the Battle Creek Air Show and Balloon Festival parking area, progressed slowly. After more than half an hour of stop-and-go traffic, the old car and crew-cab pickup truck were directed to parking spots in a grassy field. Rob sent a quick text to Shelley, telling her of their arrival.

Several parking spaces down the same row, a silver Mercedes came to an abrupt stop. Three men exited the vehicle and hurriedly began making their way towards the airshow entrance.

It was warm, in the low eighty's with light winds. The sun had burned its way through the haze, leaving a brilliant blue sky with few clouds. Corina applied sunscreen to a squirming Liam's face and arms while suggesting the others protect themselves, similarly, as it would be a long day in the hot sun. Soon, they all began a leisurely walk down the long row of cars, with David and Jenny walking together side by side, behind the others.

Sunni abruptly stopped and stared at the back of a parked car.

"Rob, that silver Mercedes, looks just like Carlos's car," she said and grabbed his arm.

"I bet there›s a lot of silver Mercedes here today; they're not that uncommon," replied Rob calmly.

Pointing, she said, "Look."

"Florida plates," replied Rob, with a frown. "Do you remember anything about his plates?"

"No, I never paid any attention," she replied nervously. "On the bottom, it says Alachua County."

"That's where Gainesville's at," Rob said as he stared at the car.

"Lots of people come from all over for this show. Is there a problem?" Wayne asked.

"What's going on?" David said as he and Jenny walked up.

"You remember when Sunni told us about her crazy ex-boyfriend in Florida? This looks like his car; it has Florida plates and from the right county," answered Rob.

David looked at Sunni questioningly and said,

"Do you seriously believe he'd follow you, all this way? Why would he do that?"

"There's a lot you don't know," replied Rob. "The guy might be involved in something bad, not saying he is, but, well, he might."

"So, what does she have to do with it?" David bluntly asked.

"You can see the girl is scared," Jenny spoke up, touching his arm.

"There might be a lot more to it; that's all I'm trying to say," said Rob.

David and Jenny walked off towards the air show entrance while the others lingered near the Mercedes.

"Why were you so short with Sunni back there?" Jenny asked her father.

"You wouldn't understand, Jenny," he answered quickly.

"Try me; I'd believe almost anything at this point."

"I look at her, and I see the people who shot me down; they stole my life, our lives, together. Yeah, it was wartime, but that war was little more than a week ago for me. Why she's along on this trip, I'll never know. I wish it would have stayed just Rob and me."

"It's not Sunni's fault, Dad, or her family. They had nothing to do with it. You're not being fair," Jenny calmly replied.

David stopped, turned, and looked at his daughter.

"Fair? Not fair is they stopped me from coming home to you and your mom. I missed over 70 years of life with you both because of people like that!" said David loudly, pointing back towards Sunni. "Just allow me some contempt for those who destroyed our family."

Sunni walked quickly towards David, closely followed by Rob.

"People like that, huh? People like me!" she shouted and stepped closer to David.

As he began to walk away, Sunni grabbed his arm and turned him around.

"I don't have to apologize to you or anyone for who and what I am. Or where my family and ancestors came from, or what I look like! Nobody around here who looks like me, including me, is responsible for what happened to you in the war, mister. I'm getting sick and tired of you trying to guilt me by association for something that happened more than forty years before I was even born!"

David stared at the angry young girl with no emotion.

"I've been nothing but good to you these past several days, and believe me, a lot of the time, it didn't come easy."

"Whatever," said David, with a shrug of his shoulders, then turned and walked away, alone.

Sunni lunged at him but was quickly restrained by Rob.

"I am so sorry he is treating you like this, Sunni," said Jenny as she put her arm around the young girl, who by now was shaking with anger. "He's just so bitter, and I don't know what it's going take for him to let it go."

"I don't even care anymore; hopefully, he'll be gone soon. Gone, gone, gone forever!" Sunni said sharply.

"Yes, gone again, forever," Jenny softly replied.

"Oh Jenny, I'm so sorry," said Sunni quietly, quickly adding, "I wasn't thinking."

"I understand, really I do," said Jenny somberly, then turned and walked off to join David.

The group got in line at two different ticket booths, Sunni and David keeping a guarded distance between them. Once inside the grounds, Liam asked where his dad was. Corina answered they would be meeting up with him later. He then became interested in the carnival attractions and wanted to go on the rides. Corina and Rose looked at Rob, who nodded. Nothing was going to occur until later in the day; carnival fun could be afforded for Liam, for a time, along with the boy and the others watching the various aircraft flyovers and performances. While also providing more precious time for David to spend with Jenny and the rest of his family.

Few planes were in the air, as the airport grounds had just opened to the public, so for the moment, it was more of a carnival atmosphere than an airshow. There had been no mention of the silver Mercedes in the parking lot since the blowup between David and Sunni. Most felt, hoped, it was likely nothing more than a coincidence and no need to upset Sunni anymore than she already was, although what lay ahead, for David, was on everyone's minds.

"Daddy!" Liam yelled out when he saw his father approaching as they strolled the carnival midway. He ran towards him and jumped into his arms.

"Daddy, these are our new friends from Florida; they have a cool old car!"

"So I've heard. Hi, I'm Davy Baker," he said, reaching out to shake Rob, Sunni, and finally David's hand, after placing the boy on the ground. He lingered an extra moment with David.

"So very glad to meet you, Mr. Haynes."

"Please, call me, David."

He became lost in the moment upon meeting his great-grand-son, who had been named after him, and a fellow pilot.

"My daddy's a pilot, and he flies all over. Let's go see the car, let's go see the car, you'll really like it, Daddy!"

"Not right now, Liam; we should get something to eat, then maybe put you on some of these rides," replied Davy.

"Yay! I want a corn dog. Can I have a corn dog, Mommy? Can I go on some rides now?"

"Maybe a couple of small rides, and I don't want you eating too much and getting sick," cautioned Corina.

The group walked the carnival grounds for a time, allowing the boy to enjoy a few of the many attractions.

"Your mom and I took you to a fair once when you were little, Jenny. You were in a stroller and too young to remember, certainly too young to go on any rides," said David, as he took his daughter's hand.

"The smell, this carnival food smell, I'm glad that hasn't changed. Hot dogs, popcorn, cotton candy, all the different fun foods, the sights, the sounds, wish I could have been around when you were growing up, watched you have fun on the rides, like Liam is now," David said, with melancholy in his voice.

Jenny put her arm around David's waist.

"It's good we're together now, and look at all of your family. Multiple generations, here for you and with you. Just let go of the past and enjoy these moments, please?"

"Okay," said David, trying to smile. "We never know how long those moments will last, do we."

"No, we don't," replied Jenny. But in truth, she did.

An empty table, spacious enough to accommodate them all, was found in a large tent near various food stands, and soon they were all enjoying the carnival food experience. They dined on pork chop sandwiches, tacos, burgers, French fries, and onion rings, along with two corndogs for Liam, who begged copiously for a third, albeit unsuccessfully. Lemon shakeups were the preferred drink.

"I suppose by now, you know the entire sordid story on how I got here, in another man's body, and that you're my great-grandson," David said to Davy as they sat across the table from one another.

"My mom filled me in as best she could on the phone. To tell you the truth, I don't know what to believe. How could such a thing happen?" returned Davy, even though knowing more than he was letting on.

"Wish I knew, Davy. What I can tell you is, more than a week ago, a Jap anti-aircraft battery destroyed my plane, and I was going to die. Yet somehow found myself in Florida, seventy-four years later wearing Derek Haynes's fifty-two-year-old body, on both our birthdays."

"Do you suppose the same birthdays had anything to do with this?" Davy asked.

"Haven't a clue what any connection between us might be," responded David.

"About that," said Rob, as he slid over next to David to join the conversation. "When we stopped in Kentucky to get the Coupe fixed after it quit running? And what a coincidence that the old gentleman, Duke, and his fellow Marine buddy had previously owned that very car?"

"Helluva coincidence, what's your point?" David asked with a touch of impatience.

"Well, maybe not so much of a coincidence. When I went into the office to pay Mike, Duke showed me a picture of his buddy and him in front of the Coupe, his buddy Frank. Frank Haynes."

"Just what are you trying to tell me?" said David, turning to stare directly at the boy.

"My dad Derek has the same picture, the exact same one. I

never knew who the shorter man in it was, but the tall guy is Frank Haynes, my grandfather, from Missouri."

"Oh, wow, my mom didn't tell me this part of the story," said Davy.

"She didn't know," answered Rob.

David sat quietly for a moment, staring out into the crowd of people, strolling by in the sunlight, then slowly said,

"So you're saying there is a connection, between your family and me, after all? Your grandfather, was a Marine on Okinawa, the same time I was there?"

"That's right, and he owned that car sitting out in the parking lot, the same Ford my dad and I restored. He had a son, born many years later on the same date you and your plane were lost, your birthday. My dad, Derek," replied Rob. "That goes well beyond coincidence."

"But what does it all mean?" David asked, with shortness in his voice.

"Everything happens for a reason, David. For whatever reason, you were meant to be with the family you left behind, now, at this point in time."

"Why didn't you tell me all this before?"

"I didn't want to make things any more confusing than they already were. But you have to believe all of this was, and is, for a purpose. It has to be."

"Now what? What more purpose could there be?" David said sharply. "I see no reason for me to still be here. You need your dad back, and I need to, to move on. And you keep reminding me it's not done until it's done. Well, I fail to see how it could be any more damn done, than it already is, right now."

"We've come this far by extraordinary, unexplainable means; none of this was by accident," replied Rob. "But I'm sure it will work out for everyone."

"Oh yeah? You know something I don't?" David asked suspiciously.

"Let's go ride on the Ferris wheel, Daddy!" Liam said, almost yelling as he ran up and grabbed his father's arm.

"I suppose we better get this boy in the air," Davy said while getting up from the table.

"I want some cotton candy, too," said Liam as he pulled Davy out of the tent.

"We'll talk more, later," said Rob to David, who glared back at him.

A steady stream of planes was now airborne over the runways and surrounding area; the sound was, at times, deafening yet thrilling. It also made any conversation challenging. While moving through the carnival crowd towards the Ferris wheel a short distance away, they watched and enjoyed the various aircraft in flight.

"Can we all go on the Ferris wheel?" Liam asked his mom.

"Oh, I don't think everybody wants to go; how about grandma Rose and I ride with you," Corina replied.

"Can we get cotton candy after, please?"

"Sure, you've been good; what color do you want?" Rose asked as they stepped in line for the ride.

"Blue, I want blue; it's the best!"

"I'll go get it for him," volunteered Sunni. "Should have it here for you when the ride is over, Liam."

Sunni and Rob spotted a booth on the edge of the carnival grounds, with multiple bags of colorful cotton candy displayed.

"I'll come with you," offered Rob.

"No, you stay here with everyone; I won't be long," she replied, then turned and walked towards the booth.

With every turn of the Ferris wheel, Liam waved at the others on the ground, sometimes shouting, "Look at me, I'm flying!" Everyone smiled and waved back.

"What a wonderful day; I wish somehow mom could be here," said Jenny to David.

"I feel she's been watching over us all ever since we left Florida," David said.

"I think you're right," she replied, putting her arm around him.

After several minutes the Ferris wheel began to unload its passengers. Liam ran up to his dad.

"Where's my blue cotton candy?"

"Sunni went to get it, didn't she, Rob?" Wayne asked, shouting over the sound of a passing formation of aircraft.

"She did, and should've been back by now," Rob shouted back as he looked at the cotton candy booth, a hundred feet away, and then began walking towards it, with the others following.

Only two people were standing in line. A feeling of dread washed over him as he immediately realized Sunni was not one of them, and was nowhere in sight. After excusing himself, he stepped in front of the two waiting customers.

"I'm sorry, but was there a girl here within the last few minutes, carrying a yellow tote bag with a parrot on it? She would've been buying blue cotton candy," he said to the startled girl behind the counter.

"Oh yes, maybe, ten minutes ago? I remember the bag, told her it was cool."

"Did you see where she went?" Rob asked nervously.

"After I handed her the cotton candy, she went off with three guys who had been standing some ways behind her. She seemed sort of surprised to see them when they walked up."

"Dammit! Which way?"

"They all walked off to the right, towards those storage buildings. Is there anything wrong? Did she get lost or something?"

"We're not sure; thanks for your help," Rob replied quickly, stepped aside, then turned towards the others.

"It has to be Carlos, the ex-boyfriend from Gainesville, and he must've brought two others with him. That *was* his car in the parking lot."

"Is something wrong with Sunni? Did she get my cotton candy?" Liam asked with a frown.

"It's alright, honey," said Corina as she knelt in front of the boy. "I think, maybe, she got a little lost, so we're going to try and find her." Liam nodded his head as he looked down at the ground.

Davy was already on his handheld radio, alerting security.

"We have to find her; she's in trouble," said Rob, quietly enough so Liam could not hear.

"These guys, they might be… we need to split up and start looking."

"Security people are on their way," Davy cut in. "The Battle Creek police have also been notified. The first thing we should check is all those storage sheds."

"I say wait for the cops," David said offhandedly. "We don't know for sure what's happened; it might be nothing but a wild goose chase."

"There's no time for that," Rob said loudly. "We need to start looking, now. I'm sure they didn't come all this way from Florida, just to say 'hi' too Sunni."

"And you expect *me* to help look for her?" David asked sarcastically.

"Yes, I do!" Rob yelled over the din of aircraft passing overhead. "You still have that cell phone?"

"Yeah, why?" replied David, pulling it out of his shirt pocket.

Rob quickly snatched it out of his hand and turned it on.

"Look, if you see, find, or hear anything, anything at all you think is suspicious, press this phone button, here, got it? Then you press my name; it will call me. Let us know where you are, don't try and be a hero."

"You don't have to worry about that; it never works out," David said quietly as a World War II bomber droned overhead.

"What?" Rob shouted.

"I got it. I got it!" David yelled back angrily.

"There are several rows of storage sheds," said Davy, addressing all. "Some sheds should be unlocked, and some won't. They're all numbered, so if anyone finds anything, call and give us the number, we'll find you. Rob, you, me, Wayne, and David should split up and start searching up and down the rows, check all the doors. The others should stay here with Liam and wait for security and the police."

Jenny stepped over to David.

"Please be careful… you'll find her. I know you will."

He was more annoyed with these turn of events than concerned. Annoyed that Sunni had likely just gotten lost and disrupted everyone's day. Once again, he wished she had never come along on this trip. It was supposed to be about finding and reconnecting, with his family, not being constantly reminded of the people responsible for losing them. He had little interest or motivation in this escapade.

The four men went off together and soon split up to walk the aisles between the gray-colored steel storage sheds. David doubted Sunni was even in the area they would be searching; likely, she would quickly be discovered, wandering about the carnival at this very moment, looking for them.

"What a waste of time," he said aloud to himself.

Thoughts of doing a quick, cursory walk-through of the area entered his mind. But decided to check all doors and look inside the sheds that were not padlocked to truthfully be able to tell the others they had been searched. All had white fiberglass, overhead garage-type doors, and a single blue entry door. He found few without padlocks, and for those, he would open the entry door all the way to let in as much light as possible, then peer inside. Many were empty; others had ordinary, or unrecognizable items, with no one inside and nothing suspicious.

Scattered on the aisles fronting the sheds were a few leaves, the occasional discarded plastic cup, or aluminum can. Halfway down the aisle, he came upon something different. Lying on the hot asphalt, he saw a small, white, cone-shaped piece of paper surrounded by a sticky-looking blue stain. Kneeling for a closer look, it obviously was the remnants of melted, blue cotton candy.

"Then she must've gone this way," he said quietly to himself. "And what would she be doing here?" He thought about the cell phone. *I should probably call Rob, let him check it out.* While reaching to pull the phone from his shirt pocket, he heard an approaching rumble, and then a roar begin to echo off the storage buildings. Suddenly, a blue Corsair making a low pass appeared directly and noisily overhead.

After watching for a moment then lowering his gaze straight down from the aircraft, David's eyes quickly fixed upon an entry door to one of the storage sheds. It was blue, like all the others, much like the plane now climbing magnificently into the clear sky. On the door in chipped, faded, and barely readable white paint was a number.

Twenty-eight.

It all came back to him like a shot. Yesterday, at the nursing home, Macy said she had been watching their travels for the past week, and told him the girl, was in danger.

"Blue door, David, blue twenty-eight, save her. Save her, and be free…"

This has to be what she meant. There couldn't be any other explanation, he quickly thought. No time to call Rob; he needed to get into that shed. Running over to the door, he saw it was slightly ajar and tried to open it further, but it would not budge.

Putting an ear to the open gap, he could hear voices; sharp, angry voices and muffled cries. With a plane passing loudly overhead, covering the sound, he used his shoulder and all of his weight to try and force the entry door open, with no success. Moving, in desperation, to the overhead garage door, he twisted the handle and pulled up hard and fast. Much to his surprise, it noisily flew open.

As the plane rapidly sped away, it became quieter in the small, stuffy building. There was the smell of lumber and old tires. As he peered into the semi-darkness, a threatening voice spoke,

"This has nothing to do with you, old man. Best be getting the hell out of here, while you still can."

David sensed the overpowering presence of evil.

"Oh, I think it does," he replied, with anger beginning to burn inside him.

A tall, younger man emerged menacingly from the darkened, left rear corner, holding something in his right hand. Slowly, he began moving towards David.

"I'm guessing you're that piece of garbage, Carlos, I've heard about. You have a young girl back there, and she had better not be hurt," said David in a low, threatening voice.

"Maybe, as I said, none of your business. What's it to ya, and how do you know my name?" Carlos responded coldly and stopped walking.

Inside Derek Haynes's body, David Hamilton's rage continued to grow. Sunni was in desperate trouble; she needed help. For a moment, he was back in the Corsair, pulling the trigger on a machine gun nest. This, too, is personal.

"She's with me," David growled, barely moving his teeth apart to form the words, then shouted, "Sunni!"

There was a commotion in the darkened corner. A desperate, pleading voice screamed out,

"David!"

Taking quick strides, Carlos moved towards him. David saw the flash of a knife blade; he quickly pulled the cell phone out of his shirt pocket and hurled it at the approaching man's face, yelling, "You son-of-a-bitch!"

Carlos was stunned as the phone ricocheted off his forehead, leaving a gash; he stopped. David lowered his shoulder and charged headlong into the man's midsection, knocking him forcefully backward into a stack of old tires, the knife spilling from his hand. He then turned left, grabbed the nearest tire, and moved quickly to the corner. Rico rose from the blackness and stepped towards the onrushing man as RayBob remained crouched, trying to hold down the struggling Sunni.

When one step away, David used both hands to swing the tire with all his strength, connecting solidly with Rico's head, slamming him backward into a wall. He slumped to the floor, unconscious. As RayBob began to stand, Sunni, reached up and scratched him, viciously, across the side of his face. Yelling out in pain, he raised his hand and bent down to strike the girl.

Taking a step closer, and with his right foot, David kicked RayBob solidly in the chin, the impact, momentarily, straightening the man. Grabbing him by the shirt, David lifted and slammed the dazed attacker into the steel wall. After several quick and brutal blows to his already bloodied face, RayBob collapsed to the floor on top of Rico and lay motionless.

All was quiet but for David's strained, heavy breathing and Sunni's muted crying. As he bent over to gently help her stand, she screamed,

"Look out!"

Quickly rising, he turned as Carlos, blood streaming down his face, charged at him, knife in hand, lunged and swung the blade, slashing deep into David's left forearm. Backpedaling and trying to keep his balance, he stumbled and fell backward into a stack of lumber. Feeling the shape of a loose 2 x 4 under his right hand, he quickly pulled a three-foot long board from the pile while jumping to his feet as Carlos advanced his attack, with David swinging the board to keep the enraged man at bay.

Sunni began crying and screaming. She could not make a break for the door; two angry men, out for each other's blood, blocked her way.

For more than a minute, they engaged in the deadly duel, a slashing movement or thrust of the knife, then a quick parry and swing of the board. Both adversaries were desperately shuffling around the small, open area, each looking for an advantage. Blood from the cut on his forearm made it increasingly difficult for David to keep a grip on the board. Exhaustion was setting in. He could not withstand this hand-to-hand combat for much longer.

Suddenly, Carlos stopped. Moving the knife from right hand to left, he reached behind his back. Almost out of breath, he spoke,

"As much as I'd like, to cut you wide open, old man, I gotta get outta here."

Pulling the black semi-auto pistol from his waistband, he pointed it at David.

Hoarsely, he said, "First you, then the girl."

"Dad!" a voice shouted out.

David's quick glance to the right revealed Rob standing in the overhead garage doorway. Carlos took a longer look then began turning the weapon towards the boy. David swiftly stepped forward while raising the 2 x 4 above his head. He brought it crashing down on Carlos's heavily, tattooed arm. An audible crack was heard as the gun went flying from his hand; he screamed in pain. David turned, slowly drew back the board, and swung it fiercely into the side of the man's head. Carlos immediately dropped heavily to the floor.

"Dad, are you hurt? Where's Sunni! I heard screaming!" Rob shouted as he approached.

Sunni slowly limped out of the darkness, her clothes torn nearly off, an eye blackened, a trickle of blood dripped from her lower lip. Rob rushed over and wrapped his arms around her as she began to collapse. Through her weeping and with a weak voice, she tried to speak,

"Carlos, he said… he said I was going to die, like the others…. he saved me, saved me. David saved me."

Wayne soon ran up to the storage shed, followed by Davy, who immediately called for police and an ambulance. As David approached Sunni, she wrapped her arms tightly around him and sobbed.

David Hamilton gently placed his arms around the young, terrified girl who was shaking uncontrollably. His wife's words again echoed in his mind. *Save her, save her, and be free…."*

Macy foresaw this, and never more would he desire to know why or how. Peacefulness swept over him, removing the weight from his tortured soul. It cleansed him, cleansed him of hate.

Soon, the women and Liam arrived. Corina and Rose took Sunni outside and tried to comfort her while waiting for the ambulance.

"David, your arm. You're hurt," said Wayne.

"You need to sit down, Dad. You're bleeding bad," added Rob.

"Will need stitches for sure, and gonna leave a scar," David said, "Tell your dad I'm sorry about his arm… when you see him."

"Will do," replied Rob, as he put a hand on the man's shoulder and nodded.

"Been a while since you called me Dad, Rob."

"Well, you look just like him," said Rob, with a grin.

"That bad feeling I had, the darkness behind us? It wasn't

Sunni; it was this," said David, waving his hand towards the three men sprawled about the shed. "It was them all along."

Rob bent over and picked up something off the floor, "Is this your cell phone?"

"Yeah, I finally found a good use for the damn thing."

They both walked outside, leaving Wayne with the 2x4 and Carlos' gun, to watch over the three hapless and bloody fools from Florida. Two security personnel showed up on a golf cart and produced a first aid kit along with bottles of water. David, exhaustedly, slumped down against the shed wall, not far from Sunni.

"Mommy, I'm scared. Did someone hurt Sunni? Liam asked, with tears in his eyes.

"She got hurt, dear, but don't you worry, everything is going to be all right," replied Corina. "Why don't you go over there and sit in that nice golf cart for now, okay?"

Jenny grabbed several bottles of water and distributed them among the men. David eagerly downed a bottle and politely asked for another. She then took charge of the first aid kit and immediately wrapped her father's injured forearm with gauze and medical tape as best she could to help slow the bleeding. Corina and Rose washed Sunni's face and arms; the young girl was still trembling. Rob knelt in front of her.

"After I got Liam's cotton candy, they came up from behind, then walked me off towards these buildings. Carlos warned me not to make any noise or try and get away, or he'd hurt all of you, starting with the boy. There was nothing I could do…," she said, her voice rising…."

"It's alright, everything is going to be okay," Rob replied as he held her hand. "They won't be hurting anyone anymore."

Wayne stepped out of the shed, carrying the yellow tote bag, setting it down next to Sunni.

"Found this inside."

The frightened young girl visibly recoiled.

"I don't want it," she said softly, putting her head down. "Dump everything out and throw it away. It belonged to a girl named Moni. They killed her, bragged she wasn't the only one, called them their girlies. Carlos counted the skull tattoos on his arm, six, then pointed to a space he said was reserved for me."

Wrapping both arms around her legs and head on her knees, she slowly rocked back and forth. Rob picked up the bag and gently poured its contents out onto the blacktop.

"We'll get you something else, Sunni," he said as he handed it back to Wayne. "Better hang on to this one, though. It's evidence."

"Carlos and those other two came here to dispose of that bag, and me," continued Sunni, without looking up. "That's the word they used, dispose."

"Do you know what happened to the girl?" Wayne asked while keeping a wary eye on the three men inside the shed.

"Outside of Archer, they dumped her body in some water, where there were gators, that's what they told me, then laughed, made jokes. Carlos said they'd just leave me here, in this shed, after, after they were done...."

"Well, that ain't gonna happen," said David in a raspy voice before taking another long drink of water.

Sunni slowly reached over and grabbed David's hand.

"Thank you," she said in a whisper.

Moving closer, he put his arm around her shoulders.

Rob's phone rang. In the distance, mingled with the noise of aircraft overhead, came the sound of emergency vehicle sirens. Seeing the ID on his phone, he stepped away from the others.

"Karli, we've had some trouble."

"What, is everything still on?" she asked nervously.

"Yes, I believe so, but David... Dad and Sunni need to go to the hospital, hopefully not for long, nothing life-threatening, just...."

"Oh my God!"

"There were some bad people who followed us here from Florida. There was a fight, Dad got hurt, he'll need some stitches, but we should be able to meet up with you all later. I will make this work."

"Oh no… what happened, Rob?"

"These guys, these three bad guys snatched Sunni away from us at the carnival. They hurt her," Rob said emotionally, his voice cracking.

"I'm so sorry…."

"She was so scared, Karli, one of the guys was her ex-boyfriend, and I, I can't say for sure, but they may be responsible for the disappearances of those girls back home."

"Are you serious?"

"As we were walking in from the parking lot, Sunni saw a car, a silver Mercedes, like her boyfriend has, with Florida plates. It scared her. She thought it might be her boyfriend's, who's really crazy, and…."

"Rob, have you seen these guys? Do you know what they look like?" Karli interrupted with a trembling voice.

"Yes, they're here now, lying on the floor of a storage shed where Dad, well, David, just about half killed 'em. They're going to be arrested; we can hear the sirens. Why did you ask me that, Karli?"

"Rob, can you describe them to me?"

"I guess so; why?"

"Just tell me," she replied, barely above a whisper.

"Two of the guys are tall; one has long, dark hair, the other shorter, blonde hair. The third one has a shaved head, not as tall, and stocky."

There was silence for several seconds.

"The shorter one, does he, does he have swastika tattoos, on his neck?"

Rob stiffened.

"How do you know that, Karli? How do you know that! Karli, Karli!"

"Rob, this is mom," said Shelley.

He could hear the muffled sound of his sister crying in the background.

"How does she know that, Mom?" Rob demanded.

"I heard everything. The one with the blonde hair, does he have a lot of skull tattoos, on his right arm?"

"He does, now please tell me how and why both of you know this!"

For the next two minutes, Rob nervously paced as he listened to Shelley's telling of the encounter at the Kentucky rest area. Of the terror they felt upon being accosted by these three vile men, how they feared for their safety, for their lives. She explained why she thought it best not to mention the incident until everything with David was finished. And how this, like so many other turn of events, could not be just a coincidence. Rob agreed.

After ending the call, he motioned to David, then stepped into the storage shed. Stiffly, he rose to his feet and slowly walked over to Rob and Wayne. Davy soon joined them. An animated conversation followed.

There was much gesturing and pointing of fingers at the three Florida men who were now conscious and sitting together, at gunpoint, on a stack of old tires, looking worried and quietly whispering amongst themselves. The conversation between David, Rob, and Wayne ended when all nodded. Davy exchanged a few words with the two security guards, who calmly took seats in the golf cart with Liam. Rose approached the open garage door and asked,

"What's going on, Wayne?"

"David and Rob have one more debt to settle," he said while reaching up for the door handle.

"The police will be here any minute now," she replied, giving him a nervous look.

"Yeah, we know," said Wayne and pulled the door down.

At first, there was silence, then the sound of muted yet angry, yelling and swearing. With aircraft flying near, few words could be fully understood. Shortly, muffled yet violent actions could be heard coming from inside the shed. The yelling intensified; there were screams of pain. Abruptly came the unmistakable sound of a body being slammed against the inside of the closed overhead door. It shook the building, causing Rose to step back while others jumped at the sudden noise. Sunni stared at the door with no visible emotion.

As the sirens grew nearer, the garage door slowly opened. David and Rob emerged, soaked in sweat, with more than a few blood splatters on their clothing. Both were red-faced and breathing hard. Wayne stayed in the storage shed, calmly watching over the three men lying scattered on the floor, again, motionless and silent. All were in considerably worse physical condition than when the door came down a few moments previous.

Two police cars came to a sudden stop fifty feet away, four officers exited the vehicles and cautiously approached, weapons drawn. Davy assured them that the threat was over, but an additional ambulance would be required for three more severely injured people inside the storage shed.

"Maybe a hearse," said Wayne dryly, as he leaned against the bloody 2 x 4, and spit.

Two officers approached the shed and, upon seeing the carnage inside, asked what had just happened.

"They tried to escape," replied Wayne, "but were talked out of it."

Within half an hour, David and Sunni had been transported to the Battle Creek hospital, emergency room. Thirteen stitches were required for the knife wound on David's left arm, along with ice packs for various other bumps and bruises. Medical personnel told him to lie still and rest, but he insisted on finding Sunni.

Antibiotics, a mild sedative, and pain medication were administered to the girl after receiving treatment for several abrasions, bruising around her left eye, and a badly swollen knee. Upon being taken to a hospital room, an overnight stay was recommended in case other complications might arise. Two Battle Creek police detectives took her initial statement then said they would talk more when she felt better. They also stated her three attackers were being treated in the emergency room for multiple, serious injuries.

By the time David and Rob found her room, the others had already arrived. They pushed past the departing detectives, who let them know they also needed to be interviewed. Rob told the men neither was up for that at the moment. He took their card, saying they would get in touch. None of this could ever be easily explained. Better to dodge any questions at this point.

"Did you call your parents to let them know what happened?" Rob asked of Sunni.

"A little while ago, I didn't say much over the phone. They're heading back and will pick me up sometime tomorrow."

Jenny walked up to David and put her arm around him.

"Mom knew this, didn't she. You always were her hero."

"The girl needed help," said David as he looked at Sunni, who was sitting up in the hospital bed. "It just took a little persuading, is all."

"A little persuading, huh?" Wayne said, with a chuckle, as he pulled a piece of paper from his shirt pocket. "I talked to one of the cops who came to the emergency room with those three bastards. He told me what their total combined injuries are; I made a list, you might find it interesting."

"Between you and Rob, they needed over fifty stitches. There

were three concussions, a fractured skull, two fractured eye sock-
ets, a sprained neck, fractured vertebrae, one broken arm, two
broken noses, several broken teeth, a shattered jaw, and the blond
dude also had two busted ribs. I don't think those boys are gonna
walk or talk right, ever again, in prison."

"Not bad, for an old guy," said Rob, with a grin.

"And his scrawny kid," added David.

"When they get released, it's straight to jail," continued Wayne.
"We told the Battle Creek cops about the connection with the missing girls in Florida. They contacted the authorities down there; a
couple of investigators should arrive within a day."

David moved to Sunni's bedside.

"How are you doing?"

"They tell me an overnight stay would be a good idea, but I
don't think it's necessary," she replied.

Liam climbed up on the foot of the bed.

"Liam, I'm so sorry I didn't get you your cotton candy," the girl
said.

"It's all right; my daddy says we're gonna go back to the air
show. Are you coming with us?" the boy asked.

"I don't think Sunni can come along right now; she needs to
feel better first. Maybe some other time," said Corina as a nurse
walked in.

"This patient needs her rest, so everyone will have to leave,
please. You can come back later this evening or tomorrow
morning."

David leaned over and kissed Sunni gently on the forehead,
saying, "I'll see you again."

Before he turned towards the door, the girl took his hand and
squeezed it. She did not want to let go. As the nurse began to
shuffle David and the others out, Sunni grabbed Rob's arm.

"I need to get out of here; you know I do."

"Sunni, you should stay the night. You've been through a lot."

"It's David. I need to say, goodbye."

Rob looked at the girl; tears were on the cheeks of her swollen face.

"I understand," he said. "I'll tell them downstairs that you'll be checking yourself out. Jenny and Rose said they'd go buy you, me, and David some new clothes. I'll bring them up when they get back; you get some rest now."

Within an hour, Sunni had signed out of the hospital over the protest of her doctor. She, David, and Rob washed up and changed into their new, more presentable, untattered, and unbloodied clothes. A new tote bag was also purchased, a simple black one, with one yellow and one red stripe. David was pleased she was joining them but expressed concern about leaving the hospital so soon.

Navy Blue No. 2 and the crew cab pickup began making their way back to the airport as the sun continued to sink lower in the western sky. An enormous crowd still remained, waiting to enjoy the hot air balloon launch and brief flight just before dusk. Davy had arranged for the two vehicles to enter the airport by the service gate and use the employee's parking lot. After everyone had exited their vehicles, Rob pulled Davy aside.

"All set?" he asked.

"Should be good to go; the others are in place. We need to start making our way over there soon," was his reply.

Liam asked if they could get his cotton candy, now, so once again, everyone found themselves on the carnival midway, with Sunni walking between David and Rob, for physical and emotional support. They slowly made their way towards the cotton candy stand, where the abduction occurred a few hours earlier. She insisted on going to the same one.

"Oh my, what happened to you?" the girl behind the counter asked Sunni. "Your friends thought you got lost or something?"

"I was lost," replied Sunni, and then added, "But now I'm found."

"By amazing grace," said Jenny solemnly.

"By incredibly amazing grace," added Wayne.

"Oh, okay. But who's this Grace person? She sounds awesome," the counter girl asked. Everyone smiled at this.

Sunni ordered blue cotton candy and gave it to the boy.

"Here you are, Liam, mission accomplished."

"Thank you, Sunni, thank you!" the boy said as he immediately began picking at the sweet, blue stickyness with his fingers.

"Speaking of missions," began Rob. "We should start heading over to the warbird area, Dad. They've all finished flying for the day; Davy says we can get close to the planes if we want and talk to the pilots."

"I'd like that," said David. "There's at least one Corsair here. Maybe, maybe if I see it up close, touch it…."

"Maybe so," replied Rob.

Liam started jumping up and down excitedly, grabbed his dad's hand, and began pulling him.

"C'mon, Daddy, let's go. I wanna see the fighters and bombers!"

Just then, a security guard drove up in an eight-passenger golf cart transporter. He was one of the men at the storage shed.

"This the one you wanted, Davy?" the guard asked.

"Yep, this one's just perfect; thanks for bringing it over."

The man nodded at David and Rob, saying,

"Glad you fella's got a chance to settle up."

"The warbirds area is at the far end of the field, near where the balloons are," Davy said. "Too far for Sunni to walk with her bad knee, so, all aboard!"

Soon, the vehicle, with Davy driving, was unhurriedly making its way westward along a narrow, paved path bordering the carnival.

"Are you nervous, Dad?" Jenny asked.

"No, everything is going to work out; I can feel it now. I'm ready," he replied while holding her hand.

Within a few minutes, they arrived at the warbird area and entered through an open gate. More than a dozen brilliantly colored, hot air balloons were laid out in a large, open field adjacent to where the military aircraft were parked. They stopped to watch for a moment.

"They're really pretty when they get up in the air, aren't they, Mommy. They look like big Christmas tree lights in the sky," Liam said.

"They sure do, honey," Corina replied.

Crews were busily hooking up large fans to partially inflate the balloons before the burners could be lit. Launch time was rapidly approaching.

"Well, let's go find your fighter plane," Davy said.

David nodded, and slowly they began weaving their way through World War II, two-seat trainers, an old Stearman biplane, two P-51 Mustangs, a Korean War-era F–86 Sabrejet, and other aircraft. Their objective came into view as they drove around a B-25 bomber named *Daisy May*, complete with cartoon character nose art.

The blue plane, with its distinctive inverted gull-wing design, was straight ahead. The same Corsair David had observed speeding low and loud over the storage sheds, now sat quiet and still, in the slowly fading light, of a Michigan early evening. On the engine cowling, in white, was the number 310, with NAVY VF-42 in large letters on the rear fuselage.

Liam quickly jumped out as the transporter came to a halt and began running towards the aircraft.

"Don't you touch that airplane!" Corina yelled after him. "Your fingers are all sticky."

"Okay," came his dejected reply.

When everyone had stepped out, David and Jenny stood together, looking at the plane.

"This is what you flew in the war. Mom has pictures of you and
your Corsair, named after her." Jenny said.

"*Macy's Magic III*, that's right. This one is a Navy plane. We were
Marines, flying off the carrier *Bennington*," David replied as they
slowly walked forward.

"Been little more than a week ago since I stepped into one of
these. Now… suddenly, it seems so long ago."

"Would you like to saddle up again, Marine?" A voice said from
behind David.

He turned to find a man in his forties standing a few feet away,
dressed in a khaki flight suit. Embroidered over one upper pocket
was the name, Rance Lenshaw. The man extended his hand towards
David.

"I'm Rance; the owners of this plane let me fly it for them at air
shows and such. It's a dirty job, but somebody has to do it," he said
with a smile. "You must be David."

"Yes sir, you have a beautiful bird here," he replied, gripping
the man's hand. "Were you serious? I mean, about getting up in
the cockpit?"

"Oh sure, you bet. Davy told me you have a special connection
to Corsairs. He said it would mean a lot if you were able to get in
and sit a spell."

David looked over at his great-grandson, who gave him a
thumbs-up.

"It would, Rance. You can't imagine how much," said David, as
he shook the man's hand again.

Everyone walked over to the right side of the plane to watch as
David climbed into the old warbird.

"You put your foot in this step, with the hinged door on the
flap, right here, then reach up…" spoke Rance.

"I got this," David interrupted.

After placing one foot on the step, he grabbed the hinged handhold door, further up the fuselage, and then pulled himself upright on the wing root. David Hamilton closed his eyes; again, he could smell the sea and the familiar mixture of aviation gas and boiler oil. The sound of multiple Pratt and Whitney radial engines warming up reverberated in his mind. A recollection of the rolling motion on *Big Benn*, with the wind blowing over his skin, took him back. It felt right. The odyssey began over a week ago, was destined to end up, right here, right now.

"Are we ready for this?" Shelley asked the three others standing with her, out of sight behind a fuel truck, fifty feet away. "Karli and I need to get our husband and father back."

They all nodded.

With David lost in thought, the group of four quietly moved towards the Corsair. From the nearby field came the low roar of propane burners, blowing hot air into semi-inflated balloons, slowly bringing them upright.

Putting his left foot in the hinged foothold on the fuselage and grabbing the windscreen, David recalled the last time he swung himself into the cockpit of a fighter plane. With calm anticipation, he hoisted himself up and stepped into the familiar surroundings.

Slipping down into the seat, he grasped the grip of the stick between his legs with his right hand, his left hand resting on the throttle controls. Looking forward, over the long cowling and past massive propeller blades, he could see wisps of clouds beginning to blend into the fading blue sky. Scanning the instrument panel, all seemed as remembered, but for the small black and white photo. The last glimpse before everything went dark and silent, saw it burning. As his mind began to revisit those final few moments of smoke, heat, and hopelessness, there came a stranger's voice.

"David? David Hamilton?"

He turned towards the voice and found a man standing on the ground, next to the plane.

"Yes, I am, more or less."

Glancing at the others, he was surprised to see Shelley and Karli, along with a woman he recognized from the office in Fort Myers. Slowly he raised his hand and gave them a gentle wave.

"It's good to see you both again," he said, loud enough to be heard over the ever-increasing noise of the propane burners. Shelley and Karli waved back, their emotions running high.

"We've met before, briefly," said the man on the ground. "I'm Doctor Bronner, Doctor William Bronner, call me Doc, everyone does. Would you mind if I stepped up there closer, on the wing?"

"Sure," said David, as he reached down towards the man.

"Thanks so much, not as spry as I used to be," he said and grabbed the outstretched hand.

Soon, he was standing on the wing root, a few feet from David.

He was a middle-aged man of average height and build, wearing blue jeans and a dark green polo shirt. There was a noticeable red mark on his graying and slightly-balding head.

"Looks like you got a good knock on the noggin, there Doc," David said with a smile. "I got one too, about a week back."

"I know; we got 'em on the same day," replied Doc.

"Is that right?" David said with surprise.

"How's your arm? I understand you had quite some excitement earlier," spoke Doc, leaning against the fuselage of the Corsair.

David, holding up his bandaged left arm, said, "Still hurts some, and I'm pretty sore all over. That's to be expected, I suppose, when you're using an older, borrowed body. But I imagine you know all about that, right?"

"Looks like Derek's going to have a scar from something he won't ever remember happening," Doc said, looking straight into David's eyes.

"So you know Derek. I've felt him, many times, trying to get back, back to his family. Like I tried to get back to mine," said David, as he looked down at Jenny.

"And you did, David, you did, and I'm so happy for you, for all of you."

"Doc, what happened to me, and Derek Haynes?"

"I'm a psychologist and have an office in a Fort Myers medical building, not far from where you fell and hit your head," Doc began.

"I was there, at your office, right?" David said, remembering back to that confusing time.

"Yes, you, and Derek," Doc replied.

"But, I don't understand, I've never met...."

"I'm also a certified clinical hypnotherapist," Doc interrupted. "I use hypnosis to treat people with various issues in their life. It works well for many of my patients. Something used in that part of my practice is known as *past life regression*, using hypnosis. I don't imagine you're familiar with that term."

"No sir, not at all. What does that have to do with the two of us?"

"On June first, both your birthdays, Derek came into the office; he'd made an appointment a few days previous. Derek has a great interest in World War II and felt an affinity for that era. He told me it was all very familiar to him and thought it might've had something to do with his father being a Marine in the South Pacific. A curiosity about what his dad went through. Or something else.

"He researched past life regression hypnosis and decided to give it a try, to see if there might be a personal connection, and possibly... a past life, from that time. It was something he had been interested in for years."

"And that's where I come in," said David, nodding. "But, why... how am I here, stuck in his body?"

"Let me tell you what happened. He decided not to tell Shelley, Rob, and Karli about his plan to undergo the regression, in case it turned out to be a bust, and wanted to surprise them if we found out anything of real interest and significance. He asked to have the session recorded, which is standard practice anyway, as patients most times have little to no recollection of what they've recalled and talked about during the regression. They often retain little more than a vague recollection, as in a dream, quickly forgotten.

"I wasn't feeling well when I woke up, but my hours are only till noon on Saturdays, and I didn't want to cancel any appointments. So I went in, hoping to feel better as the morning went on. Derek's appointment was last and was going well. Regressing quickly and smoothly back to his childhood, then birth, then beyond. In that state of hypnosis, he became a World War II fighter pilot. The fact is, before he was Derek Haynes, in a past life, he was you, David. And that is the connection binding you two together.

"Speaking through Derek, you told me of your life, the horror of war. About your family, your marriage to Macy, Jenny, and how you missed them and were so very much looking forward to going home and being with them."

"Go on, Doc."

"A standard question I ask during these regressions is *how did you come to die?* It can be beneficial for individuals in regression therapy when searching for reasons why certain things adversely affect or frighten them. This can often help to explain behavioral issues or phobias that can stem from events that may have happened, possibly, in a previous lifetime.

"When I asked, 'how did you come to die, David Hamilton,' you suddenly became panicked and animated. Putting your hands over your head, shouting, twisting, and turning, in obvious pain, saying the plane was on fire and going down, you couldn't get out, and it was hard to breathe. You were crying out to God, saying you only wanted to go home to be with your family. You'd made a promise."

David sat quietly, listening, remembering.

"I stood up, too quickly, and stepped over to try and calm you enough to be able to terminate the regression properly; you were in agony. The next thing I know, I'm waking up on the floor, with a bloody gash on my head from hitting a table on the way down. It seems I got the wrong medication for my high blood pressure the previous day, which caused me to suddenly, go out like a light.

"Later in the hospital, my assistant, Evelyn, told me how Derek didn't seem to remember who he was. Saying he didn't know any-body named Haynes and asking what was happening. Even ques-tioned if he might be in Heaven.

"I told her that was impossible; people don't get caught, don't get stuck in their past life connections during regression. Has never been known to happen before, that I'm aware of. Patients will wake up on their own, or they should, as the conscious mind naturally comes back into play. But Derek didn't.

"You came out, David, and stayed. Then wandered out of my office, a fighter pilot who had just gone through a terrible experi-ence and became trapped in another man's body, lost and con-fused, seventy-four years in the future. I'm sorry for what you had to go through; it must have been incredibly traumatic."

"Hard to believe and understand, but now I know," said David, sitting up straight. "It's not your fault, it's nobody's fault, but with-out help from Rob and Sunni, I would never have been able to be with my two girls, together again as a family, one last time. And now, to say my goodbyes, which is why you're here."

"Yes, that's why I'm here," said Doc, nodding.

Rob stepped up to the Corsair.

"You need to know, Duke, at the garage in Kentucky... he and his buddy Frankie Haynes, my grandfather, were on Okinawa."

"Yes, and I'd like to think somehow I helped out those boys at one time or another. Guess we'll never know."

"You did, Dad. Duke told me the entire story. The bright reflection you saw, it was my grandfather trying to signal you with a mirror."

"No, can't be; I saw that man go down in a blast of machine-gun fire."

"Somehow, he wasn't hurt; Frankie survived that day and the war. And you turned your plane back, saving lives, including my dad's future father. It's all connected, and it was always meant to happen, this way. My dad, and his family, my family, exist because of you, and we helped you get back to yours, as promised. Full circle."

"I don't understand...." David said, his voice cracking.

"So this has been a gift," spoke Doc. "For the sacrifice made that day, to save others. You earned this; it has to be the reason you're here. How it all came about, came to happen, will likely remain a mystery, but I'm certain it is far beyond our human ability to comprehend."

"You came home to us. Mom always said you would; she never gave up hope," spoke Jenny as she stepped closer to the plane and reached up.

David took her hand in his.

"I got to meet you," she said with a trembling voice. "We were all together. For a wonderful, brief moment, we were a family again. Everything is going to be all right now. I love you, Dad."

"I love you too, Jenny, and your mom, more than you can ever imagine."

They held hands in silence, neither wanting to let go. They allowed their hands to slip apart, and Jenny stepped back.

Rob reached his hand up, saying,

"It's been quite an adventure."

"Sorry you had to go through all this, Rob," replied David.

"I'd do it all again; it was my honor. You are one hell of a man."

"Take good care of your mom and Karli, Rob; they've had a tough time. And your dad, he's gonna be very confused. And tell him, tell him that I'm sorry for the disruption in his life, and that he has a wonderful family."

"So do you, Dad. So do you," replied Rob, almost in a whisper.

David Hamilton looked at Sunni, who stood quietly with the others, her head down.

"Sunni, Sunni," he said softly. Slowly raising her head, their eyes met. "Come up here with me, please?"

She walked up to Rob, who, with Doc's help, helped her up onto the wing of the Corsair.

"Never thought I'd ever say this, but I am going to miss you, Sunni Omora."

"You saved my life," she replied, reaching out to touch his hand.

"You saved my soul," David said emotionally. "And gave me the gift of peace, forgiveness and made me realize how precious life is. Every life, so now I can move on."

"Take that peace with you, David, she said through tears."

Rob helped her down, and she, again, stood with the others. David looked at them for a moment, then raised his hand, saying,

"I will miss you all."

"Mommy, is my grandpa David going somewhere?" Liam, quietly, asked Corina.

"Yes, he has to leave us, soon," she replied.

"Is he, going to fly away in that blue airplane?"

"No, honey, we have to be real quiet now."

"But…" Liam began; Corina gently put a finger to his lips.

Doctor Bronner stepped closer to the cockpit.

"David, you ready?"

"Yes sir," he replied, then looked at Rob, "Almost done."

Rob somberly nodded.

"Sorry, I don't have a nice comfortable couch or chair for you," said Doc.

"No place I'd rather be than sitting right here."

"By the way, you owe me three hundred dollars for the past life regression hypnosis," Doc said wryly.

"You're going to have to take that up with Derek. I left my wallet in 1945," David replied with a grin.

Everyone smiled at this exchange, taking some tension from the moment.

"I don't get it," Liam said.

Wayne tousled the boy's hair and replied, "We'll explain it to you, someday."

"Alright," began Doc. "You need to become as comfortable as possible, lean back, relax all your muscles, lower your head, chin lightly on your chest, hands together in your lap. And listen to my voice. Take a deep breath, then slowly release it. As you release, feel the tension begin to leave your body."

David took a breath and slowly let it out.

"Listen to my voice. Keep breathing as you are. A deep breath and slow release. Breathe in, breathe out. Remember this, with every breath; you will become more relaxed, your arms and legs will begin to feel heavy. You will not be asleep. You will be awake and turning your thoughts inward. Listen to my voice. Keep breathing and focus your mind on a pleasant time in your past. A pleasant place, a memory that is precious to you. Breathe in, breathe out."

David Hamilton took two more breaths as he began to focus on the spring day, at the bungalow, in Grand Rapids.

"Breathe in, breathe out."

He felt the sun's warmth, saw blue sky, puffy white clouds, leafy trees, and emerald green grass in the yard. A gentle breeze blew softly over the three of them.

"Breathe in, breathe out."

Macy was sitting in the tree swing, holding Jenny on her lap. He, standing behind, one hand on the rope, the other on his wife's shoulder. The scent of her cherished rose garden in the air mingled with her perfume.

"Breathe in, breathe out."

Neighbor Tom, right hand on the tripod-mounted camera, left hand frantically waving a toy bunny, to get Jenny's attention.

"Breathe in, breathe out."

"Look at the bunny, Jenny; the bunny wants you to give him a smile," said Macy.

"There, that was a nice one, good smile, Jenny!" Tom said.

"Such a good girl, Jenny. Mommy and daddy love you so much!"

"Yes, we do, forever and ever," he said, kneeling and looking into Macy's eyes.

"Breathe in, breathe out."

Putting his arms around both, he gently kissed Jenny on the forehead, turned, kissed Macy's lips, and repeated, *"Forever, and ever."*

"Focus on the vision," said Doc. "You are going to breathe in and breathe out, three more times. "

The image froze in David's mind.

"At the end of the third breath, you will leave this man's body and go to that vision. Your purpose for being here is complete. You will be released and free to go. You will be at peace."

Shelley, Karli, and Evelyn stood quietly together, holding hands.

"What if it doesn't work?" whispered Karli.

"It will work," said Evelyn as she squeezed her hand.

"Breathe in, breathe out."

David Hamilton took a breath and slowly let it out.

"Come back to me, David," Macy spoke to him in the vision.

"One."

"Come back to me, now."

The image became more vibrant in David's mind. He took another breath. As he began to let it out, Doc said,

"Two. Breathe in, breathe out."

Jenny, standing below them, eyes closed, slowly lifted her head upward while also taking a breath as her father drew in his third and last.

"I'm waiting for you, David. Come to me," Macy said, with a voice like music.

In his vision, David leaned in to kiss her. As he began to exhale, their lips touched.

"Three."

All gathered around the plane could see the man's body suddenly straighten; his head began swiveling back and forth.

"Derek, is that you?" Doc asked.

"Yes, of course. Who else would I be?" Derek Haynes responded, looking at the man.

"Doc? Doc Bronner, what are you doing here? Wait, what am *I* doing here? And just where the hell is here! Am I sitting in an… airplane?"

"Daddy!" Karli cried out as she ran to the plane and reached her arms upward. Rob and Shelley quickly joined her, all smiling through tears.

"Mommy, why did that girl call Grandpa David, daddy?" Liam asked Corina.

"You see, Liam, he's not Grandpa David now. He's a nice man named Derek, and that's his family with him," replied Corina.

"But, he still looks like my Grandpa David and sounds like him too," Liam came back.

"I know, honey. Grandpa David, well, he just, changed," Corina answered uncomfortably.

Liam threw his hands up in the air, then brought them down,

slapping the sides of his legs. While shaking his head and looking down at the ground, he was heard to say,

"I am so confused...."

"What are you all doing here? Where are we?" asked Derek as he began to reach out of the cockpit with both arms and touch his family.

"Ouch, son-of-a-bitch!" he yelled, looking at the tightly wrapped bandages on his left arm. "What the hell happened to me!"

"It's gonna take some time to explain, Dad. You've been, gone, for a while," said Rob.

"Gone? What do you mean, gone?" his dad questioned.

"Mommy, look!" Liam said, pointing at the sky. "The balloons are flying; they're so pretty when they light up."

Multiple brightly colored balloons had begun their ascent, slowly drifting upward into the twilight sky. Flames from the burners brightly lit the inside of the balloons, shining through the colored fabric, making them come alive with a warm glow.

"Hot air balloons, seriously? And who are all these people?" Derek asked, looking at the small crowd gathered below him.

"We're at an air show in Battle Creek, Michigan, Derek. You're sitting in a World War II Corsair fighter plane," replied Doc.

Rose felt her cell phone vibrate and stepped a few feet away from the group to answer it.

"Really? The last thing I clearly remember is going to your office this morning, Doc, for that regression thing I'd scheduled. And now you're telling me, apparently hours later, for some ungodly reason, I'm in the state of Michigan at an air show, with a bandaged arm? Somebody's got some explaining to do," said Derek, raising his voice.

"Well, it's been more than hours, actually, dear," Shelley spoke up.

"How long then?"

Shelley and Rob looked at each other, then turned towards Derek.

"More than a week," Rob said.

"What!" Derek said in amazement as he stood up in the cockpit. "That can't be; what is going on... how do I get down from here?"

Rance Lenshaw stepped forward, saying,

"Let me help you down, David. It's kind of tricky," then turning to Rob, he quietly remarked, "Yeah, just what is going on?"

Derek, with a quizzical look on his face, asked, "Who's David?"

Rose slowly walked over to her mother.

"Mom...."

"Well, it's done. But I'm so happy for the Haynes," Jenny said in a tired voice. "We need to tell Rob and the others we're going to be leaving, and...."

"Mom, Macy's gone," interrupted Rose. "She passed away a few minutes ago. That was the nursing home on the phone."

After hearing Rose's sad news, the rest of her family gathered around the two women. Jenny gazed at the balloons, drifting lazily upward into the sky while slowly moving away in a line of alternately glowing colors. A feeling of peace, and finality, came over her.

"I'm going to miss her; we all will," Jenny said, looking at the others. "She had been waiting a long time, for yesterday. So much of her life has been waiting; that's over now. The three of us were a family again. It's all she ever wanted."

Rob walked up and asked,

"Would you like to come over and meet my dad, Jenny, all of you?"

"I don't think that would be a good idea right now, Rob," replied Jenny. "Just too much for him to take in, so soon. You'll need to start helping him understand what's happened. We'll be leaving soon, going back to Fowlerville. Maybe we can all get together again, someday. All of our lives have become so connected...."

"The nursing home called, Rob. Macy just passed away, so we need to be getting back," said Rose.

"Oh no, I'm so sorry to hear that," he replied as Sunni walked up.

"Sorry to hear what?"

"Macy passed away, so they're leaving for home," answered Rob.

Sunni stepped over and gave Jenny a long hug.

"Are you going to be alright, Jenny?"

"Roses. I was breathing along with my father on the final count. There was a scent of roses, and her perfume. It was unmistakable. I could feel mom's presence, watching, waiting. Smiling.

Jenny looked again into the sky to see two red, glowing balloons nearly side by side, silently drifting upward and away, in the darkening sky.

"They are together now, again, forever and ever."

Jenny and her family said their goodbyes at the airport and departed for Fowlerville; the others returned to the motel where Shelley, Karli, Doc, and Evelyn, had been staying. Tomorrow, Monday, they would begin their journey home. Upon returning to Florida, time would be needed to address what had transpired the previous week and a day.

Rob and Derek, alone in Navy Blue No. 2, talked on the drive to the motel, and there was one burning question Rob needed to ask.

"Dad, during all this time, where were you? I mean, was there any awareness of what was happening?"

"No, not really," Derek began. "There was no sensation of time, none whatsoever; it was very confusing, like a long, strange, never-ending vague dream I could not wake myself from. I remember trying to find you, to find out what was going on, but something, someone, kept blocking me, pushing me back. Seems like I talked to you once, briefly, but you weren't making any sense, then I got pushed back again. I tried to get out, to fight my way back, to wake up, but I just couldn't. Then all of a sudden, I'm more than a thousand miles from home, in Michigan, tired and sore, with stitches in my arm. Gonna need a lot of catching up and some damn good explanations. I've totally lost a part of my life, for cry'n out loud."

"That's for sure, Dad. We're so, so happy to have you back." Rob said as he reached over and put his hand on his father's shoulder. "We'll do all that we can to fill in that blank spot."

The following morning, the Haynes family began packing up the old Ford Coupe and white Toyota in the motel parking lot. Doctor Bronner told them to call his office once they returned home and were rested, to set up an appointment. All would be welcome to meet with him; he would play the past life regression video; it would be a good starting point. Then they would talk.

"No more hypnosis, right?" Shelley, seriously, asked.

"No more hypnosis," Doc laughed.

He walked over to Sunni and put his arm around her shoulder.

"You should be there too, if you can."

"She'll be staying in Michigan for the summer, Doc. Maybe after she returns to school in August, if she returns," said Rob, dejectedly.

Sunni took his hand.

"I am going to school and will be back in Florida, soon," she said, looking up at him.

"You're not staying here?" he asked, pleasantly surprised.

"Won't be getting rid of me that easy, Rob Haynes. Soon as I heal up some and deal with the investigation, I'll be flying back to Gainesville. So, you going to come up and see me sometime?" she asked, moving closer and putting a hand on his chest.

"I have a better idea; why not travel a little farther and come stay with us in Fort Myers. We'd love to have you," said Shelley, then looked at Rob, who nodded a thank you.

"I'd like that, I'd like that very much," said Sunni, as she stepped over and hugged Shelley.

"This will be great!" Karli excitedly said. "We can share my room; it'll be fun. Wow, just, wow. We can be like, sisters!"

"All righty then," Doc Bronner said and clapped his hands. "I'll expect to see y'all when you're ready."

"Probably should get going; you can drive the first shift, Rob. Your old dad's pretty sore and not well-focused at the moment," said Derek. "Sunni, are you going to be alright, here by yourself? We can stay until your parents arrive, if you like."

"They'll be here in about an hour, and my mom, well, she's a real drama queen and will probably fall all to pieces when she sees me, and nobody wants to watch that," she replied, making a face.

"Our plane doesn't leave until early afternoon; we can stay here, maybe help explain at least a few things to her parents," said Evelyn.

Derek walked over to Doctor Bronner and shook his hand.

"Well, Doc, from what I've been told so far, it's been quite some adventure."

"Yes, Derek, David, or whatever your name is, it most certainly has, like no other," Doc said, smiling.

"I'm sure hoping someday, you, or someone, can explain to me just what that adventure was, exactly," replied Derek, with more than a tinge of irony in his voice.

Shelley and Karli hugged both Doc and Evelyn, thanking them

profusely for all they had done, then walked over to the white Toyota.

"You just follow us; we'll set the pace, try and keep up," yelled Derek after them. He looked over at Rob, holding Sunni so tightly that her feet were barely touching the ground.

"We gotta get going, boy. You need put the nice little girl down, now."

"Yeah, I know," replied Rob.

"I'm going to miss you," Sunni said.

"Going to miss you too, but it won't be too long, right? You take care of yourself and then come back to me, young lady, you hear?"

"I will, I promise," she replied, putting her head on his chest.

After a last kiss, he turned and walked towards the Ford.

"Rob, one thing," she said, seriously, as he paused by the car.

"What's that?"

"Don't pick up any hitchhikers," she giggled.

"Never, too risky. You never know what's gonna happen!" he replied with a laugh.

Soon they were on Interstate 69 South, the rearview mirror reflecting Shelley and Karli following, a few car lengths behind.

"How fast, Dad, the usual sixty-ish?"

"Oh hell no, the speed limit's seventy; let's go for it," replied Derek, holding up a fist.

"You sure?"

"It seems to have come all this way without much trouble and is running fine. I bet this old timer's in a hurry to get home. Lord knows I am," he wearily responded.

Just then, the car horn honked. Twice.

"I think Navy Blue No. 2 is happy to have you back, Dad," said Rob, knowingly nodding his head.

The boy had not touched the horn button.

"Yep, beep, beep. Let's go home," Derek replied.

After a few miles had been clocked on the speedometer, he asked,

"You spent more than a week with this fighter pilot guy, me, apparently, in a former life, this David. What was he like? What did you talk about?"

"It was weird, especially at first," said Rob, as he put both hands on the steering wheel.

"After finally realizing, well, that I was no longer talking to you, I decided to take him wherever he wanted, needed, to go, hoping that would be the end of it, and you'd come back. He was a very confused and tormented man."

"How'd he ever convince you who he was? Sounds insane."

"He told me all these things; it was like a confession, about being a fighter pilot, from 1945, it was nuts. I kept thinking it was you, with possibly a brain injury. It was scaring me half to death."

"What changed your mind?"

"He gave me dates, places, names. So I searched online to prove he, you, didn't know what you were talking about and was just mixed up after smacking your head on the sidewalk."

"Guessing that didn't work?"

"Quite the opposite. All the things he was saying matched up. Although I still believed maybe you were just repeating things you could've read or watched before. Then I found the carrier he named, his squadron, and combat records."

"And?"

Rob took a breath and began.

"He'd given me the name of a friend of his, a pilot he watched die, and the date. The man's name was in the records, had a D, dead, under fate. He'd died on the day David told me. Then he asked if there was a record of any Corsairs lost on June first, 1945. June first, both your birthdates."

"Was there?" asked Derek, tentatively.

"Yes, and I'd hardly begun reading when he gave me the number of the Corsair he was flying that day. It matched. That couldn't have been something you'd know, not something that obscure.

"You're kidding me!" Derek replied, stunned.

"He got real nervous, asked for the pilot's name and fate," Rob continued.

"What did he do when you told him? It must've been devastating."

"That's just it, Dad, none of that information was there, no name or fate at all, totally blank. We couldn't put a pilot name to that lost Corsair, presumably his. Made a believer out of me."

"I'd like to see those records sometime, Rob, if you saved them."

"I printed out a bunch of information, should all be in an envelope, in the glove box; thought it would be a good idea to bring them along."

Derek pulled the envelope out and began thumbing through the papers.

"It was upsetting to him, not knowing for sure," Rob continued. "He needed to see an official written record of what happened, a confirmation. David told me the support mission on June first was his final flight of the war and was headed back to the ship for the last time, but turned back when he saw a group of Marines in trouble. The man and his plane took out a machine gun nest and saved a lot of lives, including your.... Well, he saved a lot of Marines that day."

"My dad was a Marine on Okinawa, you remember? He never spoke about it much," said Derek while looking at the papers.

"Yeah, I know," replied Rob.

There would be a time to tell his dad, in detail, of all the happenings surrounding the different players in this surreal saga, but it need not be this day.

"All he received for his bravery and effort was to get blown out of the South Pacific sky, and no one even knows his name; I couldn't find any record, official or otherwise, showing that he ever existed. And that bothered him, a lot. Nobody, now, knows what happened, what he did—just another forgotten, anonymous casualty of war.

"Say, there's this guy in Kentucky we met on the trip up here; you should meet and talk with. I know he can fill in a lot of the story. He said David deserved to get a medal for what he did. Well, he didn't know it was David, not yet. See, he was there, so...."

"He did get a medal, Rob. The Navy Cross," Derek said, looking down at the printed copy of the combat history.

"No, no one knows who he was or what he did. That's not in there; there's no name on that record, Dad," Rob said calmly.

"It's right here, Son, on the mission records for his squadron. It's what you printed out," Derek said, pointing at the paper.

"Can't be; there's only the plane type, number, squadron, and date. You must be looking at something else; that's all there was on the page I printed," replied Rob.

"Nope, there's an asterisk next to pilot's name; Lieutenant David J. Hamilton. Under fate, of course, there's a D, says so right here."

"Can't be...."

"On the next page, it says he got the Navy Cross, and why, look," said Derek as he held it up for him to see.

Rob took a couple of quick glances and then focused back on the road.

"I've never seen that page before, never printed it out, I'm sure of it. Read it to me."

"It says," Derek Haynes began.

"For meritorious action against enemy forces of the Empire of Japan, on 01 Jun 45. While flying a sortie over the Japanese held

island of Okinawa, Lieutenant David J. Hamilton selflessly and courageously intervened and halted a sudden and savage attack upon a contingent of Marines pinned down by heavy machine-gun fire, sparing many lives. As a result Lieutenant Hamilton exposed himself and his aircraft to enemy anti-aircraft fire and was subsequently brought down by said fire, suffering the tragic loss of his life. For this act of valor and sacrifice, Lieutenant David J. Hamilton, posthumously, is justly and proudly awarded the Navy Cross.

"It's dated November 14, 1945."

Rob smiled, shook his head, slapped the steering wheel, and laughed.

"Well, son-of-a-bitch, just one more unexplainable surprise after another with that guy."

He stuck his left hand out the window, made a fist, and began shaking it in the wind.

"Yes! Yes!" he yelled. "I know you, David Hamilton! I know you! You were alive; you existed! You made a difference!"

"I, I don't understand... Rob," said Derek, confused by his son's outburst.

"On the way home, we're taking a side trip on some two-lane roads and stopping at a small town in Kentucky," said Rob. "Gotta see a man, about a man, an old car, and an unfinished story."

END